A CHOIR OF LIES

ALSO BY ALEXANDRA ROWLAND

A Conspiracy of Truths

A CHOIR OF LIES

Alexandra Rowland

SAGA PRESS

LONDON SYDNEY **NEW YORK** TORONTO NEW DELHI

12/19
927

SAGA PRESS
AN IMPRINT OF SIMON & SCHUSTER, INC.

1230 AVENUE OF THE AMERICAS, NEW YORK, NEW YORK 10020

SAGA PRESS and colophon are trademarks of Simon & Schuster, Inc.

For information about special discounts for bulk purchases, please contact Simon & Schuster Special Sales at 1-866-506-1949 or business@simonandschuster.com.

The Simon & Schuster Speakers Bureau can bring authors to your live event. For more information or to book an event, contact the Simon & Schuster Speakers Bureau at 1-866-248-3049 or visit our website at www.simonspeakers.com.

Book design by Nicholas Sciacca

The text for this book was set in Adobe Jenson Pro.

Manufactured in the United States of America

First Saga Press trade paperback edition September 2019

10 9 8 7 6 5 4 3 2 1

CIP data for this book is available from the Library of Congress.

ISBN 978-1-5344-1283-5
ISBN 978-1-5344-1285-9 (ebook)

To Macey and Freya:

I *genuinely* couldn't have done it without you.

STERRE DE WAEYER'S MANOR

Nauwgracht

VAN ECHTEN

High
Bridge

'T HOGEWIJN

Vergracht

Coppel
Bridge

COPPEL
SQUARE

Spijlgracht

Westengracht

THE LEES

Mid
Bri

ROJKSTRAAT

GUILDHALL

South
Bridge

Westenwielgracht

Bardengracht

THE SUN'S RE...

SHIPSHOME

WEST

NORTH

lengracht

Oostengracht

ORTITUDE

E ROSE
D·IVY·INN

PROSPERITY

Oude-Kanaal

RASLAND

STROEKSHALL

Offices of
Sterre de Waeyer

EAST

Oostenwielgracht

Middengracht

ARBORFRONT

THE SEA
OF STORMS

HEYRLAND

All right . . . I suppose things like this usually start with an apology of some sort.

ONE

my former master-Chant thought we shouldn't write down the things we know. I don't know if he was right. I don't know if I agree. Rather, I don't agree entirely, but I don't disagree entirely either. I'm still exploring all my options. But one option must be to write a little down, because here I am, writing, even though I'm not really supposed to. The argument he gave was that mere ink and paper can be lost or destroyed or *taken* from you.

These won't get taken from me. These are mine, and I'll burn them up once I'm done with them. And anyway, if he cared so much about what I do, he shouldn't have—

I won't write it. I can't. ("Can't" here meaning both "I don't want to. I refuse to. I won't face it" and "If I *were* to face it, there would still be no language in the world with strong enough words to make myself understood. Whatever I wrote would be a work in translation, and it's just not linguistically possible.")

There's a kind of magic in writing down the things you know. It makes mere ink and paper into weapons. It makes them a mind, in a way: A paper copy of a mind with some of the mental abilities that its writer possessed—persuasion, or charm, or insidious destruction.

But paper can't think and ink can't adapt—they are an arrow shot into a foggy night by a blind man. At least this way, I know that there's no one in front of me, no one to be struck and killed by a stray bolt carelessly shot, and no witnesses. And even though there's no one to hear my words, no one to see what I'm doing, no one to care at all . . . Sometimes, I'm going to lie, even here, when I'm all alone: I'm a Chant now myself, after all, and Chants are liars.[1]

But first, something true.

---

1   You little shit. I'd argue with you, but you've already proven your own point, haven't you? And not just a liar, but an oathbreaker (and in regards to that: Fuck you very much, thanks). Why am I even bothering with this? Why even waste the ink to call you a shit and an oathbreaker? You've already run off—at least you know how to abscond in the night like a proper Chant. It's not like you'll ever read anything I write here. It's not like you'd particularly care about it even if I did catch you. But . . . Dammit, I'll have the last word, even if you aren't around to witness me getting it. The last word and the satisfaction of yelling at you the way I want to, and what does it matter that you won't ever hear me? You never heard me before, so it's really no different.

TWO

A truth: I wonder if it was right for me to become a Chant.

Another: I think it changed me. I think I'm different than I used to be.

Another: When I was becoming a Chant, finishing my apprenticeship officially, my master-Chant led me through the rites to sink my homeland beneath the waves and unname myself.[2] But I'm afraid, now, that I must not have meant it hard enough,[3] because I still feel like I have my name. I whisper it into the dark sometimes, and it feels like I'm breaking a tenet, though the tenets of the Chants are few and vague and abstract.[4]

Chants are—

They—

This is difficult.

Chants are storytellers, right? That's what I'm supposed to be doing. I'm supposed to be a collector and a curator.[5] The things humans make up are delicate when they're out in the wild. Stories

---

2   I don't even want to think about what that man told you were "the rites." It was horrific enough the first time I heard it. Can you really even use the word "led"?
3   Gods and fishes, every time you mention that man and what he did to you, I want to tear something apart. Of course you didn't mean it! How could you have meant it in those circumstances? You were *coerced*.
4   I rest my case. He didn't teach you anything. I *did* keep telling you.
5   NO!

and languages and secrets, they have a lifespan. If no one passes them on, then they die with the last living person to remember them. A Chant tries to—

They go around—

They learn stories, and they tell them to other people. And when an apprentice becomes a master-Chant in their own right, they give up their name and their homeland. They have to. There's no other option; they have to do it.[6] I think this is because . . .

Why, why is this so hard?

It's because you need to put yourself aside, if you're going to be a Chant. You have to be humble. You can't put too much of yourself into the stories you're telling; that's what my master told me. Because they're not *your* stories. You're just an empty vessel. So you have to keep yourself separate. I think that's why we unname ourselves.[7]

But people call me Chant now and I still think they're talking to *him*. My master-Chant. Chant isn't *me*.

This is a mess, isn't it? Everything in my head is a big tangled knot. I'm not doing a good job of this so far.

I always do this. It's my weakness—that's what my master-Chant used to say. I talk too much about things that aren't important, I babble, and I get sidetracked.

———◆———

There's no translation for what I'm thinking and feeling. Why can't I stop talking about him? Why do I have to keep carrying him around with me? Why can't I just *forget*? I don't want any of this anymore, I—*why aren't there words?* Why can't I just excise it like a surgeon

---

6   Your bias is showing.
7   Sort of? But not really. Why are you bothering to chatter about this? If this is your idea of explaining yourself, my patience is already wearing thin.

cutting out a tumor? Or exorcise it, more accurately—naming the evil thing to gain power over it and casting it into salt water to burn it away. Why can't I name it? Why isn't there a word that means the same thing as . . . I don't even have a metaphor to lay hands on.

"My heart scrubbed raw with sandpaper." There, that will do. "Drowning on dry land, feeling like the water is about to close over my head at any moment, frantic and panicked and scared." Or even, "Lying down in the middle of a deserted road and crying and scream-ing until my throat bleeds." Or, "So much anger and hurt and anger and fear (and anger, and anger, and anger) that it chokes me, that it paralyzes me, that I fall down crying again because I *just—can't—do anything* with it, and there's nowhere to put it down, so I have to hold it in my heart, and there's no one to turn it against except myself—so settle in, self, and hang on."

But all right. I have to get it out somehow, excised or exorcised. I have to put it somewhere besides my own heart, or it really will choke me. Sooner or later it's going to start getting literal. I can put it here on paper, and later maybe I'll throw the paper in the sea—good clean salt water to unmake my hurts from the world.

Let's see if I can pick all these knots apart and weave them into something shaped like a story. And I'm going to lie, because Chants are liars. I won't be able to help it. I'm going to lie on purpose, and I'm going to lie by accident, and it's going to feel better than the truth, sometimes, and I'm so, so tired of not feeling better.

I'm going to write down my real name here,[8] because it strains to burst from my lips and the tip of my pen like a flooding river of

---

8   *I beg your fucking pardon?*

snowmelt in spring, and I want more than anything to take it back, to take *me* back, to go back to the way things were when I was . . . him. And I can't. It's done. It's over. It's lost to me, just like the ancient Chants lost their homeland and couldn't ever reclaim it. My name, too, has been erased from the world. That's the whole point of the rites, isn't it? It's to remember what they lost. It's supposed to feel like this.

Whenever I introduce myself now, I say, "Call me Chant."

But my name used to be ~~Ylfing~~[9]

---

9   How *dare* you. What the hell are you *doing?* I won't stand for this. There—I've scratched it out. One little thing I can do to save you from your folly.

~~THREE~~ [10]

---

10 I threw section three into the fire, just so you know. Took me a couple tries, because it kept splatting to the floor, and then it turned out it was too soggy with tears to burn. So your master, asshole that he was, tricked you and lied to you and used you as a pawn, and you got to watch him sell out a country and all its citizens to save his scrawny neck. And even now, years later, you're beset with guilt? You *know* what sort of a person he is—why bother with all this melodrama? Accept it, learn from it, and let it *go*.

FOUR

A Happy Memory[11]

---

11   This section was also completely irrelevant, so I took that out too (also, the title of this story is mediocre at best). Did you reread anything you'd written before you shoved this mountain of damp paper into my hands and ran out the door? Why did you think I'd care about some boy named Beka in Xereccio? Why did you think I'd care that he was cute and he liked you and that for the first time in your life you didn't care? So *maudlin*! I already want to slowly peel the skin off my face, and I'm not even a tenth of the way through this. (I'm forced to admit that the part describing the dragon-hatching was interesting from a professional perspective, but it really could have done without all the self-pity.)

FIVE

A Good Story[12]

A very long time ago and half the world away, a little boy named ~~Ylfing~~[13] went fishing with his friend Finne. Finne had the most beautiful eyes of anyone in the village, ~~Ylfing~~[14] thought, and lips as pink as flower petals, and hair as buttery yellow as the topaz in the ring ~~Ylfing's~~ mother wore.

The fish were slow to bite that morning, so Finne said, "There is an old man come to the village out of the hills. Have you met him?"

"No," ~~Ylfing~~ said. "I didn't know about him. A trader?"

"A strange trader, if he's that."

"Does he buy or sell?"

"Both, but all he's interested in are stories. He said that for a place at a fireside, he'll weave you tales of faraway lands and heroes you've never heard of. Fill his belly and he'll fill your ears all evening." They

---

12   For my own reference—the title recalls the last line of the previous section: "My Chant said many times that it doesn't matter whether something happened that way in real life, as long as it's truer than truth, as long as the story is good. See, that's my problem. I tried to tell you a happy story instead of a good story. Let me try again." I'll bet five guilders that this isn't a good story either.

13   *Must you?*

14   STOP.

were quiet for a time, and they caught several fish each before either of them spoke again.

"Is he good?" ~~Ylfing~~[15] asked, because the Hrefni have an eye for skill.

Finne nodded seriously, looking at the water, and said, "I think he may be the best that anyone has ever seen."

And he was. By all the heroes, he was.

He was a master-Chant, and he didn't seem to have any other name. ~~Ylfing~~ heard him telling stories, and he took to following Chant through the village whenever he had a chance. He barely spoke to Chant at first, just watched, rapt, and listened to Chant talking to the others, asking for stories and trading his own in return.

And on one glorious shining night of summer, a few weeks later, when the sky got no darker than twilight, Chant turned to ~~Ylfing~~ and said, "I'll be leaving soon."

He said, "You listen well."

He said, "I heard that you told a few of my stories to your friends."

He said, "You're special."

He said, "Would you like to come along with me as my apprentice and see all the wonders of the world?"[16]

And ~~Ylfing~~ found that he would like that very much.

"It isn't easy," Chant told him. "And it's not like your life is

---

15   I swear to all the gods, every time . . . You know what this is like? It's like someone flashing their naked body at me for cheap titillation. That's what this feels like. I've gone back and scratched every instance of that name, like I'm throwing my cloak over the naked person so nobody else has to be embarrassed. You should be ashamed of yourself.

16   Wait, this isn't clear—how was all that handled? Did your master talk to your parents at all? I have a haunting suspicion that he just stole you away in the night, and I really hope I'm wrong about that. That would be *appalling*, and . . . ultimately, unsurprising. Though it does cast an entirely new light on the way things ended between you.

here—we'll be each other's only family,[17] and we'll move from place to place."

So he went to his friend Finne, and ~~Ylfing~~ told him, "The Chant wants me to be his apprentice. I'm going away."

"Goodness," said Finne, his eyes shining. He didn't understand how far away ~~Ylfing~~ was going, but neither did ~~Ylfing~~. "An apprenticeship to *him*! You'll learn all his stories?"

"I will," said ~~Ylfing~~.

"Good," said Finne. "When you come back, you'll be the best anyone has ever seen. You'll probably be taken to every Jarlsmoot, and you'll be named the chief skald every time."

"But first I must learn," ~~Ylfing~~ said.

So he left.

He was young, he was stupid, he was kind and affectionate, and he thought everyone else in the world must be the same way he was, more or less. He thought Chant was the same way.[18]

---

17 Deeply unsettling.
18 Deeply, deeply unsettling.

SIX [19]

---

19   This section was also summarily thrown into the fire—you wouldn't mind that, though, would you? You were going to burn them yourself. It needed to be burnt, anyway; it was too depressing for words. That passage about how you woke up, a lone Chant for the first time, and began walking until you came to the first cross-roads, whereupon you sat down and sobbed for an hour because you couldn't decide which way to go? Unbearable. I couldn't bear it. Might as well have slapped a title like "Nobody Loves Me" on it, you pathetic wretch. And by the pillars of the world, boy, it was like you didn't even notice that cart driver that passed was trying to help you— you could have hitched a ride and had company. But no, you take the other path to avoid the one person you met on the road and you mutter stories to the wind to make *yourself* feel better, as if writing them down wasn't bad enough. What other heresies are you going to confess to?

SEVEN

Enough!

I'm starting over! I'm sick of myself! Here's the only part that matters: I wandered for about a year and a half after I parted with Chant, and I kept to myself as much as I could on the road and hated every time I had to tell a story to someone else. I wanted something that belonged to me, and the stories were all I had. But I have to eat, and I don't carry coin.

Enough of wallowing[20] in the past. I'm in Heyrland now.[21] I arrived three months ago. Heyrland is a city-state on a tiny, swampy peninsula off one corner of Vinte, across the channel from Avaris. They've built dikes all around, to keep out the sea when the new moons bring the king-tides every solstice and equinox, and they dug channels and canals all through the city to drain the water out of the swamp and make the ground dry enough to build on. I expected it to be smelly, but it's not nearly as bad as I imagined—it just smells of water and salt and, faintly, dead fish. No worse than the seaside is, and much better than most other cities, where the filth just gets thrown into the street. The streets themselves are clean—people wash them every day, and they're all neatly paved with bricks or cobblestones,

---

20 Apt choice of words.

21 Ah, *last!* At last we approach the important part! It only took thirty-five pages to get here, counting the ones I threw in the fire!

even in the poorer parts of the city. I see servants scrubbing the front steps of the houses, polishing even the hinges on the doors, and the dikes and canals are just as meticulously maintained—they take care of their city.

The houses are all crammed so close together that there's not even alleys between them. Only the very wealthy folk have gardens. But there are plants and flowers everywhere—even the poorest houses have window boxes of herbs for the kitchen, and others have ones with flowers dense and bright. There are clay pots on every balcony with hanging vines, and there are trees by some of the canals.

I'm tired of wandering. I'm footsore in my heart. Every time I come to a new place, I feel like I'm grasping for something that I can't quite reach. When I arrived here, I was too exhausted to keep going, so I decided to rest, and here I have been since then, the last few months. I do what I've always done, what I learned from Chant: I help with little chores in exchange for a roof over my head and a corner by the hearth where I can sleep, and when I have to, I tell stories to fill my belly.[22] It's simple, I guess. At least, it's familiar. Safe. It's what I know how to do.

This next part is difficult to admit, even silently written down. Words on a page are a strange thing, I'm discovering. When they move from behind your eyes to in front of them, they become more real. Dreadfully real.

Here's what I'm scared to write down: I think I'm getting tired of telling stories.[23]

---

22 I've asked you this before, but really, why don't you have any money saved up? Why haven't you invested in a horse and cart? Why walk everywhere? Why was your master so obsessed with eschewing material possessions? The ancient Chants owned all kinds of things.

23 Oh for *heaven's sake*. This is ridiculous. You're a human being. Humans don't get tired of stories, and if they did, they'd stop being human. Get *over* yourself.

No, that's not quite right. I'm getting tired of telling stories *to people*. And there are so many people in this city—that's why I'm writing things down now, because I can't tell stories out loud as I walk through the streets without being overheard, without someone taking an interest, without them eavesdropping—stealing from me, *taking* from me, just like Chant was afraid they'd take it if I put it on paper. Write it down, and you can keep it secret. You can make it yours and yours alone.

There. There you have it. There's the truth. I'm tired of it.

I think my audiences have been able to tell, lately. Fewer and fewer people have been listening to me, like they know I don't want them to, like they know I begrudge them every word I'm obliged to give them. The meals I get in payment have grown scantier in turn—a crust of day-old bread and a flat look instead of a bowl of stew and a smile. People want a performance; they want you to give them something of yourself. I ache for the day I speak the best story I have and no one listens to me.[24] I dream of it sometimes, of standing in a crowded room and having no one look at me, no one pay any attention at all, as if I were a ghost. I'm getting close, I think. I'm nearly there.

But I still have to eat.

So I've had to find something else to do, as much for the practical purposes of having money for food as it was from a growing surliness with the whole idea of sharing myself like they wanted me to. I wonder why I never noticed that when I was younger—that audiences snap and snatch at you like ravenous dogs, that they'll consume you if they can, that they can suck even the marrow from your bones and leave nothing behind. Once you open your mouth and give them a piece of yourself, some of them think they're entitled to the rest of it.

---

24 You should have been more careful what you wished for.

It takes too much heart, and my heart now is as empty as a desert.[25]

But I still have my brain. I still have years of experience traveling the world and all the practical knowledge I'd gathered or that my master-Chant had seen fit to bestow upon me.

Heyrland is governed by the guilds, the most influential of which is the Guild of Merchants. The city has a very nice harbor, well protected by the dikes, and they do a sprightly trade as an intermediary stop between the nations of the Amethyst Sea to the north, and the Horn of Puihajarvi to the south, and beyond that the Green Gulf, the Gulf of Dagua, and the Sea of Serpents. In short: many ships, from many places. They even send ships out to the Ammat Archipelago from time to time, far off over the eastern horizon.

Lacking any better ideas, two weeks ago I went to Stroekshall, the headquarters of the merchant guild, and offered myself up as a translator for hire. They weren't at all convinced, at first—such an established institution has translators aplenty, but most of them speak only three or four languages at most. Five is considered very good, and six is impressive.

I'm fluent in eight, conversational in another twelve, and can recognize and make myself generally understood in nearly thirty more. My master-Chant said that I had something of a knack for it, and I guess that's true. I used to pick them up as quick as anything, when I

---

25   This is a poor metaphor. The desert is full of things. Oases have insects and fish and small creatures, and in the rest of the desert there's the beasts beneath the ground, and the Ondoro and the Urts in their walking huts with their flocks of goats. And the dragons, which you should have known about considering *you spent twelve pages crying about them.*

was young—I think I was chattering comfortably in Nuryeven within four or five weeks of our arrival, and Umakh only took me three. The language they speak here, the Spraacht (which is a word that literally just means "speech"), took me a little longer, mostly because both the grammatical and social gender systems are particularly complex. (I'm not sure how I'm going to represent that in this language. I'll figure that out later.[26])

The merchants wanted me to prove my competence, of course, so I had to pass their tests. They brought in some of the other translators, and they turned them loose on me.

I should write about that, shouldn't I? That's a proper Chanty kind of thing to write about.

Hah. "Proper" Chanting. As if it matters to anyone but me.[27] What have I got to prove, right?

---

26   Yeah, why *did* you pick Xerecci as the language to write in? You're sacrificing a lot of the nuance of the Spraacht for the sake of your whimsy.
27   Sigh.

EIGHT

Stroekshall is an immense yellow-brick building by the Vasa Canal, five stories tall, with a giant carved door on each of its four sides. It's one of the only buildings that you can walk laps around. There's a wide swath of cobblestones surrounding it, dotted sparsely with a few trees and tiny grassy areas, like miniature parks. It's always packed with little groups of people rushing around and making business happen.

I went in through the south door, sky blue and twice as tall as I am. A burly *vrouw* at the door asked for my weapons, but all I had on me was a small personal knife, the sort everyone carries for any trivial task that might require it. I mostly use mine for trimming my nails or skinning rabbits I've snared when I'm traveling. It's nothing that might be dangerous, but even so, she took it from me, and gave me in exchange a leather disk with a number stamped on one side.

The inside of Stroekshall was cavernous and terrifying. It was like one of the huge cathedrals in Vinte—the middle of the hall was vaulted all the way to the roof, with galleries on every side, like you see in some taverns or theater-houses, and people were hanging over the railings of the galleries and shouting at other people above or below them. On the main floor, there were people running about everywhere, their arms full of papers and ledgers. The din was incredible, as was the sheer amount of frantic energy.

I only realized I'd stopped on the threshold when someone jostled me and snapped for me to move out of the way. I stumbled into a young *vrouw* who was flying past, and a couple of the account books in her arms slipped and fell to the floor.

"Oh, shipwreck!" she snapped.

I scooped up the books for her as quick as I could. "I'm looking for employment," I said, speaking quickly as I helped balance the ledgers in her arms again. I had a feeling she'd run off if I took too long to ask. "Where would I inquire?"

She jerked her head towards the stairs. "Top floor. *Mevrouw* van Meer." And then she was gone. No one stopped me as I went up the steps. The upper stories were somewhat quieter, though they weren't at all separated from the noise below, and they were no less busy.

I found *Mevrouw* van Meer at a horseshoe-shaped desk, occupied but not as frantic as those around her—if anything, she seemed . . . weary? Perhaps just bored. She did have a great amount of paperwork arrayed about her, but her hair was neat and tidy, without the wisps falling in disarray around the edges, like that of the agitated folk running around the main level of the hall. She didn't at all believe me when I told her how many languages I had, and when I offered to prove it, she sent an aide below to gather up all the translators who were available.

Within twenty minutes, I found myself in the midst of a crowd of people, all shouting at me at once in their different tongues—Araşti and Xerecci and Echareese and Bramalc and Vintish and Tashaz and Botchwu.

Though the noise and intensity dazed me, my tongue was quick, and I had been keenly trained for something like this since I was barely out of childhood. I answered again and again, flashing back and forth from language to language like a minnow in the shallows.

And it helped. I felt more awake than I had in months—it was all the parts of reciting stories to myself by rote, with none of the ravenous audience. It didn't involve my heart at all, nor did it require me to give anything of myself away. It was just my brain and my tongue and my ears. I could *relax* doing that.

Some of the translators hated me, or seemed to—a couple of them stomped off grumbling about *smug upstarts*. I don't see how I could have been smug; all they'd been shouting were questions or declarations about the price of grain or fish or cloth, which I relayed from one person to another, as I had no idea how to guess such things.

And at the end of it all, *Mevrouw* van Meer looked at me and said, "You know the manners to go along with those tongues too, don't you?"

"Yes, *mevrouw*," I said. She would have seen—and I'd noticed—my body language shifting with the words without my even needing to think about it, which was only sensible: Language is as much physical as it is verbal. You can't use Vintish gestures with Xerecci words—it wouldn't flow right; the rhythm would be all wrong. And besides, it wouldn't make sense to anyone listening. *She* knew that; she'd seen how I folded my hands neatly in front of me when I spoke Botchwu; how I dropped my eyes politely for Tashaz; how I reached out for Xerecci, anchoring the exchange with a touch to the speaker's arm or elbow to indicate they had my attention.

"Hm," she said. "You're too good to be here," which was kind—she did seem like a warm person when she wasn't trudging through all that paperwork she hated. She sent me off with a letter of recommendation and directions to the offices of her friend, *Mevrol* Sterre de Waeyer, a merchant who was headquartered only a street or two away. But by the time I found it, the day had already waned away to evening, and the only person at the offices was a clerk, who told me to come back the next day.

I collected my knife from the guard at the door and returned to the inn where I'm staying to help the innkeeper, *Mevrouw* Basisi, with whatever she required of me. Sometimes it's mopping the public room, or sweeping the innyard, or scrubbing the front steps, or repairing the shingles, or fetching and carrying deliveries from the street to the cellar or from the cellar to the kitchens, or emptying chamberpots into the canal. Sometimes it's just sitting by the fire and turning the roast on the spit while her cook, Stasyn, does the more complicated dinner preparations.

That day, the person who usually minded the bar was sick, so it fell to me, though I would have preferred to be emptying chamberpots. The public room was busy, full of loud foreign merchants and louder local regulars. I'd already had more than my fill of noise and shouting at Stroekshall, so of *course* I ended up getting strong-armed into Chanting for a new group of merchants who had just arrived from Pezia—two weeks now, they've been here, and they're as obnoxious and excitable as they were when they first arrived. *Mevrouw* Basisi has been letting them play music every night in the public room, which I suppose is her own decision—and it *is* better they entertain themselves than call on me to do it for them.

I would have just kept silently pouring drinks for them, not saying a word, not volunteering myself at all, but *Hecht* Neeltje, one of Basisi's regulars, was there, solidly drunk on one glass of beer. He's very small and slight, and has no tolerance whatsoever, and he gets gregarious when he drinks. He gave me away—started chatting with the Pezians, and when they asked him what sort of entertainment there was to be had that late at night, Neeltje (immediately and with great excitement) pointed right at me and said they should ask me for a tale.

He's only ever heard me tell stories when he was deep in his cups; I don't mind him so much, because when he's like that, he doesn't have the attention span to stick around for more than a minute or two, but he is annoyingly convinced that I say interesting things, and he's always ushering people towards me.

"Go ask him for a tale," he burbled to the Pezians. I attempted to demur, but Neeltje insisted and insisted, and my resistance began to draw attention. I caved; I had to. I told them a short one, "Oyemo and the Ghost," which was all wrong.[28] I was telling the story in a warm, well-lit inn, surrounded by convivial people and noise, with the smell of good beer and better food in the air—even if I'd bothered to tell it *well*, it wouldn't have worked. It was wrong for the setting and it was wrong for the audience too: a bunch of people newly arrived in town, excited to be here, but maybe a little homesick too—I overheard a few of them asking Basisi if she knew how to make a particular famous Pezian dish.

They didn't want ghost stories about broken promises. They wanted something warm, maybe something heroic. Something about home and hearth and hospitality.[29] Even better, something Pezian. I could have told them "Marsilio's Gift," but even thinking of it now makes me want to leave the room.

So I gave them Oyemo, and watched with a dull, resigned kind of satisfaction as their eyes glazed over and their attention drifted away, one by one, until the only person left listening was a young man about my age or a little older, with curly dark hair cropped just under

---

28   No shit.

29   At least you've got that basic skill. At least you can tell what the right story is and isn't—I'd love to be annoyed with you about picking the wrong story on purpose but . . . Hell, even I have to admit there's reasons to do that every now and then. I'll content myself with being annoyed with your reasoning, then, since I can't in good conscience be annoyed at your actions.

his ears and arranged with wax or oil in artful dramatic sweeps, and gleaming dark eyes that didn't waver from me for an instant, even when my voice dropped to a mumble and I rushed through the ending. Something about him screamed *flirt*, a guess that held up as he spent the rest of the evening trying to buy me drinks and *talk* to me. There was a time, long ago and half the world away, that gleaming eyes and dramatic hair might have been enough to turn my head, and if that hadn't done it, then his unabashed interest probably would have.

I didn't want to hear him flatter me pointlessly and insincerely. He would have said how good the story had been, how fascinating it was. Clearly it wasn't—it was wrong on every level, by design. He had no idea what the story could have been, if I'd scraped the barnacles off my heart and given the story to him as it should have been, like this:[30]

---

30   Oh gods, please tell me you're not about to write it down.

NINE

Oyemo and the Ghost[31]

This is an Oyemo story, and like all Oyemo stories it begins at sunset, with the last light fading from the tops of the acacia trees.

Oyemo was traveling by themself again, on the trail of an abomination that had been plaguing a nearby village. Every month, when Mzuzi, the quick moon, was fully dark, the abomination came, passing through (or over, perhaps?) the acacia-thorn fence as if it were nothing but a loose array of sticks, and sucked the life from someone in the night, leaving them to be found the next morning, a withered husk, mottled with bruises.

After three months, they summoned Oyemo, and Oyemo came.

It was a night when Mzuzi was full dark, and Jida waning gibbous. The skies were clear and cold, and Oyemo wrapped their famous tale-blanket closer around their shoulders, waiting and listening.

They spotted the abomination quite suddenly. It slunk about the thorn fence, patting it and crying softly, and Oyemo got to their feet and strolled across the empty sward. They went right up to the fence.

---

31   Goddammit. Is nothing sacred?

"Please," it said, and Oyemo saw immediately that it was no abomination, just a common ghost.

"What do you require?" Oyemo said.

"Please, I'm so thirsty. Please."

"For what do you thirst?"

"Please, give me water. You promised. You promised."

"I don't promise anything to anyone," Oyemo said kindly. "You'd best move along. Look how clear the sky is, how open and easy your path is. Go into the heavens and find a lantern that has burned out."

"I'm so thirsty."

"You are needed above. There are flames to be lit and tended."

The ghost moaned and wailed and pleaded, beating its hands against the thorn fence, clawing at the branches, and though its hands went right through the wood and thorns, it didn't seem to notice, trapped by its own belief that the fence was impassable. Every time it pleaded, Oyemo denied it, until at last its anger grew too much and it flowed through the fence and flung itself on them. But Oyemo flung up their right arm, covered with swirling patterns of scars, places their flesh had been cut and packed with the ashes of certain magic herbs that protected them from all manner of dangers both mundane and supernatural. The ghost could not hurt them. Oyemo wrestled the ghost into submission, but it was a wild thing by then and could not speak to tell Oyemo its name. When the dawn cracked over the horizon, the ghost vanished, and Oyemo yawned and went to bed.

The next month, when Mzuzi was dark again and Jida was too, Oyemo waited by the thorn fence, idly braiding a length of rope made of grass-fiber and starlight. The ghost appeared again, moaning and crying, begging for water. There was not enough moon- or starlight to see clearly, even with Oyemo's eyes, but they could see the ghost was thin, terribly so. It looked withered. *Like the bodies?* Oyemo wondered.

"What is your name?" Oyemo asked.

"I'm thirsty," the ghost pleaded. "Father, you promised, you promised. You left me."

"I have no children," Oyemo said. "And I cannot help you."

"I'm so thirsty. Please. Please."

Again Oyemo denied it and denied it until it was enraged, and it came through the fence. Oyemo fought it back until sunrise, entangling it in the rope of grass and starlight, but it was so thin that it slipped out of all their knots. At sunrise, it vanished.

The next month, when Mzuzi was again dark and Jida waxed gibbous, Oyemo had a silver basin that they had filled with water several nights before and left out at night to gather the light of the stars and moons. They sprinkled certain magic herbs across the water and waited for the ghost. It appeared by the fence as expected, and Oyemo said, "I have some water here."

"Please!" the ghost cried. "Please! Father! I'm so thirsty!"

"Where were you left? Why do you thirst?"

"The well," the ghost whispered. "The water became poisoned. You left; you told me to stay with the goats. You promised to bring water. You promised you'd come back. Two days, you said." The ghost's voice had become angrier and angrier. "On the third day, I killed a goat to wet my tongue with its blood. And the fourth, and the fifth. The other goats started dying. Their blood was thick and dark and sluggish, as parched as mine. On the twelfth day, I laid down in the shade and died. Why didn't you come back for me, Father?"

Oyemo shook their head. "A broken promise is a terrible thing. Come through, lost one. Come and drink." They had laid the grass-and-starlight rope in a snare-circle with the basin at its center, and when the ghost came through the fence and bent its head to the surface of the water, drinking deep in huge gulps until its belly bulged, Oyemo tightened the snare and caught it. The ghost sighed, long and low, and raised its face. Oyemo could see it now, the starlight in the water lighting it from the inside—the ghost was a young boy, fifteen or sixteen, and his eyes were clear now.

"You're needed above," Oyemo said kindly. "There are lanterns to be lit and tended. You're needed."

"Yes," the ghost whispered, and turned his gaze to the sky. "Is my father there?"

"Go find out." They loosened the snare, and the ghost slipped out of its loops, becoming blurry and indistinct, and it rose in the air and wriggled like a minnow into the sky.

Oyemo left before dawn, taking no payment from the villagers, and in the dark of the next moon, they sewed the ghost's tale into their blanket with silver thread like starlight.

TEN

Before I write about Sterre,[32] I have to explain something else. I thought for a long time about what tongue I wanted to write this in. It had to be something besides the Spraacht, to add a layer of protection should these pages be found or glimpsed accidentally, before I have a chance to burn them myself. So I weighed my options: The cold distance of Dveccan, to keep me disciplined and unbiased? The expressiveness of Echareese, like a pure scream of feeling on the page? The easy poetry of Avaren?

But here I am writing in the soft flowing lines and curls of Xerecci.[33] My handwriting isn't too bad. The decision was really just ... anything but Kaskeen. Anything but my master-Chant's native tongue.

Xerecci is comfortable. Cozy. Familiar. It's flexible and adaptive, I don't need a special pen, and the alphabet is designed for swift writing, like pouring a thought out of an inkwell. I don't have to slow down much, writing in Xerecci. Hrefni, my mother tongue, doesn't have a writing system of any kind of convenience (just runes, which

---

32   Oh good, we're getting even closer to the point. I don't have much patience left, and I'm just bracing myself for another goddamn weepy tangent or another new bit of heresy.

33   If I were you, I would have picked Echareese, especially if you were planning on being so whiny.

are rudimentary, more for labeling things than writing at length), nor the complex vocabulary I imagine I'm going to need if I want to untangle the mess I've made of myself.

The downside of Xerecci is that I'm working in translation,[34] and there's differences between the Heyrlandtsche and the Xerec ways of looking at the world. Xerecci, you see, has only three grammatical genders: he, she, it.

I don't feel confident in saying that I entirely understand the Heyrlandtsche gender system quite yet, and I'm hesitant about asking anyone for fear of causing offense. So I've just been keeping my ears and eyes open as much as possible, my mouth shut as much as possible, and, when I *am* obliged to speak, minding my grammar and my manners as scrupulously as I can.

Here is what I can say with certainty: the Spraacht has six grammatical genders.

I *think* that goes the same for social genders, but I haven't quite pinned down what all of those are just yet. There's *mannen* (addressed as *Heer*) and *vrouwen* (addressed as *Mevrouw*), which seem to be the two that you can find pretty much everywhere; and there's *nietsen* (*Mevriend*), who are people without gender—also pretty straightforward. And then there's *vroleischen, tzelven,* and *loestijren* (addressed as *Mevrol, Andeer,* and *Hecht,* respectively), which are the ones I'm still getting a handle on, and I don't want to make any assumptions about them before I've kept my mouth shut and my ears open a little longer. I could compare each of them to other people I've known and the ways people do things in other places I've been, but that doesn't feel right. *Similarities* don't mean it's the *same.* Each place has to be

---

34   Which was, again, your choice. I don't know how you think you have a right to complain about something you *chose.*

understood on its own terms. That's what Chant taught me—people aren't the same everywhere. They're different everywhere, and that's a good thing because it means I have a job.

The point of all this was just to reason my way through a linguistic issue: Sterre de Waeyer is a *vroleisch* and uses the *vroleisch* grammar when she speaks and writes in the Spraacht—a grammatical nuance that Xerecci definitively lacks. Therefore, because I heard one of clerks in the de Waeyer offices speaking Vintish and refer to Sterre with *"pas,"* here I will use "she" since that is the closest translation. This whole detour has been far more complicated than necessary, but I think this is important and I wanted to make sure I had everything straight and clear in my own head.[35]

Onwards.

---

35   Again, Xerecci isn't a great choice for this, if such precision mattered to you. Why didn't you just write in the Spraacht? You could have just called Sterre by *zse* and had done with it without explanation. You didn't *have* to do this work in translation.

ELEVEN

The next day, I went back to the de Waeyer offices. Sterre, I found out, is one of the richest people in the city and one of the most successful merchants. She's stout, strong as an ox even though she must be pushing nearly sixty years old, and as full of fire as anyone half her age. She always wears such nice clothes, too, with froths of ruffled lace at her collar and cuffs, and bright buttons all down her front, and fine rings, different every day except for one—a silver ring with a flattish cabochon of honey-colored amber, etched with a cameo on its underside. And she's a span and a half taller than I am, which has been catching me off-guard these couple weeks that I've been working for her so far—I've gotten used to being one of the taller people in the room the last year or so.

She's so busy that I probably would have been made to wait a long time if, when I arrived, she hadn't overheard me telling one of her clerks about the letter of introduction *Mevrouw* van Meer had given me. She came charging out of the open door of her private office. "You!" she boomed at me. "Van Meer sent you?"

"He has a letter from her," her clerk said, and I held it out. Sterre came forward and snatched it out of my hand, ripped it open on the spot and read it, one hand on her hip. "Hm," she said after a minute. "Hm! That bitch usually knows what she's about, I'll own to that." She looked me up and down. "Skinny thing, aren't you?"

"I suppose so."

"Says here you've got a good dozen or so languages."

"I do."

"She wouldn't say something that outlandish without verifying it." I nearly replied to agree, but she was peering at the letter again, and I don't think she would have cared about whatever I said. "Oh, and she thinks your manners are nice." She looked up at me then, giving me a hard look.

"I do my best, ma'am," I said.

"Good." She folded up the letter and shoved it in a pocket of her skirt. "What's your name? Van Meer didn't seem to have verified *that.*"

Ylfing, I wanted to say, I almost said.[36] "I think she was too busy for formalities," I said. "Call me Chant, please."[37]

And within the hour, I found myself installed at a clerk's desk towards the back of her offices, near her private chambers, reading contracts and bills of sale in a dozen languages and translating as meticulously as I could into the Spraacht, the language of Heyrland.

⸺⸺⸺◆⸺⸺⸺

I've been working for Sterre for several weeks now, translating the things that she wants me to translate. It's been good to get away from Chanting, from doing the things that I always thought I had to do, that I was trained to do. It's been a relief to use my skills in silence, without an audience. Even when I'm translating aloud between her and a business contact or a customer, I am blissfully invisible. Merely

---

36   I SWEAR TO ALL THE GODS.

37   What's *wrong* with you that that's so hard to say? It's been more than a year since the end of your apprenticeship.

a tool at *Mevrol* de Waeyer's disposal. I don't have to think, and I don't have to make any decisions.

I probably would have gone on in that way for a long time except Sterre found out a few days ago what a Chant is, and what they do.

TWELVE

It happened quite by accident. Last week a new shipment came in, and if I had thought the offices were busy before, that was nothing. There were more bills of sale to translate, and letters, more people to speak to, more mindless errands to run. Before, there hadn't been much speaking to anyone, except for casual conversation as the few clerks and I passed through the offices together, but with the arrival of the shipment, there were sailors and captains and merchants from other places.

One of the arrivals was a ship that Sterre had been awaiting for a long time; several months, in fact. It had come, at last, from the southwestern side of the Sea of Serpents, and it bore a cargo of the standard luxuries that you might expect—cloth and spices and unusual things from far-off places. But it held something else, something strange that I hadn't expected to find somewhere like this.

I walked in one day and saw Sterre and one of her captains bent over a filthy, twisted, ugly thing on her desk. It was thick with damp soil that crumbled onto the immaculate varnish.

Sterre looked up when I came in all prepared to settle at my desk, and she gestured me over. "Chant," she said. "Have a look at this."

"What is it?"

"A flower." I must have made some kind of expression, because she and her captain laughed. "We brought in a few crates of them last season and they did well," Sterre said, touching the root fondly with one finger. "Very well. People like lovely new things, and we Heyrlandtsche love our horticulture particularly."

"What kind of a flower is it?" I asked.

"We call them stars-in-the-marsh," said the captain.

There's this feeling when you almost remember something, when it's right on the edge of your brain and if you move too suddenly it might fall off and plunge back into the dark below, out of your grasp forever.

"Lovely things," Sterre said. "Really lovely. A little clump of long thin leaves at the ground, and one tall stalk, waist-height on your average person, about hip-height on me. And at the top of the stalk . . . " Sterre made a blooming gesture with her hand. "A single flower, blue-white. And in the dark, it glows. Just a little, just a shimmer, like starlight."

"And they smell like rotting death," the captain laughed. That feeling of familiarity tugged at me again. "Bugs love 'em, though. They fly right in, get stuck, and then the plant sucks them dry."

"The smell's a small price to pay," Sterre said with a grin. "Master Janssoen bought twenty of them last time. You can smell his garden from a street away, but I'll be shipwrecked if it isn't the prettiest one in the city. They grow in great wide fields in the wild, I'm told."[38]

"Where?" I asked. "Where did you get them from?"

"Kaskinen," she said, and that's when my heart stopped.

"Oh," I said. "Oh. Yes. I know these. I've heard of them."

She and the captain both blinked. "Have you indeed?" she said. "I suppose I shouldn't be surprised, a young world-traveler like you. Have you seen the fields yourself?"

I hadn't ever mentioned traveling to her, but she must have

---

38   True. Lovely sight. Bring noseplugs.

deduced it from my languages and manners. I shook my head. "My master-Chant told me about them once, that's all."

"I beg your pardon? Your what?"

"Oh. My—my master. The man I was apprenticed to." Damn me. Damn it, Chant.

My slip there led through a winding conversation of confusion and clarification, and eventually the captain wandered off to attend to his ship, and I was left with Sterre, who kept coming to my desk to ask me more questions—she wanted to know about my master-Chant, who he was, when he'd seen the fields of stars-in-the-marsh, whether we could write to him to ask about them. Or, better yet, if we could send for him to come here.

These last two hit me right in the gut, and I couldn't help but choke out, "No. No, we can't. I'm sorry."

"Are you certain?"

"Yes," I said firmly. "Anyway, I wouldn't know how to find him even if I wanted to. Chants don't stay in one place for a very long time."

And then she gave me a puzzled look, and I remembered I was trying to avoid explaining to her what a Chant was. *Too late*, I thought, but then it turned out that perhaps it wasn't too late: "Oh, you must mean your family," she said with a sudden laugh. "Funny surname, Chant is, but I suppose it's yours." Another faintly puzzled look, laced with amusement. "This whole time, you've never told me your given name?"[39]

Cold gripped my heart again. "Um. No, I haven't."

"Well, what is it? I can't go on calling you Chant now that I know the truth."

"You can," I said quickly. "You definitely can."

---

[39] If you tell her, I will scream so loud you hear me from . . . wherever it is that you ran off to.

"But I don't call any of my other workers so coldly," and she waved her hand at the rest of the offices—which is true, she really doesn't do that. She is a very fair and kind employer; she calls all her workers by their given names, and they do the same to her. She inquires after their families—I even once saw her write out a note of condolence to the young daughter of *Heer* Quirijn (one of the clerks), whose puppy had died. "Do you dislike your name? I know something about that." She laughed loudly. "My first one always chafed like ill-fitting boots. If you don't like yours, you could always pick a new one."

"No," I whispered. "I like my name very much. I just . . . can't tell you."[40]

"I don't follow, lad; you'll have to be more clear."

"I'm not allowed to tell you my name," I said. "I gave it up. I don't have it anymore."

"Eh? What in the world are you talking about? Family tradition?"

"Chant isn't my surname," I said, abruptly too exasperated to bother with the pretense and evasion any more. "It's a title. It's what I do. It's what I am."

"A translator? An excellent translator under the employ of the best merchant in the city?" She put her hands on her hips and gazed down at me, half-smiling.

And then I had to explain—only a translator by accident, really. She'd been more accurate when she called me a world-traveler, and then I had to fill in the rest, all the things she wouldn't have been able to guess—carrying stories from one place to another like her ships carried goods, learning the ways that people were in one place or another, going somewhere new and looking at it until I understood it.

---

40   Whew. Floods of relief.

"I'm a storyteller," I finished. "That's the simple version. That's what I do to keep myself fed."

"Until you decided to take up translation work."

I shrugged. "It's a job."

She tapped her fingers on her arm. A contemplative expression had come over her face. "Tell me a story."

My heart sank. "I really ought to finish the—"

"There's time," she said. "Go on, storyteller; tell me something."

I braced myself, and closed my eyes. "A very long time ago and half world away, there was a man named Zaria who, being in the mood for fish stew, took his net and his fishing pole and went up the mountain to a certain pond he knew of—"

"Stop."

I stopped, opened my eyes.

"Why are you telling me that story?"

"It was the first one that came into my head." *Mevrouw* Basisi had served fish stew the night before and I'd thought of it, had mumbled it to myself as I ate.

"You don't seem like you care about it. Why tell me a story you dislike?"

"I don't dislike it. I just . . . don't like telling them *to* people anymore. I needed a break; that's why I went to look for translation work."

"So you dislike that I asked," she said, without rancor.

"I meant no offense, *mevrol*," I murmured.

She hummed thoughtfully. "Up you get; follow me." She led me into her office and shut the door, then fetched out a pair of tiny glasses and a bottle of peket. "Have a drink. You look like someone's about to lead you to your execution." She said nothing more until we had sat in silence, sipping our respective thimbles of peket for a time. "What kind of a story is it? Funny, sad?"

I shrugged. "Depends how you tell it. I could make it either one, depending."

"On what?"

"On what I needed it to be. It's a fable, a . . . cautionary tale."

"And against what does it caution?"

"Making deals carelessly. It's called 'The Trout of Perfect Hindsight.'"

The corner of her mouth quirked. "Start it again. Tell it properly."

"A very long time ago and half the world away—"

"No," she said, and topped up my glass. The peket was heavy, almost oily, tasting strongly of juniper. "You got so stiff just then. Two words in and you were as stiff as a day-old corpse. Drink, then start again."

I obeyed, more bewildered than anything. "A very long—"

"Still no!" She slapped her open palm on the desk. "What is this between us that you're so formal and toneless? Slouch down in your chair," she said, pointing at me, and I had to. "Put your feet up on the desk." I did, and she mirrored me with a grin, crossing her legs at the ankle. Her shoes were bright red leather with sparkling jeweled buckles and a gilt heel, not that she needed to be any taller. "Try again. Casual, relaxed, like you're gossiping. Like you're letting me in on a secret."

A glass-and-a-bit of peket had warmed my blood. I took another sip, and closed my eyes. The room was so quiet that it was easy to pretend like there was no one else with me.

"So . . . A very long time ago, and half the world away, there was this fisherman, Zaria, who lived in a drafty thatched cottage halfway up a mountain." And then I told "The Trout of Perfect Hindsight." I told it like I'd tell it to myself, all alone in my room in *Mevrouw* Basisi's attic or on the road in between two nowheres.

And when I had finished, when Zaria had eaten what always

turned out to be an unexpectedly expensive pot of fish stew, I opened my eyes again and met Sterre's gaze.

She was sitting back in her chair, but when I finished, she rose, her hands clasped behind her back, and paced slowly once around the room, looking thoughtful. "You said your master told you about the stars-in-the-marsh," she said.

"Yes," I replied, too surprised by the change of topic to prevaricate. "Some."

"Could you tell a story about that?"

"Yes," I said slowly. "But I'd rather not."

"And I'd rather you did," she said.

"Respectfully, *mevrol*, you've hired me as a clerk and a translator."

"What's going on in your head? You're resistant. Why?"

"It's not something I enjoy anymore."

"Anymore, you say. So you did enjoy it, once. You must have, to have been apprenticed for it." I said nothing. Sterre made her way around the desk again and perched on the edge, her arms crossed, studying me. "So the matter is merely to help you enjoy it again. Or otherwise to give you enough incentive to do it regardless of enjoyment. So what would do it for you? Money? I suppose it is only fair to offer you more money for additional services."

"I don't care about money."

"If you say so. But seriously: name the thing that would incline you to my point of view."

"I don't want anyone to look at me," I said sharply. "I don't want the attention, I don't want—I can't do it. I'm sorry, *mevrol*. I just can't do it."

"Poor lamb," she said, her voice gentle, coaxing. "Of course. I understand. Pretty thing like you, they must look at you like you're a plate of strawberries and cream. Of course you're sick of that kind of attention. I can quite relate."

"I just want to be left alone," I said.

"Do you? Truly? There isn't any part of you that wonders what it could be like? That thinks about taking that hunger that's directed at you and using it like a tool? Redirecting it, building something with it?" I looked up at her, puzzled. "Hunger is everywhere, *heerchen*. The more you feed it, the greater it gets. I'm sure you've noticed that."

"Yes," I whispered. "That's why I'm tired. That's why I can't. I fed people's hunger all I could, and now there's nothing left."

"There's plenty left. When people come starving to you, looking at you like you're strawberries in sweet cream, you don't give them *that*; you give them something else. You convince them they want the apricots next to you. Or the expensive bottle of galardine. Or the exotic new flower bulbs your employer has just imported." The corner of her mouth quirked. "Right? Bright *mannchen* like you, you understand. Don't you?"

"But I'd still have to—"

"It would be different. I'd bet a hundred guilders it would be different."

"No bet," I whispered, simply because I didn't have a hundred guilders, but she smiled, triumphant.

"I thought you'd understand," she said. She pushed off the desk and put one hand on my shoulder. "Besides, *heerchen*, you'd be doing it for me, not for them." I closed my eyes, breath going out of me all at once. Her hand grew weightier. "Is that it? Is that what makes it all right? You'd have a reason. A *purpose*. And you wouldn't have to think about it. I'd guide you. I'd tell you what to do."

I opened my eyes, looked up at her. How many times had I felt untethered, drifting, lost at sea? How many times had I stood and cried at a crossroads?

"Can you do it?" she murmured. "Can you be very brave for me, *heerchen*?"

"I can try," I said faintly.

"There, that's good. That's very good. That's all I ever want—just you trying your very best." And then she smiled very, very wide. "When they show you their hunger, whatever it is, tell them they can sate it with these flowers."

———————◆———————

And that was how I ended up in the market square, sitting on a blanket on the ground by one of Sterre's rented market stalls, where she sends her lieutenants to make public appearances to represent her to the common people.

She wants me to be a Chant. She wants me to tell stories about the stars-in-the-marsh so that more people will buy them, so that she can drive the prices up. She says people pay more when there's some reason to care about the product they're buying. She says they care more when there's a story, and she's not wrong. So that's what I'm supposed to do now. I'm supposed to tell stories about the flowers. I'm supposed to be a Chant.[41]

I haven't decided how I feel about it. But I promised her I'd try. And there is something to what she said, convincing them to take a flower instead of my heart. It makes it . . . bearable. Almost. And the pleasure and approval she takes in my work, the way it matters to her, that makes it bearable too.

But still I need something for myself. And still I need a place to think, to work it all out, a walled garden to tend, tucked away from the world, secret and safe and mine.

---

41   This is perverse. You let her use you and your skills and your holy calling for her own personal gain. For swindling people into *buying* something. Have you no shame?

THIRTEEN

echt Neeltje's lover left him today. I heard all about it—I had to help tend the bar, because even though *Heer* Ambroos (the usual aleman) was there, most of his attention was taken up in managing Neeltje. Part of his job is to listen, I guess, just like it's part of a Chant's job.

I couldn't help but overhear, and it seems I'm still enough of a Chant to be nosy about things that aren't really my business. It was sort of instinctive.

Ambroos eventually decided to stop serving him any more alcohol, and *Hecht* Neeltje sat there slumped at the bar, as dejected as I've ever seen him. He didn't even ask me for a story, or gush to someone else about how *they* should ask me for one, which was probably the most significant sign that something was really, really wrong.

"Can you watch him for a minute?" Ambroos asked me, as the night was wearing on. "Gotta take a piss." He left before I could say anything, so I stood somewhere in proximity to Neeltje and wondered what Ambroos expected me to do about him while I cleaned glasses and wiped down the bar. (Ambroos was getting tired of Neeltje's misery, I think—he's one of those people who doesn't have much interest in romantic relationships, though he will listen to his patrons' other woes all night long.)

"Gimme a drink," Neeltje said. He was slurring still. Hadn't sobered up much at all, by that point.

"Ambroos cut you off."

Neeltje sniffled. "You ever been alone?"

"Yes," I said.

"Really alone, I mean. Alone-alone."

"Yes," I said again, and a dozen stories about the lonely long roads between nowheres presented themselves. I held my tongue.

"You know when you're the most alone, though?"

"When?" I wondered when Ambroos was coming back. Likely he had stopped to smoke, or gotten caught by *Mevrouw* Basisi or one of the other patrons.

Neeltje set his elbow on the bar and held up two fingers, surprisingly steady for the amount he'd had to drink. "Two days after somebody's just ditched you without explanation."

He might as well have punched me across the face. I swallowed hard and hoped my voice wouldn't crack. "Why two days?" I asked, and my voice did crack after all.

"'Cause the first day, they're still there." He flailed one arm towards the empty seat next to him. "You know. The shape of them. The space they take up. Even if they're not in it, you're used to that place having a person standing in it. It hurts, but you're not really, really alone then. Two days, though, you start realizing."

My mouth was dry. "Realizing . . . ?"

"That they're not coming back. That nobody is ever going to stand in that place again, not the way they did, not taking up the same kind of space they did. Then," he said, beginning to cry again, "then you're the most alone."

I gripped the edge of the bar hard enough to hurt my hands. The only other option was to sink to the floor and cry myself. Gods, how is it possible for someone who doesn't even *know* you to say something like that, something that pierces to the core of you, strikes you in a place that you thought no one else could ever really understand?

"Yes," I said, swallowing hard. "I know. I've been that alone."

Neeltje looked at me, his eyes red and puffy, tears pouring down his face. "Someone left you?" I nodded. "What did you do?"

"Cried a lot. Kept walking."

"One foot in front of the other," he said with a sobbing sort of laugh. "That's what my brother said. *He* doesn't know about being alone."

I took one shaking breath, then another. I reached out and touched Neeltje's hand, just the tips of my fingers. "It won't hurt forever," I said. "You're going to be okay. One day at a time." Useless, stupid, bland platitudes, but I wish I'd had someone to tell me even those during my two-days-later.

"Yeah, I know." He thought they were useless and bland too.

"Look, do you—do you have anyone you can talk to about it? Someone besides Ambroos, and when you're sober. You should. You should talk about it. Even to your brother, even if he doesn't really understand it." He made an uncertain noise. "And you should get out of the house and go somewhere besides here. You should go out and do something, or make something. Something that makes you happy, something that has nothing whatsoever to do with the person who left you."

"How am I supposed to do that?" He scowled. "The only reason I made it here was for the drink. You know what I did all day before I got here? Lay in bed and stared at the wall and just—*existed*." He spat the final word. "Hard enough work just to exist. How am I supposed to do anything else?"

"Force of will?" He rolled his eyes. "Yeah, I know. Spite, then."

Neeltje squinted at me. "What do you mean?"

"You get out of bed, wash, put on clean clothes, and eat, and the whole time you pretend like you're telling that empty space that's watching you, 'See? I'm fine. Look how fine I am. *Shipwreck* you.'"

"Is that what you do?"

"Yes," I lied. "Go show them you can live without them. Go do something wonderful, just on the off chance they hear about it through the grapevine and realize what a terrible mistake they made when they left you."

That made him laugh, at least, and then Ambroos came back and I managed to run away before Neeltje sobered up enough to realize what an awful wretch of a hypocrite I am, or decided to demand a story from me, as he always eventually does.

I'll have to do better about avoiding him. He got too close there, hit too near my heart.

Thing is, I think it would be good for me if I did talk to him. You know, if I pulled myself together and took some of my own advice. Talking to him would almost certainly make me feel better, even if I didn't tell him any of my own troubles. I feel a little different just from that one brief exchange earlier, just from telling him what he should do (mostly I feel uncomfortable and embarrassed, like I've walked out into the street without any trousers on, but considering I haven't felt much of anything lately but gray and soggy, that's still *something*). I don't think I helped him very much—hell, I probably didn't help him at all, really. Ambroos had already done most of it. But . . . He could have understood me.

It's so stupid, isn't it? Pathetic. To feel like that one little thing is so damn important, as if something that small can make any difference, in the grand scheme of things. To think that some stranger in a bar can possibly change anything for you just by *understanding*, like empty empathy is worth anything.

Look at me, look at this: Poor little Ylfing, sitting all on his own in an attic, crying because someone made him feel a little less alone for one fucking second, and he was too scared of it to stick around and let them.

~~Stupid, miserable child. Stupid, stupid, stupid.~~

No, none of that. I hear Chant's voice when I write things like that, and there *are* limits to what I'll put up with from myself. I won't stand to let him bully me, not here, a year and a half and a thousand miles away from where he left me. Absolutely not. I really must be more sharp with myself about—about not being sharp with myself like that, I guess.

I don't know if I can manage carrying on out of actual *spite* quite yet, like I told Neeltje, but I can handle sheer, bloody-minded obstinacy. I can put one foot in front of the other and trudge between two nowheres. What other choices are there? I have to keep paying work—I have to eat, after all, and at least while I'm here in the city, I need a place to sleep.

———◆◆———

Speaking of sleep, now that I've calmed down and had some, though fitfully and only for an hour or so—I've been dreaming. The same thing every time, though it's not every night, and lately it's the only one that I remember when I wake up. The first time was right after Sterre showed me the star-in-the-marsh bulb. I suppose it must have unsettled me enough, seeing something that's so much a part of the ancestry of my line of Chants.

The dream goes like this: I'm in the middle of an endless marsh. It's the dark end of twilight, and the sky is clear and empty. All around me, the stars-in-the-marsh are blooming, glowing gently in the dark, and I smell them—rotting meat, just as the captain had said. Every time, I wake up choking.

Tonight when I woke up, I lay in the dark and tried and tried to remember what Chant had told me about them. It can't have been much—he wasn't interested in plants. I know they're hardy. I know more about them from Sterre—they take five or six years to flower from seed, but the bulbs can be uprooted in their dormant season and moved about. I know that sometimes the bulbs grow offshoots, and those can be separated from the mother bulb and will bloom after only a year.

If Sterre got them from Kaskinen... That's where the Chants settled first, when they came out of Arthwend after it sank beneath the waves in the cataclysmic flood. They made landfall in the Issili Islands, on the Jewel Coast, and then (finding, I suppose, seaside living not to their taste) trickled up the archipelago to what is now Kaskinen. They were marsh-dwellers before, the Chants' people— perhaps they brought the flowers with them. Even if it's not true... It's a good story, right?

If all my years of apprenticeship taught me anything, it's more important to tell a good story than a true story.[42]

---

42   What's best, of course, is to tell a story that's good *and* true, but I don't suppose that would matter much to the likes of you.

FOURTEEN

Almost every day, I go to the market square, which the locals call the Rojkstraat, and I tell people about the stars-in-the-marsh. I'm supposedly there to help translate for Sterre's employees, but only locals come to the Rojkstraat, and everyone knows the Spraacht fluently, even the locals for whom it's not their mother tongue.

The Rojkstraat is like every other market I've seen. It's not special. There's nothing to remark upon.[43] There's rows of tables, and

---

43 What in the world is wrong with you? The Rojkstraat is one of the biggest open-air markets in this hemisphere, and it's only because the Heyrlandtsche are so exquisitely well organized that it seems smaller. Do you know how many people go to the Rojkstraat every day? Thousands. There are crowds, but it's never *crowded*, and the sheer volume and variety of goods rivals anything you might find even in Araşt—I can go to the Rojkstraat and buy a pound of Zebid coffee and Arjuni cardamom and turmeric, or a gallon of Nuryeven menovka and Vintish galardine, Cormerran wool and Genzhun silk and Avaren linen and Ammatan seawich, or Oissic olive oil, horses from Umakh or Qeteren ... I could go on. And that's only the things you can buy; that doesn't even touch on all the musicians available for hire, the street illusionists, the fire-eaters, the six different varieties of fortune-tellers, the priests on the street corners declaiming the words of Kas or Sannesi or Mindu, the coffee shops and tea gardens and public houses where dozens of merchants haggle out contracts and gamble with each other on the fate of their ships to ensure that they don't lose all their capital should the unthinkable occur. It's a world-class market, and *you* dare to say that it's "not special." I would ask whether you are blind, but that would be an insult to blind people, who could still experience the Rojkstraat in the sounds and the smells, in the cobblestones under their feet, in the feel of cloth under their fingertips,

some of them have awnings above them, and there's people playing music for coins, or telling fortunes. It's exactly like any other market. It's open every day of the week, except during the stormy season, when the rains come too frequently and too heavily for anyone to linger out-of-doors for very long.

I have to go every day for the half of the week that Sterre rents her table there, because she said so, and when I arrive, I find her majordomo, *Heer* Teo, and I do whatever *he* tells me. And what he tells me is to sit on the bench, or on a blanket on the ground, and tell stories, whet the hunger of the ravening crowd, and then turn them over to Teo when they're ready.

But they pay me. There's that, at least.

The stars-in-the-marsh are *very* popular. There's almost always a crowd of people around our table, placing orders for the roots. Of course we don't have the actual product out there in the open; I get the impression that they think it's vulgar. People pay for the things they want, and then everything is delivered to their houses in neat little parcels. That is, that's how the comfortably wealthy people do it. Poor people buy and carry just like anywhere else, and their markets are even less remarkable than the Rojkstraat.[44] And very wealthy people, people like Sterre, they don't go to markets at all—the merchants, or the merchants' representatives call at the manors to offer their wares, or the rich folk host private salons.

Sometimes I'm required for those as well. Sterre hosts a small

---

in the jostle of the crowd around them, in the warmth of the sun on their faces, in the taste of a hundred different kinds of street food from dozens of nations of the world. No, you're not blind. You're not even an idiot, because there are soft-witted people who delight in the Rojkstraat too—I have seen them! No, you are something evil: You're someone who let himself become *numb*.

44   I just sighed so loudly that Arenza heard from all the way across the room and asked if I was all right.

gathering of society figures, fifteen or twenty of them, in a fine parlor of her own house, or in someone's garden, and it's more of a party than a market. More about making an appearance and strengthening connections with people, rather than buying and selling. I hate those even more, because people talk to me there in a way that they don't at the Rojkstraat—they want to know something about me, or they tell me how talented I am. Sometimes they flirt with me. At the Rojkstraat, they listen in silence and then move on, or they talk to Teo and pay him for the bulbs. It's better that way. They barely look at me.

And they don't ask my name, not like Sterre's rich friends at the salons. There, they say, "And who are you, young man?" And I have to say, "Call me Chant," again and again. And again. And every time, it feels like I'm lying to them. I used to make friends so easily, when I had my name. I used to feel connected to people. I used to *care*.

Who *am* I? Who have I become?

When did I forget how to love the whole world? When I was seventeen, when I was ~~Ylfing~~,[45] I would have thrown myself at Heyrland with my arms outstretched. I would have made six new friends every time I left my room. When I was seventeen, I could have spent an hour in an alley and found ten things about it that were special, or at least interesting.

And who am I now? Just Chant, not ~~Ylfing~~. And a Chant is tired and jaded.[46] A Chant has seen everything the world has to see, and found it tiresome.[47] Or has at least found the people in it tiresome.

Another thing—to go back to the comparison of Rojkstraat versus salons—the Rojkstraat people throw coins at my feet, and the

---

45   Please stop.
46   Go fuck yourself.
47   That's not a Chant problem. That's a *you* problem.

rich folk never do. Not that I spend my money on anything but food; I'm still doing chores in exchange for the right to sleep in the attic with the dust and the spiders, and one small window that looks out over the innyard and the canal.

I suppose I'm spending money on ink and paper now, too. Telling stories compulsively to no one, alone in a dark, dusty, miserable room.[48] Because I can't stop. Because I can't forget how much comfort and happiness I used to find in stories, and there's no one telling them to me anymore—it's as weak and pathetic as hugging myself for lack of anyone else doing it.

There's one other thing I've spent money on. I bought one of the roots. Teo said it would grow in a pot, if I watered it enough. I don't know why I did it. I had the money for it, and I wasn't spending it on anything else. I don't even particularly like the idea of it—it's just an empty pot of earth now, but when it sprouts I'll have to look at it, and when it blooms I'll have to endure the smell of it, and every time I see it, I'll think of my master-Chant telling me the stories about it, about Kaskinen.[49] Until then, it's just a pot of empty soil sitting in front of the window, where it can get some light, and every day I go down to the rain barrel outside the kitchen and bring up a bowl of water to pour over it.

Maybe I shouldn't have even planted the flower. Maybe I should just have the pot of empty soil and carry that with me wherever I go, like I carry the absence of my name. But there was something about it that felt compelling. Something about the idea of—oh. When I

---

48 That's a sin too. As bad as telling stories to the wind. You're wasting them, writing them down like this. Words on a page are dead things, like the corpses of butterflies.
49 Why choose to torture yourself like that? Forget about him. He is nothing to you now, or he ought to be nothing.

became a Chant, part of it was symbolically sinking my homeland beneath the waves. Cutting off my bonds to my old self and my old life, giving up my name.

I think planting the flower was so important because it's the opposite of that, in a way. It's just one little thing, and it won't make much of a difference to anyone but me, but there it is: growing something, instead of throwing it away. I suppose we'll have to see if it helps me at all. Between the flower and these writings, I'm going to have to come to some kind of conclusion. I wonder if I'll be someone new by the time it blooms. I wonder if I'll be able to be Ylfing again.

FIFTEEN

I tell the stars-in-the-marsh stories eight, nine, ten times a day now. Sterre knows her business. She knows what people want, and she knows how to sell it to them. It seems like every day there's more and more demand for these ugly, wretched things. Sterre has a few blooming in her garden, and I've seen them at the salons. They smell like rancid meat, but when twilight falls . . . they do look like stars. Like starlight. As long as you don't breathe, it's easy to see how beautiful they are. The glimmer of white-blue light is strongest in the center of the flower, and when you stand at a distance as the breeze sways their stalks, they seem to twinkle.

We're very close to selling out of this last shipment, and Sterre's been scheming about how to keep the money flowing until the next ones come in. She's worried that the fashion will turn before the next ships arrive.

None of that is my concern. I just sit on the blanket, and I tell the story again and again, as if I were a clockwork automaton, and when I go to sleep at night, I dream of them, night after night—I dream of being lost in the wetlands, surrounded by the stars-in-the-marsh, their stalks soaring taller than I am as I slosh through the deep muck up to my thighs, up to my hips or my chest, every step a struggle. The smell is stale, thick, oppressive. I can't breathe, but I can't stop moving either. I can suffocate in the air, or I can slip beneath the surface and drown. And I keep moving, looking for something and hoping that someone is looking for me. No matter where I turn or which direction I struggle through thick, mucky water, all I see are the woody stalks and the low knots of leaves and the dark sky above me. No moons, no stars but the flowers, shimmering blue-white, giving me just enough light to see that there's nothing to see, there's no end in sight.[50]

And as I wrote before, I wake up choking—not every night, but lots of nights.

I don't think I can go on like this.

---

50   Oh come now, even *you* aren't so obtuse as to miss what this dream is trying to tell you. I'm sure you noticed it eventually. If not, I'll give you a hint: *You knew what you were doing was wrong. Stop it.*

SIXTEEN

I've been staring at this page long enough for my candle to burn down a full inch. Gods, look at my handwriting—look how shaky and unlovely it is.[51] I'm going to have to copy this out on fresh sheets.

But this . . . this, I have to write down. And I don't think I can just talk about it in summary like I've been doing. I think if I don't write it all down, I'll convince myself it was a waking dream. But it happened.

It happened. I know it. She was real.[52]

I went to the Rojkstraat today, just like every day. I sat—no. Slower, Chant. Tell it right, if you're going to tell it.[53]

I went to the Rojkstraat today, just like every day. Today was Watersday. Busy, but not crammed with people as it would have been on Firesday or Stonesday.

Today I . . . saw something. Someone. They were at the other end of the Rojkstraat from me and Teo and our arrangement. I didn't even notice anything unusual until Teo grumbled about it—

No. Slow *down*. Tell it *right*. You know how to do this, Chant.[54]

---

51 Yeah, it's really bad here. I can barely read this. It's giving me a headache.

52 I'm going to *scream. Who? Who was real?* And does it involve the flowers at all? I expect not! Either skip this and get to the point, or at least make it a good story if I have to suffer through it!

53 Only what I've been telling you the *entire time!*

54 That *definitely* remains to be seen.

I sat on my blanket in the shade of the awning and folded my legs tailor-style. Teo hadn't brought a cushion for me today. He forgets, most of the time. I make do on the bumpy, uneven cobblestones, and I don't complain.

I declaimed the stars-in-the-marsh story twice, and then I got up to stretch my legs. Teo handed me a jug of cold tea—he prefers it to water, I've noticed. I drank deep, wiped my mouth, and handed the jug back to him. He took it, glaring across the Rojkstraat, hardly paying me any mind at all. "You might as well sit and rest your voice, Chant," he growled. "No use competing for attention with the new, fresh thing."

"What fresh thing?" I asked.

He jerked his chin to indicate. I looked over, and then I noticed that the crowds were slowly drawing away from our end of the market, towards the other.

"What is it?"

"Who knows?" He sat back in his chair and crossed his big, thick arms. "But it'll ruin our morning's business; I can already see that plain."

I felt a glimmer of—something. Maybe just habit: a Chant's job is to go and look at things and listen to them. "Shall I go find out?" I said.

Teo shrugged. "If you like. No use for both of us to just sit here, not when everyone's off gawking." So I went over. It was strange—I hadn't walked the breadth of the Rojkstraat very often. I hadn't felt immersed in it.

At the other end of the Rojkstraat there was a big crowd of people—big for a Watersday, anyway, maybe eighty or so. And at the center of it, there was a boxy cart, something like a traveler's cart, or a tinker's, though there were no horses to be seen. It was painted blackberry-purple with yellow-and-gold trim,[55] and there was a little set of steps leading out the back end, and one entire side had been folded out and set on legs to make a little stage. And there was a woman sitting on the stage with her legs crossed tailor-style, just the same as I'd been when I sat at the booth with Teo. She was perhaps forty,[56] with iron-black hair shot with gray plaited in one long rope, long enough that the tail end of it fell on the stage in loops around her hips. Her clothing was a strange mix of fashions—a bizarre garment[57] that looked like a Xerec-style crossed-front vest on the top, but with long tails in front and back, like a Vintish waistcoat, which would reach to her knees were she standing; a pair of baggy calf-length trousers, something like the short pants worn by rice farmers in Map Sut and Genzhu. Her arms and feet were bare and golden-brown. All her clothes, like the cart, were in shades of purple, and she wore bright gold bangles at her wrists and ankles, and six gold earrings in each ear, and her clothes were sewn with little metal sequins all over so she glittered like anything. Her dark eyes were marked heavily with kohl.[58] Her hands rested on her knees, her back very straight, and she looked steadily out at the crowd. There was an unlit candle in a holder in front of her.

I found myself pushing closer, towards the front of the crowd, and then I noticed, belatedly, that there were two young people sitting on the ground below the stage, playing music. A girl with a goblet-drum across

---

55   Oh! It's *me!* You're talking about me! Good gods, were you really so unsettled? Your handwriting here is still awful.

56   Forty-six, close enough.

57   It's not bizarre, it's comfortable. I designed it myself and had it made! I don't see how you have the call to be criticizing anyone's clothing anyway—*you* go around in threadbare homespun.

58   All this detail! Were you perhaps jealous? No one's stopping you from wearing pretty clothes, Chant, or from wearing kohl or jewelry if the whimsy strikes you. Whatever happened to those togs that Sterre made you wear for the auction?

her lap, and a younger boy with a long, thin stringed instrument (which, if I had to name, I might tentatively identify as a langeleik) across *his*.

"Attend, attend," cried the girl with the drum. "Attend a sight you'll never see again! From far and wide have we wandered, and seen all there is to see! My mistress knows the secrets of the world, and every story ever told! You'll tell your children tales of this day! You'll never see our like again!"

The woman on the stage leaned forward and cupped her hands around the candle. She breathed softly on it, and when she took her hands away, there was a flame. Scant applause like scattered grain ran through the crowd—some folk must have thought she was another illusionist, or perhaps a performance-mage.

Every story ever told, the girl had said. I felt my gut twisting. I felt sick. I didn't want to hear any stories. I turned away.

"Make my cobblestones ring with copper and silver and gold," said the woman on the stage, "and I'll make your heart ring in harmony."

I felt all the breath go out of me. I felt something in me cry: *Stay, stay, stay*.[59]

And I thought, *She has a presence, that one. Master Chant would have told me to listen to her. He would have told me to watch. She has tricks worthy of study.*

And I thought, *I wonder how she does that with her voice, so she sounds like she's standing right beside you.*

"My name," she said, "is Mistress Chant."

Oh, I thought.

---

59   I confess, it is rather fascinating to see all this from your perspective. I saw you that day too—I saw a pretty young man with strikingly tired eyes come through the crowd, and he looked at me and my cart and my apprentices, and then he turned away. That's what made me notice you. Hardly anyone turns away like that. One in a hundred people. If they're not interested, they never even approach. But you approached, and then you were about to leave—and that, I noticed.

SEVENTEEN

I turned back. I set my eyes on her and I didn't look away for the next hour. I don't even remember blinking. I cast my copper with the rest of the crowd and made her cobblestones ring.

I don't know if she made my heart sing back, as she'd promised. It was thundering too loud in my chest to hear anything else. She told stories until the candle burned down—stories both familiar and strange, stories I gulped down like a fish gulps water. She told "Priya, Majnun, and the Wondrous Blue Panther," and "The Twelve Tasks of Tyrran," and one about a skeletal horse that challenged travelers to singing contests, and one about a girl who went into the Sea of Sun to make a deal with a sand demon, and then she told some real stories about recent occurrences: about the coffee harvest in Zebida, about the birth of the new crown princess in Araşt, about an earthquake in Dvecce. She told us about the king of Inacha, whose kingdom lies across the tops of five thousand square miles of mountains and karst peaks that rise like pillars from the earth, and about the web of bridges that lace his kingdom together, and the great windmills they've constructed to pump water up from the ravines below, and the way they therefore worship the wind as the source of all life.

I could only stand and listen, my heart and ears straining towards her like a thirsty ghost struggling across an acacia-thorn fence, gulping down her stories until I realized that I was doing just what I hated my audiences doing. I forced myself to look down, to fix my eyes on my worn-out shoes, the cobblestones beneath my feet. And yet I couldn't help but steal glances, now and then—desperate, helpless sips instead of the frantic gulps.

At the instant the candle's flame drowned in its shrunken puddle of wax, she stopped, rose to her feet, bowed, and retreated into the cart. The boy and the girl—her apprentices, I imagine, and I was flabbergasted that she'd have two of them[60]—yanked on some ropes on either side of the stage, and it closed up neatly.

"Come back tomorrow!" the boy shouted. "We'll be here again tomorrow!"—which of course gave lie to their assertion that it was a sight the audience would never see again.

I went back to Teo, who scarcely seemed to notice that I'd been gone, and I sat on my blanket and stared at nothing until Teo asked me why I was crying,[61] and whether I could stop doing that and start hawking the stars-in-the-marsh, since folks were beginning to wander around again.

So they're going to be there tomorrow. She's going to be there tomorrow. Mistress Chant.

Another Chant.

---

60   Really? Seriously? Even from the beginning? How many times are you going to disparage me for my teaching practices? They have nothing whatsoever to do with you. There's nothing whatsoever in all our teachings that says a Chant should only take one apprentice at a time. My own grand-mistress had three for a brief time— one was getting close to ending their apprenticeship, and they helped teach my mistress-Chant and her apprentice-brother. They were *family*. And you, time after time, spit on that as if I'm doing something wrong.

61   Oh for heavens' sake.

EIGHTEEN

Please, please, please don't let her be there tomorrow. Please don't let her come. If there is anything in this world or a higher world that might feel sorry for me, please don't let her come to the Rojkstraat tomorrow.

My master told me I'd likely never meet another Chant—though now that I think of it, maybe that's not what he meant. There *aren't* very many of us (though how would we know that for sure?), but . . . Maybe he meant I'd never meet another one who was willing to take on an apprentice,[62] because that's what I was when he told me. I was just about that girl's age . . .

I don't know what he meant, I guess. And it's too late to ask him now, even if I weren't inclined to leave town in tears were I to find out he was here. *Her* being here is bad enough.

Another Chant. By the sand and sea and sun, I never even imagined I'd meet another one. Perhaps . . . Should I introduce myself? Is there etiquette? Honestly, I'd rather stay in my rooms until I hear she's left town.

I'm being torn in two. What would I even say to her, if I were to say something to her?

---

62 No, he meant you weren't likely to ever meet another one, period. This was a once-in-a-lifetime opportunity that the two of us stumbled onto, and you squandered it because of your pathetic broken feelings. We'll never have this again. Why didn't you *care*?

Hello, I'm a Chant too.[63]

Hello, my name is Chant.[64]

Hello, Chant. I'm Chant. Will you understand me? Can you tell me what's wrong with me? Can you help me?[65]

You're a Chant. Please, tell me what I'm doing wrong. Is it supposed to hurt like this? Does it ever stop?[66]

Oh, damn my eyes, all of that sounds stupid.

I won't say anything to her. Chants don't stay in one place for very long, and she looked like she had a system. That cart, how smooth and quick and well-practiced their motions were ... They've done this a thousand times. They've designed their lives around traveling, to go from place to place frequently and in comfort.

In comfort.

Chant and I never traveled in carts like that, besides occasionally hitching a ride on the back of a passing farmer's wagon. We never dressed in fine clothes like that. We never carried so many belongings with us—nothing like those instruments her apprentices had, for one thing, and I saw glimpses of other things inside. Since I was fourteen and left home to chase the horizon, I've only owned one pair of trousers and two tunics at a time. One pair of boots. One cloak. One bag, to carry food for the road. One small knife, one small tinderbox. And Chant carried even less than that. Only the stories in his head and the clothes on his back. He went into the world with the faith that he could catch himself with his wits and his quick tongue alone, and nothing else.

---

63 I would have said, "By Shuggwa's Eye, *are you really?* Come, brother-Chant, let me embrace you!"

64 I would have said, "And so is mine. Well met, brother-Chant. We should talk."

65 I would have listened. I would have tried.

66 No, it's not supposed to hurt. It hurts because you're not doing it right, because someone screwed you up and you haven't done anything to fix yourself.

I wonder what he'd think of her, if he saw her.

No, I don't wonder. I know. He'd sniff and purse his lips in that way he had. He'd call her a pretentious upstart. He'd tell me that she cared about things that don't matter—purple carts, and baggy silk trousers, and purple brocade vests all sewn with gold sequins—rather than the important things, the stories. He'd hold his arms out to show me; he'd say that he's never needed peacock-finery to keep an audience's attention. He wouldn't like her. He didn't really like anyone, I don't think.[67]

I hope she leaves soon. I hope I never see her again.

I'm going to see her again, aren't I? I hope I don't make a fool of myself in front of her.[68]

---

67   And even after everything, that matters to you, doesn't it? It still matters what he thinks, or what he would have thought if he'd been here for you like he should have been.
68   Oh, don't worry. You definitely did.

NINETEEN

I dreamed again last night, after I came home from the Rojkstraat: in this one, my foot slipped on something, and the water closed over my head in a rush, and I was flailing and drowning and grabbing at the roots of the stars-in-the-marsh to haul myself above the surface, but the roots tangled around my hands, around my legs, and I—

I woke up, and by the distant noise of the public room below, I thought it must have only been an hour or two that I was asleep. I couldn't bear the thought of trying to sleep again so soon, so I went downstairs and sat at the bar and stared dully at the back wall with the full intention of exhausting myself with waiting—if you stay up late enough, eventually your eyes mutiny against the rest of your body and you can trick yourself into a dead-deep, dreamless sleep.

The aleman knows, by now, to ignore me, and the Pezian merchants were making a racket on the other side of the room again and taking up all of his attention anyway. I sat there, waiting for the sandpaper grit in my eyes, thinking of . . . her. She told stories like she was sipping wine from a brimming cup, like the people in the crowd were offering up baskets of bread and fruit for her to eat, like they offered up their own hearts, instead of snatching for hers.

Abruptly, I turned to the aleman. "*Heer* Ambroos," I said urgently.

He looked over. "Need something, Chant? A drink?"

"I'll give you a tale in trade for a glass of peket." Why not? Seeing her, listening to her, had shifted something inside me.

Ambroos was dubious. He'd heard my stories before, flat and dull and not at all worth even a thimble of peket. "I'd prefer coin, if it's all the same to you," he said, which should have been a relief.

"I'll take the deal," someone said, sliding onto the bar stool next to mine. "A glass for each of us." It was that Pezian, the one from before, the flirt who had listened even when all the others had drifted away. "Sounds like a great bargain to me," he added with a boyish grin.

"I'm afraid I'm not in the mood for flattery today, you should know," I said, suppressing a wince when I heard how stiff and cool I sounded. "I was only going to practice something on *Heer* Ambroos."

He paused for a mere moment and smiled. "Oh. All right. No flattery, got it." I glanced at him as Ambroos pushed our cups in front of us, each containing a finger of caramel-colored liquor. I've always had a knack for people, for sensing good intentions. I wish I was equally as good at sensing bad ones, but those get complicated. But this person, this bright-eyed Pezian with the boyish smile and *flirt* written behind him in letters of fire ten feet tall ... He'd hesitated. And then, a little awkwardly, as if he were still practicing a new dance step he'd just learned, he'd made a choice. A deliberate one. And ... sincere. It struck me as odd. He was obviously unaccustomed to being declined—he was young and lovely and rich and of good family, and I didn't need to be a Chant to see *that*. And he was unaccustomed to accepting it with such good cheer, but he was practicing that now. Intentionally. I only spotted it because I've been trained to watch people so closely, to pick up tiny cues, ones maybe they didn't even notice they were giving away.

"Would you like me to leave?" the Pezian asked when I hadn't said anything for a moment. "I was just joking about the bargain, you know. Here, I'll go."[69] He stood up in a rush, his smile turning apologetic and still so very careful. "Tell your tale to *Heer* Ambroos as you'd meant to. The drink is on me."

"Sit," I said. He'd do. He wanted to listen, and he was polite enough to be sent off with a word if he turned out to be too much trouble.

He sat, and I brought the cup of peket to my lips and drank, studying him over the rim of it and wondering once more if I could figure out how to tell a story by taking something rather than giving something away, the way Mistress Chant seemed to.

I lowered my cup, rolled it between my palms. "A very long time ago and half the world away ..." I told him "The Trout of Perfect Hindsight" as the bar emptied and Ambroos wiped down all the counters and tables, locked up the doors, and banked the fire. I mostly watched the Pezian boy, but I saw Ambroos, too, the way he tilted his ear towards me, the way he smiled now and again. He finished his work long before I finished the tale, and came back to lean against the bar with his cloth slung over his shoulder, quiet and attentive. "That's a good one," he said when I finished. "Why don't you tell that one more often, instead of the others?"

"What's wrong with the others?" asked the Pezian.

Ambroos shrugged. "They're not as good. You been practicing, Chant?"

"Something like that," I said, after a moment where I forgot again that *I* was Chant. It ... hadn't felt like anything. Hadn't hurt, hadn't wrenched at me like I'd expected. It had been hard before, some of the

---

69   Hm. This offer of graceful retreat is to his credit, even if you're right about him learning it intentionally. A gentlemanly skill.

times when I'd told stories in the public room, when I first arrived in
Heyrland. There had been drunk people (regulars of the inn, I know
now) who knew that I knew stories, who demanded a particular tale
from me and then watched me like a pack of dogs might watch a
dripping slab of fresh meat. It hadn't gone well, those other times. I'd
resented them for their interest and attention—and yes, I know that
was ridiculous—and so I'd flattened myself, deadened the story so
they wouldn't care about it. That, that had hurt. But this? Just numb.
Intellectually mechanical, like an automaton, rather than anything
that tugged at some heartstrings. I suppose it's an improvement—
better to be numb, a blank page, than to feel sick or spiteful. It was
like . . . washing clothes, or cleaning a fish, or braiding straw for a new
pair of shoes.[70]

"Well, keep practicing, then. In the meantime: Out, gentlemen,"
he said. "If you're going to sit up all night, do it in your rooms."

I pulled myself onto my feet. "Good night," I managed.

"Maybe you could give me a bottle of something?" the Pezian said
to Ambroos. "Some of us might get thirsty again if we're awake for
too much longer."[71] He cast me some kind of glance, but my sight had
grown blurry with weariness and I was already moving towards the
door. Last thing I heard as I reached the steps was Ambroos snick-
ering at something under his breath—maybe something the Pezian
had said. I didn't dream any more.

---

70   It's not a heartstrings kind of story, though. I don't know what you expect.
71   Sweetheart, he was trying to buy you a drink. Just like before, when you were
tending the bar.

TWENTY

The Trout of Perfect Hindsight

A very long time ago and half the world away, there was a fisherman named Zaria, who lived in a drafty thatched-roof cottage halfway up a mountain. Living alone, he dressed as he liked, and did as he liked, and ate as he liked.

One day, he decided that what he would like to eat was a big pot of fish stew, so he took his pole and his basket and went a little ways down the mountain to a pond he knew of, where he thought the fish must grow big and fat and very tasty.

Zaria cast his fishing pole into the lake seven times, but felt not even a nibble on his hook, and every time he pulled in his string, even the bait was still firmly attached. Zaria scratched his head and scowled. The day had worn on to evening, and Zaria's stomach panged with hunger. He could not bear the thought of walking all the way back up the mountain to his little cottage with nothing to show for the day's work, so he decided to cast his line out one more time.

Just as he was about to, he saw something large moving beneath the water. He scrambled back from the edge, and a beautiful silvery-rainbow speckled side breached the surface. A rolling round eye looked right up at him.

"Lightning strike me where I stand!" cried Zaria. "What I wouldn't give to get that beauty in my pot!"

"You oughtn't say such things," said the fish, gurgling from under the water. "Someone might hold you to it."

"Might they?" Zaria said, edging forward carefully so he could peer into the water. "And what do you know of such things, fish?"

"Enough," said the fish. "I know of bargains and regret."

"Do you indeed?" said Zaria. "How did you come by that knowledge?"

The fish bobbed up to the surface and peered right back at Zaria with its big round eye. "When I was very young, a thousand years ago, a flaming stone fell from the sky and crashed into the woods nearby. It shattered into pieces and several of the pieces fell into the pond. They glowed with a light that was not a light, and they stank of a smell that was not a smell, and they itched with thorns that were not thorns when you swam too close to them. I swallowed the shards, and became what I am, and when I dreamed, the great sea god, the King-of-Fishes, swam up out of the depths and told me of things that no other fish has known."

"You're a magic fish," Zaria said, to be sure he understood. "A heaven-stone fell here and granted you magic powers. Is that right?"

"Right enough, if you're an idiot," said the fish.

"I probably am," said Zaria, who felt himself a reasonable man. "But how would I know? You can help me, then, since you're the smart one here."

"What obligation have I to help you?"

"I'm a stranger in need on your doorstep," Zaria said. "You wouldn't turn me away, would you?"

"I suppose not," the fish replied. "What is it that you need?"

"I'm terribly hungry, and I was hoping to catch some fish for stew. Do you know where I can find any?"

"There's no more fish in this lake," he said, full of regret. "It was getting rather crowded, what with how large I'm getting. But that's what comes of magic powers."

"Sorry, what does?"

"Hindsight," said the fish. "That's my magic power and my great knowledge of the world. I have perfect hindsight."

"Ah," said Zaria, who was suddenly no longer entirely sure that he was the stupid one of the two of them. "So how's that work?"

The fish sighed again. "As even an idiot might expect. As soon as I act on a decision, I have the supernatural wisdom to see every part of where I went wrong and how I should have done it differently. But my curse is that I cannot use my powers in advance. I only know what I should have done after I do it."

"Huh," said Zaria, thinking wildly about the pot he had at home and the amount of stew that could be made with even a single steak from this fish. "How about that."

"Yes. So now I see I shouldn't have eaten all the other fish in this lake, you know? I ought to have left a few to keep me company."

"How terribly lonely that sounds," said Zaria. "And what an awful shame."

"Indeed," said the fish, sighing a great and wistful sigh. "So now you see my plight."

"Yes," said Zaria. "You'll probably starve."

The fish jerked in the water, looking wildly up at Zaria. "Wait a moment! *What?*"

"Well, won't you?"

"Of course not; I can eat the bugs that land on the surface of the water. I can eat small birds, too. In the spring there will be ducklings."

"What about when you eat all of them? Then there won't be anything left and you'll waste away to nothing. Even your magic powers won't save you from that."

The fish jerked again. "Is that true? Is it?"

"It sounds right, doesn't it?" said Zaria innocently. "But I could help you if you liked, if you agreed to help me."

"How?" said the fish.

"There's another lake, only a couple miles away. It's bigger, and it has more fish in it. I could carry you there, and then you could help me catch some of them for my stew."

"All right," said the fish. "How shall we accomplish this?"

Zaria picked apart his wicker fish basket and formed it into a large, loose cage or harness, which would support the huge bulk of the fish while hanging from Zaria's shoulder on the basket's old strap. Zaria indicated to the fish that he should jump into it, and the fish did so. "I just have to make sure you're secure," said Zaria, and tightened several of the ties so the fish could not even squirm.

Immediately the fish went very still and said, "I've made a terrible mistake." He said nothing more.

Zaria hiked back up to the cabin, killed and cleaned the fish, and brewed up a huge pot of stew in his cookpot with the fish's tender, pink-snow-colored flesh. He cut the rest of the fish into steaks and hung them in his smoker, and by the time he was finished, the stew had rendered down into the richest, thickest white broth, redolent with onions and leeks and mushrooms and potatoes and many other good things, the morsels of fish as flaky as you could hope for.

Zaria ladeled himself a generous bowlful of the stew and took a giant bite.

As soon as he swallowed, he set the bowl down sharply, looking down at it in dismay, and said, "I've made a terrible mistake." For in eating the flesh of the fish, Zaria had gained its magical power of perfect hindsight, and lived out the rest of his days knowing exactly what he'd done wrong at all times.

TWENTY-ONE

For the last few days, thankfully, Sterre has requested me to attend her at the salons for a while instead of assigning me to the Rojkstraat—I wouldn't have counted it such a stroke of luck if it had happened last week. Before I saw Mistress Chant. Before I became very interested in avoiding the Rojkstraat at all costs, hoping that she might move on before I went back. But luck runs out sooner or later, and there wasn't anyone in this world or a higher world who felt sorry for me, and thus I was sent to the Rojkstraat again today. And, as I feared, Mistress Chant was still there too.[72]

I didn't move from my blanket in the shade of the booth. I shut my eyes tight when I saw her cart pull up across the square and the people gather around. A bigger crowd than last time. We could hear the music even as far away as we were; it went on for longer this time, and the audience was clapping in rhythm to it. I heard both of the apprentices singing, sometimes alone, sometimes together, though it seemed the boy sang more often. I was too far away to hear the words clearly, but he had a strong, clean voice. Both of them did.

Then, quiet, which must have been when the Chant was telling stories.

---

72 When was this? You're not very clear about when things happened. I was at the Rojkstraat a lot.

Then, much later, the crowd dispersed, and I thought I could relax.

My tongue may as well have turned to wood in my mouth when the girl-apprentice[73] appeared before me. I stumbled in the midst of my story and tried to cover with a fit of coughing. Teo silently handed me the waterskin, and I availed myself of it simply as a delaying tactic. But then I handed it back and I had no more excuses, and so I started up again. She watched me with her arms crossed loosely, and I . . . I don't know where my mind went. I don't know what came over me. I finished the stars-in-the-marsh story—this version, one of six or seven that I kept in circulation, was little more than a paean to the endless, achingly beautiful, glittering fields of the flowers that one supposedly could find in Kaskinen, like the gilded streets of the mythical city of Euridah. I claimed to have seen them myself, to have brought the roots to Heyrland with my own hands and found a sympathetic ear in *Mevrol* de Waeyer. I told all manner of lies, but that was what Sterre wanted me to do—to lure them in with words, whet their appetite with visions of wonders they'd never see themselves, and then offer to sate them with a morsel. But today, instead of encouraging the audience to inquire with Teo about purchasing flowers of their own, I just . . .

I don't know what came over me. I started a new story.

It felt awkward in my throat and mouth, as if it were made of uncomfortable corners, and I cringed and cringed to hear myself. It was "Jump-up Jalea," and it wasn't at all right in any respect—not the right tone, not the right style, not the right anything. I could tell as soon as the first words left my lips, but by then it was too late to stop or change my mind, and I had to tell the rest of it while my face burned with hot humiliation. It was nothing like whispering stories to myself, not even

---

73 Her name is Arenza.

anything like Chanting for the evening patrons at the inn, or for that Pezian boy. It felt foreign, disconnected, clumsy.

The girl-apprentice tilted her head a little as she listened, and I did the best I could, though it felt like the story was fighting against me, like it didn't want to come out. It felt like fishhooks ripping at my insides as I forced it from my lips.

When I was done, she turned on her heel and walked off into the crowd, and Teo only said, "You'd best stick to the other one, Chant." And though I was flustered and kicking myself for choosing so poorly, again I stupidly thought I could relax. I thought she'd been bored. I thought that I wasn't worthy of calling myself Chant, telling a story as badly as that one.

Stupid. Stupid.

Stupid because she[74] reappeared a few minutes later, and this time she had her Chant in tow. I felt like crying. I wanted to run away. I wanted to fling myself at her feet. I wanted to chase her away. I wanted to take her hands and beg for her advice.

I swallowed my fear because that was the only thing I could do. I swallowed my tears because it wouldn't have done to cry in front of Teo, who might tell Sterre, who would think less of me—not to mention that the Chant would have thought less of me too.[75]

I told the stars-in-the-marsh story again, a variation that appealed to the Heyrlandtsche tendency towards humanism: a congeries of the personal virtues that the flowers symbolized, comparing them to

---

74 Ah, this is that day—that was two or three days after the first time we saw each other.

75 Ugh, you really think the worst of people, don't you? I wouldn't have *thought less* of you. I just wouldn't have thought anything about you. I would have simply marked you as some sweet young amateur, doing his awkward, inexperienced best. In fact, I might have admired things about your performance—your projection, or your emoting. That's quite different, you have to admit!

Araşti prayer-nuts, a small visual and tactile reminder of a moral ideal one is pursuing or espousing. *Look at the flowers*, I said, *look upon them and become a better person.* I exhorted the audience to inquire about prices with Teo. For a wrenching moment, I thought about opening my mouth and telling another story—how often does one Chant meet another, after all? I felt (and still feel) like I should have done something different. I should have told one of my best ones—I should have *had* a best one to tell, something grand and powerful, something that could shake the foundations of the earth. But those have never been the kind I like. I've never gotten my head around them. I like fables and fairy tales, small and quiet and soft and cozy, with their deep meanings tucked into their pockets and sewn in the hems of their coats. Suggested, rather than explicit.[76]

So instead of telling another, I got to my feet and told Teo I needed to step away for a moment, and he was so busy with his customers that he didn't even notice. I carefully avoided eye contact with the Chant and her apprentice, and I tried to slip away through the crowd.

I found an opportunity to glance casually behind me and nearly leapt out of my skin. She was right behind me, and her hand was outstretched as if she were about to tap me on the shoulder.[77]

"My apologies," she said. "I didn't mean to startle you."

"It's nothing," I said, averting my eyes and turning away. "Please excuse me."

"Actually, I was wondering if I could ask you a few questions."

I swallowed and did not look at her. "Sorry, madam, I'm terribly busy—"

"Are you?" she said. "Because you just told your partner there

---

76   Nothing wrong with your reasoning here. There's a lot to be said for a story that's still revealing new secrets to you on the fifth or fiftieth or five hundredth retelling.
77   You make it sound like I was stalking you like some street pickpocket!

that you were taking a break to stretch your legs. I'd be happy to walk with you."

Of course. A Chant should have sharp ears and sharper eyes. "Just a quick break, really. Sorry."

"Ah," she said. "Then perhaps I could buy you a spot of lunch when you're finished here. Beer too, if you like."

"I'm not hungry," I said. "Sorry."

She was not at all deterred: a Chant should be tenacious. "Then what if I were to pay you for your time?"

"I have no need of money."

"Hah! You're set on eluding me, aren't you?"

I risked a glance over my shoulder. "It's only eluding if you're giving chase."

"Fair point, master storyteller. Well, I will leave you be, then. Perhaps I'll come by tomorrow and see if your mood towards my offers has changed. You may have your pick of them."[78]

I should have just thanked her absently and walked away. I didn't. I hesitated. "That's . . . generous of you," I said.

"Not at all," she replied, smiling brightly. "We share a profession, you and I." She didn't know how right she was, and it made my breath catch in my chest. "I was hoping to do business with you—a pleasant kind of business. Trading stories, yours for mine. My girl Arenza heard the one you told earlier."

"Nothing special," I said quickly. "Just a silly thing I picked up somewhere."

---

78 This is not really how this conversation went. I wasn't so pushy—*you* acted strange the whole time, and I started getting concerned for you. You seemed so scared of me. And I didn't say I *would* come back the next day—I *offered* to come back another time, but you left that part out, didn't you? It didn't fit with your story about being bullied by the scary other Chant.

"We didn't think it silly," she said. "An interesting variation on 'The Tattling Girl.' Perhaps related to 'Sela and the Wolves'—it sounds like it was something from . . . Kirmiri, maybe? Do you remember who told it to you?"

My master-Chant, I thought to myself. *And he had it from a woman from Ffefera named Marain somewhere in the Mirror Passage—you were nearly, nearly correct.* "No."

She looked at me for a long time before she smiled again. "I see. That's a shame. I would love to hear what other variations you might know."

"I don't think . . . That is—it wouldn't be very interesting for you."

"I beg to disagree. And how would you know what's interesting to me, anyway?" Her eyes glittered. I couldn't get a read on her. I couldn't tell if she was being pushy or merely friendly.

I was floundering. I wanted to run away and hide in my attic room. "You've probably heard all my stories anyway," I said. "A Chant like you would—" And I bit my tongue and felt all the blood drain out of my face.

But a Chant must be sharp-eyed and even sharper-eared. "A Chant like me, you say?" She'd come alight. Even more intense. She took a step towards me, and I found my back scraping against the wall. "You know Chants." Not a question.

"Nope," I said quickly.[79]

"You do. Knowing the word is not so unusual—my apprentices shout it to the crowds day and night. But they say *Mistress Chant,* as if it were a name. And you said—"

I darted away down the Rojkstraat, or tried to, but she caught my sleeve and held me fast.

---

79   If you're so convinced that all Chants are liars, why aren't you better at it?

"You said *a* Chant. Not a name." She looked at me hard. "And what's *your* name, young one?"

My mouth had gone dry. I couldn't speak.

"I wonder," she whispered. "I wonder if you still have your name. You must yet have it, mustn't you? Or perhaps you are just freshly without it. That would explain why you blush like a new bride." Her grip was tight on my elbow, and she looked like she'd just pulled a treasure out of the river on a fishing line, her eyes warm and shining. "Ought I congratulate you? Where is your master? I will congratulate them too."

"I need to leave," I said. "Teo will be wondering where I am."

"Ah yes. Teo. Will you tell me what Teo calls you, or shall I go ask him myself?"

"Please," I said. Begged. "Leave me be."

"Why? We're the same, aren't we? Every moment, I see it more clearly—what other call would a young man, barely more than a boy, have to be telling stories in a market half the world away from his homeland? Norland or Smoland, isn't it? Or Hrefnesholt."

"Let me go." She released me. I took several steps back. "I promise I'm of no interest to you."

"But you are. You're the most interesting thing in the city," she said. "I'm right. I know it. I can read it in your eyes. You're a Chant too." I must have looked like a hunted animal. She took two steps back, held up her hands.

"Yes," I said, wrenching the confession out of my gut. "I am."

"Then we *must* talk."[80]

I couldn't even say that I didn't want to, because part of me did

---

80   Once again, I didn't say it like that. You're making me out to be so pushy and rude. I suppose when you say "All Chants are liars," you're actually just talking about yourself specifically.

want to. If that part hadn't existed, I could have just run away. I could still just hide somewhere in the city until I hear that she's gone. "I need to leave," I said again.

"I'm not stopping you," she said, except she was—she was standing there in my way.[81] "But your master? Are they near?"

"No," I said. "My master and I separated." All at once I realized how tired I was. Not only that, I realized that I'd *been* tired. Days, weeks. Months. I'd been tired since long, long before I arrived in Heyrland. Ever since I gave up my name, or longer.

"Oh." She was surprised, perhaps confused. I don't know why. I didn't want to know.

"Goodbye, Mistress Chant."

"I hope to see you again, Master Chant," she said in reply. It fell on my shoulders like a cudgel. I kept walking. I was too tired to say any more.

---

81   *No*, I wasn't. Why the hell were you so scared of me? I was very careful not to make any sudden movements near you, or to stand too close to you—the whole time, you looked like you were about to cry and run, except I couldn't tell whether you wanted to run *away from* or *towards* me. I gave you your space, as much as I could. I asked you questions—reasonable, simple questions—and you stood there and let me ask. You didn't run away, so what was I to think? And now you accuse me of *bullying* you like this, when I did nothing of the sort.

TWENTY-TWO

It's been weeks now since I started working for Sterre. It's going well for her—the flowers are so fashionable lately, it seems like everyone admires them. I don't know how so many people have the time and money to care about flowers. I don't have the energy to go figure it out.

I go to the salons, I go to the Rojkstraat.

Mistress Chant is still around. She's in fashion now. She gets invited to salons too, apparently. I found that out today.

Sterre brought me to her friend's house—a big one in the middle of the city, with a huge garden. He's a famous tailor; I don't know how a tailor affords a house like that, but that's how things are in Heyrland. At parties like today's, I follow Sterre around like a dog.[82] I hover at her elbow, or I kneel at her feet when we're all lounging in the garden or the parlor—I'm little better than a servant in their eyes, so I don't get particularly gracious treatment. Sterre introduced me to *Heer* van Vlymen as if I were a treasure for her to brag over. She'd brought a few other people too, other friends of hers that she wanted to introduce to each other. She had little showy facts about each person that she used over and over to introduce them. *Mevrouw* de Voecht, for example, was deeply involved in falconry, and Sterre brought that

---

82 Oh good, you're aware of that.

up again and again, as if it were the only thing about her that was interesting. *Heer* van Vlymen, I found out no fewer than seven times, was the only tailor in the city whom Sterre trusted with her personal wardrobe: "My quality of life improved *so* immensely once I met him, dear," Sterre would say to someone in a confidential tone, as if that person were the only one she had ever told this story to. "I've got a very particular figure, I'm not too proud to admit, and it takes some doing to make a frock flatter me as it ought. I really thought I'd have to resign myself to coats and breeches if I wanted to cut any kind of dashing figure, because simply no one else could quite manage to make the patterns right for me. But my dear, dear van Vlymen has never flinched from the task. He's a jewel—he could fit petticoats to a boulder," she said with the same laugh, over and over, always the same little story. She always went on longer about van Vlymen than anyone else, and I suppose it was because he was the host—so she had to wax poetic about the elegant way van Vlymen had of fitting cloth to her broad shoulders when all the other dressmakers had never managed to do anything but make them look ridiculous in comparison, and so on. "And it's all thanks to him that those awful puffed sleeves fell out of style," she finished. "Not a day too soon, either. Good riddance to those ugly things!"

I would have drawn conclusions from that—she was performing, making herself out to be light and sparkling as she sailed around the salon, a social butterfly whose only care in the world was the state of her clothing and the whimsies of fashion. It would have been an effective mask (and I saw that most people either believed it, played along with it, or else had masks of their own), except I kept noticing little moments. Moments where she might touch someone's shoulder or elbow and lean in a little closer, lowering her voice, concerned. "I heard that you lost one of your ships recently," she said to one person, *Mevriend* Jehan, who was drawn and grayish with stress. "Are you all right for money? If you need a loan, please don't hesitate to reach out. I know you're good for it." From anyone else it might have been a subtle snub, but Sterre evidently meant it with all sincerity, and Jehan knew that. They shook her hand, assured her they were fine, and promised to ask her for help if they needed it.

Those moments kept happening, once every few minutes. "Is your mother recovering from that nasty illness of last winter? I sent her a basket of nice things a few weeks ago. I hope it cheered her," and, "I heard young *Heerchen* Pieter's goldfish passed. He must be brokenhearted, poor mite. May I send him a letter of condolence, or would that upset him?"

And then after these little enclosed moments of genuine care and intimacy, she'd go back to her performance, loud and colorful and charming by design.

At today's party, I drifted around as though in a fevered haze, feeling like I'd done hundreds of these so far. I had told the stars-in-the-marsh story, as I was commanded to do, and then I sat quietly and had nothing to do but listen.

"Yes," Sterre said, "we're doing amazingly well. They're all the rage, of course, and they're only getting more so by the day."

Heer van Vlymen agreed heartily. He was a short person, a *mann* with spindly legs and a great large belly, and he wore enormous amounts of frothing lace at his wrists and neck, and bright jewels on his fingers and ears, and shining silks encrusted with embroidery. He had a great energy to him like a twittering bird, and he spoke in sudden outbursts as if each time he was holding himself back until he could bear it no longer.[83] It was exhausting, but I had no choice but to endure in silence. "Indeed, everyone talks of nothing but your flowers, Sterre my dear. I even overheard my upstairs maids talking about their plans to buy some for themselves!"

"Well, they'd better buy soon if they plan to," Sterre said. "We've sold out of the current shipment, and we've nearly sold out of the shipment that hasn't arrived yet."

"Have you indeed!" one of the other guests said. "However did you manage such a thing?"

Sterre shrugged. "It was simple, really—when people already know that they want something, and they know it's on the way, they don't mind laying down their money to *ensure* that it's theirs when it arrives. It saves the hassle of crowding in front of my offices and fighting and elbowing to get inside—you remember a few years ago when that artist came through, *Mevrol* Alyden Gelvooht? I'm sure we all remember the dreadfully unfortunate incident that happened when everyone tried to buy her work at once. The riots! Such a vulgar display." A murmur of agreement went through the room, and Sterre took the moment to sip primly at her lemonade. "My way is much more genteel, I think you'll find."

"But what of mishap? What of accident or damages, like shipwreck?" This from a young man with a marked foreign accent— Pezian, perhaps, or Bendran. I dropped my eyes to my lap and remained still and expressionless. I suppose he hadn't noticed how the people here regard "shipwreck" as a crude word, a curse.

"Hush!" Sterre said, echoed by several other people. "Gods forfend. There are of *course* stipulations for catastrophe on either side.

---

83   Hah, all right, I have to agree here—that's a fairly apt description. And now I know which salon this was—you're about to complain about me again, aren't you? Poor little Chant, was I *mean* to you? Five guilders says that's how you'll frame it.

Am I the sort of person to demand someone pay up if half their family has died of plague, or if their house has burned down? Please! I respect my fellow citizens—are we not all siblings and cousins? Do we not all shelter each other from the storms? Do we not have a moral duty to bind together to keep back the waters? I'm an honorable and upstanding person. I strongly resent any suggestions otherwise."

I, for one, hadn't heard anyone suggest anything like that, but a few people around the room said, "Too right!" under their breaths, so I gathered that perhaps the foreign man wasn't popular in this particular circle.

"In all my contracts, *both* parties are adequately protected, I can assure you. It's a very elegant and civilized solution to the problem. To several problems."

The man cleared his throat. "I apologize, ma'am, I spoke without thinking. Of course you've put a great deal of thought into this."

"I have, *Signore* Acampora," Sterre said primly. "And if you would like me to explain my thoughts on how these contracts for future sales work, I would be more than happy to do so. But it's a terribly dull affair, not suitable conversation for garden parties at all. A matter for clerks and lawyers!"

"Oh, don't be so modest," *Heer* van Vlymen said. "Your methods are always ingenious."

Sterre smiled and inclined her head, gracious. "I wouldn't want to burden all these good people with technical language. I tell you, it makes even my head whirl to think about all that."

There was a soft murmur of objection from the guests, and *Heer* van Vlymen gestured around. "See, Sterre dear? We're terribly eager—we're hanging off your words."

"Well, if you insist. It's quite simple. These contracts of future sale essentially say that you have paid for the right to claim a certain amount of the product upon its arrival in the city. A receipt in advance, if you will. As I mentioned before, you get to skip all the vulgar parts of going to a shop and fighting with other people for a limited amount of the product. The most excellent thing, however, is that I'm selling it at a discount. If it is bought with one of these contracts, of course."

Heer van Vlymen cackled. "The infamous Sterre de Waeyer, cutting into her own profits? I never thought I'd live to see the day! Someone go check the dikes; they'll crumble any day now!"

Sterre smiled indulgently as good-natured laughter rippled around the garden. "In a way, dear sir, but consider: you're saving yourself money by removing risk for me, which allows me to reduce my operational costs and therefore lower my prices accordingly. You see, a merchant's greatest fear is that she will go to all the trouble and expense of importing goods, only to find that there's no demand for them upon their arrival. She then spends money storing them in a warehouse while they molder, while the rats get into them, while they age and get dusty. Perhaps they sell slowly, and she barely breaks even. Perhaps the damp gets in and spoils them—let's use the example of cloth, since our good host is known so well for his creations. Aernoud, my good man, if I bring in a shipment of linen twill, but you've just turned the fashion to Vintish silk jacquard, then I'm out of luck until the fashion turns again, if it ever does. How am I supposed to know when that will be? That is, of course, what I employ *you* for." They grinned at each other, and Sterre raised her glass in a modest toast to him. "But perhaps you and I talk, and you say that you're prepared to pay me to bring you several bolts of silk jacquard. Then the sale is done, and I've already made my money on it. *You* like this deal because you know exactly what you're getting and when. You know that the supply will be there for you—you can plan your business accordingly and kindle a burning rage for silk jacquard before it even arrives. And

I too like this deal because I'm not taking a risk. It's closed and tied up neatly in a box."

"And so the only risk is"—van Vlymen cleared his throat—"incidents on the voyage."

"Indeed. Unavoidable and unpredictable. But those are easily accounted for with an insurance policy."

"Oh, don't tell me you patronize those coffeehouse charlatans!" one of the guests cried.

"Are they charlatans?" Sterre replied sharply.

"It's gambling! Uncouth and vulgar in the extreme."

"Perhaps—but it seems to me that more ships come in than not, wouldn't you agree? And when they do, everyone is happy and the money comes rolling in. And what's a few hundred guilders when everything is rosy? Once you think of it as an operating expense, it seems a lot cheaper, doesn't it? And if everything turns out *not* to be rosy, well! You've saved yourself a cargo of heartache, and no mistake."

"I would trust *Mevrol* de Waeyer's judgment in business matters more than my own eyes," van Vlymen declared. "So let us lay this to rest before we ruin the day with silly arguments, eh? I have a particularly rare entertainment for you all today, dearhearts, just you wait. Henrik!" he called to the butler standing at the door. "Bring in the lady, won't you?" He turned back to us and twinkled. "Such a discovery. My assistant, Theodora, was visiting the Rojkstraat a few days ago and found her, and as soon as she told me about her, I knew this would be just perfect for our little gathering."

I had mentally floated away, listening to all this conversation more from force of habit and training than any desire for or interest in the knowledge. But hearing *Heer* van Vlymen mention this, I sat up very straight and wanted very much to leave quickly and quietly, before *she* arrived.

I knew it would be her. The other Chant.

And so it was. Her apprentices had donned neat, modest Heyrlandtsche clothes in muted colors with their instruments carried on their backs, but she herself wore the same colorful, outlandish performance costume she'd worn at the Rojkstraat. She glittered in the candlelight.[84]

"Friends and honored guests, may I present Mistress Chant! A world traveler and a storyteller of no little skill, here to regale us with songs and tales of far-off lands and wondrous deeds."

"Surely such a person would be suited more for a lingering romantic dinner party than a gathering of businessfolk," someone said. His voice dripped with amused disdain, and I couldn't help but feel a pang of anger on Chant's behalf.

"I'm sorry, you said her name was Chant?" Sterre said, sitting forward. She nudged my shoulder with her knee, as I was sitting on the ground quite close to her. "A relation of yours, Chant?"

Mistress Chant's eyes fell upon me then, and I saw a glint of something in her eyes.[85] "Ah, my esteemed colleague," she said. "No, madam, no relation. We are only siblings in the way of monks in a monastery who call each other brother and sister out of respect and shared faith."

"Huh," Sterre said, eying Chant. "I think he told me something about that once. It's a title, isn't it? Not a name. Right?" She nudged me again, and I nodded silently. "I thought you said it'd be too much trouble to find another one of you. Hah! A negotiation tactic, I suppose. Deftly done, my lad. Respectable work. Well, here we are, then." She sat back, and I didn't have to look to see that she was having

---

84   Good god, you're tiresome here.
85   Yes, it's called *being pleasantly surprised to see you.*

another one of her brilliant business ideas. "Mistress Chant, after your performance, I would love to discuss a matter with you. But after." She wanted to hire her, I could tell already. She wanted a little corps of Chants on her payroll, peddling all kinds of prosaic and mundane goods as if they were priceless treasures. The stars-in-the-marsh are one thing—at least *they* really are special—but I could imagine her doing the same thing for cloth or nails or wood or bricks, now that the proof of concept had proven so effective.

Shipwreck the flowers. To hell with them.

Mistress Chant dropped an elegant curtsy in the exact correct Heyrlandtsche style and gestured to her apprentices. "These are my wards, Arenza and Lanh Chau. Before I begin, they will play and sing for you."

I sat quietly, with my eyes downcast and my hands folded in my lap, and we listened as the apprentices settled themselves, checked the tuning of their instruments, and began.

After only a few bars of music, I felt Sterre lean forward, and I felt the warmth of her breath on my ear, close enough to send unpleasant goose bumps down my spine. "You must help me, when she's finished."

"Hm?" I said back, as softly as I could.

"She's a friend of yours?"

"No," I whispered. "I met her once at the Rojkstraat, a few weeks ago."

"Are there any other Chants nearby?"

"Not that I know of. There's no way for me to know. We wander."

"We? *You* seem quite tame and content to be still." I had nothing to say to that. "I want to convince her to work for me. Do you think she would?"

"I have a feeling she wouldn't."

"Nonsense—look at her clothes. Ridiculous and gaudy, nothing of substance. And in comparison, her apprentices', plain and poor. And their instruments are worn and battered." I disagreed, but I didn't dream of saying so aloud. Mistress Chant's apprentices had dressed to the station they were expected to hold—two servants-of-sorts, just as I was. And Mistress Chant herself was a hired entertainer. It was appropriate for her to dress in fine bright clothes, and to wear jewels that would catch the light and our eyes.[86] She was a Chant, after all. Stories weren't all she held in her mind—she also had these little twists and turns of etiquette that let her sail through any level of society with comfort and grace, regardless of whether she was garbed in silk or wool or burlap. She would have been trained for it, just as I was. "She'll do it for enough money, mark my words," Sterre whispered.

"Yes, *mevrol*," I replied. I glanced up at just the wrong time and caught Mistress Chant's eyes—she was looking at me and Sterre, thoughtful, concerned or perhaps disapproving.[87] She didn't look away, didn't pretend like she hadn't been watching the exchange between me and my employer.

The apprentices played slower songs. They were already the center of attention; they had no need to grab for it with bright jigs and folk-songs. These that they played were elegant, restrained, genteel. I had heard songs just like them at almost every salon that Sterre had brought me to. I didn't find anything remarkable about them.

When they had played three or four songs, they bowed, and Mistress Chant politely applauded with the rest of the audience

---

86   A Chant should be eye-catching. Well, Eye-catching, anyway.
87   No: Suspicious. I didn't like the way she positioned you around her, sitting on the floor by her knee. I didn't like the way she leaned into you or whispered in your ear. Do you know what that looked like? Like you were a dog sitting at her feet, a cherished pet to be doted upon or scolded as the whim took her.

and stepped forward. Henrik came into the room, carrying a small, knee-high table, which he placed near the middle of the room, and Chant claimed one of the cushioned chairs to move closer to the table. Henrik produced a small candleholder from his pocket with a thumb-length knob of candle stuck in it. Chant took this and set it carefully in the exact middle of the table, and she lowered herself slowly into the chair.

They were already hanging on her every movement. She was so deliberate. She moved in exactly the way that she meant to, and everyone could tell. She lit the candle with a snap of her fingers, and folded her hands in her lap.

She looked around the room and made eye contact with each of us in that same deliberate way.

I wondered why she always lit the candle. Every time I'd seen her in the Rojkstraat, she had a candle before her, just as she did now.[88]

She hung her head, breathed deeply. Rolled her neck, exhaled. And then she began.[89]

---

88 I needn't answer you here, because you asked me directly later on, as I recall.

89 Oh, you'd better not. You'd *better not* do what you're about to do. Gods, I don't want to look at the next page. I could just set this whole thing aflame right now. The hearth is right there. Ah, Lanh Chau, bless him, just brought me a strong drink. Precisely what I needed to get through this fucking ordeal.

TWENTY-THREE

Naturally, and unsurprisingly, she told different stories here than she did in the Rojkstraat.[90] That's just common sense. There are stories that can hold an audience of forty that can't hold an audience of fourteen, and vice versa. My Chant taught me about this, lectured for ages and ages about picking the right story for the audience. Like a pair of boots, he used to say, stories were. Some fit you just right. Some rub and chafe until you're blistered. Some keep out the damp. Some you can boil and eat if you're really hungry. But you have to know how to fit them. You have to be able to look at your audience and understand them and what they want. You have to meet their hunger head-on.

Mistress Chant knew her craft well, of course. She wouldn't have been able to support two apprentices if she didn't.

I ought to copy down the stories she told, I suppose[91]—I ought to copy down any stories I hear, for lack of anyone to practice them on verbally until I've committed them to memory, and also for the lack of any inclination to do it that way. It still feels too tender. It's too soon. I'll do my best to remember them until it's time to write them down, if that time ever comes. Maybe later, when I'm feeling better, when

---

90   Oh thank the gods. I thought you were about to copy down everything I said. Not just floods of relief but torrents.

91   No! No, don't you *dare*. I swear it: I'll burn these pages, and then I'll come after you and burn you too.

I have the strength for it. But those stories aren't important to *my* story, and that's what I'm trying to muddle through right now—what I'm going to do, and where I'm going to go. And, most difficult of all, who I'm going to be—because who you are is just the stories you tell yourself about yourself, and the intersection of all the hurts you've ever had and how you survived them.

So, for my own future reference, I suppose I'll at least make a note of *which* stories they were:[92] First, one about a band of mercenaries during the war between Vinte and Bramandon, a century ago—the mercenaries cleverly crept into the Bramandese camp at night and poisoned the commanding general and averted a battle that their side would have surely lost.

Then, "The Tale of Peregrine Lee," a story about a woman who led a crew of miners to chisel a tunnel through a mountain that lay between two countries who longed to make peace with each other.

And finally she told a Heyrlandtsche story about seven siblings during a famine. I thought that, particularly, was strange—why tell them a story they already knew? And I could tell that they knew it by the way they smiled and relaxed and nodded along. Why?[93]

---

92 Ugh, if you *must*.

93 Ah, young Chant. There are things you haven't learned yet. Sometimes a Chant tells stories to bring the world closer to itself, to make it smaller and cozier, to make it easier to understand. But sometimes you don't need to bring the whole world in— sometimes you tell a story for another reason, to please your audience or to make them more . . . *themselves*. People *like* stories they know, because they emphasize an existing belief. I told "The Seven Siblings," a Heyrlandtsche story, because I was speaking to Heyrlandtsche people. And the Heyrlandtsche people have certain ways about them— they believe in community. Of course they do: their entire existence for the last five hundred years has been a battle, themselves against the water. The sea is hungry, and if their vigilance slipped they would be flooded, swept away, overcome. So they build their dikes and their windmills, and drain themselves a garden from the tidelands. And if one of those dikes falls, the water comes in, and the city drowns, and people lose their homes—or die. They do not have the *luxury* of refusing to care about each other.

She was very good, naturally. I could recognize that. But she didn't set my heart on fire. She didn't make me lean forward to reach for the words as she spoke them.

The girl-apprentice, Arenza, spent the entire time kneeling off to one side, her hands folded on her lap just as Chant's were, her back very straight, her expression attentive but impassive, giving no reaction—why? Didn't she like the stories? Did she even care about them? And if not, why was she with Mistress Chant? When I was an apprentice, I threw myself into emotion with my whole heart. I remember leaning forward when my master told a story, propping my chin on my hands, my whole attention centered on his words, as if I could inhale them quicker that way. I gathered words up like armfuls of wildflowers.

Arenza held herself still and let it all wash over her like a river.

The other apprentice, Lanh Chau, sat on the floor by Mistress Chant's chair and provided musical accompaniment to her stories. He cradled the langeleik across his torso, his fingers tipped with pointed brass picks mounted on rings, which made his hands look clawed, yet strangely graceful. He used these to pluck the strings of the instrument, first softly like plinks of rain falling into a barrel, growing louder and more melodic as the stories mounted in intensity. At each dramatic moment, he rammed his picks across the strings with a sound like a jangling thunderclap.

I hated it. I hated it so much.[94] All of it, it's just—showing off! The thing with the candle, and the stiff rituality of it, and the music. The music, particularly, is all wrong. It's all wrong! This isn't how it's

---

So I told them stories about that. I told them about the Vintish mercenaries and about Peregrine Lee because those too are about cooperation and community. We learn who we are from stories. I was reminding them who they were, and they were pleased to be reminded. They were pleased to hear stories that fit in with what they already knew to be true.

94   There's no accounting for taste, I suppose.

done! I've seen performances in playhouses, and they have musicians sometimes too—I've never liked it. It's always been distracting.
Artificial. Overwrought. How is someone supposed to listen to the
story if someone's blanging away at the same time like that? You can't
give your full attention to the music or to the story—it's split in two,
and neither of them deserve that.[95]

And to be perfectly honest, it seems lazy.[96] Music is pure emotion
in a way that stories aren't, and when you put a story to music, you're
forcing an emotion onto it. My Chant wouldn't have liked it. The
whole point of carrying stories around is that people react to them
differently depending on where you go—what's the point of that if
you're *telling* them how to feel with music?[97] You're just yanking them
around by their feelings then. If you have something worth saying,
you should be able to say it with just words. You shouldn't *need* anything else, if you're good enough.

And yet there she was, cheating.[98]

Once, my Chant and I were traveling, and we came through a
village that had just been wrecked by a powerful storm. All the roofs
had been torn off; many people and animals had been killed. It was
terrible. And my Chant went to the middle of the village and sat on
the debris-strewn steps of their ruined and rotting temple and started
telling stories for the villagers. He held them in *thrall*.

---

95   You were certainly upset about this, weren't you? Don't you think it was child-
ish to have such a tantrum about it like this? You were so cold and still at the salon;
I barely even noticed you when I was performing.

96   I'm raising my eyebrow at this. You're one to talk.

97   Because sometimes the effect *matters*. Sometimes you want them to feel with
precision, and music is the way to do that. Words are fluid and shifting and soft.
Words can be misunderstood. Music strikes at the heart of you and expresses what
can't be said in words.

98   I beg your pardon? That's a strong opinion for a heretic and a blasphemer! This
is a level of hypocrisy I genuinely wasn't expecting.

I don't think Mistress Chant could have done anything like that.[99]

Not without her apprentice plonking away on that damned langeleik.

At the end, or what I supposed to be the end, she rose and bowed to the company amid quiet yet sincere applause.

I felt tight all over. I hadn't even been watching her for most of it; I'd been staring down at the parquet floor, keeping myself from twitching or tapping my fingers, keeping myself from reacting at all. I wanted . . . something. I don't know how to describe it—you'd think I'd be better with words.

When you think of wanting someone, that's supposed to mean romance, or at least sex. This was *decidedly* neither of those, obviously, but it was still a kind of wanting. I yearned towards her, towards her knowledge and her assurance and her field of influence. I felt pulled towards her as all things are pulled towards the ground, as the tides are pulled towards the moons, as astronomers say the planets are pulled towards the sun.

And yet my yearning woke a tearing anger in me, a flood of pain and grief—what was the use in yearning? What was I yearning for? That she'd take me with her? That she'd extend the wing of her protection over me as it was over her apprentices? And was *that* what I yearned for? To be her apprentice? To be hers?

Too late for that. Already made my vows, already sank my homeland beneath the waves—a year and a half, it's been. I can't take that back, even if I want to. I can't go home like that, can't go back to something easier and more comfortable, where there was someone to rely on, someone to take care of me, someone to tell me anything I needed to know.

---

99   Want to bet?

And even if I could, *she'd* just cast me aside eventually too.

I was full of grief and yearning, full of anger and resentment, and I wanted nothing more than to catch her sleeve and—and what? What then?

I could do none of those things. The best I could manage, the *only* thing I could manage, was to catch her attention, to put myself before her and say *Here I am*.

I wanted it, and I didn't want it. I was dying of thirst and afraid of drowning.

There were so many people here, so many people to whom I didn't want to say *Here I am*. No choice, though. My tongue stirred before I could decide that I didn't want to speak after all.

"A very long time ago and half the world away," I said, not loudly and not looking at anyone, not moving from my seat on the floor by Sterre's knee. The applause hadn't even quite died down yet, but I spoke, sounding calmer than I felt. "There was a"—Sterre stiffened, next to me—"a city made of bronze and glass."

Mistress Chant's attention snapped to me, and the noise quieted; the few conversations that had started faded away again like the falling tide. She stood there, tall and still, and listened, and I was only a few sentences in when she sat, snapping her fingers at her apprentice. He handed the langeleik over to her without a word and she laid it across her lap, using her fingernails to impassively pluck a song out along with the story, matching her pace and tone to mine, building and releasing tension. It was like ... dancing. Like she, indulgently, was allowing me to lead.

She kept pace so easily because she knew the story, of course. I wasn't telling her anything new. But she seemed pleased, and she was looking at me, and ...

Ah. Perhaps that was why her apprentices sat stiffly and

betrayed no emotion. She'd trained them to listen without taking, without grabbing it from her and stuffing it into their mouths like spoiled children in a fairy tale. She did the same now—sat quiet but for her fingers dancing across the strings of the instrument.

I had no sooner spoken the last word of the tale[100] than she set the langeleik on the floor and began: "In the ninth century since the fall of the house of Cwlladda, as it is reckoned half the world away in Fyrndarog and Calabog, there was a great plague that swept across those green, quiet lands."[101] Sterre had leaned forward, and one hand had fallen heavy on my shoulder, gripping hard, but she froze when Mistress Chant began to speak again.

The apprentice gave me a rather pointed look and glanced at the langeleik. When I made no move to take it, he brought it onto his lap again, as a child might eagerly pull a puppy close.

So it went. When she ended,[102] Sterre started forward again and nearly spoke, but I interrupted and began anew myself: "Many years ago, there was a pirate known as Xing Fe Hua, famed around the Sea of Serpents for his adventures and exploits. He captained a ship, the silver-sailed *Nightingale* . . ."

And Mistress Chant just quirked that half-smile and played the langeleik. And when I was done, she handed it to her apprentice and said, "When the world was young and the gods were first scraping the mountains up from the flat earth and laying out the rivers like ribbons

---

100 Oh, thank goodness. Dodged an arrow there, didn't we? How ridiculous it is that I should feel so grateful and relieved that you displayed a minor piece of decency in not writing that down.

101 Bracing myself. Come on, brother-Chant, you managed not to fuck up with the previous one . . .

102 . . . And I sag with relief! Two for two! Though to be honest, I'd prefer you didn't even write these few sentences either, but I'll take any port in a storm. This *is* the lesser of two evils.

across the land, there was a hero named Namhala: the same Namhala who stole fire from the underworld, the same Namhala who invented the lyre and the barbat, the same Namhala who taught the birds to sing. This is the tale of the song that broke the world."

And then I: "A very long time ago and half the world away, the god Uion lay with a mortal woman and begat a son, called Tyrran." Mistress Chant rolled her eyes at this one, and I suppose I couldn't blame her—"The Twelve Tasks of Tyrran" is rather long and bland. It's one of those stories that all Chants should know, simply because everyone knows it. Even if they don't know Tyrran, they know a Tyrran-like figure from their own folktales. Still, it will hold an audience reasonably well. It's dry meat and potatoes without sauce or seasoning—it will feed your hunger, but you won't remember that meal a week from now.[103]

And then she, keeping the instrument this time, rather than handing it off to her apprentice, opened her mouth and sang "Goblin Market Whiskey" and "The Maiden's Reply to the Goblin Merchant."

I don't know why I don't usually sing or why I haven't bothered to learn songs like I've learned spoken stories—I suppose it's simply because my master didn't either. Maybe he didn't need them. Maybe he thought they were too easy or too . . . something. Too late to find out what he thought, anyway.

In response, I told a story about the Umakh, the nomadic tribes of the far north. I spoke of a boy I once knew called Syrenen, who taught me to shoot a shortbow from horseback, and about his mother, the famous falconer, who could ride all the way to the horizon, one-handed, with a golden eagle strapped to her other

---

103 Apt description. I concur.

arm and held out to the side for hours and hours without tiring.[104]
Mistress Chant had opinions about this, I could tell—she was disappointed that I hadn't followed her when she'd tried to turn us
towards songs,[105] but she seemed to accept it. She didn't sing again,
just matched me tale for tale, playing the langeleik to accompany me
except for the few stories I gave that were personal memories, mine
or ones borrowed from my master, one or two that he'd borrowed
from his—the unsettling wonder-tales sailors brought back from
long voyages far over the ocean where there was no land in sight for
days in any direction.

I was tiring a little, and increasingly annoyed at the presence
of the audience, who would insist on clapping after every story and
calling for another, as if they had any part in the conversation that
we were having. They were quieter for her stories than they were
for mine, and they'd liked the songs—a few times, someone quietly
suggested that another song would be nice, but Mistress Chant and
I politely ignored them and kept circling each other in words and
tales.

Here I am, I said to her again and again. *See, this is what I'm capable of. See me!*

I suppose her demeanor of impassivity overlaid with faint amusement was what drove me to the next one. "I'm Chant," I said, addressing
the audience for the first time with a quick glance from the corner of
my eye. "And she's Chant. Perhaps you are wondering what a Chant is
and does." Her expression flickered, and I charged along. "A very long

---

104 Hm, oddly, I don't find myself objecting to a secondhand-shop summary like
this one. Again, the less of three evils, I suppose. Or perhaps I'm merely becoming
resistant to your particular brand of heresy.

105 Yes, I was, a little. I wanted to test your range. But you were set on speech over
song, and that was fine. I'd wanted to talk to you like this, to trade stories like this—I
was content to do so on your terms, if that's what it took.

time ago and half the world away, there was a vast land in the southern reaches of the Unending Ocean, and it was called Arthwend."[106]

Mistress Chant stood up abruptly, smoothing the skirts of her long waistcoat and folding her hands before her. "I yield," she said smoothly. "We have monopolized the attention of the room far too long, don't you think?"

The tale crumbled to ashes on my lips. Sterre surged forward again, seizing my shoulder. "*Heer* van Vlymen certainly has other entertainments planned, I'm sure," she said, her voice a little too loud, a little too harsh. "But I find myself wanting to stretch my legs."

"Oh, a few!" van Vlymen replied cheerfully. "But a turn about the garden sounds just the thing to clear the palate—shall we all go out for some fresh air?"

Sterre rose to her feet, pulling me up with her by my arm. "Just the thing indeed! Chant, accompany me, won't you?"

I followed her out of the parlor through the ornate Vintish doors to the wide paved patio that overlooked the garden. She turned back to me, but several others had indeed followed us out as well—she pulled me farther along, down the small flight of steps on the side to one of several cozy nooks tucked within the ornamental trees and bushes. "What was that about?" she hissed. "Where were those *manners* you supposedly had?"

I couldn't pretend I didn't know what she was talking about. She wouldn't have believed me—she knows I'm not stupid. It *had* been a little rude, what I'd done: Our host had provided us with a light

---

106 That is not a story for rich folks' parties. That is not a tale for just anyone to hear. And it's certainly not something you ought to be putting down on paper. Out of all the stories in the world, that one is the only one that's truly ours. It deserves to be treasured and cherished particularly, not bandied about in front of an audience so you can win a friendly little contest.

entertainment, and . . . well, Mistress Chant was quite right in that last comment that she'd made. We had monopolized the attention of the room. It was different for her, of course—*she* had been invited. Hired. I was just a guest, and not even that. A guest of a guest.

I dropped my eyes. "I'll apologize to *Heer* van Vlymen," I said. "I got carried away."

"Carried away?" she demanded. "You embarrassed me in front of my friends and two dozen potential new customers.[107] What must they think of me?" She pressed her fingertips to the center of her forehead. Her skin had grown florid with anger.

"No one seemed to mind," I said.[108] "It's not a disaster. I would have stopped if anyone was bored." But they hadn't been bored. I would have been able to tell. I would have felt the weight of their attention drop off my shoulders.

"You will apologize."

"Yes, I said that I would."

"And you won't pull a stunt like that again." She dropped her hand and met my eyes. "Do you understand? Besides the social faux pas, you mustn't ever let them know that you're angry like that. It embarrasses us, makes us look weak. Reckless. Careless. Do you think people will trust me with their money if they think I'm that kind of person, or that my employees are that sort? I don't mean to scold you like you're a child, but you *must* follow my lead more carefully in the future—can you imagine how this would have gone if the party had been hosted by anyone besides such a close friend of mine? An outburst like that could have shipwrecked us."[109]

---

107 That's a little hyperbolic. No one minded that we took up all the attention of the room. We were doing our jobs, after all.

108 There, see! Exactly! Even you knew.

109 Raising my eyebrows at this.

I closed my eyes. I could have been angry. Perhaps I *should* have been angry. Perhaps I should have argued with her about the sort of expertise a Chant possesses, the kind of insight I could offer her.[110]

Relief isn't quite the right way to describe what I felt in the wake of her words. I was too tired and heart-sore for that. It was more of an aching regret that I'd had to endure at all, for so long and all alone—and now here was Sterre rebuking me for doing something wrong, and instead of angering me, that made it all right. She was so controlled, so careful not to actually shout at me, but I could see she was angry, which meant she was frightened. Frightened, because she'd been counting on me to help her, and I'd stumbled. It mattered to her that I do it properly. It mattered.

"I understand," I said. "I'm sorry. I'll do better next time."

She let her breath out slowly. "I don't know where else you've been before this, Chant, but there's certain ways of doing things in polite society."

"Yes," I said, nearly giddy. "I shouldn't have let her get to me."

"Is that what happened? She got to you?"

"I got to her too. We were trying to outdo each other. Sort of. It was an argument."

Sterre subsided then. "And you won. You won, because she yielded."[111]

The trickling thread of euphoria vanished. "No. Not . . . not really. She just wanted to stop me and that was the easy way to do it." I glanced over my shoulder, through the branches of the bushes

---

110 There's no point in arguing with people like *Mevrol* de Waeyer. It would have been a waste of breath.

111 Rolling my eyes here. Though I suppose someone like *Mevrol* de Waeyer doesn't get to where she is without an ironbound thirst for competition, so we can't really blame her for being . . . like that.

and trees. I could just see a corner of the railing around the patio, and the shadows of people milling about. I could barely hear soft conversation, and I wondered suddenly if Mistress Chant was going to try to talk to me—she'd objected to the Arthwend story, enough to interrupt me in the middle of it. She'd probably want to scold me too, but the thought of that soured my stomach.

Sterre treated all her employees like family. She looked after them, kept them close. I was one of hers. Mistress Chant, on the other hand, had no claim on me at all, and so she hadn't any right to scold, not like Sterre did. Sterre rapping my knuckles like this meant she was pulling me closer into the family; Mistress Chant's would mean she was shoving me away, denying me my place.

"To anyone else in the room, it looked like you won," Sterre insisted. "Right?"

"You'd know better than I," I replied absently, still looking off towards the patio. "But the others weren't angry or bored or insulted. They were curious. They wanted to listen to us." I shrugged. "If it looked like I won, then that's extra prestige for you, isn't it?"

"Even so, I won't have you speaking out of turn like that again," she said. "If you can't be fit to be seen in public, then you won't be. No more parties, unless I have your word that this won't happen again."

"I'll be good," I said mildly, turning back to her. I found I wanted to please her. Didn't care about the parties in the slightest, but I cared about that.

Sterre gave me a sharp look—she clearly didn't entirely believe me. "See that you are," she said. "There are no third chances."

She swept away. I stood in the cool dark shade for a time, surrounded by the greenery, until I heard voices approaching—party guests, strangers. People I didn't want to see or speak to. People who would definitely want to speak to me, if they saw me. I ducked through the bushes and emerged on the other side of the artificial thicket, farther away from the house.

I found myself among a stand of chest-high shrubs with a shallow pond on the other side, surrounded by the graceful curve of a cobblestone walkway like a moat around an island. I crouched beside and behind the shrubs, sitting on the stones that bordered the water, and settled in to enjoy the solitude while I had it.

I was ready for it; I was willing. I reached out to gather a moment of peace and sweet stillness close to me, and . . . felt my heart grasping at nothing, like fingers catching uselessly at a wisp of smoke.

This happens from time to time. There are days when I feel more awake and present in the world than I've been for years, days when maybe it doesn't matter so much that an audience wants to eat me alive. There are days where I find enough within me to try, at least. I thought this was going to be one of those days—I'd shrugged off the presence of the audience in the parlor, I'd even been a little eager for Mistress Chant to listen to me.

But it was that moment of giddiness, the ghost of euphoria I'd felt in the conversation with Sterre—it had faded away and left me plummeting, harder and faster and further than I'd expected.

I dropped my head into my hands and let emotion wash over me, let it swamp me. No euphoria now. All I could think of was Sterre, and belonging, and . . . him. My old master. I hurt. Gods, gods, how I hurt. I hurt now, thinking of it.

Grief. I was grieving. That's what that was. I couldn't put a name on it until just now as I was writing it down. It's been grief this whole time. Three years of it. And now, only now, the dawning realization: My master didn't make me a Chant because I was ready. He did it because he was sick of me. He did it because he wanted to be rid of me. I would have no place here if Sterre hadn't decided that I did.

I sat there behind the shrubs and tried to think of what I should do. I stared into the water, ringed all around with lily pads and ornamental rushes speckled with tiny pink-white flowers. In the deepest part of the little pool, I could just see the twisted shape of several stars-in-the-marsh bulbs half-buried in mud at the bottom, their roots spreading out through the water in delicate tangles. One of them had a shoot that had grown just tall enough to break above the surface of the water.

Obviously, that was where Mistress Chant found me. I looked up when I heard footsteps, and I knew who it was a moment before I saw her. "Hello again," she said. "Brother Chant."

I stood up. "I didn't know you were coming to the party. I would have excused myself from the invitation. I'm sorry."

She cocked an eyebrow at me. "Is there some reason why we can't both be here?"

"No," I lied.

"Good. I've been hoping to speak to you again."

"I see." I swallowed. "Your performance was interesting." That was all I could manage for compliments. But I felt, desperately, like I needed to control the conversation, to get her talking about herself so she wouldn't have a chance to ask anything about me. Easy enough for a Chant. It's the first trick you learn. "The candle . . . thing. Why do you do that?"

"What do you mean?"

"The candle. You always have one."

"Well, yes."

"Why?"

She gave me a puzzled look. "Because that's the way to do it. That's how Chants do it."

"That's not how I do it."

Even more bewilderment. "Why not?"

"I've never even heard of it. I don't understand what it's *for*."

She was laughing at me now, I could tell.[112] "You sound like an apprentice. No offense." I flinched anyway. "Do you want me to explain to you as if that's what you were? It's an anchor. It's important. I don't know how else to describe it to you if you don't instinctively understand it."

The anger and the hurt got the better of me. "I guess you must not be a very good teacher, then," I said quietly.[113]

"Mind your tongue, little brother," she said mildly, raising one eyebrow. She clearly thought nothing of me.[114] "A story needs two things to live: a teller and a listener. If you go out into the wilderness and tell a story to the wind, what's the point of it? It dies as it leaves your lips. And that is a sacrilege. Now, think of every time you've heard someone ask for a story—'Grandma, grandma, tell us the one about the princess and the singing sword.' It's . . . domestic. Enclosed. Warm. Home. Stories live by hearthfires; it's not right to tell a story without a flame—not a serious one, for a serious audience. I light the candle to make my space a home for the people asking me for stories. That's sacred too."

"I don't know anything about sacrilege. I don't—" I nearly choked, but I forced myself to look at her, to speak. "I suppose I don't think things like that are necessary or important." And then, with another huge effort: "I think it's wasteful, actually. Pointless."

"Excuse me?"

"Nothing my master taught me about Chanting had anything to do with sacred things," I blurted. I wished immediately that I hadn't. I didn't want her to know anything about me. Mistress Chant's face looked like distant thunder. "He was . . . elderly," I scrambled to

---

112 You give me no credit at all, do you? As I recall, at that point I was mostly confused by you.

113 No, brother-Chant, you snapped. Like an animal trapped in a cage.

114 It is so tiresome to be constantly villainized like this. I'm not the careless, thoughtless person here, *you* are.

explain. "He was always very practical. Prosaic. He wasn't interested much in the frills and fripperies of things."

"The fire isn't a *frippery*. Making a home-space isn't a *frill*."

I hadn't said that it was, but—well, it was. It is. All this about *stories live by hearthfires* is . . . quaint, I suppose would be the word.[115] It's a deliberate performance of coziness, and a performance like that can't be genuine. "I don't think he would have thought stories to be as fragile and vulnerable as you do, that's all. He thought they were strong. He thought they had power, sometimes power far bigger and farther-reaching than anything he was able to contain. He didn't mind telling stories to the wind." But what I should have said was this: People tell stories everywhere. They tell stories in the fields and in barns and on street corners. They tell stories in banks and on ships and in temples. They tell stories in summer and in winter, by sunlight or moonlight or starlight, or in perfect darkness. Stories don't need to be coddled by the fire, because they have warmth and life in themselves.

The only true part of what she'd said was the first part: that you need two things—a teller and a listener. Except she was immediately wrong about the implication. You don't need two *people*. You can tell yourself a story. You can be teller and listener both. There's no way to tell a story to the wind alone, because whoever is there speaking it is hearing it too.[116] "He didn't try to make them more special than they are," I went on. "He let them be plain if they were plain and valued them just as much as the grand ones or the lovely ones."

"That's unthinkable to me."

"He would have seen the candle as a piece of unnecessary excess. A waste of time," I said. "Like clothing or possessions."

---

115 Go fuck yourself.
116 ~~Wrong! You I don't Except that Fucking upstart!~~ Well, now you have me fuming, and I will *begrudgingly* concede the point.

"Once again, I beg your pardon?"

"Well, you know. Like the fancy cart you have, and the fine clothes. He taught me that a Chant shouldn't have such things."

"Whyever not?" Her eyes flickered across me. "Is that why your clothes are so shabby?"[117]

"A little," I said slowly. "Yes."

"Did your master just go around naked like a beggar?"

"No, of course not. He always wore a long tunic and a coat. And usually shoes[118]—he used to tell a story about a pair of turn-toe boots he was given in Map Sut. He wore them often until they were stolen."

"A long tunic, a coat, shoes," she said, voice flat. "That's all?"

"That's all. He didn't need anything else but his mind and his tongue."

"That's ridiculous, though;[119] that's—" Dawn broke over her face. "Ah! I've figured it out—goodness, that solves a lot of mysteries. But I see now: You're not *actually* a Chant."[120]

I felt as if she'd pried open my chest with a crowbar and stared straight inside at my innermost secrets and my deepest fears. "What?"

"You met a Chant once, or—well, maybe not even that. You heard about a Chant once from someone else, and you thought that sounded like a great idea, and so you've just taken the name for yourself to make a quick coin. Disgusting and despicable behavior, but

---

117 I didn't say "shabby"; I said "plain."
118 *Usually* shoes. *Usually.*
119 It *is* ridiculous. The ancient Chants were splendid to look at—the stories my line tells say that their clothes glittered with ornament, that they painted their faces, that they wore bells and bright colors and jewelry, all to catch Shuggwa's Eye. And *your* line? Faded rags from the secondhand shops! Which Chant in your ancestry was it that set aside our primary function?
120 Ah, how innocent I was! Ah, for the days I really thought you were a simple fraud instead of a heretic!

none of my business, and fortune will judge you as it will. But just as a free hint, from one professional to another—ditch the story about your master-Chant, young man. No one's going to think it's plausible. And if you ever do run into another Chant, well—maybe you can save yourself a repeat of the embarrassment."

"I'm not making it up," I said. "I was apprenticed to a Chant, and I'm a real Chant now too. I traveled with him until my apprenticeship was done. We went all over—"

"Oh, my boy . . . No. You seem sincere, so I'll take that at face value, but that makes it worse." She pitied me; I could see it. That was more embarrassing than all her accusations. "Your *master*, if he even existed, was the charlatan. That's a shame. You should definitely stop telling people you're a Chant."

"But I *am* one!"

"Young man, what are the Chants?"

"Wanderers, storytellers, people who remember—"

"No," she said flatly. "They're holy people. Priests. That's what we were thousands of years ago; that's what we are today. We were intermediaries to our god." She eyed me. "I suppose you don't know about the Chants' god either, if your master was so *prosaic*, as you say."

"You mean Shuggwa." The very instant I said that name, I felt a chill run over me. I was prickling all over with . . . anger, I guess. Sometimes when I'm telling stories in front of a big crowd, my skin crawls with the weight of all those eyes on me. That's almost what this felt like, standing there with her judging me, measuring me. It was like I was being *seen* by a thousand people.[121]

---

121 Just came back here from a couple hundred pages farther on to check whether I remembered this part right and . . . Well, shit. I'm going to have to flip through and find all the other times you mentioned this feeling and see if my theory holds water. If it does . . . Gods and fishes, Chant.

Her eyes narrowed, though. I'd gotten her with that one—chances are, I wouldn't have known that name if I weren't what I claimed to be.[122] I might have known Skukua, the puckish trickster figure who comes up in tales from Kaskinen and the Issili Islands. But Skukua had evolved from something else, something much older and much darker: Shuggwa, the god of the ancient Chants. We *were* intermediaries, thousands of years ago.

"I'm a Chant," I said. "As real as you are."[123]

"How can you be, if you don't observe any of the rites? And you're so young besides—when did you sink your homeland beneath the waves? How long ago? And how long were you a journeyman? And where is your master?"

My stomach lurched. I clasped my hands together, squeezing hard so she wouldn't see how they shook, so she wouldn't think I was *afraid* of her. I ignored almost all these questions and tipped my chin up.[124] "What do the rites matter? We travel the world, learning the ways people are in one place or another—is it so unthinkable that Chants of two distinct lineages might be as different as regular people are? I learned our ways from my master, and he learned from his, and she from hers, and so on. I've come by my ways as honestly as you did." My cheeks stung with the same low, simmering heat of anger that had set my hands shaking.

"No," she said. "Because we all started out the same. Somewhere in your line, someone decided that certain things just weren't important, and they stopped teaching them. Your line has been corrupted

---

122 I was narrowing my eyes because I was annoyed with your tone. Calm down; stop thinking yourself so ingenious.
123 No. I refuse you. I reject you. I renounce and abjure you. A Chant would have had more care. A Chant would have thought about what he was doing.
124 It's fine. I got my answers eventually, didn't I? I wonder if you'll deign to write that part down.

and perverted from what it was meant to be and to do. By all that's safe and secret, you nearly told them about *Arthwend*—"

"Chant!" someone called from across the garden, and Mistress Chant and I both leaned around the shrubs to see who it was— Sterre. She waved me over.

"Excuse me, sister-Chant," I murmured, still brimming with the prickling sensation of eyes on me, and stepped around her. She followed close behind me once again.

"You could change," she said. My own master was up to his nostrils in wiles and guiles, so I heard it as clear as rainwater in her voice too. "Corruption and perversion is a choice, after all. If you're so set on saying you're a Chant, then do things the right way and teach them to your apprentices."

"How am I supposed to learn what the right way is?" I said. "Even if I wanted to learn, who is there to teach me?" She made a low noise of disgust, and I knew I'd been right—it's not like she would have taken me on. "And I don't have apprentices," I added.

"Of course you don't. Quite right too—you're in no shape to take responsibility for someone, and you're practically a child yourself. But one day." I didn't tell her that I'm never going to have an apprentice.[125] It wasn't any of her business anyway. Nothing I do is any of her business.

"*Mevrol*," I said to Sterre as we approached. "How can I help you?"

She clapped me on the shoulder, harder than I liked. "Catching up with your colleague, were you?" She was very good—you couldn't tell from her voice that she was still angry at all. I only felt it in the odd pressure and tension of her hand. Sterre wouldn't show the cards in her hand to anyone by accident, after all.

---

125 I look forward to reading the part where we argue about that—if you even admit that it happened, that is, since I so obviously *won*.

Mistress Chant smiled. "My brother-Chant and I are only newly acquainted."

"Is that right? I would have thought folk like you would know each other well."

"Quite the opposite, *Mevrol* de Waeyer. Chants only meet each other rarely. There are so few of us, you see—only a few hundred in all the world, I'd guess, though I don't have any real way of knowing."

"What great fortune I've had to meet both of you, then," Sterre said warmly. "We should toast, the three of us, to this rare blessing." Sterre summoned one of van Vlymen's servants and had them bring us each a tiny cup of the best Vintish brandy,[126] which we sipped for each effusive toast that Sterre offered. "And now, I have something of great importance to discuss with you." She gave Mistress Chant a serious look. "Since you're acquainted with this young man, you must know that he has been in my employ for the past few weeks. He's been worth every guilder I've paid him."

"Has he indeed," Mistress Chant replied. I set my jaw and met her eyes steadily. This too was none of her business. Plenty of people do what I'm doing, selling a skill for monetary compensation. It's no different than building cabinets or making lace or painting a mural for a wealthy patron's commission. It's no different. It isn't. It *isn't*.[127]

"He has! So I would like to offer you a similar arrangement as the one I have with him."

"You'd like me to hawk your flowers on the street?"

---

126 It was *galardine*, for gods' sake, not brandy. I don't really expect someone your age to have a discerning and developed palate, but come *on*.

127 Uh-huh. Keep telling yourself that, kid. By all means, take silver and gold from people who thought your stories good. Take payment in food or beer or shelter or services. But you know how I feel about this.

"Not just the flowers! My Chant[128] has that well-handled—no, I've been thinking about expanding the business. The people have responded so well to his methods that I'd like to do the same for other things: I also import a great deal of cloth, as well as perfume from Tash, Vintish wine, Oissic olive oil, and whatever those Araşti highway robbers that call themselves merchants will let me abscond with. What say you? I can tell you're a person of the world like myself, and if you know nearly as much as your colleague does, I believe we could all expect to reap impressive profits from an arrangement like this."

"I will have to decline," Mistress Chant said politely.

"Ah, but I haven't yet laid out the *numbers* for you. The most important part, hey? See, I give Chant here twelve stuivers per week,[129] plus a meal every day that he's working for me. I think you'll agree that's more than reasonable."

"Perhaps it is. But I am quite comfortable, and my time is fully occupied these days."

"Ha! A trick as old as the bones of the earth, but a classic. All right—sixteen stuivers a week."

"No, thank you. But you might want to offer that to my brother-Chant,"[130] she said, tilting her head at me. "He seems to be more concerned with worldly matters than I am, and now that he knows you're willing to pay that rate, he might feel slighted that you haven't given him that much already. Especially," she added, "since he's worth so much to your business. Or were you going to offer me more

---

128 *Her* Chant, she calls you, like you belong to her, like she owns you.
129 What the hell did you need money for, anyway? You dress like a pauper, you're thin and bony, you don't seem to care for drinking or gambling or bed companions, and you were earning room and board at the inn with chores. So where was it all going?
130 I hope to all the gods I can name that you didn't take it. She shouldn't be permitted to think a Chant can be *bought* like this. At least, not for such a scanty price. I've advised kings, and she thinks to pay me little more than what a laundress makes.

still? I think my brother-Chant would be very interested in hearing further offers."

Sterre wholly ignored all of this but the part she found most objectionable. "You're really not interested? I could make you very wealthy."

"Wealth is not something that motivates me. And I have existing duties to attend to."

Sterre fell silent. When she spoke again, her voice was cool and clipped. "That's disappointing."

Mistress Chant nodded. "I can see that it would be. I can only offer my sincere regrets."

Sterre dropped the conversation with a scant few more obligatory pleasantries and excused herself. I made to follow her, but Mistress Chant caught my elbow.

"If you're really a proper Chant, you'll put some thought into what you're doing," she hissed, leaning close to my ear. "If you're going to sell yourself and your great calling like this, the very least you can do is to get a respectable price for them. Instead of letting people like her think that it's something *cheap*."

I tugged my arm away from her. "She's right, you know," I replied. "You are a person *of the world*, just like her."

"I dismiss your insult. She knows the value of things. She knows your value, but do *you*?" I was quiet. I couldn't answer that. "If you come to your senses, come talk to me. Truly. You think I harbor some ill will towards you, but I don't. So come and talk. I'm staying at the Rose and Ivy Inn, on Groenstraat."

I turned. I left. I hope she moves along soon, out of this city and out of my life. I hope I never see her again.[131]

You know what? I've just decided: to hell with her—any hell, I

---

131 Surprise! Now I'm glad I stuck around, purely for the satisfaction of having tortured you for so long.

don't care which one, even though in Xerecci that only means "the desert" colloquially. This language doesn't have a lot of good ways to curse someone. Shipwreck her, then, as the Heyrlandtsche say. Maybe I'm a bad Chant, and maybe I feel like my name didn't leave me when it was supposed to, and maybe I should have stayed in Hrefnesholt. But I made choices, and I *am* a real Chant, and so was my master. I had my apprenticeship. I did my duty; I said my oaths; I unnamed myself and sank my homeland beneath the waves. I'm as real as she is. It's not my fault that I was taught other ways.[132] I don't think candles and fine clothes make her any better than I am.

I'm a real Chant, and nothing she says can take that away from me. I said before that it's none of her business. It's nobody's but mine—and Sterre's, I suppose. *She* gives a damn about me, at least. She wants me around, because she thinks I'm good at my job. She doesn't pick at me like I'm a troublesome scab.[133]

And anyway, so what if I *had* just made it up? What if I'd met a Chant once and decided to take it onto myself without any of the rites, as she accused me of? Would it matter? It's *mine*.

---

132 No, but it is your fault that you're choosing to stay ignorant and useless. If you hadn't been so proud and haughty, I would have taught you everything you needed to know.

133 Ah, true. She doesn't, does she? You're right—she doesn't pick at you like I do. She doesn't challenge you. She lets you wallow. She doesn't push you to grow or change. All you have to do is mindlessly obey. You'd found a comfortable equilibrium here, hadn't you? She fit a yoke to you and got you in your traces, and you were ready to pull the load along without ever once looking back to see what it was made of.

And then I had to come along and spoil it, didn't I? That's why you were so furious here and in the garden, all blazing eyes and clenched jaw. I asked you all the right questions to throw you off your balance, and you dug in your heels and clung to whatever shitty story you could tell yourself to keep things warm and safe and comfortable and easy, rather than anything that would have made you strong and invulnerable, like I told you later. Hmph! When you wrote, "Chants are liars," you really were just talking about yourself, weren't you?

TWENTY-FOUR

S terre didn't speak to me again until we were in her carriage, on the way back to the eastern quarter of the city, where her offices and apartments were located. "You know," she said, "I hope you didn't feel stung by my offer to your colleague. I've been meaning to give you a raise. You're more useful than I had originally anticipated, and I was going to make the offer whenever I found another Chant to hire."

She didn't know that there *were* any other Chants nearby to hire, so that was a lie. "That's generous of you, ma'am," I said. I didn't care about the money. What's a few extra stuivers worth to me? I'm fed and clothed, and there's a roof over my head. I have a warm place to sleep. What use do I have for coins?[134] But I thought of how holier-than-thou Mistress Chant had been, and of how it would infuriate her if she only could have overheard this conversation, and I said, "I'll gladly accept whatever you offer."

"Sixteen stuivers a week, then."

I could have asked for more, and she would have given it to me. I probably could have asked for twenty-five, but I was angry. I *am* angry. I'm not all those things that Mistress Chant accused me of, and just because I get paid for work that I would have been doing anyway doesn't mean that I'm selling myself. There's nothing wrong with what I'm

---

134 What use indeed!

doing. She just thinks that because her master-Chant gave her some strange opinions. I don't think Chants are holy people,[135] at least not anymore, because I've met holy people: monks and martyrs and hermits. There's something about all of them that's not quite of-this-world, and Chants and stories are the most of-this-world thing that I know.[136]

So she's wrong. Mistress Chant is wrong. I'm a proper Chant. I don't know what she thinks *she's* doing, but it's a lot more grand and gimmicky than Chanting should be.[137] You don't need a fancy cart[138] or musical accompaniment by two apprentices. You don't need a candle[139] or nice clothes.[140]

That's what my master was doing: Stripping it down to the basics. Discarding everything but the core, important thing.[141] Maybe his master taught him that too.

You know, I don't care if I meet her again or not. If I do, I won't be afraid of her next time. I'm as real as she is, and she calls me *brother-Chant*,

---

135 Entirely, literally wrong. Chants were priests and intermediaries to Shuggwa in the height of his power! They were *chosen* by him, and they were safe from all his mischief and misfortune. *My* line never ceased in our devotion.

136 Seriously? That's your argument? You have a feeling, so therefore you're right? "I feel normal and worldly, so therefore all Chants are worldly." And what's this nonsense about stories being prosaic? You ought to be ashamed of yourself—where are you getting these wild conclusions from? Thin air? Have more discipline.

137 *Gimmicky?* Oh, you mangy whelp, it's a good thing you've already left town, or I'd thrash you from here to Novensok.

138 What else are you going to do? *Walk?* Carts make travel easier; that's what they're *for*.

139 You do if you're doing it right! Chants are connected to fire. Stories live by hearths and campfires, and we ought to respect that. The candle is a *symbol*. Symbols are important.

140 I'm going to scream. Yes, you do need nice clothes. At least, you do if you're going to show devotion to Shuggwa. The whole point of Chants is to occupy his attention, and you do that with stories and songs, and loud speech, and rude *fucking* words, and bright clothing or jewelry so as to catch his Eye. The nice clothes aren't a *vanity*, they're a *necessity*.

141 As far as I can tell, he was discarding everything *including* the core, important thing.

like I'm an equal to her. Because I am. I am! She's already admitted it. So next time, I won't let her push me around. Next time I'll argue with her properly.[142]

I worked to get where I am. Whether or not it was the right choice, whether or not I'm broken and full of regret, that's irrelevant—I could give up Chanting next week, and it doesn't change the fact that I'm a Chant *now*. I could give it up next week and it won't change the fact that I *was* a Chant; I earned it fair and square. So I say again, and I'll say it as many times as I have to: she can go get shipwrecked for all I care, or she can go into the desert or to hell, her and her cart and her smug opinions.

. . .

Shit. Something I scrawled up above caught my eye and I've been staring at it for a long, long time.

I could give up Chanting next week.[143]

I had such a good petty outrage going, and then I had to go and write that and ruin it. Is that what I've been refusing to think about this whole time? Do I want that?[144] Have I been keeping secrets from myself this whole time?

I could give it up. There's nothing stopping me. I could take my name back. I could be me again if I wanted to. I could do *anything* I wanted to, and all I'd have to do is break some oaths and walk away from something important.[145]

I have to stop writing now, or I'm going to start crying and ruin the ink.

---

142 Ha. Ha. Ha. Ha. Ha. Ha. Ha.

143 You could! You should! Do it! You don't deserve to go on that narcissistic little quest you came up with. You don't deserve to stand where they stood. If I'd kept talking to you after you handed me these pages, I'd wager you would have said something about *finding yourself*, wouldn't you?

144 I don't know, but *I* sure want it.

145 Oh come now, chin up! You've already done all those things every single day since you sank your homeland beneath the waves! Surely you've got loads of practice at it by now.

TWENTY-FIVE

Two more of Sterre's ships arrived today, and that's all there will be for the next few months. The solstice is coming in two weeks, and with it the summer king-tide, and then the stormy season is going to close the ports, for the most part. Some people, desperate people with more brains than sense, make a run for it, trying to outsail the storms and make it to safe harbor in time, but it's wiser to stay put. The small hurricanes that blow in from the sea drive ships aground and batter the buildings, sometimes tearing shutters and roofs off and always flinging debris around everywhere. *Mevrouw* Basisi told me that if we get a bad storm, I'm to come out of the attic and sleep in the kitchen, well away from the fire—if the wind is bad, it can come down through the chimney and blow embers and ashes around the kitchen. She told me not to worry overmuch about it—the canal systems mean that if the waters rise to flooding, at least they drain away quickly too, and everyone has little boats and coracles to paddle around in the canals, so the water isn't that much more of an issue.

Oh—I haven't talked about Basisi before, have I? She's a Heyrlandtsche and N'gakan *vrouw* and she owns the inn with her spouse, Nicasen Eenyart. She's short, heavyset, very strong, and very serious. A canny businesswoman, too. I don't know Nicasen; they've never come to the inn. They and Basisi live a few streets away, in a proper townhouse. Basisi handles all the day-to-day running of the inn, and Nicasen handles the accounts. I gather that they have some trouble leaving the house, but I'm not sure why.

Anyway, Basisi is already moving her dry goods out of the cellar and into one of the guest rooms on the second floor—that was one of the tasks I've been helping her with these last few days, in the spare hours I have in the morning before heading to Sterre's offices or the Rojkstraat, or in the evening when I return. The strange Pezian flirt turned up again this evening and got underfoot while we were working, crowing to Basisi about how delighted he'd be to help out. He trailed after us and did carry a couple things, but mostly he just stood around trying to sweet-talk her, even though she's married and was having none of it. He kept giving me these looks, too, like he wanted to turn on me next, but I was busy and making quick trips up and down the stairs. I didn't much care to help him practice his obvious *quest* of learning how not to inflict himself upon people.[146]

When we paused for dinner, he followed us into the inn's kitchen without being invited, which *I* thought was rude. Basisi was having a grand time yelling at him, but if she'd really wanted him gone, she would have hauled him over one shoulder like the sacks of potatoes in the basement and dumped him in the common room with his family, the other Pezians. She's a very straightforward sort of person.

"Why are you *here?*" she demanded of him after the third time he'd compared her smile to dawn breaking over the spires of the Palazzo della Colombe in Astimo.

"Why wouldn't I be here?" he asked cheerfully. We hadn't offered

---

146 Oh god, I wish I could meet this young man and commiserate with him about what an obtuse, self-involved prick you are. I'd buy him a drink just to hear him tell this story from his perspective.

him any food, but he didn't seem to mind. He sat with us at the little table that was wedged into the back corner of the bustling kitchen and folded his hands neatly on his knee. "I'm enjoying my evening with the two loveliest creatures in the city."

"I guess you can't be accused of having a type," I murmured, and Basisi snorted—she is the polar opposite of me in every physical respect.

Saying anything was probably a mistake, because the Pezian turned his limpid eyes on me. "Do you wish me to be quiet?"

"We wish you to be good company, if you're going to be company at all," Basisi replied sharply. I tipped my head towards her to indicate my agreement and kept eating.

"I can be good company," he said. "I've been told I'm very agreeable."

"You'd be more agreeable if you talked less."

He smiled. "No one else is saying anything," he pointed out.

Basisi nudged me with her elbow. "Say something. Quiet this young fool."

"*I* don't have anything to say."

"See?" said the Pezian cheerfully.

She nudged me again. "Talking is your profession, isn't it?"

"Is it?" the Pezian said, turning his bright eyes on me again. "Is that why that *loestijr* the other day made you tell us that story about Oyemo and the thirst-starved ghost?"

I made a noncommittal noise and scraped up the last of my soup, wishing I'd lingered longer over it.

"Still hungry?" Basisi asked. "You've been working hard."

"No." But there was an idea, a chance to escape the chatty Pezian. "I'll get back to work now."

Basisi waved dismissively. "Hauling sacks and boxes through the kitchen during the dinner rush? I think not. We're done for the night."

"I'll go down and sort things to make it easier tomorrow, then."

She shrugged in reply and pointed her spoon at the Pezian. "Go help, if you're going to help."

He practically jumped out of his chair. "I can do that!"

I must have been giving Basisi some kind of *look*, because she smirked at me and said, "Have fun! The common room is yours if you feel like it, later." I sighed and turned away, making my way down the steps to the basement with the Pezian on my heels. We'd left the two lanterns burning. The light was dim and flickering, but enough to navigate the space without tripping.

"What did she mean about the common room being yours?" the Pezian said, perching on a crate by the steps.

"Nothing," I said. "It's not important."

"I don't mind how important it is. I'm curious about y— about . . . about what she said." *Curious about you*, he'd been about to say, and then he'd changed his mind. I supposed it must be part of that quest of his I'd intuited with my Chantly instincts. There was just something a little off in the way he'd flirt furiously, then back off, then flirt again, as if he was trying to figure out how other people's boundaries worked by patting around in the dark for them. If I'd had to guess, I'd say that he'd recently gotten his fingers burned for coming on too strong. Maybe by a potential conquest. Maybe he'd just been scolded by a few elders from the flock of his cousins. Maybe he'd just decided on his own to try to be better.

"She meant I could go out and tell stories if I wanted some spare coin," I said, picking up an empty crate and beginning to pack wine bottles into it. "I do that sometimes. Or I used to, when I first got here. Not as much anymore."

"Oh, are you going to tonight?"

"No."

"You don't need the money? That's good."

"It's not about the money."

I expected him to say something, but the silence stretched out, empty and expectant, like an open palm.

"I just don't feel up to it," I muttered.

Sick? he could have asked. *Tired?* But there was just quiet. I glanced over at him. He had his hands clasped between his knees, his feet swinging gently. He was watching me without any shame, just . . . curious. As he'd said.

"It's complicated." I think I was challenging him, daring him to ask, to push, to grab for a real answer. Maybe even to volunteer information of his own, to say he knew how I felt. He sat still, biting his lip a little and watching me work. "Nothing to say now?"

"Did you want me to say something?" he asked mildly. "I can, if you'd like me to. Would you?"

I shoved wine bottles in the crate, letting them clatter and clink against each other. I didn't care if they broke. I wanted them to break. I wanted wine running over my hands like blood, maybe the sharp bite of a glass shard in my fingers. I sat back on my heels, and let my hands fall into my lap. *Did* I want him to say something? "I don't know."

"All right."

We said nothing. The candles flickered. Hollow footsteps passed across the wood floor above our heads. We could hear the muffled noises of the inn's common room, people talking and laughing.

We said nothing.

Until I said, "You remembered the story. The one about Oyemo."

"And the one about the trout of perfect hindsight," he said. Surprised me. I'd forgotten he'd heard that one. Another minute passed in silence. "Would it be all right if I said something?"

I turned my hands palms up, shrugged one shoulder.

"You seem sadder now than you did earlier, when you were work-ing with *Mevrouw* Basisi. Is it because of me?"

"No," I said, still staring blankly into the crate of wine bottles. "Nothing to do with you."

"Oh, good." I thought that was going to be the end of it, that we'd sit in silence again, there in the nearly dark. "You don't have a good face for it, you know. Being sad."

"What do you mean?"

"Some people are prettier when they're sad. They look delicate and . . . I don't know. Wistful. Like a flower in snow."

"You're saying I'm not pretty?" I said, just about managing wry. "*That's* a new strategy."

"I'm saying you look like you've spent most of your life laughing and that's what your face is used to. Sad doesn't *fit* right on you. It looks like you're wearing someone else's coat."

I looked at him, utterly bewildered.

"I think you started getting sad again when *Mevrouw* Basisi poked you and told you to talk. Or when I asked about the story from before." He put his head to one side. "Why?"

"It's complicated," I said again, my voice no louder than a whisper.

"You don't like telling stories?"

"I love stories."

"But you don't like *telling* them?"

I could only shrug, helpless and empty. "That's what I do. What I'm supposed to do, anyway."

"Seems like it's taken a lot out of you. It's nicer to listen some-times, I think."

"I don't get to listen much anymore. People only want to take. No one wants to give."

He fidgeted, picking at the cuff of his knee-breeches, no longer looking at me so intently. "Perhaps they're intimidated. Perhaps they think you're not interested in listening because you're so good at it already."

Do you think that? I could have asked. *Do you have a story that you think I've already heard?*

And then maybe he would have said yes. Maybe he would have given me a shyer version of that boyish smile that made "flirt" spring up in letters of fire behind him. Maybe he would have told me, if I'd asked, about dawn over the spires on the Palazzo della Colombe, about the first time he'd seen them, about who he'd been with. Maybe he would have told me, if I'd asked, about the voyage from Pezia, or about how his parents met, or a memory of eating his favorite food. Maybe he would have told me about his first love, or that he'd never been in love, or that he hoped he never fell in love at all. Maybe he would have told me something true and precious and secret, something just for me, something the size of a baby bird to nestle safe into a warm, wool-padded box in my heart.

But I didn't ask any of this.

"I'm going to bed," I said. His face fell, but he nodded and hopped off the box. I blew out the lanterns, and we went up the stairs, him ahead of me, glancing back over his shoulder every few steps like he thought I'd vanish.

I'll finish the rest tomorrow.

———◆———

Mevrouw Basisi and I moved the rest of the wine, the potatoes and flour, and the cured meats today. We've let most of the barrels and jars stay in the cellar; they're all well-proofed against damp—the cellars are almost waterproof themselves, else they'd be completely unusable when the king-tide comes, instead of mostly unusable. Basisi says the waters rise an inch or two above the lip of the canals, but usually no farther, what with the windmills pumping day and night to keep the flood outside the dikes. There's even backup systems, in case the winds stop and the waters start rising too high—they get people to come in and crank the pumps by hand. And people *volunteer!*[147] I thought they must use prison labor, but Basisi says that people just show up at the dikes to help; even when all the pumps are manned, more people arrive with buckets and start bailing like the city's a row-boat with a leak. Everyone knows how important it is to keep the waters down.

Everyone seems secure but . . . *prepared.* They're not relaxed, but they're not stressed either. They're just ready. Or perhaps I should say they're *at the ready.*

I expect that at the very worst, we'll have damp socks. Everyone keeps giving me advice, knowing I'm a foreigner—they're all terribly worried that I'll do something stupid, not knowing how storms work. I can't talk to anyone without them firmly explaining to me that I must be careful to stay out of the canals, that swimming in them will definitely make me ill.[148] I suppose they're used to foreigners having foolish ideas—the canals are just as any other river in any other city: filled with human waste. You wouldn't want to swim in that. They always tell me that if the canals flood, I should be careful not to walk

---

147 Yep. They do. See: those stories I told at van Vlymen's party, particularly "The Seven Siblings."

148 Hah, I get these explanations too. Every new person I meet mentions to me that I shouldn't even touch the canals if at all possible, shouldn't dabble my feet in them, shouldn't breathe near them or acknowledge they exist. . . . I've taken to play-ing a little game. When someone starts earnestly warning me about the canals, then I say in an innocent and confused voice, "You mean I shouldn't drink from them?" and then I see how many different colors their faces turn before they realize that I'm joking. I really would like to meet whatever batch of idiot foreigners decided to bathe in the canals and traumatized the Heyrlandtsche so permanently.

through the water without wet-boots. Everyone seems to have a story about someone they knew who had a little cut on their ankle and went walking in the flooded streets, and then had to get their whole leg chopped off when the tiny cut took a virulent and horrific fever.[149]

Needless to say, I will be very careful. The floods bring other illness too, everyone says—I don't know if I can believe it. I've heard so many different arguments for the causes of illness and the treatment thereof that I don't know what's real anymore. In Genzhu and Map Sut, they say it's an imbalance of the humors, but even *they* disagree about whether it's six humors or eight and how the imbalances come about.

But as the saying goes, when in Araşt ... If the Heyrlandtsche say the tides and the flooding make people sick, then I shall assume they know what they're talking about.

Everyone's making preparations for tides and storms, but that hasn't stopped them from buying up Sterre's stock at all. She had signed so many contracts of future sale before the ships arrived that nearly their entire supply of stars-in-the-marsh was used up in fulfilling them. She is delighted. We had two boxes left after deliveries today, and as soon as people know that there's any available, they'll buy them up in a trice.

---

149 Hah! You're right again. They do *all* claim to know someone who lost a leg or a hand because a minor injury got a little splashed with dirty water. And yet, you look around on the street, and the instance of missing limbs is roughly the same as it is anywhere else: a few people in every crowd, rather than the full thirty to fifty percent of the population that they would have us believe.

TWENTY-SIX

While I'm still in a reasonably good mood:

I promised myself I'd make some notes on the stories Mistress Chant told at the salon when I was feeling better. I'll do that now before the tide turns.[150]

1. The one about the Vintish mercenaries. Technically mercenaries employed by Vinte, not all Vints themselves. Mercenary captain's name was Fintan Iarainn (of Calabog/ Fyrndarog, by the name); was supposedly secretly in love with one of the Vintish ministers of war (le Paon, I think?). (Mistress Chant downplayed this, but it could be played back up—I like romances, even if she doesn't.)[151] Iarainn hears that General Catuen's army is sieging Fort Cielisse and leads his men through the forest. Sneaks into the general's camp (how???), poisons the general with aesica (herb native to Bramandon) to sow uncertainty among the army and make them think there was a traitor within their own ranks. Fighting breaks out among the captains, army splinters, Fort Cielisse holds against the siege until the rest of the reinforcements arrive. Lots of stuff about

---

150 Goddammit.
151 It's not about the romance!

loyalty to an adopted homeland, etc. (Personally, I'd like it better if le Paon was inside the fort when it was being sieged.[152] No idea if le Paon is male, female, other. Could possibly find out in Vinte someday?)

2.   "The Tale of Peregrine Lee." Peregrine Lee's husband dies in battle. She starts digging a tunnel through a mountain to connect the two warring countries, makes it easier for them to make peace with each other. At first, everyone thinks she's wasting her time, then one by one, some miners come to help her. Kind of boring, and no internal logic—what does the tunnel do? Why does it help? Why can't their diplomats just walk over or around the mountains? Why not build a road? Needs more information to make sense.[153]

3.   A Heyrlandtsche story—seven siblings living in a very poor cottage are starving during a famine. Three times, people come to their door to ask for help: First, a prince who had been set upon by bandits and separated from his caravan; they bind his wounds and send word to the caravan. Then, a merchant whose cart lost a wheel; they help her repair it, and notice also that her horse has thrown a shoe. Then, a beggar with a little dog whose leg is broken: they fix the dog's leg; they offer the beggar clean clothes and a bath; they give him the last crust of bread that they have. A few days later, the siblings are hungry, so they go to their neighbor's house and ask for help; the neighbor gives

---

152 It's not your job to change it! Again, it's not about the romance! If le Paon is in the fort, then Iarainn's motivation isn't loyalty to a group or a community, it's just fear for his lover.

153 It's not about what the tunnel does; it's about the act of building it.

them a bowl of chicken bones and a pair of onions. They go to
their other neighbor's house, and receive a cabbage. They go to
a third neighbor's house and receive a bunch of carrots and a
few cups of barley. They make everything into a soup, and take
bowls back to their neighbors, and for a day, they eat well. Then
a few days after that, the prince returns. He gives them a sack of
coins; they try to protest, but he says he wants to help them as
they helped him. The next day, the merchant returns. She gives
them seven laying hens and a barrel of potatoes; they protest,
but she says she wants to help, etc., etc. The next day, the beggar
returns. He gives the siblings a basket of berries he has gathered
from the forest. The siblings, humbled at the sincerity of this
small gesture, accept it and ask the beggar why he bothered with
it. The beggar says that there isn't much he could do to thank
the siblings for their hospitality, but he wanted to care for them
as they had cared for him, and picking berries was one little
thing he could do for them. (This was the best one.)

I'll do the rest another time, maybe.

———◆◆◆———

Today was a good day: I was working as a translator again, instead
of a Chant. It was such a relief to be away from all that, and I kept
thinking about what I was writing a couple days ago: *I could give up
Chanting next week. I could.*

Well, not if I'm still working for Sterre. She won't let me stop being
a Chant yet.[154] It matters too much to her that I keep talking about these

---

154 And what did it matter what she wanted you to do? She didn't own you. You
could have left at any point, you know. That was *your* choice. You could have quietly
left town in the night, like any self-respecting Chant does when they run into trouble.

flowers as if they're a sacred relic, as if possessing one will somehow solve all the ills a person might have and resolve all their insecurities: *Buy stars-in-the-marsh! Your business will prosper, your children will be beautiful, everyone will like you, and all the sex you have will be above average!*

But now, with the futures contracts, the sales have already been made, so all she needs is for me to go with her porters to the houses of the buyers whose mother tongues are something other than the Spraacht. We go over the contract, confirm the amount, collect the papers, and distribute the roots to them in neat brown parcels, and then we leave.

A funny thing happened today, though.

We were going up to the house of the ambassador from Tash. I wrote before about how close the houses are crammed together—even the ambassador's house. Even the servants use the front door for everything. The houses are too narrow for another door (in some of them, you could just about touch both walls if you stood in the front hall with your arms outstretched to either side—they have to haul furniture up from the outside, using a hook on the roof gable and a pulley, because there would be no way to get it upstairs otherwise), and any doors that were sunken below the level of the street would only flood uselessly as soon as the king-tides came. Besides that, if there *is* a back door in the house, it only leads into a garden the size of a blanket, and you'd have to go through a lot of other people's gardens and over dozens of walls and fences if you wanted to reach it from the outside. Only the incredibly rich, like Sterre and *Heer* van Vlymen, have gardens big enough to walk around in, and even those are located a ways outside the city proper.

It's nice, I think, not having a servants' entrance. It makes everyone equal. And people keep their front steps clean—scrupulously clean! They scrub their front steps more thoroughly than they scrub their dishes. That kind of cleanliness, of course, is rarely true about side doors in other cities. Servants aren't allowed to toss slop out the doors carelessly here, because it would befoul the street. They just go a few more steps and empty the pots into the canal.

This is all a long way of describing why we were waiting on the ambassador's front steps, me and Gillis, one of Sterre's porters. The big cart waited behind us, watched by four armed guards so no ruffians could sneak up and ransack us for our precious cargo. We rang the bell, and the door was answered by a person in simple Glass Sea clothing (covered from head to toe, with only their hands and arms below the elbow exposed), whom I greeted in the customary manner. "We've come with the flower roots that Ambassador Kha'ud ordered. Stars-in-the marsh, very fine quality," I said in Tashaz. As we were both to be considered servants, I did not completely avert my eyes in deference, instead politely pinning my gaze to the slope of their left shoulder.

Of course the ambassador was fluent in the Spraacht, but they were important enough and such a valuable customer that Sterre considered it an imperative of courtesy to send a translator. Safer, too, to make sure that everyone agreed and understood each other in two languages. Less chance for mistakes. "Are they available to settle the contract?" I asked.

"I'll find out. Wait here." We were accustomed to having to wait a few minutes on the steps—the houses are too small to have waiting rooms for merchants, servants, and parcel-deliverers, and of course you don't bring just anyone into your parlor.

We didn't wait long; the servant came back promptly and showed us up to the office, where the ambassador sat on a gold-embroidered cushion on the floor at a knee-high table. They wore the open-fronted robe appropriate to their station, cream-colored with woven patterns in shades of blue around the cuffs and collar and at knee-level, with a matching headscarf covering their hair and mouth, bordered with a tasteful and understated fringe of silver seed-beads. Beneath the robe, a long tunic, loosely sashed around their waist, dyed in the unmistakable shade of Vintish indigo.

I bowed in the proper style and came down onto my knees as well, so we'd be able to talk comfortably. "Good afternoon, Ambassador," I said, demure as protocol demanded, my gaze respectfully lowered. "We have your order prepared." I gestured to Gillis, who carried a wicker basket full of damp earth and bulbs. "Do you have the contract to confirm?"

The ambassador folded their hands on the table. "I do not. I passed it along to my friend *Hecht* Mathys van Zandwijck, the city water-warden."

"Passed it along?" I said. "I'm sorry, I don't understand."

"I sold it to him."

"Sold it. Why?"[155]

"He said that there weren't any more contracts available for this shipment, and he's been desperate to get his hands on some of these exquisite specimens. A passionate gardener, he is," they added. "So I offered to sell him my share. Somewhat unorthodox, but I don't think it will be too much of a problem, will it?" Their voice gave nothing away, and of course I could not glance up at what I could see of their face, but their hands were fiddling with a stylus in a way that showed just a hint of uncertainty.

I looked at Gillis, who just shrugged. "I don't see why it would be," I said slowly. "So . . . you didn't want the flowers anymore?"

"Oh, I did. I assure you, I did. But *Hecht* van Zandwijck was so disappointed, and it mattered more to him than it did to me." I heard

---

155 Aha, now I see. This is where it all started going wrong. Well, *wronger*—you'd been going wrong for weeks by this point.

a smile in their voice. "I confess, I made a tiny little profit on it too. A hundred and fifteen guilders I paid, for ten bulbs. Van Zandwijck insisted on rounding it up to a hundred and twenty out of gratitude."

"That was kind of him," I said.

The ambassador paused and tapped one elegant finger against the tabletop. "So," they said slowly, carefully. "It doesn't cause any problems? Selling a contract on like that?"

"No," I said, blinking. The difficult thing about Tashaz is remembering to emote with your hands instead of your face. No one looks in your eyes, except your most intimate friends and relations or particularly rude people. "Why would it? The money has already been paid to us, so we don't mind who we deliver the flowers to. If everyone's happy and in agreement, then so are we. I'll have to check with *Mevrol* de Waeyer, of course, but I can't imagine that she would have any objections...."[156]

"Excellent!" the ambassador said heartily. "Tell *Mevrol* de Waeyer that I'd like to do more business with her. I definitely want a few more of those contracts-of-whatever-she-calls-it before the next shipment is booked up."

"Contracts of future sale," I said.

"Right, future contracts."

"But you know the next shipment isn't coming until after the storms?"

"I don't mind at all."

"All right. I'll mention it to her. Do you know where we could find *Hecht* van Zandwijck?" We were given an address in the Coppel

---

156 Oh, brother-Chant. Dear sweet naive little brother-Chant... Your problem, you see, was that you let the story get out of your hands. You told a story too big for you to handle, and it ran away from you like a wild horse. You should have been more humble.

Square District, on Bardengracht, and Gillis and I went there promptly, where van Zandwijck received us and our delivery with great enthusiasm.

As he was showing us out again, when all had been settled, I turned to him. "I was just wondering—you bought the contract from Ambassador Kha'ud. And you paid them a little extra?"

"Well, that's only fair, isn't it?" he said. "They were being inconvenienced. Anyway, they're a good friend of mine. Have been for years. And one favor deserves another, doesn't it?"

"I suppose so," I said.

There's something about all this that doesn't sit quite right with me. I can't put my finger on it. It feels . . . almost familiar. It feels like something I know about, like a familiar tune whose words I've forgotten.[157]

It's probably nothing. I'm so tired, and I haven't been able to focus. Tomorrow is just going to be more of the same. We'll walk all across the city until I'm footsore and blistered—and that's saying something too, because there was a time when Chant and I would walk all day long, only stopping to eat. It's been years since I traveled like that—he'd started slowing our pace a few months before we even reached Nuryevet, started taking a few more opportunities to hitch rides with passing carts and caravans. And after I sank my homeland beneath the waves and set out on my own, I'd go only a few miles a day on foot, stopping well before I was tired. Living in the city these past few months has been naturally even more sedentary.

Or maybe it's just that I'm getting old. Nineteen or twenty and I'm getting old already.[158]

---

157 No, that was just your conscience. It was trying to tell you, "THIS IS A BAD IDEA!" but of course you were too busy wallowing to pay any attention.
158 Oh, for gods' sake. Don't start with that.

TWENTY-SEVEN

I told Sterre about Ambassador Kha'ud and *Hecht* van Zandwijck's little arrangement. It was still nagging at me this morning, and I thought that she might have some kind of insight about why it was so troubling. She didn't, of course. She just laughed. "That's wonderful news!" she cried. "I'll send word to double the size of the next shipment."[159]

"You're not worried about people selling the contracts back and forth?"

"Of course not. It means people want them badly enough to haggle each other for them."

"But what if someone else gets the same idea?" That wasn't the problem. I'd said it out loud and I could hear it wasn't right.

"Whatever do you mean?" she demanded.

"If someone buys a lot of bulbs this year, then next year they'll be able to sell the seeds, won't they?"

"Oh." Sterre scoffed and waved me off. "That's nothing. The plants take five years or more to bloom from seed, and the bulbs don't grow offshoots every year. If you're worried about competitors, we won't have serious trouble for years yet, unless someone goes to Kaskinen

---

159 Can you hold on for just a moment? I need to go bang my head against a wall.

and finds my secret supplier.[160] And by then I expect they'll be out of fashion anyway, or I'll have imported so many that the canals will be choked with them." She laughed. "Imagine that!"

"I'd rather not,"[161] I said, thinking of the stench.

"And travelers would come from far and wide to see the wonderful canals of Heyrland," she said. "Moreso than they already do, I mean. How romantic that would be, to row down the canal full of stars in the twilight."

There's no arguing with her. I don't think it would be romantic. I think it would be smelly—the canals are dirty, nothing you'd want to drink from or swim in, as I've mentioned before, but they don't smell that bad. Just musty, especially at low tide—the Heyrlandtsche have a great deal of experience in managing their water flow, and there are currents running through the arteries of the city and sweeping all the filth out to the harbors, to the locks and pump systems, and thence to the sea.[162]

Speaking of the flowers, the root I bought from Sterre weeks ago has sprouted. Already it has four spindly leaves, and its stalk is only a few finger-widths high. It's still green and lively, too—it'll darken to brown and go woody as it gets taller, and then one day

---

160 Has she *been* to Kaskinen? It's not exactly hard to find stars-in-the-marsh! You just . . . find a marsh. And then you follow your nose. And then you wonder why you were thinking that this was a good idea. The sort of things that people decide are *luxury items* are really completely arbitrary.

161 Ugh, nor I. Heyrland is quite pretty, as towns and cities go. They have all this greenery hanging around, all these neatly manicured trees in tame tiny plots along the streets, and the water plants growing in the canals, and the ornamental plants that they drape down their balconies. It's as if the whole city is one of those public parks they have along the rivers in Vinte. Do they really want to spoil that with an overlying smell of rotting meat? And the bugs! Don't get me started—they'd be up to their eyebrows in flies and mosquitos.

162 If only you could apply your good taste for the prosaic to more elevated matters.

I'll have to get rid of it or it'll stink up the whole inn. Maybe I'll sell it to someone, like the ambassador sold theirs to *Hecht* van Zandwijck.

I don't know what I'd do with the money, though. Perhaps it's a silly idea, and I should just give it away to someone who could make better use of it.

TWENTY-EIGHT

I need a break. It's too much.

That dream, I keep having it—not every night, but five in seven. I wander through the swamps, sloshing through water up to my thighs, or my waist, staggering and falling. I'm wet from head to toe; I'm covered in mud and miserable. My clothing sticks to my skin, and my feet are bare. I have the impression that the sucking mud beneath me stole my boots days or miles ago. It's no use, anyway. I push onward, too tired to cry, wanting only to stop and rest.

But I can't. When I stop, I start to sink. I keep moving. There's no stars above me but the flowers. There's no wind.

I walk, and I walk, and I push my way through the stalks. They grow so thick I can't see more than a couple feet in any direction. Some of them, when they grow in deeper water, have long roots that tangle around my legs. There's nothing living in the swamp but me and the stars-in-the-marsh and the occasional cormorant that I glimpse as it paddles past me through the stalks—it doesn't struggle like I do, of course.

I drag myself onward, and every morning I wake up more exhausted and drained than when I went to bed. And then I drag myself onward out of bed, and I drag myself to Sterre's offices or the Rojkstraat, and I drag myself through the day.

I'm so tired. I can't go on. This has to stop. Something has to change.[163]

---

163 I wish you'd been able to talk to me. I wish you'd been *smarter* about this. I tried to tell you! How many times did I try? At the beginning, when you first saw me, you were thinking of asking me for help. Was it pride that kept you from doing it, or sheer cowardice? You could have changed things. You could have changed at any time. But you held yourself back, waiting and waiting as the point of no return rushed ever closer. If you'd been honest, if you'd had a little less pride, you wouldn't have had to suffer through all this. You could have stopped—well, you probably couldn't have stopped it outright. Might as well try to stop the tide. But you could have averted it, or you could have just . . . left. You didn't owe Sterre anything. That was all just the story in your head fucking you up.

TWENTY-NINE

Another day as translator. There was a small riot outside Sterre's headquarters; some people had found out that she still had twelve stars-in-the-marsh roots left, and they were trying to fight over them. Not very effectively, since there were three or four different languages spoken, so most of the insults went over everyone else's heads. Sterre sent me outside to sort them out—it was very much like that test at Stroekshall, where all the translators came and stood around me shouting, trying to muddle me up in chaos and confusion. This was just the same—people tugging on my sleeves, catching my hands, trying to tell me they'd pay so much for just one root. I suppose I was a little distracted, but I kept up pretty well.

I just kept telling everyone else how much the others wanted to pay for the roots, because that's what I thought I was supposed to do. Someone would say "Fifteen guilders!" and I'd translate that into the Spraacht, Tashaz, Araşti, Vintish, and Avaren, and someone else would say, "Shipwreck that, I'll pay twenty!"[164]

I guess it was a better thing than letting them come to blows in the street? Nobody got hurt this way.

---

164 It is so strange to look at this from my position. I was here for all of it, I saw the whole thing, but you tell this story bit by bit, in pieces as things happened. It gives me a strange warping of perspective—like the sort of eye-bending vertigo you get when you look up into a very large, very tall dome or vaulted ceiling inside a temple.

And eventually everybody else drifted away and there were just two people left, and somehow, *somehow* they'd argued each other up to seventy guilders per root and the two of them had begrudgingly agreed to split the twelve roots between them.

Sterre was *thrilled*. Seventy guilders apiece! She hugged me as if I'd *done* something, as if I'd told them one of my stories.

"All I did was translate," I tried to tell her. It was pointless.

"Nonsense!" she cried. "My good *mann*, don't be so modest! That was excellent! I've never seen anything like it!"

"Translation? But there's lots of people at Stroekshall who could do that."

She cupped my face between her hands, which I didn't particularly like. I endured. I didn't want to be rude. "I hadn't even planned on holding an auction until the next shipment came, but you! Look at you! You walked right out there and took the reins like it was nothing! You brought them to heel without a blink! I should have known—I should have accelerated my strategy the moment you walked in the door—you're fanning the flames like nothing I've ever seen!"

"I mean," I said. "That's my job. Getting people to pay attention. And knowing how to talk to people."[165]

"My dear *heerchen*, I'm going to have to expand your responsibilities again. You're too good to be wasted on street hawking. Any idiot could do that. You, dear, you were destined for greater things."[166]

---

165 I'm getting tired of writing some variant on, "Seriously? *Really?*" every time you say something like this, so from now on just assume that I'm doing that every time.

166 I don't know how you can accuse *me* of being pushy when *Mevrol* de Waeyer was right there, haranguing you and making wild improbable promises.

"No more storytelling on the street?" I said, just to be certain I understood what she meant.

"Never again, *heerchen*! I have more important things for you now!" She hugged me again and sighed blissfully. "Every time I think I've got a handle on your capabilities, you go and surprise me again. First the stories, now this. You and me, my dear, we're going to make Heyrland the capital of the world."

"Um," I said. "How?"[167]

"Well, if the stars-in-the-marsh keep selling like that—if *you* keep selling them like that, the way you just did, then when the storms are over ... We'll go on an expedition, you and I. We'll take a voyage and travel about to find something new and exotic, something no one's ever heard of, and then we'll bring it back here.[168] I can't see that people would care about the flowers next year; they'll likely be sick of the stench of them, ha-ha!"

"A voyage?" My gut had twisted the moment she said it. I didn't want to go with her. I didn't want to go traveling, or hunting for new things no one had ever heard of. It was too much like Chanting. "I'd rather not, if it's all the same to you. . . ."[169]

"Oh, what's this about? Seasickness? It's really only bad for the first few days and then your stomach settles. Trust me, you'll have a lovely time."

---

167 Greed, deception, conspiracy. How else do you think?

168 She was awfully presumptuous, wasn't she? I hope you eventually did something about that. *Before* the end of things, I mean, before you walked out of the city or wherever it is you've gone. But I suppose you must have—you did come around towards the end, you did change your mind and do the right thing. And I suppose you would have had to fight with her to get her to allow that.

169 People like her, you can't give them a soft refusal like "I'd rather not." You say "No thank you," and then you hold firm. You didn't owe her anything. All she was doing was paying you for services. She shouldn't have tried to run your life or demand that you attend her on voyages.

"No, it's not that."

"You're not afraid of the sea, are you?"

"No, ma'am. I've been on voyages before." I shook my head. "Never mind. I'm sorry. It's still so early; we don't have to make any decisions about this now. Forget I said anything."

"Hmph." She narrowed her eyes at me. "All right. For now." Still peering at me, she went off back into her office, and stopped right on the threshold. "Chant. I really thought that it'd be another few months until they were ready for an auction. Why do you think they fought like that?"

I looked up at her. "What do you mean?"

"I've been a merchant my entire life. I've never seen anything like the reaction to these flowers. But today people nearly came to blows over them—why is that?"

I shrugged. "I don't know why people want what they want." I barely know what *I* want these days. "But just now . . . they got frantic because there were only a few left, I think."

"Hm," she said.

"That seems obvious. Is it?"[170]

"It's good to say obvious things out loud sometimes," Sterre said in a strange voice. "It makes you think about them in a different way."

"What do you mean?"

"If I import chickens, there's a selection of things to worry about. I worry about having too many, because then I can't sell them and I've lost money. I worry about having too few chickens, because then I've lost an opportunity for more money. The best thing for me, or so I've always thought, is to guess as accurately as possible exactly how many chickens will be required, no more, no less." She put her

---

170 Yep. It is.

head to one side. "I was always so focused on getting the exact right number of chickens that it never really occurred to me that having too *few* chickens might actually ... create future opportunities." I stared at her, waiting for her to finish her thought. She only looked thoughtful, and then sly. "I think I'm actually going to halve the next shipment, instead of doubling it."[171]

I felt another tickle at the back of my brain, but I brushed it aside. "I'm sure you know best," I said, because she probably did.

"I do," she replied, coming back to herself suddenly. She pointed at me. "Which is why I won't hear you turning down a place on the expedition. We'll go in the fall, if all goes well. After the summer storms have passed."

This, of all things, struck a sour note—I've been walking for years. I just want to rest. No voyages for a while, no more trying to chase the horizon. At the same time, I can't imagine staying in Heyrland for the rest of my life. I don't know that I can imagine staying anywhere for the rest of my life. I only ever meant to stay here a few months—a few *more* months, now. And then I'll drift off somewhere else. Maybe just the next town over. Maybe go inland to some border town on the marches of Vinte or Bramandon. Somewhere quiet, where no one will bother me—no, but that's not right. You can't be invisible in a small town. I'd better go to another capital, then, when I'm done here. "What if I don't want to go?" I said quietly.[172] We just looked at each other for a long, long time.

"As long as I'm paying you," she said, "you'll do the work you're assigned. No?"

"Yes."

---

171 Can you hold on a moment? I need to go bang my head against the wall again.
172 Attaboy, Chant.

"So if I say you're coming with me on the voyage, then you're coming with me. End of story."[173]

"There will be other voyages, won't there? I can go on the next one. I don't think I'll be up to leaving in the fall."

She smiled. "Of course you will be," she said. "You've been working so hard lately. You're just tired. We've all been working hard. You'll feel better after a rest—the king-tide is coming, and likely some storms, and you'll get a lovely holiday then. You can curl up at home and nap or read a book; that's what everyone does. You'll have plenty of time to relax, and I expect by the fall you'll be feeling as antsy and fretful as the rest of us. You'll want to get out of the house and have some adventures." She patted my shoulder. "Trust me, *heerchen*. I know how you young *mannen* are. And I know how *you* are specifically. You'll want to wander again, and if I don't arrange some outings for you, you'll wander right over the edge of the world and then I'll never see you again. Can't be having that."

I didn't reply. I returned my attention to the translations she'd requested earlier.

Maybe she's right. Maybe I'll be fine after the storms pass. And I know that one day I will wake up and feel my feet itching for the road again, just as she says. If I leave, then I'll be alone again, and I won't belong anywhere. So perhaps she's right to be thinking of the future, to plan for a way to let me wander a little—with a purpose, even—and then to come back. To come . . . home, I guess. I suppose if I stay long enough, eventually this will begin to be home. How

---

173 Is this how normal people live? People who aren't Chants? Do they really just sign their souls away to people like de Waeyer? You should have been more firm with her. She's not your superior. In the old days, she would have been very polite to her local Chant—she would have been a little scared of you, scared that you might become angry with her and turn Shuggwa's Eye upon her. She would have respected you in the old days.

long will that take? A year? No, longer than that. Three years? Five years?

But ... maybe she's not right. Maybe I won't feel any better by autumn. If she tries to force me to go with her, I don't have to, not really. Not if I'm willing to sacrifice belonging—I've done that before and survived, and I could do it again. I'll just leave.[174] I'll go somewhere else. I don't need this job. I can do something else. I can go somewhere else. I can be someone else.[175]

I can stop Chanting next week, if I want to. Maybe.[176]

Maybe not. I don't think I can get away from stories, and I don't think I'd want to. They're too deep in me now, in my blood and bones, and tangled in my hair like brambles.

Maybe I don't know what I want.

At the end of the day, I rushed out of Sterre's offices onto the street and let my feet take me where they would.

Which was, apparently, to Mistress Chant.[177]

---

174 Good.
175 See previous note in regards to sighing heavily and at length.
176 Do it, then. I dare you.
177 Oh, it's *that* day. I wish you'd be more clear about the passage of time! It'd be more fun to anticipate my next appearance rather than being ambushed by it, but you have a tendency to ambush people with things, don't you?

THIRTY

I found Mistress Chant at the Rose and Ivy, as she'd told me. Her cart was stationed on one side of the innyard, and I saw her younger apprentice sitting on the back steps of it, plucking at the strings of an instrument shaped like a tiny lute with a long, reedy neck. "Hello," I said. He looked up at me and blinked.

"Oh, it's you," he said. He had the glossy black hair and the accent of southeastern Map Sut. "Chant's been waiting for you to visit."

"Here I am. Is she around?"

"Inside," he said, jerking his head towards the door of the inn. "Do you hate her?"

"No," I said quickly. He quirked an eyebrow at me. "Does she think I do?"

He shrugged. "She thinks you're mad at her. She's frustrated with you. And she told me not to speak to you, but . . ." He used his free hand to brush down the front of his torso as if he were sweeping off dust in one long movement—a *se-gko*, the gesture of politeness or greeting in Map Sut, and I was a little amused to see it. In time, he'll give up the ways of his homeland, just as I did, and adopt and discard local customs as often as he changes his shirt. "I'm Lanh Chau." No surname, I noticed—an orphan, I supposed.

I sketched a short bow in the Heyrlandtsche custom—his *se-gko* hadn't been terribly formal, so my bow wasn't either. "Pleased to meet you."

"Arenza thinks you're handsome."[178]

"Arenza is . . . the other one?"

"Yes. My apprentice-sister."

"It's very kind of her to say so," I said awkwardly, not sure what else I was expected to say.

"She told me she was going to flirt with you if she met you again."[179]

I laughed awkwardly. "Perhaps you could find a moment to drop a word in her ear. . . . I wouldn't want her to be embarrassed. My preferences don't run to women, you see."

He nodded thoughtfully. "I'll tell her. So do you just tell stories?"

"Isn't that what a Chant does?"

"Chant says it isn't, not necessarily. She says there's lots of different things in the world that need to be collected and remembered, and one Chant can't attend to all of them. She says that we can take specialties, if we want."

I felt a little dizzy—culture shock. I thought I'd gotten over that a long time ago, but I suppose that was when I still had Hrefni culture sticking to me. Now it's just Chant culture, or what I *thought* Chant culture was, if we even have something that can be called that. "What

---

178 Oh, that boy! I'll smack him upside the head if I catch him pestering her again. He's got a very Chantly natural inclination to assume everyone's business is *his* business, but now he needs to learn that not all subjects require his nose shoved into them.

179 This is probably a lie. He just wanted your attention. Arenza might have thought you were handsome, but she's too reserved to say anything about it. She prefers to hang back and watch a situation, like someone sitting beneath a tree on a lazy day with a fishing rod—the fish will bite or they won't, Arenza thinks. We're working on it. I'm hoping she and Lanh Chau can learn from each other.

do you mean by 'specialties'? I don't think it's right to decide something isn't important or worthwhile. . . ."

He gave me a flat look. "Chant says it's better to concentrate on
one thing and learn everything about it."

"So what's your . . . specialty?" I asked. He was just a kid—young
for an apprentice too, maybe twelve. I didn't feel right making arguments against his philosophy. He wasn't *my* apprentice.

He tapped the belly of the instrument that wasn't a lute. "Music.
When I'm a Chant, I'll go all over, collecting songs from people
instead of stories. Chant says that's good, because people forget about
songs a lot." He gave me a meaningful look, judging me from my toes
to the top of my head. I expect he got that look from his Chant.

"That's a little limiting, don't you think?" I said before I could stop
myself. Apparently I was arguing with him after all. "The way I was
taught, Chants should leave themselves open to receive any kind of
thing, whether it's stories or songs or secrets."[180]

"But you don't know songs."

"I know *some* songs. Everyone knows some."

"You wouldn't sing at the party, though."

"I don't know them well enough to perform in a setting like that.
I haven't gone out of my way to learn them or practice them, that's all.
It hasn't come up—I learn what comes up."

Lanh Chau frowned at me, then shrugged. "You think my way is
limiting. I think your way is unfocused and lazy."[181] I was taken aback,
and after that he seemed to have dismissed me from his attention

---

180 Seriously? Really? You think you can come up to *my* apprentice and start med-
dling with their training? You think you're entitled to criticize *my* methods or *my*
teachings? You should count yourself lucky I never heard about this. We would have
had a *row* and no mistake.
181 Hah! That's my boy! He's impossible to impress or intimidate. He has no
patience, and he can spot bullshit like yours from a mile away.

entirely. He plucked away on his instrument, and I wandered in a daze into the inn.[182]

I spotted Mistress Chant almost immediately. She was sitting quite near the door, playing a hand of cards with her other apprentice, Arenza, and a couple patrons of the inn.

My Chant never approved of gambling. He didn't hold with money-dealings of any sort, not on a personal level. He'd carry coin if he had to, but that was very rare, and he always tried to get rid of it as quickly as possible. He had so many friends in every land we traveled to that there was always someone willing to do us a small favor, and Chant was an expert in playing small favors off one another like movements in chess until he had a big favor in his hands, like getting a ship's captain to allow us passage to wherever we needed to go, even though the best we could hope for was a corner of the crew's berths, and not even a hammock to curl up in.

Remembering the intricate dance of favors as I watched Mistress Chant play her hand probably made me more inclined to be sociable. A friend can be a lot of things—a shelter, a savior, a tool.[183] A friend is a good thing to have, even one who seems to half-hate you.

So I pulled out a chair and sat down, and Mistress Chant glanced at me, and then glanced again and blinked, wide eyed. "Brother-Chant!" she said, more brightly than I'd expected. Part of me had thought she'd launch right into excoriating me for some other per-ceived failure or shortcoming. "What a pleasant surprise."[184]

---

182 He did tell me that he thought you were soft. This must have been why.

183 A *tool?* Well! That's not selfish and manipulative of you at all. People aren't tools, Chant. But *you* knew that, didn't you? You're not the sort of person to phrase something like that. This is one of the bad things you inherited from your master, isn't it?

184 You know what? Yes. It was a pleasant surprise, though I suppose you wouldn't believe me. I was surprised and I was pleased. I thought we could finally find a moment to talk properly. I thought we—plural, both of us—could come to an

"Hello. I was in the area, and ... I thought we could talk. You said ..."

"So I did, so I did." She introduced me to the other people at the table—a pair of *nietsen*, Maarsi and Annan (I noticed instantly that they were married and seemed to be having a silent, ongoing spat, but Maarsi was sorry and Annan was about to forgive them); a *vrouw*, Cilla; and a Vintish woman, Liliane. I don't think Mistress Chant was very close with any of them. She was just being polite because one or more of them had something interesting to tell her and she was going to tweak it out of them.

I saw my old master do it a thousand times. I could have recognized the play from across the room by her posture alone.

Chant sent Arenza off to get something for me to drink, and offered to deal me in to the next hand, which I declined. "Are you sure? Well, perhaps we had better wrap the game up, friends."

"What, already?" Liliane said.

She shrugged. "I wasn't expecting my colleague to visit, and I have so been looking forward to having a conversation with him."

Sociable, I reminded myself. *It can't hurt anything to make a friend. Maybe it's all been a funny misunderstanding and we'll find some common ground in our ways.*[185]

I watched them finish up their game, and then Chant drew me outside, back to the cart. Arenza followed in our wake, quiet and expressionless and watchful. Chant knocked on the side of the cart as we came up. "Lanh Chau, fetch out a couple cushions, would you?"

He flung from the door several battered, stained ones, clearly

---

understanding. But let's just see how you framed things, eh? Let's see how you do with casting me as the villain in this next part. Let's see how you convince yourself that nothing I said in this bit was right or worthwhile. You hated every word I said that night; I could see it then and I can see it now.

185 No one wished for that more dearly than I. And yet ...

intended to be thrown on the ground and unceremoniously sat upon, and Mistress Chant and Arenza nudged them into the shadows in the space between the cart and the inn wall, as if they intended it to serve as the receiving parlor in a fancy house. A moment later, Lanh Chau hauled out a large brass bowl, roughly the size of a soup tureen but perfectly round, with gently curved walls. "No need for that," Mistress Chant said. "Put it away."

"But I'm cold."

"You're going inside in a minute," she said, nodding towards the inn, its open doors spilling warm light and noise across the yard.

Lanh Chau looked taken aback. "I don't get to stay?"

"No."

He burst into a flurry of rapid Sut in a dialect I couldn't make any sense of whatsoever. From context and the odd, trip-trapping, tongue-twisting rhythm, I'd guess it was some variety of thieves' cant.[186] In any case, Mistress Chant understood him perfectly well and responded just as nimbly, and at last he huffed and picked up the bowl. "Can I show it to him first?"

Mistress Chant gazed impassively at him.

"I'm going to show him," Lanh Chau declared. "He'll be interested. I bet he hasn't seen one before." There was a wooden baton lying in the bottom of it; Lanh Chau clanged it against the side of the bowl, producing a pure, resonating sound like a struck bell or a gong, then ran the baton steadily around the lip of the bowl, chasing the vibrations so they went on and on and on, unceasing. Within moments, a faint glow began to pool at the bottom of the bowl, like sunlight on an inch of rippling water. The glow grew brighter until we

---

186 Not bad. Pretty close. Closer to a general gutter-tongue than a thieves' cant specifically, but the distinction is often blurry.

A CHOIR OF LIES

could have read printed text quite comfortably, and a few moments
after that I noticed a cozy warmth emanating from it as well—not as
warm as a fire would have been, not nearly warm enough to cook on,
but a delicate, springtime-sunshine kind of warmth. And the whole
time Lanh Chau went on with the slow, steady circles of the baton
around the lip of the bowl while it sang and sang.

"Bet you haven't seen anything like *that*, have you?" Lanh Chau
asked, greatly satisfied. "They're *rare*."

"No, I haven't," I said politely. "It's lovely." But it was a little like
the dragons in Xereccio[187]—the beauty didn't strike my heart in the
way it should have. "A fine and wondrous item."

"A gift from the king of Inacha," Arenza said.[188] "We find a great
many uses for it."

"Better'n candles," said Lanh Chau. "Your arm gets sore after a
while, though. And the light and the warm don't last. They stop when
you stop." He set down the baton, and indeed the light faded out after
a few heartbeats. He eyed me. "You don't look impressed."

"I'm very impressed," I assured him.

"You don't *look* it." He glanced at Mistress Chant and said something else in that unusual dialect of Sut. She answered, and he looked
me up and down again, dubious as all hell.

"Enough now," Mistress Chant said. "Enough bragging and pea-
cocking. You showed him. He's impressed. Away with you both, and
leave us to talk."

---

187 Oh, that was in those pages I burned, wasn't it? In my defense, they didn't seem
relevant at the time or like something you'd ever mention again.

188 I expect that I'm about to be scandalized. I cannot bear to look at the next page.
I dread looking at it. When I look, I'm going to see that you've copied down the story
I told you in the same words that came out of my mouth. I would have been pleased
and flattered to find out that you'd relayed my little story to someone else, but *copying
it down*? Copying down one that's *mine*? Just beyond the pale.

"I don't mind if they stay," I said.

"See?" Lanh Chau said. "It's fine. I want to listen."

Mistress Chant narrowed her eyes at him. "If you must," she said slowly. She added something in that Sut dialect—it sounded sharp, nearly a rebuke, and the only words I managed to snatch from the tangled snarl of unfamiliar language were "aware" and a phrase that I thought might have been one I knew—just pronounced with a funny accent—which could have meant, depending on context, *reversal, torque, perversion, to tilt one's head, tacking a ship,* or *a fencing volte.*[189]

Lanh Chau grumbled in reply but nodded and perched on the steps of the wagon. The iron lantern that hung above the door shivered with the vibration, making the shadows and patches of light on the ground fly and flicker until they settled once again like a flock of sparrows.

"Arenza?" Mistress Chant asked, turning to her. "Are you going inside, or are you going to argue with me too?"

Arenza considered this slowly and with great deliberation. "I'll argue with you," she said after a few moments of intense thought. Mistress Chant sighed.

"I really don't mind," I said. I thought that if she was going to yell at me, she might modulate herself a little in front of her apprentices.

"We might as well sit," she said flatly. "So, Brother-Chant. You finally grace us with your presence." She pointed imperiously to one of the cushions, which I took.

"I'm not here to fight," I said. She only glanced meaningfully at Lanh Chau, who nodded.

"So what are you here for, then?"

---

189 What I said: "Be mindful that he's got some screwed-up methods and attitudes. I don't want you getting ideas."

Perhaps I should have let her send Lanh Chau and Arenza inside. They watched as silent and still as they'd been listening to Mistress Chant's stories at the salon. It was unsettling, almost creepy. I tried not to look at them and cleared my throat. "Just to talk, I suppose. How . . . have you been?"

Lanh Chau murmured something in Sut, a more standard dialect, which I managed to make out: *Is that the best he can do?*

She gave him a sharp look. "We're fine. Getting settled in."

"Oh—you're going to be staying a while?" I didn't know how to feel about that. Nerves and frustration and despair and, strangely, relief. I could make a mess of this conversation but still have enough time to try again if I had to, if I really wanted to. Again and again until I got it right.

"Probably well into autumn," she said. "And then we'll head north to warmer climes before it gets too cold—Tash, maybe. *Some of us* have fussy constitutions." She glanced accusingly at Lanh Chau. "And you? How long are you staying?"

"I haven't decided yet," I said weakly, still processing "well into autumn."

"You'll be here through the stormy season, at least," she said confidently, as if she were telling me what my orders were, instead of guessing my intentions. "You won't want to get caught on the road in a tempest."

"Maybe more than that," I said. "Maybe a few years. Maybe longer."

She frowned. "You find the Heyrlandtsche so interesting?"

"They're all right. They're as interesting as people are anywhere."

Her frown deepened. "A young lad like you, you ought to be scampering about from one end of the earth to the other. Use all that youthful energy while you have it."

"I've already done that with my master. I've seen plenty."

"You hadn't seen our bowl, though," Lanh Chau said suddenly. "I could tell. You'd never seen anything like that. And you didn't even ask us anything about it. Chant says you should always ask questions when people show you something they think is nice."

"Hush," said Mistress Chant, without heat.

"Oh," I said. "It didn't seem like the important thing at the time."

"It was a present," Lanh Chau said.

"From the king of Inacha, yes. Arenza said."

He gave me an expectant look that faded gradually into outrage. "You're not going to *ask*? It's from a *king*, and you don't want to know anything about it?" He looked incredulously at Mistress Chant, who shrugged. Lanh Chau threw his hands in the air and repeated that Sut phrase they'd used before—the one that meant something like *torque–tacking–tilting head*.

"Perhaps he's met his fill of kings," Arenza murmured. "*You* wouldn't know."

"I haven't," I said quickly. "I meant no offense. If you'd like to tell me about it . . ."

"There," Lanh Chau said, smug and satisfied. "Go on then; tell him. Tell him how we got it."

THIRTY-ONE

The King of Inacha

everal years ago," Mistress Chant said,[190] "only a few weeks after Lanh Chau had become my apprentice, we were traveling east from Map Sut, following one of the tributaries of the Ganmu River, and we came into Inacha. The king was having some trouble with the ambassadors from Genzhu—"

"He's *always* having trouble with the ambassadors from Genzhu," Lanh Chau spat. "Because Genzhuns are greedy cheats." He was Sut, so of course he'd think so, quite understandably. The Genzhun empire sprawls across the entire, vast Genmu River Valley and all its tributaries, except for those two tiny kingdoms: Map Sut at the root of the river delta, and Inacha off by the mountains to the east. Year after year, both of them just barely manage to fight off the Genzhun armies and diplomats, and every other generation or so, one of them falls and is absorbed for a time, until it manages to shake itself loose once more. Even for an empire, the amount of money it takes to conquer just one of them is unfathomable—they're both blessed with an *extremely* inconvenient (and therefore defensible) landscape, as well as allies at their backs who are very much invested in suppressing

---

190 Fuck you. Seriously, really, truly this time: fuck you.

Genzhun expansion campaigns. A particularly motivated monarch with a few years of good harvests and robust tax seasons can manage taking one, barely, but so far they've never been able to hold it long enough for their grandchildren to see.

"The nature of this particular trouble was related to a so-called peace treaty which the Genzhun diplomats had put forward, which appeared at first glance to be a welcome opportunity for Inachans everywhere to take up a new hobby besides sharpening spears and fletching arrows for the next summer's siege. But the king of Inacha had a feeling that something was wrong, and he had a feeling that his advisers might be keeping secrets from him," Mistress Chant said. "Now, I'm an old friend of His Majesty; I spent a summer as a court troubadour when I was new to Chanting and he was new to his kingship. We became very close. So when I turned up on the palace doorstep, I was given a warm reception, even considering I had Arenza and Lanh Chau tagging along on my apron strings."

Lanh Chau whispered loudly, "I saw 'em *kissing*." Arenza bit back a laugh and glanced at Mistress Chant, who was completely unaffected.[191]

"As I said," she continued in a voice like honey, "we became very close during my time in his court. He knew that he could trust me. He asked me to look at the peace treaties for him, and of course I agreed. It took me a week or two, and it would have taken longer if I hadn't had Lanh Chau along to help read the damn thing—I speak Genzhun, of course, but I never bothered learning to read it. There were two copies, quite usual in this sort of situation: the Genzhun copy and a translated Inachan copy. Now, the translation was

---

191 Not so unaffected if I had known what you were planning on doing. This was *mine*; this was part of my heart, and you just took it and killed it and pinned it down like a dead butterfly.

technically correct, but there were a few key differences between the treaty when read in translation versus in the original. The Inachan version stipulated that upon signing the treaty, the two kingdoms would exchange symbolic gifts of silver and copper to mark the new friendship between their countries. And in the Genzhun version—"

"It said that Inacha had to give Genzhu all of their mines!" Lanh Chau burst out. He slapped his hand against the side of the wagon.

"Hush," Arenza said sharply. "You stole the end from her."

"They're greedy fish, the lot of them!" Lanh Chau went on. "Like fish in a pond! You throw in some breadcrumbs, and the Genzhuns appear out of nowhere and *gobble gobble gobble* until it's all gone!"

Mistress Chant laid a quelling hand on his arm. "I showed His Majesty the discrepancy, and he had his advisers executed, and he had the Genzhun diplomats packed off home with a letter requesting that if the empire wanted to engage in a game of sneaky tricks, they could at least do His Majesty the honor of sending competent players."

Lanh Chau snorted. "And then he threw a big party for us, and he gave us this bowl, and we ate *so much food*—"

"Here we go," Arenza whispered to me. "Brace yourself."

"I memorized the menu," Lanh Chau declared. "First course: a salad in the Araşti style, greens with goat cheese and walnuts and figs, dressed with a pomegranate balsamic vinegar reduction. Pale white wine. Second course—"

Mistress Chant folded her hands in her lap and gazed off into the distance with an expression of exceeding patience.

"—a soup, chicken and cream and onions, flavored with makrut lime leaves and ginger. Also, a selection of sweet peppers and pickled mushrooms, preserved in olive oil. Third course—"

Arenza rolled her eyes and sighed.

Lanh Chau continued doggedly. "*Third course.* Fresh river trout poached in rice wine with ginseng. An assortment of baked turnips and parsnips from Sharingol. Roast pigeons stuffed with oranges. Fourth course!"

"You'll have to forgive him," Mistress Chant murmured to me. "He was living on the streets when I met him. Food is very exciting to him."

"Roast pork, tender enough to fall to pieces, with an oily chili-ginger sauce. Roast peppers and cherry tomatoes, lamb kebabs flavored with garlic and sumac, and those Araşti rice things rolled up in grape leaves—what are they called? Dolmas!"

"Nearly done," Mistress Chant said.

"Fifth course, a clear chicken broth flavored with lemongrass. Sixth course, fresh bread of seven types, with herbed butter, honey butter, plain butter, five infused olive oils (chili, cumin, basil, malisess, orange peel). Seventh course, tiny fowls the size of my fist, one for each of us, with an orange-ginger glaze, served in nests made of twigs of carrots and potato and beets. Eighth course, twenty different sorts of dumpling—some with meat, and some with just vegetables, some with a combination, some with juicy sauce inside; some baked, some steamed, some fried. Ninth course." And here he held up his hand and started ticking things off on his fingers. "Sweetbuns with custard filling. Sweetbuns with apple jelly filling. Honeycakes. Sticky sesame cakes with red bean filling. Baklava of two varieties, cashew and pistachio. Miniature dome cakes with almond whipped cream. Egg custard tarts. Fruit ices—peach, strawberry, and rambutan. And cool jasmine water to drink at the very end." He fell silent and looked at me expectantly.

"It sounds amazing," I said politely. What I wondered most was how deeply into debt the king of Inacha had thrown his kingdom in order to offer a spread of such exotic variety—rambutan in Inacha is ... not unthinkable, but not what you'd particularly regard as affordable, either. And makrut lime leaves—that's not a plant suited for the Inachan climate either. "It clearly made an impression on you. Does the king of Inacha have an Araşti cook?"

"An Araşti and a Sut," Mistress Chant said, nodding. "Behnou Atil of Şehir and Oung Te Jue. They don't get along," she added wryly. "Hence the, uh ... *assortment* of things. They're very passive-aggressive with each other."

"Have *you* ever seen that much food at once?" Lanh Chau demanded.

"I don't think so," I said. "But now I'd like to."

"I ate all of it."

"All right, if you're not going to be quiet as we agreed, then scat," Mistress Chant said, shooing him away. "I was hoping to talk to my brother-Chant about more than just food."

"*Why?*" Lanh Chau demanded, aghast.

"Away with you! Arenza, go with him."

"He mentioned something about specializing in songs," I murmured, as soon as they were out of earshot. "I've never heard of such a thing, but why would he pick that, of all things? Hasn't it occurred to him that he could do food instead?"

"I'm planning on mentioning it to him when he's older," Mistress Chant said. "Preferably after he's sunk his homeland beneath the waves, and after he's had a few years as a journeyman. The plan is to tell him right as I'm hugging him goodbye and he's about to go off on his own, so he won't be my problem anymore. We'd never hear the end of it if that thought occurred to him.[192] So don't you dare breathe a word. I'm waiting to see if he thinks of it himself."

---

192 Too right. He likes music very well, but food is something deeper and more visceral for him. I've never known someone to enjoy food with the ferocity that he does.

I nodded. "Sister-Chant," I said, with some difficulty. "Can I ask you something?"

"By all means," Mistress Chant said.

"Why did you take a second apprentice?"

She quirked an eyebrow at me. "He picked my pocket quite deftly, and then he came back a few minutes later, angry and demanding to know what I thought I was playing at, carrying foreign coins around to entrap young street rascals into their own downfall or some nonsense like that. Arenza and I had just come from Mangar-Khagra, and we were in Sou Yun Pin, a small town near the mouth of the Genmu delta. We were planning to go upriver, and I—"

"No, no, no," I said. "You already had an apprentice. Why would you take a *second* one?"

She frowned, puzzled. "Why shouldn't I have two apprentices?"

I resisted the urge to fidget. "You've got to admit it's unusual."

"Unusual," she said.

"My master only had one at a time, so I was just wondering why—I mean, it's so difficult and time consuming to have one, it must be even worse with—"[193]

"Do you have an apprentice, brother-Chant?"

"No."

"Have you ever had one?"

"No," I said. My mouth was dry.

"Did you plan on taking one soon?"

"No."

---

193 I'm going to nip this in the bud, because I know where you're going with this. You're going to say that I was *mean* to you, that I was scary and intimidating and hurt your feelings. I did nothing of the sort. *You* were getting snobbish and rude, asking me how I could manage two apprentices. Condescending. That's the word I'm looking for. That's what you were being.

"Ever?"

I looked away. "I can't," I said, even as I heard my master-Chant's voice ringing in my head: *It's part of the job, training the next one.*

"You can't," she said. "Interesting."

"Why are we talking about me? I just wanted to know why you'd—" I gestured in the direction where Lanh Chau had stalked off.

"Why I'd *what?*"

"Never mind. I was just asking a question. You don't have to be . . . like this."

"Like what? What am I being?"

"Nothing," I said. "Let's talk about something else. Maybe we could talk about the flowers. That's kind of what I came here about."

"The flowers," she said flatly. "The ones you're selling your soul for."

"Yes," I said. I fidgeted under the weight of her disapproval. *What does it matter to her, anyway? It's no business of hers. And, on the other hand, what if she's right? What if I'm doing something wrong?* "Do you mind? Talking about them?"

"I don't know what you expect me to tell you," she said slowly. "You seem to know all about them."

"There was an incident today," I said, wincing. "And something felt off about it. I just wanted to talk to you."

"Where was this incident?"

"In Sterre de Waeyer's offices."

"The incident was related to you conning hundreds of people out of their money?"

"That's not what we're doing," I said, flushing so hard my cheeks stung. "We don't control them; we can't convince them to buy if they don't want to."

"But you can present them with a beautiful platter of lies, and when they make decisions based on false information, that's not your fault?"

"Well—"

"Well nothing. Why did you come here?" she asked sharply.

"Today there was nearly a riot in front of the store, and I was the only one who went outside to chase them off. They ended up bidding with each other for the bulbs."

"And?"

"And I thought it was strange."

"Yes, it is strange that you'd pick flowers, of all things, to fan the city into a hysteria. Of all the luxury goods you could have offered them! Not rugs or perfume or clothing. At least clothing has a purpose: it keeps you warm or dry. Flowers do nothing but look pretty, and some of them smell pretty. These don't even do that."

"They eat bugs," I offered, feeling a little desperate.

"Oh, sure. Sure, yes. But to eat them, they first have to attract them. This city is going to be miserable in a year's time or so, if you keep going at the rate you're going."

"I'm just doing what I was told to do."

"And you think that means you have no responsibility? You have *knowledge*, Brother-Chant. You know what you're doing isn't quite right—I can see it in your face. You're miserable with your knowledge. And you're making a *choice* to do it anyway."

"What else am I supposed to do?" I said.[194]

"You were *supposed* to make wiser choices. You were supposed to think about the ways stories can be twisted and perverted. You were supposed to be *better*."

"Well, I'm not. I'm not better. I'm just me, just—" I swallowed

---

194 You didn't *say* it, you *snapped* it.

hard. I'd almost said *Ylfing*. "Just the same as I've always been. I'm not
wise, or special." I gave up being Hrefni when I sank my homeland
beneath the waves, but once you have a culture of *realistic assessment
of your own skills* in your bones, it's hard to break the habit: "I'm certainly not the best Chant in the world, but I'm not the worst either.
I'm still learning—you said so yourself. You said I had things to learn.
So what right do I have to make decisions about what's best for Sterre
and her customers? Why should I dare to think I know better?"

"Because you *do*. Because you hold something in your hands that
could be a weapon. Or a flower. Or a rope. Or a wall. You have something, and someone allegedly showed you how to use it, once."

Once. Yes. I knew how to use it—I knew how to bring a city or
a nation to its knees. I knew how to betray the people who loved me
best. I knew how to flee in the night with a country burning and dying
in my wake. I'd been taught *that* very well. My master-Chant was a
fine teacher in those regards.

The objectionable thing was choices. We did *terrible* things. We
made choices that weren't ours to make. And Mistress Chant was
right when she said that I was miserable with the choices I was making
now. Before, when I was younger and following dutifully in my master's footsteps, I could have claimed ignorance. I do claim ignorance
for all that. I couldn't have known what would happen—I was young.
Sixteen or seventeen. I thought everyone's intentions were as good
and well-meaning as mine. And I'd never seen what stories could do,
the way they could be like rust overtaking a metal tool, or like a trickle
of water cutting through rock, or an invasive plant devouring the
landscape before my eyes. My Chant made choices, ones that affected
the lives of *everyone* for hundreds of miles in every direction, and the
only person it benefited was him. And me, I suppose, but I wasn't the
one with my neck on the executioner's block.

I couldn't have known, then. But now . . . Now I do know better, but once again, what *right* do I have to make choices for someone else? What right have I to say to Sterre that she doesn't know her own business, or that what we're doing is somehow hurting someone? We can't know that for sure. We're not responsible for how they spend their own money. If they want to spend seventy guilders apiece on stars-in-the-marsh roots, why should we stop them? Even if it's a bad choice? Even if it means they go hungry for a few weeks? And how could we *possibly* know that it would? What does "ruin" even mean? Maybe it means something different to her than it does to me, and what right have I to tell her that her definition is wrong? Sterre is a smart person. She's cautious and thoughtful. She's blisteringly competent. She cares about people. She'd know, if things weren't going the way they were supposed to. And I don't think she'd ask me to do something if she knew it was going to hurt someone.

"You don't value your gifts at all, I think," Mistress Chant said in a low voice. "You said yourself you have no plans to take even one apprentice. This suggests to me that you don't think your knowledge is worth passing along. Am I right?"

"No," I said. "No. It's worth it, but I—I *can't.*"

"Why?"

"It's not time yet! I'll know when it's time! I can't just—" I bit off the rest of my sentence again: *I can't just stop doing this.* Because I can. And I might. I buried my face in my hands. "You don't have to attack me," I said when I'd gotten my voice under control.

"*Attack* you? Who's attacking you? I'm offering you a chance to argue your points and defend your beliefs. It's an opportunity, Chant."

The name made me flinch. Hard.

"Are you all right?" she said suspiciously, after a beat of silence.

"I'm fine."

She narrowed her eyes at me. "You twitch like a blueash smoker. Are you? You're doing yourself no favors with filthy habits like that, not as a man and not as a Chant."

"It's a good thing I'm not, then," I said.[195]

"You'll end up in some decadent Araşti incense parlor if you're not careful."

"I like Araşti incense parlors," I said, just to be contrary. I've never actually been to one,[196] but I've caught the heavy scents in the air sometimes when I'm walking in the foreign quarters of one city or another, or I've seen a narrow, dark little shop tucked in between two busier ones, colorful hangings draped across its windows and the characteristic orange-and-green tassel hanging from its doorknob.

"Then you won't mind it so much when you end up there," she said.

We bickered for a while longer, the conversation circling further and further down into resentment and anger, until we'd had enough of each other and I left.[197]

---

195 *Snapped.*

196 Ah-*hah!*

197 I . . . beg your fucking pardon? That's it? You've left out all the important parts! You've left out all the parts where you explain, where you tell the truth, where you speak aloud of all the things that made you who you are. And that's the problem, isn't it? You'll speak it, but you won't write it down, because of that thing you said before, about how words on a page are terribly real. Oh, sure, you'll linger over the trivial, soft, easy things like the singing bowl and the banquet in Inacha, but gods forbid you talk about anything real! That would be too hard, wouldn't it? You'd have to be vulnerable. Really, truly vulnerable, not just this miserable self-pity. Ugh! Wretch! Coward! Do it right for once in your life, Chant—here. Here, I know. I'll fucking do it for you, and then if I ever run into you again one day, I'll shove these papers in your face so you can see how it's done. Are you watching, Chant-in-the-future? Are you paying attention?

THIRTY-ONE ½

For the Benefit of Lazy Chants Who Were Abandoned by a Roadside Far Too Young

*A*nd now that I've actually begun, Brother-Chant, I must be honest with myself: You'll never read this. You've run away. My annotations thus far are all in vain—and this, too, is futile. Every "you" I write is a waste of ink.

And yet, here we are. Here I am.

So far in this miserable stack of pages, you've already committed several heresies and offenses, but possibly the worst of all is lacking the discipline to tell the story right. Lacking respect for your audience, even when you thought you were only telling this story to the wind.

So this is addressed to you, but I have no choice but to admit that it's for me. I'm the one who has to live with herself after this. I'm the one who will be lying awake at night and grinding her teeth about this gap you've left so cavalierly.

So let's just fix it, shall we? For the sake of me being able to get a good night's sleep, if nothing else.

———◆———

A very long time ago and half the world away, by which I mean a few months ago, right outside the inn where I'm sitting and writing this, two Chants sat down together and told stories.

The first Chant was older and wiser, and she had seen many marvels in the world, from the Mirrors of Zeva guarding the harbor of the Araşti capital, to the cliffs at the Straits of Kel-Badur and the Library of Anyaoh. All her stories were proper stories, tales of distant lands and wondrous things, memories and people and precious treasures.

The second Chant was young—too young to be a Chant, really, certainly too young to be a Chant all on his own—and he had pointlessly huge eyes like a starving baby seal that somehow made the first Chant simultaneously want to punch him and pour a bowl of soup down his stupid gullet until he stopped looking like he thought someone was going to . . . well, like he thought someone was going to punch him, really. All his stories were the lies he was telling himself in every breath and every heartbeat.

———◆———

All right, no, enough of that. Can't keep it up, not for this, though it would have been funny.

Ugh! This writing stories down thing is even stranger and more uncomfortable than I thought it would be. Unnatural, this is.

Let's try again, and let's jump right to the relevant part. I don't have time to ramble for pages and pages like you do, Brother-Chant, and the innkeeper only gave me a few spare sheets of paper when I asked.

The relevant part, then. Yes.

You kept—

No, I don't like that either. Doesn't feel right.

He kept twitching and flinching, one moment blushing scarlet with shame or anger, and the next staring at me with those big blue baby-seal eyes, helpless and hopeless, like I was holding his true love for ransom. Like I had some kind of answer to the greatest question of the universe and I was about to destroy it.

"Are you sure you're all right?" I said. I thought about pushing him, about telling him, *Of course you're not all right, I can see you're not all right; pull yourself together and tell me what the fuck is wrong.*

"I don't like fighting."

"We're not fighting; we're arguing." He twitched again, like I'd pinched him, and looked wretched. Well, more wretched. "What's the matter? Why do you keep doing that?"

I watched him struggle to find words, perhaps even to decide whether to speak at all. "It's nothing. I don't want to talk about it."

I threw up my hands. "What is the point of this? Why do we keep failing so miserably at having a conversation? I'm here, I'm talking, I'm trying to meet you somewhere in the middle, and you . . . There's something wrong with you. Something seriously wrong with you, and it isn't just the willingness to sell out to Sterre de Waeyer, or the lack of discipline, or the obvious inexperience and refusal to take responsibility. You claim to be a Chant, and you can barely talk to me. How can you be a Chant if you can't feel your way blind through a conversation? You ought to be able to do it as instinctively as breathing, or like one of the decorative automatons the Vintish king has in the palaces at Montcy and Ancoux." He cringed into himself with every word I spoke, and it only made me more and more irritated, until finally I snapped, "Didn't your so-called master teach you anything?"

Then, then he looked up at me with some fire in his eyes. Less starving baby seal, more starving young wolf caught in a hunter's trap. *Finally,* I thought. *Finally.* "He taught me enough," he said.

The boy didn't like to fight, he said, but he was angry about something and he was doing a damn good job of repressing it. But all you need is one spark to build a bonfire. I cupped that spark of his between my fingers and blew on it. "I doubt it," I said, letting all my contempt come through. "I've seen no evidence of that yet. He didn't teach you shit. But you knew that. You must have known that, if you decided to strike out on your own so early."

He drew himself up, then, his spine stiff and prim and proper. "I didn't strike out on my own," he said. He was pale now, but his eyes were flashing. "And I don't want to talk about him."

"Any Chant worth his salt would have seen that you weren't ready to go it alone yet." I was goading him, drawing him out. Plain as day, everything had something to do with that master of his. That was the one thing I'd found that got him properly mad.

He tossed his hair out of his eyes and gave an artfully careless shrug that did nothing at all to convince me. "He thought that I was. It's been a year and a half that I've been alone now."

Now . . . That gave me a bit of a turn. "How old are you, boy?" I demanded.

"Nineteen or twenty."

"He set you loose when you were eighteen?"

"Roughly. Yes," he said stiffly. "Nearly nineteen, I'd guess. Hard to keep track when you're traveling."

"By the gods of the summits, why so young?"

He shrugged.

"No," I said. "None of that. I mean it. Tell me why. What did he say?"

"Why would he have said anything?"

"Because sinking your homeland beneath the waves is a pretty big project. It's a time commitment. You were from Hrefnesholt, weren't you? Forget half the world away, that's three-quarters of the world away. When did the two of you decide to turn back that direction? When did you arrive? How long did you stay before you made the choice? And in all those days, weeks, months together, heading back, what were the reasons he gave you?"

"It wasn't like that," he said. "It was quicker than that."

Terribly suspicious. "Quicker in what way? Surely you talked about it."

"No, not really. He decided I was ready, and then we did the rites and that was all. Then we parted."

"But that's not right," I said. He responded with another infuriating shrug. "You have to go home, you have to think it over, and then you do the rites. No—tell me exactly what happened."

"We were walking along one day, and we came across an old abandoned farm. It looked like it was going to rain, so we slept in what was left of the barn. In the morning, Chant said he was tired, so I went out to scrounge for food, and he stayed in the barn by himself. I came back in the afternoon, and he asked if I was still carrying my homeland with me. I had a rock in my bag, you see. I'd brought it from Hrefnesholt when I first left with him, because I knew he'd ask me to give it up one day and I wanted to be ready. He told me once that wasn't how it worked, when he found out about the rock. He said then that we were going to go home, that he'd take me back and do the rites there. But in the barn, he asked if I had the rock. And I said yes, and he said, 'All right, let's go outside and get it over with.'" His voice wavered just a touch here. "So I followed him outside, and did the rites and sank my homeland like he told me to, and then it was over."

I was aghast. "And you were fine with that?"

"I did what he asked me," he said.

"But you should have had a choice. You should have been able to say, "'No, Chant, I'm not ready. Let's keep going a little longer.'" And, listen, I might object to everything about you, but you deserved better for your rites than a rock tossed into—what was it? A mucky millpond?"

He was quiet. He swallowed. "No," he said, trying valiantly to maintain that stiff, prim tone that sounded so wrong on him. "It wasn't a millpond. It was a trough."

"A what?"

"A trough. Like for horses." He paused, then added as if each word were being wrenched from him by some geas of truth, "Or pigs. More likely pigs, I think."

The sorts of things that come out of your mouth when you've been trained to keep asking questions even when you're shocked and horrified . . . "Why do you say that's more likely?" I asked, because that was the only thought that could fit in a sentence small enough to get out of my mouth.

"It was lower to the ground. Made of wood." He wasn't looking at me anymore. "Old wood. Mostly rotted away, actually. More of the idea of a trough that had once stood there. The legs on one end had fallen off, so it was lying crooked. On a slope, see. But it held the rain from the night before. Some of it. A few inches of it." His voice had dropped to a whisper, and I was too horrified to stop him talking. He gave a shaky laugh. "It was kind of green, actually. Algae. And there were mosquito larvae in it. Little tiny twitchy things. Chant told me what to do and say, and then I dropped my rock in the trough and that was it. I told you he didn't stand much on ceremony."

"I remember. You did say that, yes," I said blankly.

"I was—upset. I was upset, so I went to bed early, and when I woke up in the morning, he was gone. I thought he'd just gone for a walk. I waited all day, and then I slept again and he still wasn't there in the morning, and that's when I realized he wasn't coming back at all, and that I . . ." His voice cracked and he swallowed hard. "I was going to tip the trough over and get my rock back so I'd have that, at least, so I'd have something precious with me, but I—I thought it would be wrong. I threw it away. That was the point, right? You do the rites to prove you're willing to give up something, just like the ancient Chants did when they lost Arthwend to the sea. And I did. I gave it up, and I could have taken it back, but I didn't. I just left my homeland there in scummy, smelly water in a rotting pig trough, and I walked away. And that was a year and a half ago. And that's what happened."

"But why would he do that?" I asked, still too stunned to be angry. "Why would he leave you like that?"

"I don't really know," he said, with an obvious, regrettable, and failed attempt to sound airy. "We were fighting. He was tired of me. I didn't trust him anymore. I kept crying all the time."

"Why?"

"Well, it's a long story, but the short version is that a bit more than a year before he abandoned me, he incited a civil war, wrecked a country's economy, and then sold out said country to save his own neck. He got a lot of people killed or ruined in the process, and just as a final straw he faked his own death, sort of, but not dead-dead, just dead in the mind, and he didn't tell me any of it. He tricked me into carrying messages for him, and he went behind my back, and then at the end, he sat there in front of me pretending to have lost all his wits and his soul, and I wept in front of him, and I took care of him: I fed him soup and cleaned him and changed his clothes and told him how much I missed him. I grieved in front of him for days, and the whole time he never once even hinted that he was still alive in there, because—because he needed me to be lost. That's what he said. Because I'm not a good liar, he thought, and he didn't think I could keep a secret or act convincingly."

"What the fuck," I said. "What the fuck."

"I know it's stupid!" he cried. The tears that had been standing in his eyes spilled over. "I know it's stupid of me to care this much after it's been so long, and I know he did it wrong. I know it was my fault too, just as much! I should have—I should have—"

"What?" I snapped. "What should you have done? Should you have been better at loving someone who didn't love you back enough to keep you from unnecessary pain? Or been better at trusting someone who didn't trust you back enough to confide his plans? What could you have done to change what he did to you?" He buried his face in his hands, his shoulders shaking. I got to my feet and paced back and forth. "No fucking wonder you're all screwed up, what with that monster dragging you around on a string."

"He wasn't a monster. I loved him, I loved him like family—"

"Like more than family," I said. "Like more than anything. Yes, I know. And I loved my master too. I thought she hung the moons. You loved yours, and he betrayed you and let you down. He had obligations to you that he cast aside—obligations as a Chant, yes, but also obligations as a person who has taken responsibility for the care of someone else. What do you call someone who drowns a puppy just because they don't feel like looking after it anymore?"

"Evil," he whispered.

"There you have it."

In hindsight, I probably handled it badly. I should have said "It's not your fault" and "You're going to be okay" and "Do you want to talk about it?" and I should have offered him . . . something. Comfort or kindness. I should have told him that I thought he was strong for leaving the rock in the disgusting trough, even though if it had been me, I would have tipped it right over, scooped up the rock, dried it off, and found myself the prettiest waterfall to throw it into out of spite if nothing else. He was strong for walking away and leaving it there where he'd sunk it. That took a great deal of willpower and humility. I should have said so.

But I was angry. I was thinking of his master, not of him.

"You can't fix what happened," I said.

"I know! I know I can't!"

"And it's not going to get better until you pull yourself together and let go of him."

"He walked away! He left me there in a drafty ruin of a barn, sleeping in moldering hay, without even saying goodbye! I don't get the luxury of letting go of him, because he tore himself away from me before I could."

"Brother-Chant," I said sharply. "Use what you have. Rebuild yourself. Make up a story about how it should have been, set it in the forge of your heart, and believe it as hard as you can, believe until it burns white-hot, and then pour it over whatever happened before and quench it in oil, temper it so it never breaks again."

"'It doesn't matter if it happened that way in real life, as long as the story is good, as long as it's truer than truth.'" He stopped to wipe tears off his face. "That's what you mean, right?" His voice quavered. "My master used to say that."

"So maybe he did teach you one thing after all."

"I'll still remember what really happened. It'll still hurt."

"Yes, it takes longer than you've had for wounds like that to heal. But you can at least do this, keep yourself from getting any new wounds." I crossed my arms. "You already tell yourself so many stories. Make up a new one and give yourself a happy ending. The gods' mercy is given only rarely. Until that day, you make your own mercy. You save yourself."

"My master said a Chant shouldn't make up stories." I think he had mostly stopped crying by that point. His breath still came in little hitching, shallow gasps.

"Well, someone's got to, don't they?" I scowled at him. "You need to get yourself under control. You're like a caged animal, so frantic to be free that you'll batter yourself to death against the walls, gasping and crying out and never realizing that you're doing yourself more harm than anyone else has done to you yet." I glared down at him. He'd gone still, staring at the ground. "Well?" I said. "Have anything else to say?"

"No, ma'am," he said softly. He got to his feet slowly, hands clenched at his sides. "I'm sorry for wasting your time."

"Well, I've said everything I have to say too. I'm not here to coddle you, if that's what you were looking for."

"I know," he said, his voice cracking. "I never expected you to be very kind."

"I'm being kinder than you will ever possibly recognize, you pathetic little fool."

He turned away sharply and walked off.

"May Shuggwa's Eye fall favorably upon you, Brother-Chant!" I called after him, not bothering to conceal my mockery and disdain.[198]

———◆◆◆———

And that's what you should have written, brother-Chant. That was important.

---

198 Flicking back from farther along in this story to check this—oh gods, I even said it.

THIRTY-TWO

Enough. Enough. Enough.

I can't bear this anymore—I can't go on being Chant. I'm not Chant, and I'm barely *a* Chant anymore.

Enough. I can't go on.

Enough.

THIRTY-THREE

The world! The world is alive! The world is wonderful![199]
Something happened that I need to write about now,
because I'm *awake*. I'm awake, for the first time in three
years.

Gods, everything! How have I been living like this? How did
I go so long without caring about anything? The world is alive;
there are colors and smells again. I want to cry with joy, and laugh
through my crying, and fling open my arms to the whole world.
Here I am! Here I am; what have I missed? All this time I've been
sleepwalking.[200]

Last night, when I was writing all that about "enough, enough,
enough"—*was* that me who wrote it? I don't even recognize myself
there. Poor thing, he seems so sad.

It feels like someone else's hands wrote that, like I was only looking over his shoulder.

But I need to write about what happened. Yes! Now!

Last night, I threw down my pen and I cried on my cot for a long

---

199 Oh dear fucking gods, what did you get into?
200 That's a nice little way to dodge responsibility for all the shit you did when you
weren't paying attention. Nice excuse! Blame everything on your grief! You're not
responsible for anything, because you were busy being sad, right? Now bat your eyes
so everyone feels sorry for you and you'll be all set to go.

time.[201] I can't remember the last time I cried like that. I can't remember the last time I cried at all.

Last night, I came back from the talk with Mistress Chant and I cried, and it was awful, but a good kind of awful. Like I'd been holding a marsh in my heart, all stagnant and rotting, but the dikes broke and the king-tide came rushing in and swept everything away with seawater, leaving behind only salt and me, gasping for breath like a beached whale.

I felt raw and empty. I *felt*.

I was dazed. I remember, faintly, looking around this little room and wondering what I was doing here, what the point of it was. Not in a destructive, angry way, just . . . neutral, curious. And then I heard noises from down in the inn's yard, and I looked out through my window, and I saw a big party of people arriving—those Pezian merchants, with their fur-trimmed simarres, and their tall boots with the wide, floppy cuffs, and their loose breeches. They had their instruments slung on their backs, ready to make another racket in the common room, and they were so . . . bright.

That's the thing that caught me first. They were so bright. Brightly colored in their clothes, bright in emotion. They were so happy. They had always been so obviously a family, and a big one too—I only had to watch how they teased and jostled each other, or the familiar touches to each other's arms and shoulders, how comfortable and easy the men and women looked, grouped all together like that. And the even more obvious, too: There was a resemblance among them, though all I could see of it from my garret window was their build and stature and the color of their

---

201 "Now!" you say, and then promptly diverge from the story to tell us about your feelings again. That's real great, Chant. You'd better be doing *something* here. You'd better seize control of your story, whatever it is.

hair—dark and glossy among the younger ones, stately iron-gray for the elders.

It had been so long since I felt happy. It had been so long since I had *felt*, but I was feeling then, and I wondered whether I could have that, what they had.

So I left my room and I went downstairs, into the common room.

I've never written much about the inn. There's two stories, and the attic on top, but the common room is double-height. Much like Stroekshall, it's got a big central area on the ground level, and the upper part is ringed with a railed gallery. Unlike Stroekshall, there are tables everywhere, and food, and people aren't nearly so wild-eyed and harried, and the only people moving quickly are *Mevrouw* Basisi's staff.

I stood at the rail of the gallery and watched the Pezians. They got settled in, they bought food and drink, they scattered all throughout the room, and some of them found attractive companions—

And I've never written about *them*, either? What's wrong with me? Why haven't I been paying any attention? There's four companions-for-hire that come by the inn—that's what they like to be called. Their names are Avit, Orrin, Hildise, and Lijsbet, and I've met them when I was doing chores for *Mevrouw* Basisi. She introduced me once, when I first started here, and bade me be quick and respectful with anything they asked. She doesn't let most of her patrons keep tabs at the inn, but those four get to. There's some others who come by from time to time, but I don't know them very well. They all seem nice.

Maybe I'll write more about them later.

Chant used to say that I got distracted a lot,[202] and that I should learn to keep focused on one thing in a story.

---

202 On one hand, *fuck* that guy, but on the other hand, he was right. I've just been skimming the last page or two and trying not to nod off. Get to the point of things, Chant.

To be quite honest, I don't think I care about what Chant used to say anymore.[203] I'll tell the story however I like to. And why shouldn't I? No one's ever going to see this but me.

Right now, I *would* like to tell the story about the Pezians, though, and not the companions.

I watched them for a long time, and one of them looked up and saw me—and then I recognized him, I . . . Goodness, I've seen him a dozen times before, haven't I? I've *written* about him before. It was the one who sat in the cellar with me and watched me work.[204]

But I've never described *him* much either. Damn, I've been in the dark. Time was when I would have documented every line on a handsome boy's lips or his palms, every hair on his chest, every freckle on his nose.

I must make amends by doing it right: He looked up, and I saw him—a young man about my age, with bright brown eyes, kind and warm. Curly brown-black hair. Very fine dark eyes. A seafarer's tan deepening classical Pezian olive-toned skin. A wide, soft mouth. A sharp chin, clean-shaven this morning, now just shadowed with stubble. Clean, neat clothes in what I suppose are his family's colors, green and gold, not too fine, but not at all coarsely made.

He held my gaze for a moment or two, then blinked in surprise, I guess, noticing that I'd noticed him, and . . . gave me this sad, wry little smile and nodded politely.

And I decided, quite abruptly, that it was time to have even more feelings, ones that I hadn't had in ages. Enough of grief. Enough of letting Chant take anything else away from me, like he took my choices and my chance to honor my home properly before I gave it

---

203 Damn fucking right.
204 Oh, this should be good.

up, like he tore my name away from me before I was ready. Enough of him. Mistress Chant was right.[205]

I strode over to the stairs, and clattered down to the main level, and I walked right up to him, and he watched me the whole way, getting more and more . . . alarmed?

"Hello," I said. "What's your name? I should have asked before."

"Orfeo," he said in a vaguely strangled voice. "Orfeo Acampora. I introduced myself a couple weeks ago."

I have no memory of such a thing. Surely I would remember, wouldn't I?[206]

"Orfeo," I said. "Right. I'm having some trouble with names lately, sorry."

"It's all right," he said, eyes wide. "You seemed distracted at the time; I don't know that you even heard me." He was very, very still, like he wasn't sure which way to step.

"I'm not distracted now. Do you want a drink?"

"Yes? Yes. Yes, thank you. Very much, yes." He shook himself suddenly and seemed to come out of whatever moment of confusion had set upon him. With a surreptitious glance at his family, he half-led me to the bar with a hand between my shoulder blades and babbled something about wine to the aleman. I leaned on the bar and didn't take my eyes off him. "Sorry," he said, clearing his throat. "I'm not usually . . . like this."

"Like what?"

"Oh, you know," he said airily. His cheeks were pink. "Flustered."[207]

---

205 May wonders never cease!!!

206 Hah.

207 Oh no. Oh, fuck me, no. It's going to be like *that*, all squishy and romantic and disgusting. I don't want this anymore. I've already suffered through enough of your other feelings, haven't I? What did I do to deserve this?

I glanced back over at his family. I suppose there must have been something in my expression I didn't intend.

"Oh, no, nothing like that," he said quickly. "No. Not at all. They ... They'd make fun of me, that's all—actually they've *been* making fun of me already, and I just—oh look, wine," he ended desperately, pouring a great deal of wine into a glass and downing it in one go. I continued watching him, ever more curious.

"Are you all right?"

"Fine," he gasped. "This is kind of new for me, that's all."

"What is? Drinking? It's very simple, I promise."

"So funny, ha," he said, and poured himself another glass, then noticed abruptly that mine hadn't been filled even once yet, and did so with an apologetic wince.

"Drinking with another man, then?" I said, sipping the wine. It was a very good vintage—not Vintish, but good. Avaren, possibly, or Borgalish.

"Nope. I, uh, have plenty of experience with that too."

"What's new, then? Being flustered?"

"*Yes.*"[208]

"There's no reason to be."

"It's just—can I ask you something?"

"Usually when someone offers to buy you a drink, it means that it's generally acceptable to ask him about himself, yes." I added innocently, "That was a good educational point about drinking that you might not know, given your inexperience."

He huffed at me, but I could see he was holding back a smile. "Why did you—wait. First of all, just so we're clear, I'm paying for this wine."

---

208 I'm so embarrassed for the both of you. I don't even want to make eye contact with the *page*, let alone another human.

"No, I've got it. I asked you, after all."

"Yes, but I've *been* asking you."

I blinked. "When?"

The grin slid off his face, replaced by a look of amazement and shock. "I've tried *three times*! Three separate occasions! When you were working behind the bar, and when you were sitting down here by yourself late that night, and when I was helping you and the inn-keeper with the things in the cellar!"[209]

I frowned at him. "Really? You asked right out?"

"Well, no," he said, exasperated but still faintly smiling around the edges. "If I had, it only would have taken one time of you turning your back on me and sweeping out of the room, and then I would have given up."

"I don't sweep out of rooms."[210]

"Okay," he said, topping up our wineglasses. "Anyway, no, I was . . . well, I was hinting. Flirting, or trying to. I'm—" He cut himself off sharply and took another large gulp of wine.

"You're . . . ?"

"Nothing, never mind." He gave me a tight smile and set his glass down. "I was about to say something, but it wouldn't have been right."

"Say it. You were trying to flirt, and . . . ?"

He took a breath. "I was about to say that I was hinting, but not hinting very hard. It's . . . complicated. I'm trying to be a better person lately; that's the short version of a very long story." He gave me another half-wry, apologetic look from under his curls, and I felt a little butterfly-flutter in my heart. It's nice to find out you were right about people—I'd recognized he was a flirt, and that he was

---

209 That sounds right. Told you.
210 Yes, you do.

working on some kind of personal quest relating to how he spoke to people—in the way he went back and forth on flirting with *Mevrouw Basisi*, in the way he'd so obviously held himself back when we were talking in the cellar. Even numb and empty and taking hardly any notice of the world around me, I'd seen that. Chant instincts, I guess—if it had been anything else, I'm sure I would have noticed other things too, like how pretty he was, and how much he knew it, and how he smiled to say that he thought I knew it too.

"You could tell me, if you wanted."

He forced a polite laugh. "It's not that interesting, I promise. And—look, you haven't even told me your name."

"Oh." And then it was my turn to occupy myself with my wine, trying to find a few seconds to scramble a flush of terror into something orderly. I swallowed, bit my lip.

He was looking at me curiously, probably as curiously as I'd been looking at him.

"It's complicated," I said at last. "You're trying to be a *better* person, and I'm trying to be a *person at all* again. That's the short version."

He paused, and his brow furrowed. "Do you want to talk about it?" he asked, very carefully, as if he were reading a poem off a page.[211]

"Maybe another time," I said, and his expression relaxed and brightened, and I felt the flutter in my chest again, and then I recognized it. I *remembered*.

Chant used to grumble about how I fell in love three times a week if I were given the opportunity. I never thought anything of it then. I always ran at the world with my arms and my heart wide open. I remember meeting people and marveling about how wonderful they were, how kind, how interesting. I was always ready to love them.

---

211 Ah, see, he's better at this than I am.

And there were boys, and some of them thought I was a little wonderful too, and that was usually enough to get me to trip over my own feet for them. I haven't been in love with anyone for years. I don't think anybody *else* would call this feeling love—they'd call it a crush, or infatuation. They'd make it small and harmless and unthreatening, because *love* is big and scary and takes up space and *hurts*.

But it's all love to me. Or it was, in the old days.

And looking at Orfeo then, with him so deliberately and carefully trying to be a better person, I thought, *Why? Why did I kill this part of me?*

Who am I, if parts of me are dead? What's my name, indeed?

I think . . . I think you can choose, to some extent, who you are. You can take all the molding and grooming that everybody else has forced on you and you can cast it off, and choose to be . . . real. You can choose. I didn't know that until now. I didn't have to be Chant. I was thinking the whole time that I could *stop Chanting* if I wanted to, but ceasing to *be Chant* is another matter entirely. And I mean that both ways: I don't have to *be named Chant*, and I don't have to *be my former master-Chant*.[212]

So that's why I did it: I looked at Orfeo, and I whispered my secret: "My name's Ylfing."[213]

My voice was steady.

His smile widened. "Ylfing," he said—my name. My *name*. My name, passing another person's lips for the first time in nearly two years.

---

212 I'm failing to see the difference between this and "I could stop Chanting," but clearly you see a difference. I have a headache. I'm tired of trying to puzzle out what you mean. Be a Chant or don't—just make up your mind and get back to the disaster with the flowers, would you?

213 Oh no, not again. You were doing so well. What's it matter that you were strong enough to leave your rock in the trough if you're still carrying this one with you secretly?

The world came alive.

"Some people call me something else," I said. I felt wild. Adrift.

"Mmm," he said, his voice almost a purr. "I like your name, if you do."

"I do." My grip had tightened on the glass, and I felt like something was about to fall on me. My breath was short in my chest, and I longed for nothing more than for him to say my name again. Again and again and again. "I said I was having trouble with names lately," I whispered.

"And it's complicated," he said.

"Very." I drained the rest of my wine. "Let's talk about something else."

"Yes, certainly," he said immediately. "So . . . what do you do?"

A bubble of harsh laughter burst out of me before I could swallow it. "Sorry. Sorry, I wasn't—it wasn't you, it was—oh, *shipwreck*," I said, and refilled my glass, drained it again. "Orfeo," I said.

"Ylfing," he said, and my heart thumped once, hard, in my chest.

"Is it all right if we—stop?" I set my glass down heavily. "Stop pretending, I mean. I'm not okay, and you don't seem to be very okay either."

"Me? I'm fine," he said quickly.

I looked straight at him. "You're not," I said. The wine was . . . oddly, it was making everything clear, clearer than I'd managed in years. I felt more Chantly in that moment than I ever had, and my eyes felt sharp—I looked Orfeo over, just as I'd been trained. I looked at him and *saw* him. I'd already pinned him as a flirt, but now I studied him, looked right into his soul, picking out things about him and piecing together *specifics* that had trickled out throughout the conversation: the way he was more comfortable buying the wine than having the wine bought for him; how he *knew* for a fact he'd make a subtle

pass at someone three times but forthrightly only once; how he wasn't
accustomed to being flustered; his merchant family that took him on
travels far from home and how he might not be in one place for longer
than a couple months at a time . . . *Flirt*, I concluded, might have been
too mild of a word.

"Orfeo Acampora," I said, "you're a bit of a rake, aren't you?"[214]
And then, as he was opening his mouth with a desperate look on his
face, I held up one finger. He said nothing. "No, that's not quite right.
You've *been* a rake until recently. And, like you said, you're trying to
be a better person now."

"Have you been talking to my family?" he demanded.

"No. Tell me the long, complicated story."

He laughed shakily. "You mean you can't read that out of my
eyes too?"

"I can't read anything out of your eyes," I said, which I suppose
wasn't quite true. He has very expressive eyes. "I like stories. Tell me."

Orfeo caught the aleman's eye and gestured for another bottle of
wine. "Can we walk? Would you mind? I need some fresh air."

"Sure, if you like."

He let out his breath all in a rush and laughed again, steadier
now, and shook his head. "I really am trying not to be like *that* anymore. I didn't know it was so obvious."

I shrugged. "I have training. I'm good at reading people."

"Terrifyingly, amazingly so, apparently." We collected the bottles
of wine and went out from the warmth into the cool night air, and
he put his arm around my waist as we walked down to the canal. We
found a seat on some stone steps leading down to the water in the

---

214 Mm, yeah, that holds water. Only a rake would try so hard, for so long, to get a
pretty boy to drink with him.

shadow of a bridge and huddled together in the dark. It's midsummer, but the wind off the sea keeps the city cool, and in the night it's just chilly enough for lovers.

"So what happened?"

"The long version?" he asked. His voice was ... different, here in the dark. Raw, more vulnerable.

"Do you have anywhere else to be?" We'd left the glasses inside, so we were drinking straight from the bottles, passing them back and forth. "I don't."

He let out a long breath. "I'll give you the medium version. What it comes down to is that I thought as long as I was honest about what I wanted, I wasn't going to hurt anyone. Except, as it turns out, it's not that ... tidy."

"Feelings," I said.

"Feelings," he agreed. "Dammit, I don't want to regale you with all the selfish little things I did to people; I didn't want a conversation with you to be like *this*." I drank, and listened. We couldn't even see each other, cast in darkness like we were here. "I ... was making a habit of being honest about what I wanted while intentionally ignoring the idea that maybe other people's wants might change or grow. And my family ... noticed. They'd been noticing for a long time, but they always joked about it: *Oh, Orfeo, should we even ask the innkeeper for a room for you, or are you going to find a bed yourself tonight?* That kind of thing." Then, suddenly, "Do you have siblings?"

"No," I whispered. "I have no family anymore."

"That thing you did in the bar, where you looked at me and saw right through me. Siblings can do that, and cousins if you're close to them. They see everything about you, all unadorned. A few months back, we were on a voyage. Everyone was bored. We were just bickering among ourselves, keeping ourselves entertained, and my sister

Giada looked over at me and said, *Ah, but Orfeo doesn't care about anyone but himself. He'd flee for the door if his bedmate invited him to stay for breakfast in the morning, and he wouldn't even wait long enough to put on his drawers. He's cold like that."* I handed him the bottle of wine, and he paused to drink. "That shook me up. I don't think I'm cold. But I'd never seen myself that clearly before, until I was forced to."

"Would you run away without your drawers if someone invited you to stay for breakfast?" I asked mildly.

He took a breath. "Yes. Because I've done almost exactly that. And I didn't even *think* about it until Giada said that, and then I couldn't stop thinking about it. About how cold it really is to do that. About how many little hurts I've probably caused, you know? A thousand times I probably made someone feel just a little bit bad, or made their day a little worse, or spoiled the afterglow with a clumsy comment. And the whole time I was priding myself on my gentlemanly comportment as a lover. So now I'm . . . trying to be better."

"How?"

Another pause while we both drank. When he spoke again, I could almost hear him mentally tearing at himself. "Well, sometimes now I ask people if they want to talk about things that are bothering them. And then I try not to fidget and squirm when they're *naturally and understandably* emotional about things that are going on in a part of their life that doesn't have anything to do with me. I'm trying not to panic when people want a little bit of extra care from me. I'm trying to be less afraid of giving a shit about them. That sort of thing." There was a long silence between us. "What about you? You said you were trying to be a person again."

"Yeah," I said. We'd had enough wine by that point that it had dulled the ache.

"Do you want to talk about it?" he said, so deliberately again that I couldn't help but laugh, and that set him off too.[215]

"What, are you hoping I'll help you practice?" I said, bumping his elbow with mine.[216]

"Even rakes know it's uncouth to only talk about yourself," he said loftily, and I laughed again. "Go on, though. I told you all about my thing. It's only fair. I shouldn't be the only one admitting my flaws to a stranger."

So I told him. I told him about Chants; I told him about growing up in Hrefnesholt, and meeting my master. I told him about leaving, barely more than a child myself, to follow my master-Chant across the world on my apprenticeship. I told him about what happened, the real story, because I didn't have time to come up with a different one. I told him about the year and a half of walking next to Chant with the knowledge that I didn't know him at all and that he would hurt me if it furthered his interests, and then about leaving Chant at last to be a Chant myself, and about another year and a half of wandering alone, lost in a swamp, even when I was here in the middle of a city.[217]

And the whole time, he sat quietly, and nodded, and listened. He even laughed at the funny parts, because there *were* funny parts.[218] But he listened. And he didn't expect anything. He just . . . listened.

And I realized that I was telling a story. I was telling him a story, and it didn't hurt at all. It was just . . . me, prying my heart open with a crowbar and opening it to him, handing him my treasures, my

---

215 Mm, yeah, that's a rake move. I'm glad that all three of us can be honest about that. I really wasn't expecting him to admit it.
216 He absolutely is.
217 Long-winded, aren't you? And he just . . . sat there? For the whole thing? Smooth, Orfeo. Very smooth. A gentlemanly rake is an irresistible thing.
218 This is a thing that people do when they are trying to seduce you.

memories, my *self* and saying *Is this enough? Is this someone I could be again?*

And when I finished, he said, "I'm so sorry that happened to you. It sounds like you've been hurting for a long time."[219] I nodded, drained. But not *empty*. Not *raw*, like I'd been before. I felt . . . clean. Like just saying all of it aloud had made a difference, had let me purge something that was making me sick. Like it had brought the summer's king-tide rushing across the stinking swamp, and then it had pumped it all back out again. "You've been through hell, haven't you? It sounds lonely."

"It was," I said.

He shifted a little, scooting closer, so that we were touching from shoulder to knee. "I'm glad I could come sit with you." He handed me the bottle. "Sounds like you need another drink."

I knew what I wanted, but I had to pull together my courage to ask for it. "Actually, I—if you don't mind, what I really need right now is a hug."[220] His arm came around my shoulders and pulled me over, close to his warmth, and I let my head drop onto his shoulder. "Are you going to run away without your drawers if I start crying?" I mumbled.

He snorted. "Not right now. I'm pretty drunk. It'd be hard to scare me off right now."

I squeezed my eyes shut and buried my face in his neck. He smelled of sea salt and black tea and, faintly, of roses, like he'd dabbed a little perfume on his neck that morning and it had all but worn away. He gathered me in close and rested his cheek on my hair and held me tight.

I don't have the words. People aren't meant to live as I've been living, all alone and untouched and adrift—even Chants shouldn't

---

219 Hmph. Politic. Smooth.
220 I just snapped my pen in half. You pathetic wretch, can you stop being quite so *damp*?

live like that. I felt like I was crumbling to pieces and being rebuilt all at once.

It was . . . warm. Just warm.

I did end up crying after all, and he noticed before I did. He held me tighter, kissed my hair, said, "You're all right now, Ylfing. It's okay."[221]

And when I pulled away eventually, he let me go, and stroked my cheek, my shoulder, down my arm, and took my hand. "A little better?" He tucked something into my other hand—a bit of cloth, a handkerchief. My fingertips caught on the rough lines of embroidery on one corner of it, and I dried my eyes.

"A little," I said. "You're not as bad at that as you think you are, you know."

"Drunk," he said cheerfully. "Nothing frightens me when I'm drunk."

"You don't need to be frightened when you're sober, either," I said. "I'm a Chant. Running off in the dead of night is part of the job description. I'm not going to have any expectations of you." Never mind that I'm already half in love with him—that's not really any of his concern unless he wants it to be. I took another drink, finishing off one of the bottles of wine. After a moment, I threw it as hard as I could into the canal. It splashed with a hollow sound, and we watched the ripples, just visible in starlight and distant lamplight, until they died out. "I don't know what I want anymore, or where I want to go, or what I want to be. It feels like everything was taken from me. I barely know who I am now. Ylfing isn't even my name anymore, not really. I was supposed to give it up. I'm only supposed to be Chant now."

"Why?" he asked.

---

221 Yeah, he's way better at this than I am. Godspeed to him, to be honest. Better him than me.

"Because," I said, struggling to come up with an answer. "Because that's the way it is, that's the way it has to be. That's the sacrifice I made."

"What did you get in return?"

My heart stumbled in its beating. "What?"

"When you sacrifice something, you're giving something up in order to get something else. What did you get?"

I was . . . speechless. I opened and closed my mouth. "I'm a Chant now," I said. I could hear how weak I sounded.

"Why did you have to give up your name for that?"

I rallied at last, at last. "Because Chants have to. My job is to go from place to place, and learn all I can, and listen to people's stories and tell them to others so that the really important things in the world get remembered. That way they never die—people aren't ever really dead as long as their stories are told."[222]

"And what's that have to do with your name?"

"Because I can't be a person when I'm doing my duties. I don't get to have an identity, because I might get in the way of the stories, or muddle them up."

Orfeo squeezed my hand. "Why's that bad?"[223]

"Because they're *important*. They should stay untainted, the way I found them. My master used to rebuke me—I'd make up new stories about gods or heroes that I learned about, and he taught me that that wasn't right of me. So I stopped."[224]

---

222 Meh. I mean, you're not wrong, but you're not really right either. It's more complex than that. But, *sigh*, I already know you care nothing for the rites and holy mandates, so there's no point wasting the ink over theological quibbles.

223 Why's it any of his business? What call does he have to question you?

224 There's a difference, though. There's a lot of nuance missing from a prescriptive rule like that. You can make up stories all you want, but you probably shouldn't make up stories with other folks' heroes. It wouldn't be right for you to make up a new Oyemo story, for example. That's probably what your master meant; you just

"Ylfing," he said, very gently. "That's bullshit."

I shook my head. "No, it's not; it's the way it is."

"Yes, it is. You say you can't be a person because the stories shouldn't be influenced by your personness. Except they're *made* by people. A story doesn't happen without people's influence."[225] He looked at me for a long time, as if he was waiting for me to respond. I had nothing to say. "What if you've got it all backwards? What if you can't understand the stories as they deserve unless you *are* a person, unless you're personing as hard as you can?"[226]

A shudder went over me. The tugging in my chest.

I closed my eyes. "I'm glad you came out here with me," I said.

"So am I," he said, without a hint of polite deception. I could hear his smile in his voice.

I'd told him my name, and the world hadn't ended. It felt good. Orfeo had spoken my name, and I already felt closer to him than anyone else for the last three years. "When I was younger, I definitely would have noticed you trying to buy me drinks," I said.

"Oh yes?" He was pleased, and he wasn't trying to hide it.

"Yeah. I would have tripped over myself. I would have talked to you for hours and then gushed to everyone I knew about all your virtues and accomplishments."

He squeezed my hand, rubbed my knuckles gently with his

---

misunderstood. You can make up brand-new stories all you want. That's how you get room and board at royal courts, you know; you make up a flattering story or a song about the actual monarch and some heroic deed they recently did.

225 Hm, his argument is sound but this conclusion is all wrong. They're made by people, but that doesn't mean Chants have the right to mess about with them. Just like I said above, you're not the right person to make a new Oyemo story. It's meddlesome, and Oyemo doesn't belong to you. Some things never belong to us, even if we're carrying them around.

226 You don't *have* to understand a story because, again, not all stories belong to you. A messenger doesn't need to read a letter to carry it to its recipient.

thumb. "I wouldn't dream of stopping you, if flirting was something you felt like doing," he said innocently, and I couldn't stifle the bubble of laughter that rose in my throat.[227]

"I'm sorry. I don't think I know how anymore. I forgot that too." Regretfully, I made to draw my hand out of his, but he caught my fingers again at the last moment.

"Would it help if I started?"[228]

I swallowed. My mouth was dry. "Maybe . . . ? I suppose it depends on if you're any good at it. Are you?"

"I've been told I can be terribly enticing when I set my mind to it," he said.[229]

"I wouldn't want to get in the way of your efforts to improve yourself."

As if in answer, he slowly raised my hand to his lips, giving me more than enough time to pull away if I wanted, and when I did not, he kissed the backs of my fingers. He was looking at me—I could feel the weight of his eyes, even though it was too dark to see his face.[230] My heart stuttered in my chest. "How did you like your flirting, before? Jokes and teasing? Poetry? Somewhere in the middle?"[231]

"Mostly I just threw myself at boys that I thought might catch me. And I told them a lot of things about themselves that I thought were wonderful."

"I think *you're* wonderful," he said without missing a beat.[232] Young Ylfing would have swooned right off the steps and into the

---

227 At least he's not the *feral* sort of rake.
228 Rake.
229 *Rake.*
230 *RAKE.*
231 I'll give him points for elegance of execution, at least. And points for asking, too. He *does* keep asking, which is to his credit.
232 He's *very* good. Quick on his toes, and a solid facsimile of sincerity.

canal. I made some small noise, and he grinned against my fingers and kissed them again.

"You think so?"

"I do," he said. "I think you're brave for traveling all on your own. I can't imagine that. I've been beset by relations my entire life, and I wouldn't know what to do with myself if anything happened to them. I think you must be very strong, and very determined, and very disciplined.[233] And honest."

"You're guessing," I whispered.[234]

"I'm drawing logical conclusions," he said, turning my hand over and kissing my palm. "Just like you did when you looked straight through me and asked if I was a rake. Are you not honest?"

"My master always told me I was bad at lying. I guess that means I must be honest, then, yes." I looked out over the water. "I don't feel like I'm those other things though. I don't feel strong or brave. I just feel tired. And I feel tired of being tired."

"Tired of what, specifically?"

"Giving bits of myself away without getting anything back."

"Oh. That does sound hard. Like trying to get water by scraping mud out of the bottom of a well."

"Yes," I said, turning back to him.

"Mmm. But it seemed easy for you to tell me everything about yourself. Unless I'm wrong and I missed something. You didn't have to do that. I don't want you to do anything you hate."

"It was easier than the alternative."

"What would the alternative have been?"

"I would have said, *Call me Chant*." He hummed and took a sip of

---

233 Meh.

234 Yep. Cold-reading, it's called. You could say "strong, determined, disciplined, honest" to anyone and they'd think you were right.

wine from the other bottle and offered it to me. I took it and sipped too, wishing in a silly romantic part of me that was stirring to wakefulness that we were sharing a glass instead, so that I could drink from the opposite rim. That's a romantic superstition in Araşt; they call it "a kiss over a river," a charm to reunite lovers separated by circumstance or bad fortune.

"*Call me Chant*," Orfeo said. "You didn't say *Call me Ylfing*, though. You said *My name is Ylfing*. When you tell people to call you Chant, that's harder? Because it's not really you?"

I nodded immediately. "You're the first person to say my name aloud in nearly two years," I said, and he squeezed my hand.

"Ylfing," he said. "Ylfing, Ylfing, Ylfing. Ylfing." He was so firm and serious that I couldn't help but laugh, and when I started, he did too, and he caught both my hands in his and kissed my name into my fingers, my palms, the insides of my wrists until I lost my laughter in the joyful ache of my heart: "Ylfing. Ylfing. Ylfing."

I curled my fingers tenderly along his jaw and the edges of his hair; I cupped his cheeks in my hands and pulled him forward, and I kissed him, and he met me with that sunshine-smile and kissed my name into my mouth too.

It wasn't a very long kiss, but it was sincere and sweet as spring flowers, and then he kissed my cheeks and my forehead, whispering my name each time.

I was so desperately happy that when I opened my eyes, I was a little surprised to find that I wasn't giving off light. "Orfeo," I whispered back.

He touched my hair. "Now I have to practice being a good person," he whispered. "I have to tell you things."

"All right," I said, giddy and drunk and *kissed*. "Tell me some things."

"You pointed out yourself that neither of us are going to be in this city very long."

"I said not permanently, but yes."

"I think you're lovely." Sweet Orfeo. He hasn't entirely cast off his rakish ways yet, and he still knows how to flatter a person. "I'd like to spend a little time with you, but then I'm going to leave, or you will."

"That's all right," I said. I have a lot of experience in leaving people.

"I just don't want to break your heart when I go," he said. "That sounds presumptive of me, but I really don't want that."

"Why not?"

"What?"

I had to bite back a lot of responses that probably would have sent him running, like how the idea of feeling anything at all was desperately appealing, even if it was painful. Like how part of me wanted something to wrench my heart back into place, like resetting a dislocated shoulder. Like how I could love him for myself and he wouldn't need to trouble himself with it at all. "Let me worry about my heart," I said. "And you mind yours."

We sat in silence, finishing the wine and leaning against each other in the dark, not saying much. In the silence, we could faintly hear music coming from the inn—his family, a Pezian song. It was slow, a wistful joy, and Orfeo hummed along and sang the chorus in a whisper against the edge of my ear. My Pezian is really quite poor, and I only made out a few words—*my lady* and *hair* and *face* and *eyes* and *love*. "Do you want to go back in? There will be dancing soon."

"No," I said. I hoped he could hear the regret and hesitation. "I'm just getting a handle on being a living person again," I added, trying to joke. "I think dancing is too much to ask of myself today."

He kissed my hair, and then tipped my face up and kissed my

mouth too. "Ylfing," he said, as if for good measure, and I laughed a little and leaned my head on his shoulder. "I hope I can hear you tell another story before I leave."

"What sort of story would you like?" I said, returning my face to the warm crook of his neck.

"One that doesn't hurt you. One about you, maybe. About Ylfing, not about Chant."

I sat up suddenly. "Oh," I said. "Oh, *yes*." And then: "*Listen.*"[235]

---

235 Oh no.

THIRTY-FOUR

How Ylf and Tofa Slew the Great White Bear[236]

A very long time ago and half the world away, there lived a hero called Ylf.[237] He was the biggest and strongest of anyone in his village, with the bushiest beard and the sharpest axe, and his wife, Tofa, was the cleverest and most beautiful of anyone in the village. Ylf had been the great-jarl of all Hrefnesholt twice, but he had retired from governance to have adventures. This is the story of how he traveled to the ice fields and slew the Great White Bear.

Ylf's problem had always been traveling over water. His luck was spell-twisted somehow, but only in regards to boats. Even as a child, the little coracles he paddled about in the calm, sheltered inlets of the fjords would wear out, or spring leaks, and more often than not, Ylf found himself having to swim back to shore.

Fortunately, he was an excellent swimmer, one of the best in his village. But the boat problem made things difficult. He had only been

---

236 Not again! No! Another one?

237 Shit. Your namesake, I suppose? A story from your own childhood, one you knew before you ever heard a rumor of a Chant in the village. I . . . begrudgingly relent, then. If any story is yours to do with as you will, I suppose it would be this one. You own this one in a way that's more real than the others. If you want to write it down, if you think it's not as hideous as shoving pins into dead butterflies, then fine. Write it down. It's yours.

able to become great-jarl when the Jarlsmoot was hosted in his own village, and he counted himself lucky that Tofa was clever enough to win the title of chief skald and therefore bring the Jarlsmoot to him when it next came about.

But the boat problem frustrated Ylf, so one day he went up the mountain to the witch who lived in the woods. The witch lived all alone in a house with a triangular yellow door, and she kept all manner of animals around as pets and messengers and spies. When Ylf went to knock on the door, it swung open before his knuckles could touch it, and he saw the witch sitting by the fireplace with two cups of raspberry-leaf tea already waiting. "Good day, Ylf," she said. "Sit down." So he did. "What's troubling you?"

"My luck with boats is spell-twisted," he said. "It must be. I cannot even go fishing without getting my boots wet. I've endured it for far too long, and I was hoping you could help me or give me some advice."

The witch stroked her chin and looked into the fire. "The easiest path would be to avoid boats," she said with a firm nod.

"I'm not looking for an easy path."

"Hm," she said. "Well, if you're sure. I can work a spell to untwist your luck, but it's complex and time-consuming, and requires components which are difficult to find."

Ylf left her house with a quest—to travel to the northern ice fields and slay a white snow bear and to bring back its heart, kidneys, and pelt. The witch advised him to call up the sea-women from the deeps and attempt to negotiate a deal, to carry his boat to the ice fields and back and ensure that it would not sink on the way.

Ylf called the sea-women as he had been instructed, for he had no other way of reaching the ice fields, and besides that, he knew that it was never wise to disregard the advice of a witch. The sea-women live in the dark cold depths of the ocean, but occasionally they venture into the fjords—they are just like seals, but with the heads and torsos of women. They have the tails of seals, the big round luminous eyes of seals, the teeth of seals, the mottled gray-charcoal-brown skin of seals, the sleekness to let them dart through the icy water, and thick blubber to keep them warm.

After extensive negotiations, they agreed to carry Ylf's boat, but they charged him an extortionate sum: a hundred perfect pearls, and the promise that he would give them the teeth of the white bear should his quest be successful.

Then Ylf went to Tofa and told her everything the witch had said, and the price that the sea-women had asked for, and Tofa nodded. She was not at all worried, for she knew her husband was the strongest and bravest in all the land, but also she knew that he was prudent and was only too aware that even his great strength had limits. "Would you like me to come with you?" she asked.

"Very much, yes," Ylf said. "Otherwise I may run into some tedious matter involving riddles or sorcerers, and you know I'm no good at those."

"Mm," Tofa said, nodding. "I know it. You'd rather just hit your problems until they stop. You really are better off bringing me with you."

"Just so," said Ylf. "I agree." And so they paid for their passage with a hundred perfect pearls and climbed into Ylf's boat, and the sea-women carried the boat on their shoulders, so even when Ylf's bad luck struck again and again, the craft did not sink. Tofa was clever and patient, and together she and Ylf patched up every leak the hull spontaneously sprung, every tear in the sail, every snapped line, while the sea-women occasionally peeked over the gunwale and made unhelpful comments like "Did you know your boat is leaking?" and "Did you know your sail tore?" and "We think your rudder might have cracked."

On the third day, the sea became strange, and the sea-women

peeked over the gunwale to say so, and Ylf and Tofa said, "Thank you, yes, thanks, we noticed, yes." Tofa lay down in the prow of the boat and reached down to trail her hand in the water, and she rubbed the water between her fingers and frowned.

"What is it?" said Ylf.

"Foul magics, I think," said Tofa. "I've never seen magics like this before." But Tofa, being clever, knew some runes of power.

(*Here I paused briefly to explain the Hrefni rune magic to Orfeo: that nearly anyone could learn the runes, but that they were wickedly complex and required a great deal of precision and a very steady hand, of which Tofa had both.*)

Tofa spent all afternoon scratching a single rune on the inside wall of the boat, and she saw that it was perfect. She pressed her hand against it, but only a curling flicker of power ran through it. "Another problem, dear husband," she said.

"Yes, of course," he said. "What is it?"

"I've heard of this from travelers—the runes stop working once you leave the fjords." But Tofa sat and thought hard for a little while, and then got one of their waterskins and dribbled a little of the water from home on the rune, and took off her shoe so she could scrape a little of the earth from home from her sole, and rubbed that on the rune too, and when she pressed her hand to it again, the power flared up, just enough to work with. She rolled it between her hands into long strands and braided it into a rope, and then she set it about the ship. The sea-women peeked over the gunwales, but they were polite enough to know they shouldn't interrupt a woman doing a complicated task, and dipped below the surface again.

As soon as Tofa had tacked the last end of the magic rope in place, a great fog came up out of the sea and surrounded them. Ylf cursed and shook his fist, but Tofa tapped her fingers on her golden rope and the power flared up again, bright as sunlight, and burned a clear path through the fog.

And in that clear path, they saw something flying, something as big as a person, with enormous ragged wings. And when it came closer they saw that it *was* a person, and that her wings were made of the wood of wrecked ships and her clothing made of sea-rotted sails. She circled their boat three times and landed on the mast. Her skin was as gray as a corpse, and her eyes were rimed with frost, and her lips were blue. "Turn back," she said.

"Do you warn us or threaten us?" Tofa said. Ylf stayed perfectly silent while Tofa spoke, and he hunkered down next to the rudder in the stern and tried to make himself as small and inconspicuous as possible.

"I warn and threaten, both," said the figure. "Turn back."

"Why do you warn, and why do you threaten? Who are you?"

"I—witch of the north! You—too close to my territory. I warn: if you do not turn back, you die. I threaten: If you do not turn back, I kill you."

"A witch," Tofa said. "How unexpected. If we had known you lived here before we left, I'm sure our witch at home would have sent us presents to bring you."

This gave the witch pause. "Presents?"

"Great presents," Tofa said regretfully. "If only we had known. I don't blame you for threatening us, to be honest—I too would be upset if a guest arrived to my home without a token of some kind."

"Presents," the witch rasped again, slowly and thoughtfully.

"Perhaps we could find something nice for you," Tofa said brightly. "And then we'll be on our way. And next time we'll be sure to ask our witch if she'd like us to bring you anything—I'm sure whatever she sends will be *very* nice."

"Very nice?" the witch said. "Very nice. Present now."

"Hmmm," Tofa said, looking around the boat. "Well, here's something good. How would you like that as a gift?" And she pointed to Ylf, scrunched up in the stern of the boat.

"What that?" said the witch.

"That's a husband," Tofa said. "A very fine husband. Will you be pleased with that for your gift?"

"Pleased," said the witch slowly. "Pleased, yes." And then she swooped off the mast and caught Ylf up in her talons, long wicked iron things that were tied on to her legs with rope, and she flew off due north into the mist. Ylf was scared to bits to be skimming above the water like this, unable to see in any direction, and so he concentrated very hard on holding onto the talons in case she decided to drop him. He couldn't be angry at Tofa, of course—there really wasn't anything else in the boat that would have done as a present, and Tofa was cunning. She would not have given Ylf away unless she had a plan to get him back and a certainty that he could look after himself until then.

At length, a shadow loomed up out of the mist, and Ylf saw that it was the face of an ice cliff. The witch flew up to the top of the cliff and dumped him in front of a large barrow made of snow, into which was bored a little tunnel. "In!" said the witch, and Ylf obediently crawled into the tunnel. It wove back and forth, the better for keeping out the cutting winds that blew across the ice fields, and then opened into a large inner chamber surrounded by several smaller chambers. The floor was covered with fish bones, and against one wall there was a wooden rack from which hung an assortment of huge seal steaks, stiff with frost.

The witch hopped and squirmed her way in after Ylf, and pointed to a cleared section of the floor. "Fire," she said.

"All right," said Ylf, and built a fire.

"Pot!" said the witch, pointing to one of the smaller antechambers. Ylf fetched the pot, a huge cauldron, nearly as big as he was. "Snow," said the witch, and then "Melt" and "Knife." Ylf ran about the barrow-house, fetching things as the witch called for them, and finally she looked him up and down. Tapping the knife against her palm, she said, "Leg."

"I'm sorry, what do you mean?" said Ylf.

"Leg! Give leg!" shrieked the witch, waving the knife at him. "Meaty, juicy leg!"

Now, Ylf was not as clever as Tofa, but he had a little cunning of his own, not to mention a profound emotional attachment to his leg. He wrapped his long fur cloak around himself and drew away. "I think no," he said.

"Leg!" screamed the witch, scrambling towards him.

"All right, all right," said Ylf. "You can have my leg." But from beneath the cloak, he offered forward not his leg, but the long haft of his axe. The witch fell upon it with a cry and hacked it right off, shearing off the haft right below the head of the axe with one stroke and taking a good deal of the fur cloak along with it. She threw the whole mess into the boiling cauldron, laughing with delight, and as soon as she turned away, Ylf fell upon her and killed her with the axe head he still held in his hands.

He dragged her body out of the barrow-house and piled it high with the driftwood wings and all the other scraps of wood that he could find littered about her house, and he set it ablaze so Tofa could find him, if she was looking. The mist had cleared when the witch died, but Ylf couldn't see the boat anywhere, not even all the way out by the horizon. He sighed. "Well," he said, "I might as well make use of my time." So he turned away from the cliff and went in search of a white bear.

Ylf was an excellent tracker, but white bears are sneaky and cunning, and they only walk on snow packed tight, so they leave no footprints. After a few hours of looking for white bears against the white landscape, Ylf's eyes were sore and half-blinded, so he kicked some snow into a pile to shelter himself from the wind, and he sat down to close his eyes and rest for a time.

When he opened his eyes, Tofa stood right over him with her hands on her hips, shaking her head. "Here you are!" she cried. "Napping in the snow, right where I expected to find you."

"However did you get here so fast?" he cried, leaping to his feet. "I looked across the whole horizon, and I didn't see the ship anywhere."

"Of course not," she said. "The boat got much faster once the witch whisked you and your curse off, and when you looked for us, we were already at the foot of the cliff. We called and called for you, me and the sea-women, but you didn't look down."

"Well," Ylf said reasonably. "I've never been known as a very clever man."

"No," Tofa agreed. "So it's lucky that you have such a clever wife."

"Perhaps my clever wife can outwit these stealthy bears."

So Tofa, with her fresh eyes, looked about, and eventually she found a little patch of disturbed snow where a white bear had buried its droppings. She found the trail then, and led Ylf along it, pointing out scratches here or there, and finally they found a valley in the endless ice fields. At the bottom of the valley was a giant sleeping bear, bigger than any that Ylf or Tofa had ever heard of. It would have been as tall as a pine tree if it were standing on its hind legs, and each of its paws was as wide as Tofa was tall.

"Perhaps this was a bad idea," Tofa said.

"Perhaps," Ylf said. "But I have to kill that bear."

"*That* bear?" said Tofa. "Why not find a different bear?"

"We haven't found any different bears," Ylf said, quite logically.

"Now, you'll have to tell me how to kill it, or else I will skip my way down the hill and throw myself on its snout with my axe."

Tofa sat down on the snow and put her chin in her hands to think, and at length she said, "All right."

There was a rune on Ylf's axe-head that she had engraved for him years before. She spat on the rune, that being the only way of linking it to Hrefnesholt that she had, and from that flicker of power (and it was just a flicker, a bare whisper), she managed to grow the broken haft into its full length again before the magic faded. "That's all I can do in *that* regard," she said. "But I have another thought." Now, what Tofa knew was that the bear in the valley was too big to be your usual kind of bear. "We'll go down together," she said. "Just like always."

They descended into the valley together and hid behind a snow-bank. Tofa peered over the top and looked the bear over. "This land must have magic in it," she said to Ylf. "Between the bear and that witch, there's something in the earth and water here."

Ylf nodded. "I think you're right," he said. Tofa thought for a little while longer, and then she told Ylf her plan.

Together they walked out from behind the snowbank, clutching each other in awe and amazement, and came right up to the edge of the bear's paw.

"Oh goodness me, darling, look at the size of it!"

"My dear, all the stories couldn't do justice to such a magnificent creature!"

"Certainly not! I shall have to carve the portrait of this mighty beast into the shoulder-bone of an elk."

The bear snuffled and whuffed in its sleep and slowly opened one eye.

Tofa and Ylf gasped in wonder and applauded. "How wonderful! What a beautiful and terrifying creature!"

"Truly he must be the jarl of the ice fields."

The bear lifted its enormous head slowly. "Who are you?" it rumbled.

"So eloquent!" Tofa gasped.

"We're no one special," Ylf assured him. "Just travelers."

"Just travelers!" Tofa sang. "We heard tell of your greatness, and we could not rest until we came to see for ourselves. *Are* you the jarl here?"

"What's a jarl?" said the bear. Its voice was as deep as an avalanche, and it made the ground beneath their feet tremble.

"A jarl is the greatest and most skilled person in all the land. Often the fiercest and the bravest, too. Is that you?"

(*Here I had to stop to explain something to Orfeo, because I realized that to a non-Hrefni ear, it might sound like Ylf and Tofa were trying to flatter the bear, perhaps to trick it into showing its weakness—that's how it would go in any other story. But the Hrefni find such cascades of unfounded praise embarrassing and unsettling. They are very realistic about their skills and abilities. Having someone assume that you're the jarl when you're not would be uncomfortable or even shameful because it means that perhaps you were misrepresenting your skills—bragging, in other words. The Hrefni don't bother with that. It is not something that makes sense to them.*)

"Well, I don't know about all that," whuffed the bear, a little offended. "I'm no different than anyone else."

"Surely you must have the biggest paws of any bear on the ice fields?" pressed Tofa.

"That could be," said the bear, suspicious. "I am large. It is possible."

"How amazing it is to meet the biggest bear in the land!" Ylf crowed. The bear whuffed again, annoyed, and pushed up with its forepaws so it was sitting rather than lying down.

"But we should introduce ourselves," said Tofa.

"Yes! This is my wife, Tofa, the best wife I have ever had, and very possibly one of the best wives in all the land. She can match anyone riddle for riddle, song for song, and rune for rune."

"And this is my husband, Ylf, the best husband I've ever had, and . . . well, he's all right, as husbands go."

"I'm in the middle as husbands go," Ylf agreed cheerfully. "I'm still practicing."

"He has proven himself to be among the bravest and fiercest and most skilled in all the land. He was great jarl of our villages *twice*."

"What do you want of me?" said the bear. "Why have you disturbed my nap?"

"Well," said Ylf, "we were planning on killing you, if we're being honest."

"That's right," said Tofa. "But then we saw how grand you are, and we knew that was a very bad idea."

"It *is* a bad idea," the bear said. "Begone with you, or I will crush you beneath my paw."

"Now, now, hear us out," said Tofa. She had been studying the bear this whole time, and she had not yet spotted any runes that might transform the bear into this enormous monster. "We were going to offer you a deal," she said. "We were going to ask you to become our business partner." (*I had to translate the word for Orfeo. They don't say "business partner" in the original Hrefni, of course, because that's a very southerner sort of idea—they would have said* gyldbróðir *instead. The two concepts share a lot of the same trappings, but a different impetus and direction.*)

"Why would I want to do that?"

"Well," said Tofa, clasping her hands behind her back and pacing before the bear. "You never know when your luck can change, do you?

It helps to be careful. Suppose the seas grow warm and the ice all melts. Where will you go? What will you eat? If you have prepared in advance, then you need never worry about such matters. They take care of themselves." As she walked back and forth, she still looked the bear over. She caught sight of a flash of green behind the bear's ear, and upon closer inspection she saw it was a strange jewel, wedged into a snarl in the bear's fur.

The bear scoffed. "These ice fields have been here since the world was born, and they will be here until the world dies."

"Mm," Tofa said. "Well, if you want to take that chance. Such a magnificent creature like you must live for a very, very long time. . . ."

"And there was that thing we saw back at the cliff," Ylf said.

"Oh, yes," she said, greatly concerned. "That was a frightening sight indeed. The witch, dead. The cliff, crumbling into the sea. But it seems like this fine snow-white gentleman has his affairs well in hand, dear husband, so let's leave him to his sleep."

"What was that you said about the witch?" the bear asked. "Dead?"

"Dead as death!" said Ylf. "A real shame."

"*Murdered*, I suspect," Tofa said. "The ice fields really aren't what they used to be, are they, darling?"

"You're lying," the bear said suspiciously.

"I beg your pardon, we most certainly aren't," said Tofa. She held her arms out to either side. "You're welcome to sniff out the lie on me. The witch was murdered!"

The bear narrowed his eyes, but he did indeed lean down to sniff her, whereupon she lunged at the jewel behind his ear and wrenched it free. As soon as the jewel came loose, the bear roared out in fury and shrank, and shrank, and shrank, until he was only the size of a normal bear.

A normal-sized bear was no challenge for a great hero like Ylf, of course, and by the time Tofa had scuttled away behind a snowdrift with the jewel (because her strength was with cunning rather than brawn), Ylf had already killed it.

"Oh, well done!" said Tofa. "Let's take what we need and go home. I'm getting cold."

"You're not thinking of bringing that jewel with us, are you?" Ylf asked, squinting suspiciously at it. "Only I'd rather not have a wife the height of a tree, if it's all the same to you."

"It's not coming with us, no," she said, and buried it deep in the snow.

While she did that, Ylf skinned the bear and took its teeth and claws and liver and heart and as much of the meat as they could carry, and then they went back to the boat. Tofa showed him a steep, hidden path down the face of the cliff, and when they made it back to the water, the sea-women all bobbed up above the surface and helpfully pointed out that Tofa and Ylf were rather covered in blood, did they know?

Ylf took the bear's teeth from his pockets and showed them to the sea-women, and they all crowded around and cooed. "Take us the rest of the way home, and I'll give them to you then," he said.

"Half now, half later," said the sea-women, and Ylf found that acceptable. He climbed into the boat, which immediately sprang four leaks, and sighed.

A sea-woman said, "I think your boat is leaking again."

When they made it back to their own familiar fjord, Ylf paid the sea-women the rest of the teeth and they vanished beneath the water without another word. Ylf walked up to the witch's cottage, halfway up the mountains, and gave her the pelt, the heart, and the liver, as promised, and she worked a long and complex spell, involving many runes, which she laid into the raw side of the pelt. When she was finished, she wrapped up the fur again and bid Ylf take it to the best tanner in the village to have it cured, and then to make it into a cloak or mantle, which he could pin about his shoulders for warmth.

"I think I've solved your boat problem with this," she said. "I'm not the best witch there is, you know."

"I know," he said. "But you're the only one we've got."

"That is true," she said.

Ylf had the fur tanned, as he was instructed, and when he wrapped it around his shoulders and pinned the paws together over his chest, he felt quite certain that the witch had cured him. He immediately went down to the water and leapt into a boat, paddling it out a few yards.

Well, within half an hour, the boat had taken on enough water that it was getting very low, nearly sunk, but to Ylf's surprise, he found himself resting on top of the water as if it were the ground. He got up and danced around, but his feet only splashed like he was a child jumping in a puddle.

That is the tale of how Ylf the Bear-Slayer failed to undo his spell-twisted luck, but gained a magic mantle instead.[238]

---

238 Gruffly and grudgingly, I am forced to admit . . . It is a rather good story. And it clearly is precious to you. I will remember it well, and I will pass it along to another, in good time. And I'm sorry for snarling earlier.

THIRTY-FIVE

There," I said. "How was that?"

"Wonderful," he said. "Really. It made me think of the stories my grandmother used to tell me when I was very small." I smiled and ran my fingers through his hair, imagined how his eyes must be shining, judging by the sound of his voice. "But how do you feel?"

"All right," I said. I took a breath. "Fine, actually. Good. Warm." I pressed my hand flat to my chest, between my heart and stomach, right over the seat of the soul, feeling a little candle-flame of . . . I'm not sure what to call it. Contentment, perhaps, though satisfaction might be more accurate.

"That was a story you knew before you met your master-Chant, wasn't it?"

"Maybe that's why I feel good."

"Are you named after Ylf?"

"Yes. Ylfing is a diminutive—little Ylf, or Ylf's-child, but the word *ylf* means 'wolf,' so my name is also 'wolf-cub.' They don't have gods in Hrefnesholt, just heroes. There's a lot of stories about them, and people make up new ones all the time. Lots of people get named after them, too. There was a boy when I was young called Finne— that's a hero too, just like Ylf."

Orfeo kissed me again. "It was a wonderful story. *Ylfing.* I've liked all your stories so far. Do you think the others might feel better again, someday?"[239]

"Maybe," I said, tilting my head a little in thought, but Orfeo saw it as an invitation and pressed his lips to the pulse in my throat, which distracted me for several lovely moments. "If I stop feeling so tired," I said eventually, when I had regathered my wits. "It's like washing clothes these days. Tedious and grimy and exhausting, scrubbing away while the lye chaps your hands. Not the stories themselves, but having to share them with people who don't understand them."

"It wasn't always like that, though, surely."

"No," I said softly. "Not always. But I saw once what people will do for a story, the ways it can go wrong, and after that I stopped wanting to give them anything that might hurt them, or that they might use to hurt other people. And the longer I went like this, the more I thought about it, the worse it got. I probably shouldn't have let it fester like that." I swallowed, pressed my face against his hair. "But it used to be like doing magic. Rare and wonderful."

"Oh," he said, with a kind of warm familiarity that made me lift my head again.

"Do you have some? I heard the Pezians do, sometimes."

"Just a little." He raised his hands and a faint shimmer ran across them, like pale golden starlight. It lit us briefly, sparkled in his eyes like soft firelight before it faded.

I caught his hands in mine and kissed his palms. "Show me again."

He rubbed his hands together briskly, as if he were warming his fingers in winter, and flexed his hands, and then another shimmer

---

239 I'm not really interested in reading this much about your private life. I think I'll skip or skim over those bits if you keep writing about them.

ran across them. Beautiful, beautiful. "That's about all I have. A little witchlight and some nudging."

"Nudging?"

"When something already wants to do something and you just help it along.[240] I bet you can start a fire with two sticks, right?"

"Takes a while, but yes. If I have to. It's easier to carry a tinderbox and flint or alchemical matches."

"I don't need matches. Two sticks and a nudge is almost as quick. Or you can nudge a pot into boiling over, or imbalance clay on a potter's wheel. It's easier if it's already doing the thing you're nudging for, because then you're just giving it a little more momentum. But it's just little stuff, just mischief—I had a friend who could nudge a nervous horse into bolting, but she lost the knack as she got older."

"Can you use it on people?" Even drunk, I could see the dangers of that.[241]

"You can," he said. "But . . ." He put his hand against my shoulder and shoved gently. "Could you tell that I did that?"

"Yes."

"You'd be able to tell if someone was nudging you," he said confidently. "Even if you don't have magic yourself, you'd feel yourself being pushed about, and you'd know that it had happened.[242] It's like persuasion as a physical sensation—it can't change your mind or your opinions, and it can't force you to do anything.[243] Anyway, most Pezians have just a whisper of it. Do you have any?"

---

240 Well, that's terrifying.

241 Even in Pezia they call it "the Pezian curse." Using it on another person is a capital offense.

242 Did he expect you to just *believe* him about that? He's lying to soften you up. He doesn't want you afraid of him, because if you're afraid then you'd be guarded.

243 That's not quite true. But then we get into a debate about what constitutes compulsion. If someone twists your arm behind your back to make you agree to their agenda, or shoves you along in front of them to make you move, that's compulsion, even though

"No," I said, tracing my fingers over the light in his palm. "None that I ever learned. Like in the story about Ylf and Tofa, in Hrefnesholt, it's runes and sigils, too complex for a child, and they need the connection to the earth and water to work."

"Where is Hrefnesholt? I'd never heard of it before today."[244]

I took his left hand and traced the deep line that ran from the heel of his palm and curved around, ending at the web between thumb and fingers. "This is the Genmu River." I tapped the end of the line at the base of his hand. "Map Sut is here. Banh Tua to the southwest, Aswijan to the southeast." Two taps, one to each end of the lines on his wrist. "And Genzhu." I brushed my fingers over the broad expanse of his open palm and up his fingers, like the wide and verdant river basin ringed by mountains. "Inacha." I touched a single point at the side of his hand opposite his thumb. "Tall mountains here, tall enough to hold up the sky." Across his fingertips. Then, finally, I kissed the tip of his index finger. "Ulfland. And then Hrefnesholt is just across the channel, a bit farther north."

"*Really,*" he said. "North of Genzhu? That far away? Gods, and I thought I was a seasoned traveler."

"I told you Chanting took me all over," I said.

"Hrefnesholt, though, that's . . . Whew, you're a long way from home."

"Half the world away," I agreed. "But it's not my home now. That

---

it's your mind making the choice and your feet doing the walking. The Pezian curse can, I think, best be described as . . . weaponized charisma. It's very easy to use that poorly— but I expect you would have realized that too, if you were keeping your wits about you. Your master had something like that, didn't he? But he didn't need magic for it.

244 No, you know what? I'm not quite ready to move on from the previous topic yet. I've taken a few minutes to think about it, and it just keeps sticking in my head. I don't know . . . The way he talks about the Pezian curse, like it isn't that big of a deal . . . I don't know. Makes me pause. Just a little, little pause, but with someone this charming, even a little pause in your mind is important to pay attention to. It could be something. It could be nothing. I don't know. He's trying to be better, he said, but he could fall back on bad habits anytime, and he didn't *really* tell you what those were.

was part of the sacrifice too," I said, still dreamily tracing his palms. "I haven't had a home or a name since then."

"I can't imagine that. I can't imagine giving up my family."

"Six years since I left them. That grief is over. I don't think it ever really struck me. I was never more than a little homesick. Not until after I became a Chant—I think then it was real. Then it was over, and I *couldn't* go back."

"You could. Hrefnesholt is still there, isn't it? Your family is still there. Nothing's stopping you."

"I don't think I will. I don't think it's my place anymore." The air was getting cool, then, and the wine was gone, so we picked ourselves up and walked back to the inn—his family was still inside, still drinking and singing, though it had quieted down. "Do you . . ." I began, suddenly feeling very warm and uncertain. "Do you want to come up to my room? It's not much, it's just a pile of blankets in the attic, but . . . Do you?"[245]

He tucked a lock of my hair behind my ear. His smile was full of regret. "Earlier you said that *dancing* would be too much."[246]

I bit my lip and felt a blush tingling in my cheeks. "I did say that, didn't I."

"You did," he said softly. "And we polished off two bottles of wine between us, and I do still happen to pride myself on gentlemanly comportment as a lover, rake or no." He bit his lip. "But . . . I don't much like sleeping alone. What if you come up to *my* room, where there's a real bed, and I'll kiss you good night and we can . . . sleep? Just sleep."[247]

---

245 *Wow,* great job, *super fucking romantic,* inviting a boy up to screw you on a pile of blankets in an attic. I'm *sure* he was simply bowled over with that offer.

246 What's he up to here? What's his angle? He's almost *too* well behaved. Right? He went out of his way to make sure you knew he's a gentleman in the sack. I just don't know about this one . . .

247 Hmmm. Hmm. Hm. It's just a little inconsistent of him. He was making those jokes about how he'd run off in a panic if someone invited him to breakfast after

And I didn't realize until he said it that *that* was what I really wanted, more than anything, more than... whatever I'd thought would happen when I invited him up.

He had a room on the third floor, on the end of the north wing, which meant it was right under where I had my things piled in the attic. When I told him so, he said, "Oh! Do you have a pet?"

"No," I said, very confused.

"Hm, it must have been rats in the walls, then. I hear scratching at night, you see, for an hour or two, and then it fades off."

"You must have heard me writing. I don't have a desk, so I use the floor. Sorry, I didn't realize anyone could hear me. I'll—not do that, I guess, for as long as you're here."

"Oh—no, you must do whatever you need to. It didn't bother me. I've gotten used to it, by now."

We loosened our clothes; Orfeo removed his simarre; his belts, hung with all manner of cleverly worked, useful little items; his doublet; his shoes and hosen. He unbuttoned the knee-cuffs of his breeches so the fabric hung free and comfortable, and he untied the throat-laces of his shirt.

I had much less elaborate clothing to manage, but I rid myself of my boots and socks, and the voluminous, threadbare black coat, the worn neckcloth with its torn and tatty lace trim, and the equally sad waistcoat, all of which I had acquired from a secondhand shop upon my arrival in Heyrland. (In the last year, I've found value in blending in, as much as that's possible, by wearing clothes unremarkable for the place. The Hrefni pale skin and blue eyes are distinctive wherever I go—though my tendency, thus far, to stick to large trading centers means that there's enough variety of faces in the crowds that even I

---

sex, which suggests he's got a bramble-patch when it comes to intimacy, but then he invites you to stay the night? I just don't know.

don't stand out too much. In Hrefnesholt, we didn't see foreigners for months or years at a time; everyone looked much the same as everyone else. But anywhere you go around the Sea of Serpents or the Sea of Storms, and all the way up the Amethyst Coast and into the Glass Sea, it's different. People move around—boats come from everywhere to everywhere else. Here in Heyrland, I don't think they'd bat an eye if the sultana of Araşt herself disembarked a boat in full royal regalia.)

Orfeo held up the covers for me and engulfed me in his arms as soon as I slid beneath them, and kissed me good night until I was breathless and rethinking whether dancing would have exhausted me after all. But the room was dark, and the hour was late, and we *were* both quite drunk, and we both fell asleep before I could make any more decisions either way.[248]

And then we woke up this morning. His aunt or someone was pounding on the door and calling for him, and he kissed me before he tumbled out of bed and wriggled back into his clothing, leaving his pantaloons on but changing out his shirt for a fresh one, and he told me to stay and sleep as long as I liked.[249]

Right as he was running out the door, I said, "Did you remember your drawers?" and he stopped, and looked back wide-eyed. And then he grinned, all springtime sunshine, and off he went.

---

248 I just *don't know.*

249 This is driving me mad. *What is he up to?* He seems so calm and unbothered about waking up next to you—he even kissed you. Which bit was he lying about? Or ... Hm. Come to think of it, *you* might be lying. Not on purpose, I don't think, not here. But you're young, and you've got a bit of a flutter going for this boy already. Perhaps that's the source of the inconsistency. You can hardly be expected to remember every little thing or interpret it all accurately when you're beset with youthful passion.

THIRTY-SIX

I woke again quite late in the morning, cozy and warm, and I felt . . . I felt like *me*.

I feel like Ylfing again, not just some empty shell calling himself Chant. I woke up and it was like I'd really *woken up*. Like I haven't quite been in my body at all the last couple years. It's good. I don't know how long it will last, and I suspect I'm not finished grieving. But the world feels alive, and open, and bright. I can do things. I can make choices. I can choose *who I am*. I can tell myself the story I need.

And I'm not irredeemably broken, not yet. I'm still enough of a person to love someone. At least one someone, at least for a little while.

He's so lovely. This isn't going to last very long, of course—he has his family and his obligations, and I . . . well, I have my own things to do. I'm going to be terribly sad when all this ends, I know that for sure, but I think that's good. I think I won't mind being sad like that, because I'll be *feeling* something, and feelings are how you know you're alive.

But he'll be here for a little longer. I won't press him for time.

Orfeo! Orfeo with the sunshine in his hands; Orfeo who was there and ready to meet me when I turned away from the brink of despair at last, who took my hand and led me back to the world. I really mustn't waste paper on speculating about all the wonderful things about him; I'm sure I'll discover more of them and feel compelled to write them down then.

For now, here are three wonderful things that I *do* know about Orfeo:

1 ...

No, I can't even number them after all.[250] I can't even put words to them.

I realized just now that I was starving, really properly starving. I've gotten so thin and bony in the last couple years. I haven't cared about food either. But just now I asked *Mevrouw* Basisi for a big breakfast, and it was so good that I'm going to list everything she brought me:[251]

Sweet peppers, onions, and mushrooms, sauteed together in oil with cumin.

Two soft-boiled eggs.

Three kinds of sausage (thin slices of a hard, spicy red kind embedded with peppercorns; fresh pork links still sizzling from the pan that burst with juices when I cut them; and a cold chunk of beef summer-sausage).

A wedge of buttery, flaky, apple-and-plum pastry.

A thick slab of dark brown bread with butter.

Two kinds of cheese (a hard orange kind with a mild, nutty flavor; and a medium-firm sharp white kind made of sheep's milk).

Pancakes with caramel syrup and cinnamon.

A whole lemon. (The Heyrlandtsche love lemons. They squeeze them over everything.)

I ate all of it, and—can you believe it?—I could *taste* them. I asked for coffee and I could taste that too—the Heyrlandtsche like

---

250 *Thank all the gods.*
251 Do you want to take Lanh Chau off my hands, by any chance? I have a feeling the two of you would get along, if he hadn't already decided you weren't worth his time.

to flavor theirs with chicory and cinnamon and drink it with great dollops of honey and lashings of cream. It's *delicious*.[252]

I ate until I felt like I'd be sick if I had even another bite, and then I looked around and started noticing things, dozens of things, that I'd never cared to notice before.

There's a mirror above the fireplace, and it's set in a beautiful green frame carved with flowers. The fireplace and the pavings of the floor are neat, regular slabs of smooth gray stone, and I never noticed before how tidy *Mevrouw* Basisi keeps the common areas. In lots of taverns, you'd have the floors strewn with sawdust or dry, tired rushes, but the inn is so clean that the floors are bare. At least in the summer—I expect they lay down carpets or woven mats in the winter to help ward off the chill.

Mevrouw Basisi herself is so beautiful! I never noticed that before either! She's half-N'gakan, a big woman, shorter than me and round and soft all over, and she works so hard all day with her family and her staff. She has bright, cunning gold eyes; and strong limbs; and she wears sensible skirts every day that I've seen her so far; and she has excellent, luminous dark skin. Everyone loves an innkeeper, and she's no exception—all her patrons greet her warmly by name and inquire about her well-being. While I was eating my breakfast today, she watched from the corner of her eye, and I couldn't help but feel that she approved—I've been wallowing for far too long.

The innyard is a good size, too, not too large and not too small, and it has a simple iron gate at the front with two spindly trees growing on either side. Now, I won't go so far as to think that I hadn't noticed the trees. I'm sure that I had. But I definitely hadn't noticed the dozen lanterns hanging from their branches, and I had no memory of seeing them in darkness, even last night when I was out with Orfeo.

---

252 I don't care for it. I prefer teas and tisanes.

Writing all this down, it seems so silly. I hope it's worthwhile—this sort of thing went on all day. I was not required at Sterre's offices today; I've been working seven days out of eight, and this was the eighth day. I did chores for *Mevrouw* Basisi and was joyful to find that they took me all over the inn, where I could poke my nose into places and wonder about them and marvel about what a lovely place I was in. And it *is* lovely. I think this must be a very respectable establishment. I shall have to find out.

It's called the Sun's Rest[253]—I don't think I ever noticed that before either.

Orfeo arrived back in the late afternoon, and I went to him immediately and embraced him. "Thank you," I said.

He laughed. "For what? Letting you sleep in this morning?"

"You brought me back to myself. I was lost."

He drew away and touched my face. "I don't think I did that much," he said, still smiling. "You were the one who approached me in the end, anyway."

"Are you doing anything right now? Will you come on a walk with me? I've been locked up inside myself for so long—I want to go out and see the city; I want to know something about where I am."

He was more than willing, so we walked for hours along the canals, finding little twists and turns, and I chattered the whole way to Orfeo about this or about that. I exclaimed over every bridge we passed—the little footbridges spanning the canals were all so lovely.[254] I made Orfeo play a game that I learned somewhere on my travels

---

253 Oh—yes, that is a respectable establishment. I nearly chose to stay there myself, but I had an acquaintance who recommended the Rose and Ivy. I've heard of the Sun's Rest, though—I've been told the food is excellent.
254 I'm getting bored—lovely this and lovely that, and *oh how charming*, and *ah how wonderful*. How much longer does this go on?

with Chant when I was very young, still young enough to be learning children's culture, which is always different from that of the adults no matter where you go. The game goes like this: You get two pieces of grass, or two little twigs, and you and your friend drop them on the upstream side of a bridge, right in the middle. Then you run across to the other side and wait to see whose arrives first.[255] I played this with street urchins in Genzhu when I was new to my apprenticeship, and today I was just so overcome by this flush of youthful energy . . .

Well, Orfeo was very patient and willing to humor me. I think he was amused.

At length we came to a market square—not the Rojkstraat, but a similar one; there are so many markets of this kind all over town. I smelled something delicious and suddenly I was starving again, so I bought food from the cart vendor—bites of cod, battered and fried, served with the ubiquitous slices of lemon. I took a bite and started laughing, wrecked with helpless giggles that rose up from the center of my chest like so many floating soap bubbles.

"Are you all right?" Orfeo asked. He was laughing too, and that just made mine worse.

"I can taste it," I said. "It's good, right?"

"Really good," he replied. He slung an arm around my shoulders, and I leaned into his side, still quivering with mirth. "But are you?"

"I'm—fine. I'm great. I've never been so good."[256] I devoured the rest of my fish and brushed the crumbs of batter off my hands and into the canal. "I can taste things again. I can see things, notice things. It's like I'd forgotten how to see color, but here it is again, everywhere."

---

255 If there are children and a bridge over water with a current and bits of twig or grass, they will invent this game. This game is a force of nature. Literally every child in the world knows this game.

256 I don't believe you, and I don't think Orfeo believed you either.

"I'm glad you're feeling better." He dropped a quick kiss on my cheek. "What do you want to do, now that you're back in the land of the living?"

"Everything," I said. "Everything. Let's go explore the city; let's run until we find an adventure."

"There's playhouses," he said. "My uncle went to one of them the other day and saw the Marijke van Baer Troupe. He says they are very fine."

"I don't think I can sit in one place for a very long time right now. I need to move."[257]

Orfeo dropped the arm that was around my shoulders to around my waist and pulled me a little tighter against him. "We could find some dancing."

I must have lit up like the Tashaz festival of lights. "Yes. Yes, let's do that."

We trod what must have been every street in the West District, talking and ... flirting. It was easy again, effortless. I bought us food at every street cart we passed, and every bakery, until Orfeo claimed he couldn't eat another bite. I still could. Every twenty minutes, I was starving again. The whole time, I kept a running commentary about all the lovely things about him—the shine of his hair, the curl that fell on his left temple and begged to be twisted sweetly around a finger. The color of his eyes, the set of his mouth, the way he had of watching me so I knew he was paying close attention to everything I said.

And when I wasn't flirting with him, we traded things that weren't quite stories, mostly about Hrefnesholt and Pezia, and our childhoods. He told me about the Acampora Bank, headquartered in Lermo, with six branch offices in Marsania, Ponterosso, Tono,

---

257 Ah, see? You weren't happy; you were manic.

Stradenze, Serta, and Bolifetto. His family is very rich, and very influential, and very well-known, and he stands to inherit, apparently, exactly none of it. "I've got the name and the looks, but that's all," he told me. "I'm really just a minor cousin—I'm lucky to have even that much. I don't get an allowance like my cousins who are closer to the center of things do, except when I'm traveling with the family and things can be considered business expenses. I won't inherit land or property or business interests, even. My father's just a clerk at one of our countinghouses, and..." He laughed bitterly then and dropped his arm from my waist, shoving both hands into the pockets of his simarre and staring down at the cobblestones as we walked slowly down the canalside. "I'm going to be a clerk too," he said at last. "Unless I spontaneously manifest some kind of useful talent. But I won't. And even if I did, it wouldn't matter."

"Why not?"

"It's too late. Remember what I said about siblings and cousins last night. About family seeing right through you. Except sometimes they don't. Sometimes they only see who you were a year ago, or five years ago, and they never get around to noticing that you've changed." He forced a smile, tense and as unhappy as I'd been a few days ago. "They've already decided that they know what I'm like. They might try to tell you, actually, if they notice me spending any time with you. Just... be warned, and take it with a grain of salt, and if they say anything that alarms you, at least give me a chance to explain myself before you decide I'm not worth your time."[258]

"I will. But about the rest of it, couldn't you learn a trade of some

---

258 I just don't know about this one. With some people I've known, this would send me running for the hills. And with others, they really had been represented wrongly and it was worthwhile to get to know them.

kind? An apprenticeship, or . . . There are universities in Pezia, aren't there? Good ones."

"Hah. Too late for that too. I had a chance and I wasted it. I was supposed to be studying rhetoric. They'd thought I might make something of myself in politics. But I was stupid, and I didn't real-ize how things were, in the family. I thought having the name was enough; I thought it counted for more than it does. I thought it would suffice to keep me in favor."

"What happened?"

"Every three months, they'd send me money for my room and board and tuition, and I . . . lied about how much I needed and spent it on other things. Drink, gambling, fancy clothes. The family found out, of course. Sent some cousins to drag me home, where I found out exactly how tenuous my position really was. Of course they wouldn't send me back to university after that." He laughed weakly. "I just thank the gods I've never had trouble getting laid for free, because if I'd spent the money in brothels, I probably could have kissed the family name goodbye too. They wouldn't have tolerated that kind of indignity. It wouldn't do, not for an Acampora."

"But they tolerated the gambling?" I asked, skeptical. Gambling sounds like a worse offense than brothels do to me.

"Only because I was usually winning." He glanced at me. "That was the rest of the long story, by the way. The other reasons I'm trying to be better. I had the reasons I mentioned last night, and they're important, but it's . . . mostly selfish." He winced. "The only chance of saving myself from a life of wasted opportunities and dreary tedium and scant fortune is to prove, somehow, that I'm different. That I learned a lesson and I want to turn over a new leaf." He shook his head. "It probably won't happen. But that's the last chance I've got, so . . ." He shook his head, suddenly. "I'm ruining it, aren't I? Being maudlin. I don't even know why I told you all that."

"I'm a Chant," I said automatically. "It's my job to be someone that people tell things to."

"Oh? I suppose working in a tavern is a good place for that."

"It would be, most of the time. Lately, I've been . . . not myself. I haven't wanted to watch people or notice things about them. But now I'm fine!"

"Oh, good, that's a great relief. If we swing by the printer's shop, I'll cancel the order I put in last week. I decided I needed some engraved invitations to hand you next time I was flirting with you, just to make sure you noticed what I was doing."

I laughed and shoved him a little with my shoulder. "Not like that—it's more . . . looking at a person and seeing something about their character. Deep things."

"All right, tell me something about . . . her." He nodded to a person across the canal, either a *vrouw* or a *vroleisch* by the way she was dressed—a faded blue skirt and a newer-looking cream shawl. Her back was to us, so all I could see of her were her rather red-toned neck and arms, which looked very strong. She had a deep basket on her arm, holding groceries: bread; a large parcel wrapped in paper, which was probably a fish; a few other items.

"She's a laundress," I said.

"You're so sure?"

"Yes."

"Oi!" Orfeo shouted. "*Mevrouw*, pardon me!"

"Don't bother her," I said. "She's busy."

"*Mevrouw*, can you direct us to the launderer's? We're lost!"

She'd turned at Orfeo's call and studied us. "You looking for van der Wel's, Vinck's, or Zendman's?"

"Either. Do you have a recommendation?"

"Go to Zendman's," she said. "Down the way you came, on this side of the canal, and turn right at the next corner."

"A thousand thanks, *mevrouw*! You are a goddess of mercy! Should I tell them who sent us?" She shrugged and turned away. "Well, that was inconclusive," Orfeo said. "Too bad."

"A laundress," I said again. "She knew where three launderers' shops were, and she had an opinion about which was the best—her skirt is old but her shawl is new, and she's feeding her family bread and fish for dinner, so she's not of a social class to be sending so many of her things out for cleaning that she'd become a connoisseur. She was too tired to care about your flirting, and her skin was red from working in the heat, which means she just got off work. Also, did you see those arms? Only launderers and farmers have arms like that, and we're in the middle of a city."

"Her skin could have been red because she's hot," Orfeo objected.

"Why's she wearing a shawl if she's hot? She's a laundress. Trust me; I'm a Chant."

"You're an Ylfing," he replied, taking my hand again and squeezing. "And I concede defeat. Tell me something of yours now. Not a Chant thing, another Ylfing thing."

So I told him about going to the Jarlsmoot, the enormous competition between all the villages that happens once every three years, where everyone who has been named jarl of their village (by being the most valuable person with the greatest variety of abilities) comes together to try their skills against each other. I told him how it worked, how the winners of all the dozens and dozens of competitions would be recorded, and how, at the end, all the jarls would discuss who among them made the most impressive showing, and that person would be named the great-jarl.

"What kind of things do people compete in?"

"Everything—there's athletic ones: running, jumping, climbing, archery, javelin-throwing, rolling a barrel of beer up a hill, and so on. And there's material skills—weaving and carving and fishing, for example." I nudged him. "There'd be something for you, certainly."

He nudged me back. "Aren't there any competitions for someone like you? Storytelling or memory?"

"Not to be named the great-jarl. But at the end of the Jarlsmoot, one of the villages hosts a huge party, and everyone drinks—there's drinking competitions, of course, and there's competitions in singing and dancing and telling stories and jokes. And riddling! And the winner of that is named the chief skald, and at the next Jarlsmoot, their village hosts the party. I apprenticed as a Chant because I thought . . ." I felt a tremor in my vibrant mood and realized that maybe it was more delicate than I had realized. "Well, I thought that then I might be the best at stories, and I might be chief skald at the Jarlsmoot someday.[259] But I'm not even Hrefni anymore, not really."

"Why not?"

"I've been too many places. I lost the things that made me who I am. Like my name. That's all part of being a Chant, you know. You don't get to be yourself anymore. I told you about that last night."

Orfeo nodded. "Let's go find that dancing?"

"Yes," I said, relieved not to be talking about it any further. "Dancing. Yes."

We didn't find music until the light faded and the sun set, but when we did it was at one of the biggest inns, near the docks on the eastern side of the Shipshome District. It was an inn for merchants

---

259 Shit, now I'm wondering if your master knew about that. If that was, perhaps, a factor in why you didn't go home for the rites.

and their clerks, for ships' officers and their deputies, for foreign diplomats newly arrived to the city. We gave up our weapons to the attendant at the door—I only had my little old knife in its leather sheath, but Orfeo had a lovely matched pair, one markedly bigger than the other, fine things with faceted green spinels at the pommels and the centers of the crossguards, and elaborately embossed gilt scabbards.

"We used to stay here, my family and I," Orfeo said into my ear so I could hear him over the din of people talking and dancing. "But it's noisy and expensive, and it never felt like a home. Too many people."

It was crowded, to be sure, but the musicians were good, and there were a half dozen people pouring drinks at the bar just as fast as the patrons could down them.

We danced. In some places, it's uncouth to dance with the same person more than twice in a row, but at least in this inn it didn't seem to matter at all. The musicians were clearly accustomed to a great deal of variety in their audience, and they had an inclination to please each of them and the ability to match—they played a Heyrlandtsche fjouwer and Vintish bransles and Avaren jigs, which Orfeo and I muddled through very clumsily off to the side of the dance floor so that we wouldn't get in anyone's way, giggling all the while as we tried to copy what everyone else was doing. At the next song, Orfeo lit up and he whispered, "Oh, this one I know! This is Pezian." He took my left hand in his right and we . . . walked.

"Is this what Pezians call dancing?" I whispered, trying not to laugh.

"It's *stately and dignified*," he whispered back sternly, though his eyes twinkled.

(Steps to *amoroso*, for my own future reference: Four steps forward, hand in hand and apparently by necessity looking deeply into each other's eyes. Drop hands; the Lead progresses four steps forward, looking longingly back over their right shoulder like a lover tragically separated from their sweetheart, hand outstretched back to the Follow, who stands in place. Lead turns back; both point their right foot, sweep it around to the back, and sink into a deep bow or curtsey (which Orfeo tells me is called a *reverence*).[260] The Lead returns, passing the Follow's right shoulder (obviously looking deeply into each other's eyes for as long as possible), circles around behind them. The Follow goes forward four paces and turns; the Lead repeats the return. Both circle: once clockwise without touching, then once counterclockwise clasping left hands; reverence. The Lead switches their hand from the left one to the right, and then they've arrived back at the beginning and they do the whole thing over again. I think this dance is for people who have some kind of forbidden secret longing for each other. It's kind of boring otherwise, unless you have someone like Orfeo to dance with—I was biting back my laughter the whole time, and Orfeo *knew* it, the imp, and all he did was make even more ridiculous faces at me. I don't think this so-called dance[261] is supposed to be funny like that.)

We made it home eventually, and Orfeo invited me up to his

260 I'm glad to see you thinking in a more Chantly way (learning culture and things with the evident intention of remembering them), but I still can't feel easy about it being written down....Actually, I suppose I can begrudgingly be fine with this. I just stopped to ask Arenza. I was trying to get her to agree that it was strange and uncanny, but she says that there are several popular books written by famous dancing-masters in Pezia. She couldn't say whether you've done it in a similar style to theirs, as she's never read any herself, but she recalls that when she was young, one of her cousins was apprenticed to a dancing-master and used to practice the patterns in the kitchen every evening with one of those books laid open nearby for reference. So since the Pezians are already writing them down themselves, I guess I can't find harm if you do it too. It's like the script of a play, isn't it? Written down, but performed aloud. (Still strikes me in an uncomfortable place, but I suppose that's my problem and that I may well be wrong in this specific, individual situation.)
261 "So-called dance," though, hah! I have to agree; the Pezians wouldn't know real dancing if it kicked them in the teeth. Even the peasants dance sets and figures, though theirs are a bit more lively than the stately stuff the upper class do.

room again, where we piled into bed, and I wrapped him up in my arms and whispered not-quite-stories of one sort or another into his ear, and—

And I don't think I should put anything else about all that on paper![262]

It was the best day I've had in a long time. And Orfeo is wonderful.

---

262 *Thank the gods.*

THIRTY-SEVEN

Mistress Chant is angry at me again.[263]

I woke up this morning with Orfeo, and he nearly made me late for my duties at Sterre's shop. When I finally managed to pry myself out of his arms, I went up into my attic room for fresh clothes and to scribble a few pages about what happened yesterday, and then I rushed off. The clock was chiming, so I ran the rest of the way to Sterre's shop and arrived flushed and breathless and felt again that delicious *realness* and *presence* in the world that Orfeo had brought me to.

Sterre took one look at me and asked if I'd just come from a brothel, and when I stammered and blushed, she sent me off to the alley to splash cold water from the rain barrel on my face and comb my hair until I looked presentable. She shoved a parcel wrapped in brown paper into my arms when I came back inside and, pushing me into her office, said, "A uniform for you. Change into that. Quick, *heerchen!*"

I changed as quickly as I could, groaning when I unwrapped the package and saw the clothes inside. Just outside the office, Sterre was scolding one of the clerks: "If you're sick, you should have sent word!

---

263 Oh good, a bit about me! I'm fed up with you most times, but this must be . . . ah, Stroekshall, right? *That* day.

What kind of employer do you take me for, that you think I would hold it against you? No, you must go home at once, and straight to bed. And here—six duit to send out for hot soup."

I emerged from her office, stiff and uncomfortable and feeling more than faintly ridiculous in that getup, but Sterre glanced me over, beamed, and declared me absolutely perfect, which smothered any objections I might have come up with. We piled into her carriage (a tiny, cramped thing it had to be, to navigate the narrow canalside streets), and we went to Stroekshall.

It was busier than I'd ever seen it, and the carriage could barely cram through the crowds. It was no less crowded for us inside— Sterre had had the carriage's benches removed, and every bit of free space not occupied by our bodies was piled with the last crates of stars-in-the-marsh, all that remained of the current shipment. We even sat atop them. This was for safety, Sterre said. She didn't trust the slavering crowds, and she was ferociously suspicious of bandits or rioters seizing the carriage and its precious contents.

"Today's going to be special, Chant," she said. I almost didn't answer—in only twenty-four hours I'd gotten accustomed to being called Ylfing again, to having my name spoken sweetly, or kissed into my mouth, or breathed into the dark like a prayer. Who was *Chant*? Not me.

"Yes, *mevrol*," I said. I wondered if I should tell her to call me Ylfing too, but it didn't feel quite right yet. I didn't long for her to know my name the way I had longed for Orfeo to know it.

"I need you in top form, got it?"

"Of course, *mevrol*. I'm ready."

"Did you get some sleep last night?" she asked pointedly, and I blushed again.

"Yes. Enough. I'm rested, if that's what you're asking."

"Mm," she said, then nodded, apparently satisfied. "It's good to see you with some color in your cheeks, *heerchen*. Young people like you ought to be taking advantage of your youth while you have it."

"As you say, *mevrol*."

"Honestly I thought there was something wrong with you."

I blinked at her. "I beg your pardon?"

"You're a good worker, Chant, but you've been wandering around limp and listless. I thought perhaps that was just the way you were, all gray like a dishrag. I'm pleased to be wrong, and I commend your timing in getting over whatever that was about."

"Grief, *mevrol*," I said, careful not to be impertinent about it.

"Well, it's better to be past all that. You'll need all your focus today."

"I *said* I was ready."

She laughed. "And you're even feeling well enough to be snippy with me." So much for me not being impertinent, I suppose. "Good! Good. I want you full of fire today. How's the uniform?"

There are two divergent fashions for Heyrlandtsche *mannen* right now. The first is a more comfortable and conservative style, worn by the middle classes (or the upper classes in casual settings), involving dark muted colors in linen or lightweight wool—essentially a knee-length robe, open in the front and cut loose (or even baggy) in the body and sleeves, and belted about the waist. Beneath that, a waistcoat and a light linen undershirt, breeches and hosen. Understated and unassuming, quite plain, like a blank slate. People dress it up in small ways, with fancy buttons, or colorful silk hosen, or a bit of embroidery at their cuffs or collar. The collars are removable and interchangeable, and therefore very much subject to the whims of fashion. Currently, the mandated style is to wear them wide enough to drape over your shoulders, like a miniature shawl. If you're rich, then your collar is made *entirely* of lace; if you're not, it's one of several varying grades of cambric merely edged with lace—or not, as the case may be.

These clothes are the sort of thing I wear (though my collars are secondhand and not at all up to the current style). It makes me nearly invisible.[264]

The other fashion, worn exclusively by the upper classes, is a ridiculous,[265] dandyish[266] confection[267] of as many as four colors that was somehow intended to make sartorial reference to soldiers and, in my opinion, misses the mark by several . . . thousand miles.[268] It's *like* the other fashion, except that it's tailored snug through the torso, with an undeniably charming nipped waist,[269] and the skirt of the coat is much shorter, barely reaching past one's hips—more like a doublet with a wide bit of fabric as trim on the bottom hem.[270] The sleeves are huge through the arm and cuffed tight at the wrist, and it's worn with a pair of fitted knee-breeches[271] and hosen. And, as the crowning glory, if you want to call it that, the whole production is slashed all over with dozens of tiny cuts in elaborate patterns to show the fabric beneath in a contrasting color. The whole thing is topped off with a hat of varying styles, but it always has at least three enormous, fluffy ostrich feathers, imported all the way from Onendogo.

The version of this that Sterre had made me change into was

---

264 Makes you look dowdy and bland.
265 Wonderful.
266 Delightful.
267 And such a confection it is!
268 Shhh. Shhh. It's a wonderful fashion. Gods bless the tailors who invented it.
269 Agreed!
270 Mmmmm. Yeah . . . It's great. It's a really good fashion.
271 Okay, but did you ever see the ones that are shorter than that? There are some that just have really short breeches, not even halfway down the thigh, and the hosen just goes *allllll* the way up. It's a really, *really* good fashion.

stripes of blue and black velvet overlaid on silk of an intense reddish plum in the top half and pale peach in the trousers.[272] It was trimmed all over in bands of narrow gold braid, and while the hat was (thankfully) the smaller of the available styles, the ostrich feathers were abundant, all dyed rich blue. I felt ridiculous and self-conscious[273]— I've been wearing the muted and conservative style the whole time I've been in Heyrland, and secondhand items to boot, everything at least five years out of date.[274] But of course I couldn't tell her that I felt like a child borrowing someone else's clothes, swimming in all that extra fabric like I was. She might have been insulted. "It's fine," I said, trying not to fidget.

"It fits all right? Nothing scratching or pinching? I don't want you to be distracted at all today."

Again, I couldn't complain. "It's fine, *mevrol.*" It wasn't fine—I was beginning to understand why all the *mannen* I see wearing this style always *lounge* so aggressively. The trousers are too tight to bend your legs without the fabric cutting off your circulation and crushing your family jewels into a fine powder, so you can't sit comfortably in a chair like you normally would—you have to slouch, so you can stretch your legs out straight, or drape yourself across something, all louche and

---

272 So, uh . . . I don't know if anyone told you, but did you know what that looked like at a bit of a distance? The pale peach underlayer of the breeches was just about the same color as your skin, and you had matching hosen, so from across the hall it really looked like you weren't wearing anything at all under your trousers—like it was just the slashed overlayer showing bare skin beneath. You *know* that was intentional on Sterre's part, right? She dressed you up like that to be just on this side of scandalous.

273 Sigh. Of course you did. I don't know what I expected.

274 Dowdy! Moth-eaten! Just another way you're failing as a Chant—you *ought* to dress like you did at the auction, or like I do: bright and splendid and eye-catching. Sterre knows it, even if you don't! A Chant is supposed to seize the attention of the room! The ancient Chants did—it's said they wore bright colors and shining things to draw Shuggwa's Eye.

disarrayed.[275] There wasn't room for that in the carriage, piled in with boxes as we were, so I flexed my feet and tried to ignore how I could feel my own pulse in my calves. "Nobody else in your offices wears a uniform," I said.[276] "And I didn't have to wear one for the salons."

"This is different," she said quickly. "Have you ever seen an auction before? A proper one?"

"Of course."

"Have you ever seen one at Stroekshall?" she amended.

I hesitated. "No, *mevrol.*"

A smile spread across her face. "You're in for a treat, *heerchen.* And for a trial by fire, I suppose."

"What do you mean?"

"Oh—you're going to run the auction." She patted the crates piled around her. "Hence the uniform. You have to look present-able;[277] you're representing me, of course. Make me a lot of money today, got it?"

"*Me?*"

"Yes. You're the best translator in the city. Everyone else needs at least four to run an auction like ours—you'll impress them just by being alone at the podium." I must have looked like a wild, frightened animal. That's what I felt like. She patted my hand. "It's no different from what you do at the Rojkstraat, and you did a very impressive job wrangling that little crowd in front of my offices the other day.

---

275 Heavens, is *that* why? I love it. I love them, and I love it. May the gods smile upon the tailors.

276 Oh, you sweet innocent thing. You really believed her when she said it was a uniform? With trousers like that?

277 I'm *sobbing* with laughter. I honestly had to stop and collect myself. Oh gods! *Presentable*, she said! And you *believed* her, didn't you! You believed that you looked *presentable* instead of like the human version of a tray of assorted chocolates. Presentable! I have tears in my eyes!

You're a natural. Calm down." I forced myself to stop and breathe—
there wasn't anything else to do. The biggest crowd I'd ever spoken to
before was at the Rojkstraat, probably—a few dozen people, a small
crowd. In Stroekshall, there would be hundreds. "There, better. It's
going be noisy. It's going to be fast. You're going to want to try to slow
them down to make yourself comfortable—don't. You *want* it fast.
You want to push it faster if you can. Fast makes people uncomfortable, makes them anxious, makes them compulsive. You want them
panicking. You want them making snap decisions." She leaned forward. "You want them to think you're the only one in the room who
isn't terrified. Be confident. Be anchored. You want them to think
you know what you're talking about. Because you *do*. You know more
about the stars-in-the-marsh than any other person in the city. You
know how to turn a person's heart to your will."[278]

When you grieve for years, it becomes a habit. You become so
bland and flat and listless that you forget how to rise to extremes on
either end of the emotional spectrum. I wanted that flatness again—I
wanted to claim I was sick and go back to the inn and curl up in my
attic and sleep for the rest of the day.

That would have been the Chantly thing to do. That would have
been the grieving thing to do. But there was Ylfing in me again, and
the Ylfing part of me wanted to shake off the haze and run forward
with my arms outstretched. And, besides, I thought of what my
master would have done. He would have just done it. He wouldn't
have been frightened. He adored an audience, especially a captive one.
That, I think, tipped me the rest of the way over, made me angry

---

278 All right, mirth aside, and as much as I approve of her taste in clothing for
Chants, the two of you should never have been left alone in a room together. Alone,
you each have your allotment of sins. Together, your sins grow exponentially—her
greed fuels your heresy, and you both go tumbling down into the muck of petty evil.

enough to set my fear aside. I can't quite put words to it, but I felt all of a sudden like I had to do it, out of spite or to prove something to myself (by which I mean: to the memory-him that lives still in my head). A real Chant could do what she was asking, and I'm a real Chant, and therefore . . . Therefore.

Fuck what anyone else thinks. To the desert with all of them.[279]

"You can do it," Sterre said. "You don't actually have an option to not do it, of course, because I would have had to hire translators days ago, and all the others have been snapped up by other merchants at the auction by now. You're all I have. It'll have to be you. You'll do it." She didn't sound threatening, just assured. Like she knew what she was talking about. Like she was the only person in the room who knew what she was talking about.

I took a breath. "Yes. I will. I can." *Fire*, I thought. She wanted me with fire in my belly—I could do that. I'd found that again, fighting with Mistress Chant about our ways of doing things, and dancing with Orfeo. I had life in me again.

And to the desert with my master, specifically.

We had guards when we arrived at the doors of Stroekshall, and they helped our team unload the carriage while people in the crowds around us surged forward, shouting and crying out and waving their money-purses at us. "Ten guilders, de Waeyer! Ten guilders for just one!"

"Fifteen! Fifteen!"

Sterre only smiled like a wolf and led me inside. My legs prickled as all the blood rushed back into them, freed from the oppressive strangulation of the cloth that had pinched at my bent knee and the

---

279 I have mixed feelings about this, but I'm going to let it slide because "Fuck what anyone else thinks" is a personal philosophy that I hold very dear.

crease of my hip when I was sitting in the carriage. "This is a good sign. Don't sell them for less than fifty apiece—more, if you can. Remember, the others went for seventy each. And put your hat on."

"Yes, *mevrol.*"

"Drive the price high. Sing them into submission. They know who you are, and some of them have bought before. Don't harp on the story for too long—come up with something new if you can."

"I would have liked some time to *think* if you wanted new material," I said. I'd relaxed the leash on my tone, and my voice came out petulant and snappish.

Sterre only laughed again and clapped me on the back. "That's the spirit! More of that."

Inside the hall, there were even more people packed in as tight as possible, shoulder to shoulder through the entire first floor, and more of them hanging from the balconies above. At the other three doors, guards accepted admission fees—they had to pay a full guilder just to get *inside.* That's three days' wages for a common laborer, and almost a full day's wage for someone skilled, like a ship's carpenter. This fee was to dissuade people from coming just to gawk at the proceedings. Only serious buyers allowed today.

Our door was reserved for entrance by the merchants who had products to sell at the auction. There was a tall man with thinning black hair standing a few spaces ahead of us in the line with a wheelbarrow full of bolts of cloth wrapped in white muslin. A fold at the end of one bolt had fallen loose, and I saw layers and layers of jewel-like silk shining inside in shades of strangely lovely greenbrown, as clear and bright as a millpond in spring.

"Prepare yourself," Sterre whispered. "There are people in front of us, but it won't take as long as you're hoping. Be ready to go in minutes."

"I'm ready." My stomach was fluttering. I watched the stage—as she'd said, every merchant had at least four translators on stage, all shouting at once, pointing to people in the audience and taking their bids for whatever was being sold, relaying them to an accountant standing at the back of the stage. And she was right—it did move fast.

The man in front of us and his translators hauled the bolts of cloth onto the stage and unwrapped the muslin from them. They blazed with color, so bright that I could almost taste them, like berries bursting on my tongue. The translators announced that they were examples of a shipment from Map Sut, four hundred bolts in total, in these twelve different shades.

They unfurled lengths of the cloth, all silk—there was a mulberry-purple, a blue-black.... They were all two colors, flashing one or the other depending on which angle you glimpsed them at. There was one that I would have sworn was fire-orange until the merchant holding it turned towards us, and I saw it was violet. Some people in the audience cried foul play, thinking the cloth somehow enchanted or faked, but the translators shouted them down: it was merely two-tone silk, they said, woven with the warp in one color and the weft in another. No magic at all, and anyone who liked could come up and touch the cloth to see for themselves.

Of course the hall was packed too tight for anyone to move much, so the audience had to be satisfied with the confirmation of the people within the first couple feet of the stage.

The cloth sold, those twelve bolts and the rest of the four hundred, for a sum so enormous that I couldn't quite wrap my head around it.

And before I had expected, we were standing at the base of the steps leading up to the stage, and Sterre was patting me on the shoulder.

She murmured to me, "You're brilliant. You'll do fine." She was as nervous as I was, I think, but her nerves calmed mine. I watched the other translators, watched their frantic flurrying motions, and I fell into a still, quiet state.

"I'm ready," I said again, and the round of applause signaling the end of the previous merchant's turn on stage roared up as we mounted the steps, with our porters carrying the crates of stars-in-the-marsh behind us, and then it was too late to turn back or change my mind.

I didn't want to. I felt as solid as rock, and I felt as if I were flying, like I had yesterday afternoon with Orfeo.

Sterre stood at the back of the stage and handed me the list of lots that she had separated the stock into. I looked down at it, looked up at the crowd. They were quiet, dead quiet. There weren't hundreds, I saw. There were *thousands*—perhaps two, three thousand people, all crammed in here, quiet as the dead, waiting for someone to speak.

"The honorable *Mevrol* Sterre de Waeyer," the Stroekshall representative announced from the stage. "Importer of fine luxury goods from Araşt, Vinte, Bramandon, Arjuneh, Oissos, Kaskinen, Pezia, Onendogo, Cascavey, Borgalos, Tash, Mangar-Khagra, and the Ammat Archipelago! The auction will be translated today by," and he paused for the barest heartbeat, glanced at me, saw that there was only one of me. I stared back at him, blank and calm. I didn't feel like either Chant or Ylfing at that moment. I was something completely different. "Translated by *Heer* Chant," he finished.

Another round of applause, perfunctory and brief.

"Twenty lots," I announced. The stage was arranged in the middle of one of the broad sides of the hall so no one would be too far away from it. I could make my voice reach even the farthest corner. "Twenty lots of stars-in-the-marsh, of five bulbs apiece! You've heard the stories. Your neighbors' gardens are agleam with these beauties. If you leave here without these today, you will have lost. These are the very last bulbs in Heyrland! There will be no more until after the storms. These are *the very last ones*."

I paused. I let them hang off my words. My mind flashed back to last night, to laughing in bed with Orfeo as I hovered above him, just out of kissing distance, tempting and beguiling and teasing, until he whined some objection and pulled me closer. *You want me*, I thought at the crowds. *You want what I have. Come to me. Come claim it.*[280] "The first lot: bidding begins at one hundred guilders!" And my skin *blazed* with the weight of eyes on me. It was like nothing I've ever experienced.

I think that's what it must feel like when a god looks at you.

In the hall: Chaos. Chaos. Chaos. A wall of sound. Hands flew in the air all over the floor; the crowd surged forward a step. People waved handkerchiefs from the balconies above, trying to catch my attention, calling for my eye to fall upon them.

The previous merchants' auctions had been nothing like this. Those at least had been civil and orderly. This was a *tempest*.

It occurred to me that I didn't actually need to take anyone's specific bid. All I needed to do was to hold out and cry numbers until only one person remained or the wanting had been thinned enough to deal with reasonably. "One fifty!" I said—repeating myself in Vintish, in Tashaz, in Bramalc and Botchwu and Avaren and Araşti—and then, "Two hundred!" and so on. Out of the corner of my eye, I saw the Stroekshall clerk scrambling, wild-eyed, and I saw some movement out of the corner of my eye, flashes of white and black, but I didn't dare turn to see what was going on.

---

280 You knew what you were doing. You did it on purpose. I'm furious once again— and now I see why you put in all that blather about Orfeo and *falling in love*—you knew this part was coming. You wanted to soften me up. You wanted to make me sympathize with you, so that I'd forgive you a little for this atrocity.

I caught the eye of someone close to the front of the stage—she mouthed, as clear as day, "Five hundred," so I repeated that. Five hundred. Another surge of noise, a cry of despair.

Then it was six hundred. Then eight hundred. A thousand. People had dropped out now, a significant number of them, but still there were dozens—hundreds, even—who had the gold to spare on these worthless flowers. I spoke in a daze, my tongue tripping faster and faster through the tongues I knew. At length I threw in Arjunese, Oissic, Mangarha, and what I knew of Pezian.

I spoke in Kaskeen and didn't even feel the pangs of hurt that I'd come to expect when I was reminded of my master-Chant.

Mine. They were all mine. They were as ravenous as any audience I've had, snapping and howling wolves the lot of them, but all their baying was not for me, but for the flowers at my feet. I held the wolves back with my words and with their own wanting, and that was enough. I was alone, and *I* was enough.

The first lot sold for one thousand, four hundred and seventy guilders. Sterre seized my arm and turned me. Her eyes were wide, her face flushed with glee. "Chant, change of plans. Ask the buyer to come forward. Ask whoever else is willing to buy at that price to come forward." There were six of them—none of them had wanted to go higher. They'd been bidding in increments of ten towards the end. They made their way through the crowd to the sound of murmurs. No one had ever seen anything like this before. I certainly hadn't.

When they reached the stage, Sterre knelt to be closer to them, and I stood close in case she needed my services—but they were all native-born Heyrlandtsche citizens, merchants themselves or members of the Council of Guilds. "I have twenty lots of five bulbs each. How many lots do each of you want?"

And then we were finished, or so I thought. Sterre rose to her feet a few minutes later and handed me a stack of papers. I looked down at them—unsigned futures contracts. "Sell these," she muttered into my ear. "One bulb apiece, highest quality."

My mouth was dry, my hands shaking, but I turned back to the audience. It was my job, after all. "*Mevrol* de Waeyer has sold her current stock," I announced. "But because there was so much demand, she is offering contracts of future sale for the next shipment of stars-in-the-marsh." I raised the sheaf of papers over my head. "One bulb per contract. We'll start the bidding—" I paused, glanced at the accountant on the other side of the stage, who mouthed a number to me. "We'll start at three hundred guilders apiece."

Three hundred, four hundred—it seemed like they cared more about the price than they did about the amount of bulbs in the lot. They were quite happy to purchase a single bulb for eight hundred guilders when fourteen hundred for five had been too expensive.

The tempest whirled around me, the noise battered into me like a gale, but I sold the futures contracts and, at last, fell back. There was no applause now—the people weren't even paying attention to me by the end. I could see little knots of people fighting and bickering around those who had bought the contracts, begging for the winners to sell to them. It seemed some people were already regretting not buying the bulbs cheap when they could.

I've done the math, and one guilder buys around a tenth of a pound of tea in Heyrland, or two chickens, or fifteen pounds of bread, or roughly seven and a half pounds of good cheese (depending on the variety). And some of them had bought one bulb—*one single bulb*—for eight hundred guilders. Eighty pounds of tea; sixteen hundred chickens; twelve thousand pounds of bread; more than five and a half thousand pounds of cheese. You could feed an *army*. Supposing two pounds of bread, a pound of meat, and eight ounces of inexpensive cheese per person per day (and taking into account the negotiations with merchants for discounts on such large orders), you could feed a hundred and fifty soldiers for a *month* for the price of what one star-in-the-marsh bulb sold for today.[281]

I turned back to Sterre, breathless and exhausted and exhilarated, my skin still crawling, though not unpleasantly, with the ebbing tide of all that attention.[282] She and her porters and assistants were surrounded by sheaves of paper in a drift on the floor. I walked across them, looking down. They were marked with scrawled numbers written large—the noise had been at times so loud and overpowering that they'd had to hold up the amounts to communicate across the hall how high the bidding had risen.

Sterre had tears of joy in her eyes, and she caught my face in her hands and kissed my forehead soundly. "Gods bless you, *heerchen*. I knew you could do it. I knew you could."

Someone pressed a cup of lukewarm tea on me, and I drank it in a daze. It was thick with honey and the wholly unsurprising tang of lemon. "Are we done?" I rasped.

"We're done," she said. She was beaming at me like I was her own child. "You can have the rest of the day off. And here—go buy yourself something nice." She pressed a small purse of coins into my hand. "There will be more where that came from, *heerchen*, I promise you. Tomorrow's payday, and you will certainly have a beautiful reward—a bonus."

---

281 There are no words. You knew. You knew the whole time. You used your words to weave a fisherman's net, and you cast it for an evil cause. You used your words to trap and exploit hundreds of people. I'm not even capable of anger anymore. I'm just . . . desolate. This is not what a Chant should be. This is *never* what a Chant should be.

282 Except it wasn't their attention, was it? It wasn't their eyes that you'd felt fall upon you. (Hello again. Mistress Chant-from-the-future, flipping back again to check that I remembered this right. I did.)

"Thanks," I said, and dropped heavily down the steps, brushing past the line of gawking merchants who watched me pass. I fought my way through the crowd outside and collapsed on one of the little oases of greenery that dotted the huge cobblestone courtyard at the back of Stroekshall, a little miniature park. This one had a slender tree and a generous swath of grass.

It was not like anything I've ever done before, and I wanted to sit alone with it for a minute and think about it. Was it a Chant thing to do? Was it an Ylfing thing to do? Was it something in-between?

I've been thinking about it all day and I still don't know. It was like . . . nothing I've ever done before, like nothing my master-Chant told me *he'd* ever done. He'd spoken before audiences of hundreds, I know—at the very least, there was that time he was on trial for witchcraft. He was always so practical and prosaic and worldly. Even if he *had* spoken before thousands, I don't think it would have struck him this way.

This . . . this was transcendent. I've been trying to think of something to compare it to. It was nearly a religious experience, or at least what I've always imagined one would feel like. It felt like the whole world had turned to watch me, like the gods themselves had paused to glance over. It was terrifying. It was thrilling. It was more than I could possibly hold within myself, my lungs and stomach and heart and throat all brimming over at once.

My master would have scoffed at me. He would have snorted and dismissed it, flicking his hand in the way that he did when something failed to engage him. He would have said I was building it up all on my own, that it was all in my head. He would have explained it away, made it mundane and unlovely, sucked all the goodness out of it until it was as leathery and desiccated as dried meat. He would have told me why I shouldn't have bothered to feel anything.

And maybe that's all true. But, putting all that aside, what it comes down to is that doing things his way hasn't been working for me. Trying to be *him* hasn't been working.

And lying there in the grass in velvet and silk and gold braid, with all the wealthiest people in Heyrland drifting past in little groups and talking quietly to each other while regular waves of half-muffled noise surged out of Stroekshall, I looked up at the sky and thought, with some relief and an equal measure of terror, *Maybe I can still do this after all. Maybe it won't be unbearable forever.*

And then Mistress Chant came up out of nowhere and said, "Now you've done it." [283]

"Sorry," I said automatically. "What is it that I've done now?"

"That show inside. Those *clothes.* How dare you?"[284]

"You were in there?"

"I was."

I shook my head. I still felt foggy and vague—she would have had to pay money to get inside, unless she had a patron of some kind to pay for her, and considering how strongly she objected to *my* doing that . . .[285] "I didn't do anything wrong."

"You're not a Chant."

I sat up, leaned back against the trunk of the tree, and let my hands fall loose on the grass to either side of me. "Should I tell you my name, then?"

Her face turned bright red with fury. "You don't *understand.* You're not taking this seriously—you're not even taking yourself

---

283 I stand by what I said.

284 Oh, I forgot I was angry about the clothes at the time. Hm. I see why I was, but—well, I'd rather see you dressed as a Chant ought to be.

285 I paid for myself, because *I* don't turn my nose up at the idea of saving money. What am I supposed to do when I get old, otherwise? What if I get injured and can't *speak?*

seriously. Don't you have any shame? Don't you have any knowledge of the power a Chant can have? No," she answered. "You don't.
Because you've felt so sorry for yourself for so long that you don't
notice what you've learned how to do."

"Are you going to tell me what it is?"

"What were you trying to do in there? What were you playing at?
The way you batted your eyes at the crowd and cocked your hip. You
sold those flowers like you were selling yourself, just like you've been
selling yourself for *months* now."

"I do what's asked of me," I said. "Sterre didn't have anyone else
who could have done it. I was good at it, wasn't I?"

"You don't feel any remorse? You sold them *trash* and dressed it
up as something valuable."

I felt something twang inside me, and I folded my arms at her.
"I didn't tell them to bid that high. If they think it's worth that much
money, who am I to tell them otherwise?"

She spat at my feet. "You're responsible. You knew what you were
doing. You knew that a story makes a thing more valuable than it would
be by itself. You gave those flowers a story, and you let it spread like a
plague through the city. *You did that.* You just let two dozen people—"

"They're not mine. I don't control them. I told them information,
and it's up to them what to do with it. It doesn't have anything to
do with me," I snapped, and then I felt a cold twist in my stomach.
I sounded like my master-Chant. I heard it in my voice and cringed
from it. "I didn't force anyone to do anything."

"Did you see what else happened?" she said in a low voice. "After
people bought your thrice-damned flowers?"

"I was busy," I said. "What are you referring to specifically?"

She knelt on the ground near me, leaning close—looming, more
like. "You weren't the only one selling futures contracts in the aftermath."

I sat up. "What? Who else?"

"Those six people you sold the bulbs to—they're already selling offshoots before their bulbs are even in the ground. And no one who bought a contract from your hand walked out of Stroekshall with it—they'd sold them along by the time they reached the doors. People were already second-guessing themselves for not paying more. You made them that desperate."

"But they made money. None of my concern."

"People in there held a contract for less than three minutes, and then they got their money back and walked away with a fortune—twenty, thirty, fifty guilders more."

"Well, good for them. So it's not a problem—it's even less to do with me. Go yell at someone else."[286] I got to my feet and dusted off my clothing.

"It's gambling," she said. She hadn't moved. "You're beguiling people into gambling their lives, their livelihoods, on these flowers. How can you do that in good conscience?"

I shrugged. "It's not for me to worry about. They can make their own choices."

And then I left her, and went home to the inn, and found that Orfeo had left a message for me with the innkeeper—he was out with his family at the Stroekshall auctions, and he hoped to see me for dinner later in the evening.

He'd been there! I hadn't seen him. He'd be able to tell me whether I'd done something bad—Mistress Chant has such a way of chewing on the back of my brain for hours and hours after every time she comes around to harangue me.[287]

---

286 I wasn't yelling at you.
287 Good. You've admitted already that I've been right before. I was right about this too—you'd done something terrible that day.

I was angry for the rest of the day, a grudging resentment against Mistress Chant and all her stupid opinions, and that she'd come up and spoil the afterglow just when I was starting to get a handle on it. My mood only slackened when I set eyes on Orfeo, right around dinnertime. He spotted me sitting in my usual place in the second-story gallery of the inn and came up the steps, catching me with one hand on my jaw and one in my hair, kissing me soundly before either of us said even a word.

"So you were at the auctions?" I said breathlessly when he let me go.

"Forget about me, *you* were at the auctions!" he said, all delight. He pulled up a chair to my table. "Why didn't you say anything? I had no idea!"

"Neither did I until this morning," I said. "So I couldn't have said anything until I was at the doorstep of Stroekshall."

"I knew you did translation work for de Waeyer, but ... Wow. Ylfing. That was really spectacular." He was looking at me differently, like a man who has discovered an unexpected treasure.

"Was it? Someone was very rude to me afterwards." [288]

"What! What for? What did they say?"

"Ugly things. They—she. She's a colleague of mine, sort of. Another Chant." I chewed my lip. "I don't know what to make of her. She was angry at me for taking that job, I suppose, and she thinks I'm a heretic and a blasphemer. She thinks I'm doing harm."

Orfeo looked rather taken aback and gave me an extraordinarily puzzled look. "Harm? How?"

"She thinks the flowers are useless—which they are—and that I'm tricking people into wasting their money. She accused me of selling the flowers like I'm selling my body."

---

288 To hell with you!

Orfeo went very still. "Sorry, *who* is this person? A colleague? How long have you known her?"

"A couple weeks, at most. We've hardly ever talked."

"So she's all but a complete stranger. And she thinks she can just walk up to you and insult you like that?"

His outrage on my behalf was both gratifying and endearing. I reached out and ran my fingertips over his knuckles. "I guess so. I've been sulking about it all day."

He took my hand in both of his. "Put her out of your mind this instant. She doesn't know what she's talking about. You were splendid. Magnificent. I've never seen anything like that. You were practically glowing. And those clothes, those colors! Nobody could have taken their eyes off you. At least, I certainly couldn't. I've . . . never seen *any-thing* like that. Are you sure you don't have the Pezian gift?"[289] And he let the golden light flicker over his hands as if in invitation.

"I'm sure," I said.

"You were splendid," he said again. "Calm and assured and . . . and *brilliant*. How many languages were you speaking? I thought I counted five, but—well, I don't know how you managed to hear the bids in that din."

"Where were you standing?"

"Second-floor balcony, on the same side of the building as the stage was but a ways down towards the end. We hadn't even been looking at the bidding—we were only there to watch the trends. But then I heard your voice, and I was surprised, to say the least. I leaned out over the railing to watch you. I made my family watch too. We were all impressed; everyone was. We talked about you afterwards, and I bragged that I'd taken you out dancing last night." He grinned.

---

289 *Gift?* I've never heard a Pezian call it a gift.

"And then they were impressed with that too. First time they've been impressed with me in . . . well, probably ever. Uncle Simoneto told me I could take you to dinner and call it a business expense, if I wanted."

"You're exaggerating."

"I swear I'm not!" Orfeo put one hand over his heart. "Here, I'll prove it." He leaned over the railing and shouted below: "Uncle! Uncle, come here!" He'd been sitting at the bar, flirting with *Mevrouw* Basisi, I think. When Orfeo called, he looked up, and Orfeo waved him over. "Come up here; you'll want to meet my friend." I'd seen Orfeo's uncle the last few days, but Orfeo hadn't introduced me, and I hadn't felt the need to introduce myself.

Orfeo's uncle squinted up at us. "I've left my spectacles in my room, boy. Who is it?"

"Come *up*."

He shook his head and made for the stairs; he didn't recognize me until he was about ten feet away. "Good gods, Orfeo, you'd better warn a man. I didn't know him without that splendid costume." He came forward the rest of the way with his hand outstretched, and I got to my feet to shake it. He looks just the same as Orfeo, but eighty pounds heavier and thirty or forty years older. They have the same eyes, the same curls, the same cheekbones. The same tendency toward a sunshiny outlook on life. "Simoneto Acampora," he said. "It's a true pleasure to meet you."

"See?" Orfeo said brightly. "I told you I knew him." I sat back down, and Orfeo leaned close. "I can introduce you as Ylfing, can't I?" he whispered.

My stomach lurched unpleasantly, a moment of vertigo. "I—uh—no. Chant." I'd spoken before I'd really thought about it— I'd mentally reached for something solid to steady myself, and my hands had landed on that boulder I'd been carrying around. Too late to change my mind. I couldn't unsay it. I made myself smile at Uncle Simoneto. "I'm Chant," I said, and hated every letter of it.

"Yes, I know!" he said. "Did my blockhead nephew really take you dancing last night?"

"Yes, of course." I looked curiously between the two of them. "Do you often tell tales about taking people dancing, Orfeo?"

"Never in my life. My uncle is teasing me," he sniffed. Simoneto laughed—big men like him often boom with laughter, but he was nearly silent, cackling softly into his beard like a man half again his age. "Uncle, tell Chant how good he was at the auction today." It felt deeply wrong to hear that not-name from Orfeo's lips instead of "Ylfing." "I said everyone was impressed, and he doesn't believe me."

"Oh, yes," Simoneto said immediately. "Very good. Strong work, I have to say—you must have the ears of a bat and the eyes of an eagle. Not to mention a silver tongue."[290]

"Quicksilver, surely," Orfeo said, beaming at me.[291]

"And a tailor of legend," Simoneto added.

"The clothes were just what my employer asked me to wear," I said quickly. "I had no part in all that. And the rest, I was faking most of it," I said. "I'd never done that before; I didn't know what else I was supposed to do—as long as people were still bidding, it didn't matter what I said, so I just said whatever sounded likely. Right?"

Simoneto blinked, then nodded thoughtfully, a grin beginning around the corners of his mouth. "You're a smart one, then, quick on your feet." Orfeo looked back and forth between us. I could see some

---

290 Context is important. The context here is that a bunch of merchants, who are already inclined to be easily impressed by gaudy displays, think you did a good job. Are they a reliable and objective source of information in this situation?

291 Hah! The boy didn't know how right he was. Quicksilver drives people to madness and ruin, after all.

beautiful thought dawn on him, something that made him look joyful and, a moment later, *hungry*. And then, whatever it was, he went very still indeed, staring at nothing. Then suddenly he looked over again, his eyes flickering across me and then away, intense and thoughtful.[292]

"I try. I'm trained to be adaptable."

Simoneto and I spoke for a time, and when the Acamporas began settling down for dinner, he insisted that I join them at their tables below on the main floor. Orfeo spoke up for the first time in several minutes to agree strongly, seizing me by the arm and looking at me imploringly so that I couldn't help but accept the invitation. They introduced me to the rest of the family (including one young man I think I recognize—the one who was at Master van Vlymen's salon, the one who embarrassed himself). They introduced me, of course, as Chant.

The Acamporas are a gregarious bunch. They all wanted to speak to me, or tease Orfeo in front of me, which he took with an extremely funny air of dignity, but which must have bothered him more than he wanted to admit in front of me—I spotted him dragging a few of the perpetrators off to the side of the room to speak fiercely to them, gesticulating and shoving their shoulders when they laughed at him. If they tried to walk away, he caught them by their sleeves and dragged them back, or stood before them and blocked their paths until they rolled their eyes and agreed to whatever it was he was saying.

They all called me Chant, and . . . and Orfeo did too.

I found myself getting tired and upset more quickly than I had expected—maybe it was just the aftermath of the auction. I excused myself from dinner and came up to my room to write. They're still down there now. It's so early in the evening—I'll probably nap and then go see if Orfeo wants company.

---

292 I just don't know. He's up to something now, even if he wasn't before.

All right, I suppose I won't nap. Ugh! Every time I start drifting off, I sink right into that dream again. I can't go five minutes without choking for breath and feeling like I'm covered in beetles or tangled in the roots of the flowers.

I don't understand why it's pressing on me so, today of all days—the auction went well! I felt good! I felt like I'd done something right! So why is my mind throwing this at me so strongly? Why plague me with the flowers and the water, and the thick mud sucking me down, and something (a bird?) pecking and tugging at my clothes in the brief moments I can pull myself above the surface? Is that what it's going to be now? More torments?

Gods, I need to sleep. I'm restless and fidgety, and I keep looking around like there's something I'm missing, something different. Like maybe someone's sitting nearby. But there *isn't* anything, and no one comes up to the attic but me, and there's no such thing as ghosts in Heyrland, so it can't be that either.

To the desert with this; I'm going to Orfeo.

THIRTY-EIGHT

So I went down to Orfeo last night, and I invited him to exhaust me so that I'd be too tired to dream, and it . . . only sort of worked. It was different, at least. I didn't wake up choking again and again, like I had been before, so that was something.

Every time I closed my eyes, I was struggling through the swamp, the stars-in-the-marsh towering above my head and filling the air with the suffocating, fetid stench of death. The air above me was alive with buzzing insects that bit me and flew into my eyes, my nose, my mouth. I fought them off, pulling the cloth of my tunic over my face, and surged forward through the thick, slurping muck. I struggled until I was too weary to go on, falling time and again into the water until I could move no more, and then, with my last breath, my last whisper of power, I looked up.

I saw the sky. All was dark except for the flowers, and just before the water closed over my head, a cloud moved aside, and—there it was, clear in the sky as it always is, a spiral of stars hanging in the black: the Eye of Shuggwa. That's what the Chants call it.

I said, "No more of this, please. Please, no more." And then the water closed over me.

Something seized me by the collar of my tunic and dragged my head above the water—I gasped for breath and felt a breeze on my face. The air on my tongue was sweet and fresh. Pure.

I opened my eyes and saw the bird, the one that had been pecking at me before. It was a cormorant with golden-brown feathers,[293] floating beside me and holding me up by the scruff of my tunic, as if I were no heavier than a small fish. It was fanning its wings to make the breeze, and I breathed and breathed.

And then I heard something coming through the muck and the tall stalks. The sound of water lapping on wood—a boat, I thought, a moment before it appeared, pushing through the thicket of flowers.

In the stern of the boat, there was a person, sitting very still with their hands folded on their knees.[294] They didn't row—the boat just moved steadily forward of its own volition. It was a punt, I saw now, a squarish boat with a shallow draft and a flat bottom—good for marshes like these, where it wouldn't run aground even in water only a few inches deep. The figure wore a cloak of rushes and a broad-brimmed hat,[295] and a lantern hung on a stick behind them, casting their face into shadow so I couldn't see it at all.[296] The cormorant tugged me forward and jumped up onto the prow of the boat, and the moment I put my hand against the wood, the boat stopped dead, as still and steady as if it were on dry land, and the figure in the back turned their head and looked down at me.

"Please," I said. I was too weak. I could barely lift my hand above the water. The figure leaned forward and grasped me by the forearm, dragged me into the boat, then sat back in the same position as before. All I could see of them or their clothes was a tiny corner of hem by their ankle, embroidered richly in a style I've never seen before. I sat

---

293 . . . Wait. Wait.
294 Oh, what the fuck. What the fuck.
295 What the fuck. You've got to be kidding me. No!
296 No, this doesn't make *sense*. This is Heyrland; we're thousands of miles away from the seat of his power. He doesn't reach this far. There's no way he could.

up, and the cormorant croaked at me. "Thank you," I said. "I thought I was going to drown."

The figure leaned forward and brushed my cheek with their fingers.[297] "Ylfing," they rasped, so quietly I couldn't tell anything about their voice.

And then I woke up—naturally, for once, not clawing my way out from the bedding.[298]

---

297 Liar. Liar, liar, liar.

298 I'm . . . speechless. I'm *speechless*. I'm speechless at you, upstart Chant. Speechless at your ignorance, speechless that you would *deserve* a dream like that to begin with, and I . . . I can't. That was *Shuggwa*. As clear as day, that was Shuggwa—all the signs were right. The cormorant was his messenger, Ksadir. His boat was there, and his lantern, and his cloak of rushes, and the hat shadowing his face from sight. That was *Shuggwa*. Not funny, bumbling trickster Skukua of Kaskinen, but proper Shuggwa of old, from the ancient days when he was powerful and terrible, and the people of the swamp gave him Chants, favored and indulged ones, to hold his gaze and protect anyone less favored from harm at his hands.

And you! You! Upstart! You with your disregard for propriety, you with your immoral, heretical beliefs. *You*, of all the Chants in the world, you draw his Eye, you win yourself a visitation? He comes to *you* when you call? He knows and speaks *your* name aloud? What did you do to earn that? What was it that brought him to you? Was it the spectacle you made of yourself in Stroekshall, wearing those tarty clothes and batting your eyes like a maiden until every red-blooded person in the room was aching for you? You have to be lying about it. You *have to*.

THIRTY-NINE

I t's been two weeks or so since I've written anything down. I've slept better than I have in months, now that I'm not dreaming of drowning every night. Just . . . silently sitting in the boat, with the cormorant in the prow and the stranger in the stern, and myself perched on the center thwart. No one speaks, but the cormorant flaps her wings every now and then, and the air stays fresh. It's such a relief, and infinitely more restful, but . . . it's so much more consistent now than it was. Before, there would be nights here and there where I wouldn't dream at all. But now? Every night. Immediately, the moment I close my eyes, until I wake in the morning. That's strange, isn't it?[299] I'd think it was some kind of magic, except that:

1. nothing interesting happens, and

2. the only magic like this that I've ever heard of is the kind in legends and wonder-tales. Even the hugely powerful magicians that crop up at random, one every two or three hundred years or so, don't really do workings like "sending weird dreams about flowers and boats and birds and strangers to a single, specific Chant in Heyrland."

---

299 Only *impossible*.

If this were a wonder-tale, I suppose the dream would be significant—a prophecy, or something like that.[300] A message of some kind.

But this isn't a wonder-tale. It's just my life, and life is fairly mundane. Yes, *before*, it would have made sense for the dream to be a message, even if it was just from myself to myself: me, slogging through the marsh, choking on the flowers that came from my master's homeland? Easy enough to see what *that* means, because I felt like I was struggling through thick, soupy mud even in my waking moments.

Dreams are a lot like stories—they're a way for your mind to come to terms with what's happening to you, a way to look at a problem from a few steps away, the better to get a perspective on the whole picture.

Is the message just that I'm done with struggling, and that it's safe to rest now? Or that I should accept help when it's offered, even from a stranger? To be fair, I haven't been doing much of that the last few years.

Maybe it's just a weird dream, and I should stop trying to read things into it.[301]

We've had a few minor rainstorms, but I'm told they're nothing compared to what we'll get later: howling winds and driving rains that last for days sometimes. Sterre has had me working less, now that the greatest part of our work is done until the end of the season, but still there are dozens of errands to run, and contracts and papers to translate and deliver—I've seen the whole city now, all the corners and crannies. I've been to the palace, where the Council of Guilds meets

---

300 Fuck off.
301 What if you're not reading enough into it?

twice a week to make laws and rule the city, and I've been dancing a few times with Orfeo. We've walked along every canal and crossed every footbridge. Orfeo even took me to see his family's ship anchored in the harbor. We rowed out ourselves during a light drizzle and he showed me everything, from the figurehead to the captain's quarters and the orlop deck and the hold, everything lashed down solid or covered in tarps for the storms.

The tides have been rising higher, and the first king-tide arrived last night, peaking precisely at midnight when the moons, both new, were directly beneath our feet, visible on the other side of the world where it was noon, if I understand my astronomy correctly.

Just as *Mevrouw* Basisi said, we were quite dry. The water came right up out of the canal and spilled onto the streets, lapping an inch or two above the lip of some of the canals but no farther. I thought it would be terrifying, but it isn't—the water is filthy, of course, because this *is* a city of a hundred thousand people. But we have water-boots when we need to stamp about in the wet. I haven't needed to yet—I have three days off, by Sterre's command, with the rest of the clerks and workers in her offices, and that will be extended if a bad storm hits before the water's gone down. Orfeo couldn't leave either, so we've all been holed up together in the inn, quite cozy and comfortable. I catch him looking at me sometimes with a strange, thoughtful expression, but whenever I ask him about it, he gets very flustered and denies that he was doing anything of the sort.

There's one thing that's nagging at me, and that's the flowers. They're more expensive now than I or Sterre ever imagined they would be. Regardless of the increasingly inclement weather, the coffeehouses are filled with people buying and selling futures—there's hundreds of these contracts now, thousands. All the people who bought early are offering to sell their bulbs next season, when the plants can be safely uprooted and moved around.

I heard a rumor, a few days ago, of someone selling three bulbs for the price of a house. It's ... unbelievable. Sterre says that it's wonderful news, and that as soon as the ships come in a couple months from now, when the storms are over, we'll all be rich beyond our wildest dreams. She keeps promising me money. I don't really care about the money. After the auction, she gave me a small purse of gold, and all I did with it was dump it into the jar in my room where I keep the rest of my coin.

The flower in the pot in my room sprouted at some point. I haven't been up in the attic as much recently, because I've been spending so much time with Orfeo. The soil has to be kept extremely damp, so I bought a wide, shallow pan, four inches deep, and I fill that with water from the rain barrel by the kitchen door so the flower can drink all it likes and I only have to check on it once a week or so. I went up once to refill the pan, and the next time, five days later, there were four leaves and the stalk was already six inches high.

It's so strange to think that I could buy a third of a house with this one plant. I could go anywhere. I think that's why I keep taking care of it now. I could buy a cart like Mistress Chant's—ten carts, even. I could buy one of every instrument and lessons to learn them. I could set up as a merchant like Sterre or Orfeo's uncle. I could take the money and go somewhere remote and never do anything again—I could be like Zaria the fisherman, with a cottage halfway up a mountain, and I could sit on the edge of a cliff and tell stories to the wind.

And if I did that, I'd never feel anything again.

I'd never have to. Or ... I'd never get to. I'm still not sure which one of those is true, whether feelings are a burden or a treasure.

FORTY

First, a few days ago: Sterre called me into her office on some trivial matter; she wanted to crow to someone about an artist, someone she had been trying to hire to paint a still life featuring the stars-in-the-marsh, who had finally succumbed to her gold and guiles. But that's not the part I need to record.

"Whatever you're doing that's different than when you started with me," Sterre said to me as we sat on opposite sides of the desk, "you should keep doing it. It's doing you good. What are you up to? Eating better? Getting more sleep?"

"Both," I said, but I've always blushed easily, and she saw the color come into my cheeks.

"A lover, is it?" she asked, impish.

"Um, sort of," I said, clearing my throat.

She hummed and shuffled through some papers on her desk, sketches the artist had delivered earlier that day. "I'm glad to hear it," she said demurely. "As I said, it's doing you good. I can't imagine why you wouldn't confide in me such pleasant news.[302] Surely you didn't think I would object to you falling in with some nice . . ." Sterre eyed me up and down, and guessed, "*Mann?*" and I nodded.

---

302 Gods, she's terrible. Has she no concept of you as a private individual? Does she think you're friends?

"Right. A nice Heyrlandtsche *heerchen*, doing you a world of good—of course I'd be happy to hear such a thing. I hope it goes well."

"He's not Heyrlandtsche," I said. "And it's only temporary."

She paused, her brow furrowed. She sat forward. "What do you mean, not Heyrlandtsche? He lives here, doesn't he? That makes him Heyrlandtsche."

I shook my head. "Only visiting. He'll be leaving . . . sometime."

"Visiting. Pleasure or business?"

"Business. His family are merchants."

Her frown deepened. "A foreign merchant. Now, Chant, not that I don't trust you to know your business, but . . . Just be careful, all right? I know merchants better than anybody, and I know foreigners better than—" I gave her a pointed look. "Well, *almost* as well as you do, I suppose, now that I think about it."

"He's nice," I said. "We don't expect anything of each other."

"Don't let him be a distraction," she said sharply. I blinked at her—she'd been so warm a moment ago. "You have duties and obligations." I flinched. "I would hate to see you cast aside a promising career for the sake of some foreign boy that no one knows."

"He's going back to Pezia after the stormy season passes. He has duties and obligations too; his whole family is merchants, or . . . merchant-adjacent."

She paused again. "Pezia?"

"That's where they're from."

"A merchant family, you said?"

I blinked again. "Yes."

"From Pezia." She narrowed her eyes at me. "What did you say his name was?"

"I didn't," I said. She kept changing tacks so quick that I only wanted to dig in my heels and make the conversation as tedious for her as it was becoming for me.

She looked at me, expectantly, eyebrows raised. "Well?"

"Well what?"

"His name?"

"Whose name?"

"Your lover."

"Which one?"

"The *mann* from Pezia that you're fucking," she snarled. "His *name*."

"Orfeo."

"His *surname!*"

"Why do you ask?"

"Dammit, Chant!" she said, banging one hand on the table.

"Acampora," I said.

She sat back sharply in her chair. All the irritation had run out of her expression like snowmelt, and now she was once again warm and approving. "Orfeo *Acampora*. My goodness. Well done, you. Which one is he? I haven't met all of them. There was the one at van Vlymen's, but he was only an Acampora by marriage, hardly anyone to speak of. But this boy?"

"Simoneto's nephew," I said slowly, cautiously. She didn't need to know anything else, and it certainly wasn't my place to speak of Orfeo's troubles with his family.

"Hm. Young thing, then. Your age."

"Yes."

"Not married?"

The very thought! Orfeo's not the marrying type. "Definitely not."

"Hm," she said again, steepling her fingers. "Hm." I couldn't read her expression—it was still shifting from one emotion to the next, as if she was having a cascading debate with herself in her own mind.

"Do you mind if I go back to my desk?" I said, gesturing towards the door. "I have the Anagonye contracts to translate—"

"Not yet. Sit there; let me think."

So I sat there, and I let her think.

"How often do you see the Acampora boy?" she asked, nonchalant.

I shrugged. "Every day. We stay at the same inn."

Another long silence.

"Right," she said eventually, after nearly a full minute of silence. "Right. I'm hosting a party."

That was the first I'd heard of it. "In the middle of the stormy season?" I asked dubiously.

"Hardly the middle yet, is it? And really, what better time? It shall be a cozy little gathering of friends, perhaps fifty or so. Three days hence. At my country house." By this she meant the large villa she owns about an hour's ride from her offices, towards the edge of the city where it is less crowded and there is space for gardens—very near *Heer* van Vlymen's house, where we'd attended the salon. But none of this seemed to require my input, so I said nothing. "You'll attend, of course. I've already put in an order with van Vlymen for a few new outfits like the one you wore to Stroekshall. We can't have you appearing in the same thing twice." I glanced down at my usual ensemble of faded and threadbare secondhand clothes, which was one of only two sets that I own and which I have definitely worn to salons, the Rojkstraat, *and* her offices dozens and dozens of times, and still I said nothing. I could guess what was coming next, and in due course it did: "When you see the Acamporas tonight, I'll have you deliver an invitation." A smile slunk across her face. "If they try to decline, use your powers of persuasion. If they still decline, at least convince what's-his-name, the nephew. Surely you have wiles aplenty for him."

"You said you'd met some of them, though. Why not invite them yourself? Why does it fall to me?"

"Because I employ you and I'm directing you to do it," she said flatly. "All I have is an acquaintanceship—not even that. I was introduced to them once. Not enough of an excuse to invite them to my house. They're *Pezians*; you can't just walk up and introduce yourself to Pezians. They don't take it well at all. You always have to find a mutual connection to be a go-between. You're it, chickadee!"

"You want to do business with them."

"I *want* to get on their good side. Of course I do. They're one of the richest families in Pezia—they've got their fingers in everything, not just trade. Banking, politics. They could even give some of the Araşti a run for their money, if anyone could just figure out how those fucking *highway robbers* build ships that go that fast—they can even dodge the sea serpents in the breeding season, you know, that's how quick they are." She sighed and folded her hands on the desk. "The Acamporas could be powerful allies for us, Chant. You've already got one of them wrapped around your finger; knowing you, I'm sure the others are equally charmed."

"I've eaten dinner with them a couple times at the inn, that's all. They're friendly enough, but I wouldn't say they're *charmed*." Maybe Simoneto is—Orfeo keeps getting extra money from him to fund little outings with me. The rest of them just seem like they don't know exactly what to do with me. They know Orfeo and I have been sleeping together, so I suppose they must be wondering why he hasn't gotten skittish and run away yet. Orfeo was right—they really haven't noticed that he's changed. "I'm welcome at their table, but . . ."

"That's enough of a precedent! Invite them to a party—not for business, just as your guests."

"Surely it's strange for me to invite two dozen guests to a party that's not mine," I said.

She shrugged. "Bring as many as will come. Say that I gave you permission, and my hospitality is unbounded. I need them to attend. After that, I won't need your connection—I'll have one of my own. Business is business, after all, but one *can* be graceful about it."

So that was the premise.

I did as she asked. I spoke to Simoneto and I gave him the invitation card that one of Sterre's clerks had drawn up for her, and when I said that the party was to be held at the house of *Mevrol* de Waeyer, he quirked an eyebrow in interest. "Ah yes, your employer! The woman with a keen eye for flowers. When did you say this was? Three days from now?" I nodded, and his whole expression furrowed into thoughtful regret. "I'm terribly flattered at the invitation, of course, but our social calendars ... We're busy people, Chant," he said with a shrug.

"All of you?"

He laughed. "Young man, we don't come all the way from Pezia to sightsee, you know—well, not most of us. Ah!" He brightened. "There's a thought. Why don't you take that useless nephew of mine? He's really only with us for educational purposes and to look ornamental. And because he gets into trouble if he doesn't have at least five cousins holding him down at any given moment. That boy needs someone with a sensible head holding on to the back of his shirt-collar."

"*Mevrol* de Waeyer was very hopeful that at least a few of you might come to the party. . . ."

"No, no," Simoneto said, warming to his solution. "This will be good in many ways at once! Of course you want to look good to your employer; I can't blame you for that. So you'll have an Acampora on your arm to show for it—Orfeo's good at parties. A very sociable boy. Too sociable, at times. But you've already turned his head, so there's no need to worry about any youthful mischief or *escapades*. You strike me as a terribly sensible sort, even so—I daresay you could manage him if some dreadful whimsy seized him. So I can send him off by himself to get some practice at being useful. I'm assuming *Mevrol* de Waeyer has some interest in business discussions, yes?"

"My understanding is that it's to be more of a social function," I said faintly.

But Simoneto Acampora is a canny sort. He chuckled quietly into his beard in that way he had, eyes twinkling. "It's all a dance, my boy!" he said. "De Waeyer knows her steps. Very proper. Of course she wants to do business with us. But we really do have prior engagements this time. Give me this chance to toss my useless nephew into deep water and see how well he's learned how to swim. I'll be happy; you'll be happy; de Waeyer will be happy. Orfeo will grumble a little, but he'll do as he's told. And I daresay he won't turn down a chance to put on pretty clothes and squire *you* about."

• • •

Which brings me to . . . today. With Orfeo, at the party, wearing the latest uncomfortable costume that Sterre had bundled into my arms as soon as I stepped through her front door. It was made of that near-magical two-tone silk I'd spotted at the auction, an emerald green that flashed brilliant pink at certain angles, slashed and ruffled extravagantly, and laid over sheer butter-yellow cotton—*cotton!*[303]— the whole embroidered with gold.[304]

---

303 Good *gods*. For an *underlayer*? She really wasn't sparing expense, was she? If the gods truly loved me, you'd come straight back here because you'd accidentally forgotten something, and I'd have the chance to catch you and make you tell me what that felt like. Cotton, gods be merciful. I can only imagine. Even the King of Inacha doesn't have so much as a pair of drawers made of the stuff. Not even a handkerchief.
304 Green and gold, eh? Trying to flatter the Acamporas, was she?

I don't care to write it down, so I'll skip Sterre interrogating me about whether the Acamporas had accepted the invitation. I'll skip the part where she was exasperated with me when I said only Orfeo was going to come, and how she asked whether I had even tried to convince the others. She was frustrated, and I could tell, even though she tried to hide it. She's not really one to take things out on other people.

Of course she was polite to Orfeo, treating him as if he were the heir to the entire Acampora company, a young merchant prince. Orfeo was wildly flattered by the attention she paid him, how she introduced him to all the other guests and poured his wine by her own hand. He was giddy with it, which soothed my ruffled feathers and made me think the whole party might possibly have been worth it. I was happy to see him happy, at least.

For nearly two hours, Sterre made elegant conversation that didn't once touch on issues of business, walking Orfeo around the garden as I drifted silent a few steps behind them.

"Your garden is as lovely as I expected," Orfeo said. "I hear that you had quite the reputation for it, even before your recent success."

"I dabble," Sterre said, poorly feigning modesty.

"Are those the new flowers?" Orfeo nodded to a small ornamental pond that we had passed several times, which did indeed contain a dozen or two of the stars-in-the-marsh, clustered in bunches along the opposite shore. "Lovely."

"Lovelier at night, of course," Sterre said. "And terribly romantic. Perhaps you'd like to see them sometime—Chant would be delighted to bring you back to show you."

Orfeo quirked an eyebrow at me over his shoulder; he'd glanced back to watch me following them several times with an increasingly curious expression, probably wondering why I was hanging back.

This time was more . . . sardonic. It wasn't the first time Sterre had spoken for me. "I couldn't presume upon your hospitality."

"Nonsense, young man! Chant is like family to me." She kept talking about how we'd be more than welcome to wander through her gardens at any hour, but Orfeo's smile flickered.

He glanced back at me again, then gave Sterre a strange look that she entirely missed. "Ah, really? Like family—is that right, *Chant?*" He stopped and tucked his hands behind his back, turning to face me so Sterre was forced to do the same. That not-name on his lips still trickled over my skin like an unexpected handful of snow down the back of my collar. But I knew what he meant: Was she really like family if she was calling me Chant, not Ylfing?

I shrugged. I said nothing.

"Of course he is," she said, far too jolly to sound at all sincere, even to my ears. "He's very precious to me—I couldn't have had such success with the stars-in-the-marsh without him, you know."

Orfeo smiled faintly. His shoulders were set in a way I'd never seen before. "No, I don't expect you could have," he agreed.

"He's indispensable." Something in Orfeo's expression changed, like windows slammed closed. Sterre hadn't yet even looked at me, occupying herself instead with inspecting the budding fruit hanging from a small tree by the garden path. That hadn't escaped Orfeo's attention—he dropped back a few steps to stand directly beside me, nudging me with his elbow when Sterre wasn't looking. I shrugged again and dropped my eyes to the path.

"I'm glad you think so," Orfeo said. "My *uncle* had some very complimentary things to say about him after the auction. We were all very impressed with him."

Sterre paused and turned then, smiling. "Did he? How kind. I'm sure Chant has told you that we have some great plans for the future."

All at once, the Chanting parts of my brain clicked into motion. There was another conversation, a subtler one, happening beneath the one they were having with words—Sterre might as well have said, *Your uncle can go fuck himself; I've got dibs on this one.*

"Not at all." Orfeo's smile in return was brittle. "Chant isn't at all the type to betray a confidence. You're very right to trust him. I can assure you I've heard nothing about any plans, even ones that aren't secrets." *Do you really have plans? Not ones he cares about, or I'd know.*

"Oh, I wouldn't count it as a confidence," she said in a voice like sweet mead. "Perhaps he was keeping it to himself for his own reasons. You're right, though: he is very discreet. But of course one lets little things slip to a lover now and then, if one is fond of them." That hardly needed translation at all—she was nearly outright accusing him of being meaningless to me.[305]

Abruptly, I turned away and wove between the shrubs, off deeper into the garden—we were on the outskirts of the city, here, where owning a nice sweeping parcel of land was not as impossible as it would have been in the middle of town. Sterre's gardens were still limited, but more than generous by city standards.

There were stars-in-the-marsh everywhere, though. Sometimes it was just one or two tucked into a nook, a miniature swamp built into ornamental ceramic pots. I wondered how she ever managed to throw evening dinner parties; though the smell of the flowers is *markedly* fainter during the day than the miasma they give off at night, the whole garden still had a faintly sulfuric odor to it.

I found a bench, wedged between two of the miniature swamps and overhung by the curtaining cascades of a mature willow tree. I collapsed onto it, heedless of my silks and cottons, slouching because

---

305 Yep. Rude. Once again, what call does she have to be so possessive of you?

the stupid pants wouldn't even *let* me bend my legs, even at the cost of cutting off my circulation. I rubbed my hands over my face. The headache remained—it was one of those steady ones, not pounding, like there's something heavy pressing in on you.

I stayed there for I don't know how long—long enough that a few of the other guests started and finished a game of lawn-bowling on the other side of the garden. Long enough for Orfeo to come find me, swarming through the curtains of the willow, flushed and heaving with breath, his eyes blazing. "Are you all right?" he demanded.

"Me? Why wouldn't I be?"

"You ran off. After those *things* she was smirking about," he hissed, shooting a withering glare somewhere in Sterre's presumed direction.

I sighed and gestured expansively in a way that was meant to say, *Well, what can you do?*

Orfeo was not placated—he began to pace. "How dare she? Honestly, how *could* she?"

"I don't know," I said. "Did something else happen?"

"She doesn't think you're special," Orfeo said, in an entirely different voice.

"Of course she does. She does actually have a lot of plans for me. I think she . . . Well. She just has a certain way of communicating. You're from different backgrounds—of course you'd misunderstand each other."

"It's not misunderstanding, Ylfing, that's—she's an ass."

"It's nothing; that's just how she is sometimes."

He turned sharply to me, agape. "She talks to you like that all the time?"

"Not all the time. It's nothing. I don't *care*."

"I care!" Orfeo cried, and then froze, pink-cheeked and breathing unsteadily. He swallowed and looked away from me, clenching his jaw and his fists. "She shouldn't talk like that about you," he said, quieter but no less intense. "You're—you're incredible; you know that. What you did at Stroekshall and what you do every day for her. The way you are in front of people."

"Anyone could learn it," I said softly.

"No. No, they couldn't. You can't teach that." He flung himself onto the bench beside me. "You're responsible for her success. The flowers would have been a little pointless fad for gardeners and hobby botanists, and you made it something . . . bigger, and more beautiful, and important. That was you. No one else could have done it, not as quickly and certainly not as well." He took my hand. "If you don't care what she says about you, that's fine. But I do. It matters a lot to me that people know those things about you."

I blinked at him. "You're . . . more upset than I would have thought you'd be."

He bit his lip, ran his thumb over my knuckles. "It's just that you deserve better than that," he said, even more softly, barely more than a whisper. "With your knowledge and talent, you could—you could go anywhere, you know. Somewhere new."

"Yes, I know."

"Do you?" he asked. "*Do* you know? Do you know that Uncle Simoneto would snap you up in a heartbeat if he thought you were looking for work? Do you know he'd pay you whatever you asked?"

"Doing *what*?"

Orfeo's hand was a little clammy in mine. "Hell if I know, Ylfing. He'd find something for you. He'd *invent* something for you if he had to! He'd give you the best cabin on the ship home if that's what it took. He'd sleep in a hammock in the crew berths."

"Just to get me to come back to Pezia with all of you?"

"Yes. He knows you're brilliant. *Mevrol* de Waeyer thinks you're an asset—you could be an asset to Simoneto, too, and get better treatment. You could have your pick of positions in the business."

"Did he say so?"

"I know him. He would do it."

"But did he *say* so?"

"No. Not yet. Dammit, though, I know he would."

"You've been thinking about it?"

"I suppose I have."

"How long?"

"I don't know. A little while. Like I said, I think you deserve better—"

"But you didn't know how Sterre spoke to me until just now." He froze again. "You've been thinking about me coming back to Pezia, and it wasn't to do with Sterre at all."

He cleared his throat. "There would be a lot of opportunities for you in Pezia, if that's what you wanted, if you—"

"Orfeo." He flinched. "Are you all right?"

"Fine," he said. "Fine." Clearly he wasn't fine—still fidgeting, still restless as a child waiting for someone to catch them and scold them. He glanced warily at me, held my eyes for only a moment, and then all the air went out of him. He slumped against the back of the bench. "Do you think you . . . might want to?"

"Oh," I said, suddenly struck. "You *like* me. Is that what all your funny looks have been about recently?"

He fidgeted again. "Yes?" he said slowly. "Yes. Listen, I'm really sorry. I know I said this was going to be temporary—but then Uncle Simoneto liked you and you were getting along so well with the others, and I suppose I just got to thinking . . ." He glanced at me for just a moment, and I saw again that hopeful, hungry look that had dawned on his face the night I first met Simoneto. "I've never done this before. I don't know how to do this part with gentlemanly comportment."

I squeezed his hand. "I used to like almost everyone I met, so I've had a lot of practice. You're doing fine so far."

"It just sort of . . . occurred to me," he said, still not meeting my eyes for more than a heartbeat. "I just realized that it might be nice. I never really saw the benefits of . . . you know. All that. Liking someone, really liking them, enough to bring them home, enough to do that whole . . . 'I'm yours and you are mine' thing. But you're . . . you. And I saw the way you talked with Uncle Simoneto, and all of a sudden I realized how much better my life could be if you were in it." He winced. "I've just been . . . hoping? Wondering? If you might give me the opportunity to convince you that—look, I'm sorry, I *know* we had an understanding that this was temporary and that we'd both mind our own hearts, and I thought that wouldn't be a problem for me, because it never has been in the past. And I realize I'm doing the thing that I've always hated other people doing; I'm changing my mind and wanting something else, something that wasn't discussed before, and I'm *sorry*, but once I thought of it, I couldn't stop thinking about it. And I realize, I *do* realize that you're too good for me; I know that. Everyone knows it. So I guess I'm just asking you—begging, really; let's be honest, I'm begging—to give me the chance to convince you that I could be agreeable, because frankly I'm desperate."

My heart skipped several beats during this tirade, and by the time he finally fell silent, I was gripping his hand tight. I don't even think I was breathing.

"Don't decide anything now," Orfeo said when I didn't manage to come up with any words. "Please. Think about it. All I want is a chance. I don't get many of them these days and—and this is probably the last chance anyone would give me, the very, *very* last one."

"I—I don't know," I heard myself saying. I stammered some other nonsense, fragments and shards, trying to articulate what I meant, and I still don't know what I meant, but Orfeo—

"Okay," he said. He was trembling, and his grip was tight in mine, but he nodded without looking at me. "Okay. You don't have to know. I'm not going anywhere yet. I'll—" His voice cracked. "I'll leave it to you to bring it up if you want to ... say anything." And then he took a deep breath, and let go of my hand, and stood up with a diplomat's smile, a smile full of those benign small false-hoods we link together into chain mail for our hearts: *Of course I'm fine. Why wouldn't I be fine? This is not a situation that causes me strife in the slightest. I am certain. I am fine.* "I'd very much like to go home now, I think. Are you coming, or do you have other things to—"

"I'm coming," I said, standing. "Yes, I'm coming." My mouth was dry and my hand was empty, and it ached from gripping his so tightly, and it ached too for the lack of that grip now. I flexed it at my side, longing to reach out to him, longing for something solid to steady myself against, and was terribly, terribly unsure whether such a touch would be welcome.

There was a hired carriage waiting in front of the house, some-thing fine but impersonal, which Simoneto had allotted funds for—even a minor scion must be delivered to a potential business interest in fine style.

Orfeo and I sat on opposite sides of the carriage in silence and the gathering dusk, listening as the faint patter of rain began again. There was a whole hour that we could have filled with talk, but nei-ther of us said a word. I could have slipped over to his bench and laid my head on his shoulder, or coaxed his down to lie on mine; I could have kissed his forehead and twined my fingers in the soft curls at the nape of his neck. I could have told him—anything. I could have explained what was happening under the surface of me, all the thoughts wriggling like fish down in the murky depths.

He spoke again only when we reached the inn, lingering in the carriage with his hand on the door. "I want to ask you what you want," he said. "About a different matter."

"Oh?" I managed, faintly.

"It's to do with *Mevrol* de Waeyer." His voice was calm and collected now. "I wanted to ask you whether you'd like the Acampora syndicate to reciprocate her overture of interest towards us. If you want us to do business with her."

"Whether *I* would want?" I said. "What do my wants have to do with that?"

He met my eyes then—the carriage had come to a halt beneath the two trees at the innyard's gate, and there was just enough of a glow from the dozens of hanging lanterns to see him by, or at least the outlines of his features, softly limned in candlelight. He said nothing, merely waited.

"I won't get in trouble if you don't," I said. "It's nothing to do with me, and she knows it. If that's what you're worried about."

Silence. Calm, quiet, waiting.

"Why did you say it that way?" I demanded suddenly. "What I *want*. Why not ask what I think?"

"Because whatever you want, I'm going to do," Orfeo said in a low voice, and I fell still. He'd had the whole hour to think just as much as I had, and . . . I think he must have made a better use of it than I did. "Say you want us to pursue this, and I'll go inside and tell Uncle Simoneto that she's a ruthless snake and we'd benefit from an alliance with her, and that you agree."

"Will he listen to you?"

"He'd listen to the both of us, if we had an accord on this matter."

"I can't take responsibility for—for this. I don't know anything about your business, or what would be good for it. I can't. I don't want it."

Orfeo nodded slowly. "Are you saying you have no preference?"

"Yes," I said with great relief. "Exactly."

He nodded again. "Then I'm going to go inside and tell Uncle Simoneto that she's a ruthless snake and I don't like how she speaks about you, and I'll leave it up to him. But I'd wager he won't have anything to do with her."

"That doesn't make any sense," I said desperately. The coach driver knocked impatiently on the roof. "Come on, get out," I said, and Orfeo flung the door open and leapt out with more furious, focused energy than I had expected to see. He turned back sharply on his heel and offered his hand to help me alight. I'd already clambered halfway out myself, and I could have jumped out just as easily as he had, but the tight knot of worry in my stomach eased abruptly at the chance to take Orfeo's hand again, to make this whole unspoken mess a little more right, a little more sensible, with just that one little thing—a hand offered at the right moment.

I remembered the stranger in the boat from my dream, taking my hand, pulling me out of the water. Maybe that was the message.

So I took Orfeo's hand and stepped down, and got my fingers laced tight and stubborn into his before he could pull away again.

"It makes plenty of sense," Orfeo said, flipping a coin—a full guilder, I saw, as it sparkled in the lantern light—to the carriage driver. "In entirely mercenary terms, you're an investment. She doesn't treat her investment well. Therefore, she's not as good of a businessperson as she pretends she is, and we ought to be careful about climbing into bed with her. Uncle will see that immediately." He turned towards the inn, paused, and turned again, facing me, our hands still clasped. "You're going to go up to the attic and write before you sleep, aren't you?"

"Yes?" I said faintly. I generally do—either before I slink into Orfeo's room in the full dark and crawl under the covers, or after we've tumbled into bed together, returning much later, when I've made sense of myself again.

He nodded sharply. "You're welcome to join me. You're always welcome. I'd like you to know that." And then, the barest hesitation. "And if you'd rather not, tonight, I understand."

I had to step forward then, had to lay my other hand against his cheek and crowd him back against one of the trees to kiss him. "I'd rather yes," I said, *brilliantly* eloquent, between kisses. "I—Orfeo, I—" I wrapped both arms around him and shoved my face against his neck because it was easier to say the next part that way. "Before. Earlier. What you said. I just need to think."

"Yes, I expect so," he said, more wooden than I like to hear from someone I've just kissed. "Take your time."

I wanted to give him some reassurance, some kind of promise. I could only kiss him again, cupping his face in both my hands, and then he went to Simoneto, and I went up here to the attic and . . .

And that was everything. That was all of it.

Might as well do the brave thing and make it all real by putting it on paper. Might as well continue in the way I've begun:

He has feelings for me, and he wants me to go to Pezia. He thinks I could work for his family, which means he's thinking long-term. He talked about Simoneto listening to both of us, if we had an accord.

Shipwreck! Gods and fishes! Shuggwa's Eye ever-watchful! I think that's what he's getting at, isn't it? All this talk of *accords* and meeting his family and all—I just wrote earlier that he's not the marrying type, and yet here we are.

So now I get to stare at myself and wonder what sort of type *I* am. I've never gotten much of a chance to find out.

———— •◦• ————

After an hour or three of pacing, I went down to Orfeo's room. I wasn't making any progress all on my own, just circling and circling in my own head until I was mad with it.

I didn't bring a candle; it was late and he was already asleep. I climbed into the bed without undressing, kneeling by him on top of the covers in the dark. "Orfeo," I said, and kissed the corner of his mouth. He stirred and made a soft noise. "You're serious about—what you said?"

"Mmm? Yes," he mumbled.

"You want to marry me?"

He made another soft sleep sound and burrowed into the pillows. "Ideally. It'd be best."

I sat back on my heels. "Huh."

He squirmed onto his back, and the blankets moved as he untangled his hands from beneath them. "What time is it?" he groaned.

"A ridiculous hour," I said absently.

"You've been awake?"

"You didn't hear me above?"

He yawned. "Heard your pen-scratching for a long time." He paused, then added in a much more awake voice. "Lots of thoughts today, I guess. I fell asleep before you were done."

"Why do you want this?"

"Told you that already. More interested in what you want, though." He pushed himself up and reached out, his hand knocking into my knee, then my elbow, before trailing down to take my hand. When he spoke again, his voice was lower, beguiling. "I had an idea in the carriage of what I mean to do."

"What's that?"

"Give you everything you want." He pulled me forward slowly, got his other hand into my hair, and kissed me until I was dizzy with it. "There's stories to be found in Pezia," he said against my throat. "There's knowledge, and secrets. You've never been there. You haven't learned that language yet. I'd teach it to you. Like this—" He pulled me closer still, until he was breathing my breath, tracing his fingers across my face. "*Baciami ancora.* Kiss me again."

I did, helplessly. "I don't know what I want," I said into his mouth. "You can't give me everything I want if I don't even know it myself."

"You'll think of something." He pulled me again, tipping back into the pillows. "And if it's in my power, it's yours."

I resisted, didn't let him tug me all the way over with him. "I don't know if I can do it. Go with you, be with you like that. I don't know if I . . ." The words stuck in my throat.

"I'm not asking you to do it." He ran his hands down my back and sides with long strokes, like he was gentling a horse. "I'm just asking you to think about it and allow me to make my arguments. Allow me to prove you could be happy. That I could make you happy." I fell slowly into the pillows next to him, and he curled himself around me, tweaking at the fastenings of my clothes and kissing me, and kissing me, and kissing me. "Anyway, I know one thing you want," he said, and I was expecting something entirely different, but his manner softened and mellowed. His thumb rubbed along the line of my jaw, and he followed it with ghost-light, dry brushes of his lips. "Ylfing. Ylfing. Ylfing." Another kiss to my mouth, then, as warm as a hearthfire on a winter night. "Ylfing," he whispered. "Ylfing, Ylfing, Ylfing." And I could, again, almost feel my name being written back into my skin.

FORTY-ONE

The storms have come as they were expected to, and the city has settled in to wait them out. The Heyrlandtsche live so close to the sea, and there is so much commerce that comes in that way. Even with the dikes around the city, they are still subject, to some extent, to the rise and fall of the tides and the stubborn persistence of water.

I was not expected at Sterre's today, so this morning I borrowed a pair of water-boots from the inn-mistress and walked all the way out to the Rojkstraat. There were no market stalls set up, and most of the shops around the perimeter were closed too, due to the inch or two of water covering the cobblestones. People don't like walking through it, *Mevrouw* Basisi had told me—people might not, but I do. I like seeing the sky reflected on the street. I like the way the footbridges rise up above the water like lazy, breaching dolphins. I like the feeling of approaching the bridge, sloshing through the water, and climbing the slope, and then pausing at the peak of it with water streaming from my boots, and then descending the other side again. I like watching the ripples dancing out from my feet.

The only place open on the Rojkstraat was the coffeehouse, and it was busier than I expected for so early on a wet morning like this. I ducked inside, shaking the water off my boots on the threshold, and craned my neck to see over the loose crowd inside.

At the door, a burly *mann* with a great bushy beard and hairy arms, who had watched me shake the water off my shoes, held up his hand to stop me. "Weapons."

"I don't have any." I really didn't. Not even my personal knife; it wasn't that useful in the city, and I was tired of having to stop to give it to someone every time I entered a public building and then collect it again when I left.

"Bullshit."

"Check me," I said, holding my arms out to the sides. "I've got nothing."

He patted me down, sticking his fingers down my shoes to check for hidden blades, and finally grunted. "Fine, in you go." He also handed me a towel to dry off my boots with, which I suppose is quite the usual thing during the king-tide and the rainy season.

The air was thick with pipe smoke. Almost all the native Hey-rlandtsche of the more would-be artistic set smoke constantly, to-bacco from Tash or Zebida in long thin pipes made of porcelain or silver or wood, depending on their wealth. Some, who do not care for the taste or smell, still carry around an empty pipe as an aesthetic grace note. People in Sterre's circles, those so wealthy they have no need to be pretentious, consider it an unbecoming habit—Sterre herself has forbidden her employees to smoke within her offices or warehouses, or when making deliveries to her clients and customers.

The air was hazy and dim, and the pictures on the walls were yellowed. "What's going on?" I asked the *mann* at the door.

"Business as usual," he said. "Lots of folk here today to sell those flowers that everyone's going crazy for."

It wasn't an auction, not quite—there was no scrambling and fighting to make bids. Looking through the coffeehouse, I just saw serious, quiet people sitting at tables and talking in low voices. They'd pair off—sellers and buyers, I assume—and they'd each write a number on a little strip of paper. Then they'd call two other people over, hand them the number they'd written down, and the other two would retire into some dim dusty corner and compare the numbers they had.

The original buyer and seller sat quiet at their table, not even really looking at each other. One *vroleisch* I watched pulled some knitting out of her bag and entirely occupied herself, with no regard whatsoever, it seemed, for the person sitting across the table from her. At length, the two negotiators would come back with the price they had agreed to compromise on, and the buyer and seller looked at it quietly and then paid, or didn't.

Very strange.

I crammed myself into a rickety chair very near the door and watched the dance of negotiations happen. "Are they selling well?" I asked the guard.

"Well enough, I'd guess. One bulb went for eight hundred and fifty guilders earlier today."

It was inevitable, I suppose, that someone would recognize me. A *vrouw* at one of the tables took her pipe from her mouth and blew a stream of smoke to the side, studying me. I ducked my head politely to her, and she got up, pushing with one hand on the table to help herself to her feet, and came over. "I know you, don't I?" she said.

I glanced around the room. "Have you bought stars-in-the-marsh recently?"

"Yes. Yes! That's where I know you from—you're that young man who's brought all this to our attention, aren't you?"

"The same," I said. "Call me Chant."

"*Mevrouw* Katheline Valck. Do you smoke, *Heer* Chant?"

"Thank you, but no."

"You must come with me anyway," she said languidly, taking another slow puff from her pipe. "Come sit at my table."

I had no reason to refuse, so I followed her and settled myself between two people. She introduced me around the table, and everyone greeted me warmly.

"Crispin was just telling us about his flowers," she said. "Some very exciting new developments."

"The flowers until now," Crispin said. "We've always thought they were that wintry blue-white color, haven't we? All of them." A murmur of agreement went around the table. He leaned in and lowered his voice. "But they're not. There are"—he dropped his voice—"*variants.*"

Katheline raised her eyebrow, lowered her pipe. "Have you one of these variants?"

He nodded. "It bloomed in my garden just last night. It's the color of white gold, with delicate crinkling edges to the petals. And," he said, lowering his voice even more. "Less of a smell."

"You don't say," said one of the other *vrouwen*, Sabien, immediately interested. "How fascinating."

"It's quite beautiful," he said. "I'm hoping to sell it for a handsome sum. Something so rare should belong to someone who truly treasures it, not just a simple hobbyist like me."

"I've never heard of variants," I said. "But I suppose it happens."

He nodded enthusiastically. "Consider lilies—I once had a garden of sunshine-yellow lilies, and one year, a new shoot came up and bloomed maiden's-blush pink. Quite a surprise. That's one of the reasons I love gardening so much," he said, in a sweeping and grandiose tone, and his companions groaned.

"Do shut up," Katheline said. "Don't start on that again."

"You never know what's going to happen," he continued stubbornly.

"Please stop."

"Sometimes you plant blue hyacinths and they come up white."

"Crispin, seriously."

"Sometimes your cherry blossoms get frozen off and the whole crop is ruined."

"I'm sorry," Katheline said to me. "I'm sorry for my idiot friend."

"The point is!" he cried. "The point is, you never know what's going to happen. It's always a surprise."

Fortunately I managed to escape soon after that, but . . . Variants. I really have never heard of them before, and Sterre has never mentioned them—and she would have, if she'd known. She would have seen the potential value. I wonder how we two have never known about something like that.

FORTY-TWO

Sterre's offices again today. There is not much to do. The stormy season makes things slow, and the lashings of rain against the windowpanes today made us all lazy and sleepy. "Sterre," I said, "has anyone told you about variations in their flowers?"

"Eh? In the stars-in-the-marsh, or are we talking general flowers?"

"Stars-in-the-marsh," I said. "I was at that coffeehouse on the Rojkstraat yesterday, and I met someone. His flowers bloomed, and one was different."

"Well, that happens from time to time." She yawned. "What's the odd one look like?"

"White-gold, he said, with crinkly edges to the petals."

"Oh?" she said. I thought she sounded strange. I looked over, and she was sitting at her desk, very still, a peculiar expression on her face.

"He wasn't upset about it," I said, in case that's what she was worried about. "He thought it was pretty. He said he could probably sell it for a lot of money."

"He probably could," she said. She was suddenly very occupied with the papers on her desk. "Did you get his name, by any chance?"

"Crispin—I didn't get a surname. Big man. Heyrlandtsche in his accent and manner, but Sdeshe by blood, or so I'd guess."

"No, I wouldn't doubt you on those judgments at all," she said. "Hm. I think I'd like to find him. And visit him."

"Are you going to buy the flower?"

Sterre paused and looked at me. She looked around the room, at the clerks making their way through the paperwork, and gestured me inside her office. I followed, confused. "Shut the door, Chant," she said, and I did. "I can trust you, can't I?"[306]

"Yes," I said, surprised. "What's going on?"

She tapped her fingers against the table. "You'll keep something discreet, won't you?"

"Yes."

She got up and tucked her hands behind her, pacing slowly back and forth behind her desk. "You'll keep a *secret*."

"Sterre, what's the matter?"

"When I was in Kaskinen, buying that first shipment last year, I was asking all about them—care and keeping and so forth. They told me that they're good, hardy plants; they can survive nearly anything as long as you keep their roots drowned. They warned me about something, though." She cleared her throat. "They said that every decade or so . . . It's like a sickness. A plague. And it sweeps through the marsh, and it kills off most of the flowers."

I've never seen a plague. Gods willing, I never will. But I've heard of them. I've seen the aftermath—crops rotting in the field, starvation.[307] "It can't hurt people, can it?"

---

306 That's always a red flag. She might trust you, but you shouldn't trust her.

307 Yes. People die and their bodies rot where they fall, sometimes, because there's not enough others left alive to tend to them. If a plague strikes anywhere near you, just leave. Just get out. Because when people start dying, then everyone else is going to look for someone to blame. "Who brought the plague?" they'll ask. "Someone had to bring it. Perhaps it was that stranger who just came to town." That's the best kind of scapegoat, you know. Someone they can murder with no guilt or consequences. It doesn't even matter if the foreigner is barely older than a child. Plagues make people crazy; ask me how I know.

"No. No, it's just the plants." She took a deep breath. "They told me what signs to watch for—that the flowers go yellow, and the edges of their petals wrinkle, and then black speckles come up from the base of the stalk and spread over the flower itself."

I took a breath. "He didn't say that had happened. He didn't mention black speckles at all."

"But the yellowing, the petals' mutation." Sterre leaned on the desk with both hands. "I need to find out, discreetly, where he bought his root. If he bought it from me, or if somebody else happened to smuggle in a few of these."

"Why?"

"Because if he bought it from me, then when all his flowers die, he'll come for my blood," she snapped. "If I sold him a defective prod-uct, if I'm responsible for him losing a *fortune* . . . I have my reputation to think of, Chant. Reputation is everything. People know me. They know I'm reliable. They know they can lend me money because I'll pay it back, and they know that I'm careful about who I lend money to in turn. They know the quality of my products."

"So if it's diseased, let's just go to him and buy it back. We can destroy it and nobody will know."

She gave me a haunted, hunted look. "Maybe. It spreads through the water. I daresay if he has any others, they've already caught it too. We'll have to buy all his flowers, just to be safe. We'll isolate them and destroy them. If we're lucky, maybe it won't spread. Maybe it's just the flowers in his garden that have it. . . . If he planted them in pots, or if his garden is on a bit of high ground, then it's simple. But . . ." She glanced out the window. "Considering the state of things, that's more than I want to waste hope on."

The water. I looked outside too, looked at the lashings of rain, and gulped.

Nearly the entire city is covered in an inch of water, and the comings and goings of the tides, plus the city's system of artificial currents, mean that it *moves* instead of staying stagnant—the dikes keep the tides mostly repressed, but they still rise and fall a few inches. Not only that, but people water their gardens from the canals, if they're not already flooded.

Just one infected flower in Crispin's garden, and it can spread all across the city.

"What should we do?" I said. "If his flowers aren't isolated, what should we do?"

She breathed. "Nothing. We can do nothing. Nobody knows about the disease but us—we'll say that it happened because of the tides.[308] Yes. The water is filthy. Everyone knows you don't drink from the canals, you don't swim in them. You don't use the water for cooking until it's been cleaned and filtered." Which is true—each neighborhood has a great cistern of water, pumped up from the canals or collected in rain barrels. First, they skim any debris from the top and let any sediment settle to the bottom, and then they run it into the cisterns, where it filters down through layers of gravel and sand and charcoal, until clean, crystalline water trickles from the bottom into troughs. "We'll say the flowers need clean water, and we'll blame the disease on the king-tide and the rains." She nodded firmly. "That will save us."

"But . . . what about everyone else?"

"Everyone who?"

"The people who own flowers. The people who have been buying and selling. They're so *expensive* now."

"Bad luck," Sterre said, shrugging.

---

308 She deserved everything she got.

"But the people who sold futures—if their flowers die, they'll have to break their contracts. They'll lose all the money they invested. Some people will be ruined."

"Not that many," Sterre said. "Hardly anyone bet their whole fortune on them."

"How can you know that?"

She shrugged again. "They took a risk. That's what investment is about. It's not like everyone in the city has one, anyway. Only a few hundred, a thousand."

"We've imported more than *ten thousand*," I said. "And they were cheap when you started. Do you keep records of all your customers?"

"Of course not. There's a hundred thousand people in the city, Chant. And most people who bought stars-in-the-marsh bought more than one."

"You're fine with them losing money because *you* brought a sick plant in?"

"I had no way of knowing it carried the disease! I'm not morally responsible for this."

"But your reputation—"

"Yes. My *reputation* would suffer, because people are stupid and they'll want someone to blame. It's not fair, but that's how it is. I haven't done anything wrong, per se. *I* didn't poison the plants."

"I don't think it's right."

Sterre sighed and rubbed her forehead. "To be honest, Chant, I don't really care whether you think it's right. But you *must* keep this a secret. You promised you would. You *promised*."

I had promised. But I was so . . . angry. I was full to bursting with this scrambling, thorny rage, except it wasn't quite directed at *her*. At least, not solely at her. I sat there, breathing, and I kept thinking, *She's abandoning them, she's leaving them all behind, she's made them throw away something precious with a promise that they'd get something even more infinitely rare and precious and extraordinary in return, and now she's leaving them there all alone by a rotting pig trough in the middle of nowhere, just like* he *did, just like Chant did to me, and she doesn't care if it all withers up into nothing, she doesn't care, she doesn't care, she's just like him and she doesn't care—*

She's making me abandon them too.

"I'll keep it a secret," I said, trembling. "But I need to leave. I need to go home for the day. I—I just need to think."

"Fine," she said, flicking her hand at me. "Go. There's nothing for you to do here anyway. Until the rains stop, we're just shopkeepers."

I walked out of her office without another word. I switched out my thin lambskin slippers in the vestibule for tall water-boots, and wrapped my oilcloth cloak around my shoulders, and lifted the hood. I was shaking. I could barely keep my knees from giving out under me. I felt sick, and all I could think was: *Just like him, just like what we did in Nuryevet, except this time she can't even tell a story to convince me she did it to save someone. Just like him, and she's ruined everything, and now she's turning away.*

There's a trick to walking through Heyrland in the rainy season during high tide. The water was ankle-height on my way home. When the rains pause and the water is still, you can see the edges of the street. When the sun is out, it's even easier—you can tell how close you are to the edge by the temperature of the water through your shoes. In the shallows, the water is sun-warmed; the closer you get to the canal's edge, the cooler it is, as the currents bring up colder water from the darker, deeper layers below.

In the rain, all that's impossible. It's all cold, and the uneven surface doesn't let you see anything beneath it. I've walked back and forth from the inn to Sterre's offices dozens and dozens of times, and I know the way and most of the odd characteristics of the path. The best thing to do, the easy thing, is to stick near the houses where you can be sure there's solid ground, and almost every bridge in the city is arched, so that boats coming through the canals can slip beneath them. But there's a few difficult areas—a public square that I have to cross that is bisected by a canal with a flat footbridge that I can never quite find on the first try when the water is like this.

Sometimes I and other people in Heyrland carry sticks with us that we can use to tap the ground ahead when it's obscured, to make sure that we're not about to trip in a pothole or come unexpectedly to the edge of a canal, or fall into some stairwell that usually leads down from the street level to the water level—the same sticks that the blind use all year round. I had no stick with me today, so I wrapped my oil-cloth tight around me and pulled the hood low over my face and felt out my way with my feet, step by step. It was very slow.

I didn't mind. It gave me time to think.

My sick feeling was overcome by a rising tide of fury. I let my anger grow and surge and batter at the walls of my head like the waves crashing on the dikes. *Leaving them,* I thought, *leaving them, leaving them, leaving them.*

It doesn't fucking matter how I feel about audiences; it doesn't matter if they're baying for my blood or snapping at my heart like hungry wolves. You don't just leave someone behind when they need help.

I can't do that again. I can't let it happen right in front of my eyes.

———◆◆◆———

Fuck you, Chant. Fuck you for leaving me behind, fuck you for leaving Nuryevet behind after you'd sold them out to save your own miserable neck.

I'd curse you in Xerecci here, Chant, I'd say *go to the desert,* and mean it with all the venom I could muster, but you loved the desert; you loved the warmth. So: To the ice fields with you. To the top of the tallest, coldest mountain with you. Wherever you are, I hope you *freeze*.

You left me because I stopped loving you. Isn't that right? You used to puff yourself up like a smug little bird when I admired something you did, and after Nuryevet, I stopped. After Nuryevet, I could only see a man who thought his life was worth more than other people's.

I *saw* you. I saw through all your lies and your veils and your smokescreens and your thin little excuses. And you couldn't stand it, couldn't stand watching me watch you every day, couldn't live with yourself while I was standing next to you and *grieving* for what you'd—we'd—done. You ran away from Nuryevet, and then you ran away from me to escape what you'd done, to escape your guilt, because you weren't strong enough to take it, not years and years of it, not long enough to see me to the end of my apprenticeship as it should have been.

Isn't that right? *Isn't it right?* Come the fuck back here and *admit* it, you monster, you coward, you weakhatefulhorriblecruelselfishconnivingpoisonousBASTARD.

But I'm never going to know if that's right. To the coldest, darkest hell with you. *I hope that you freeze.*

Sterre may have held the money, but I was the one with the power. I was the one who put a story to the flowers and made them valuable—I was the one who convinced people that the flowers were some kind of miracle, that buying a flower would *fix* something that was broken about their lives. I was the one who convinced them that there *was* something broken in the first place! And I hadn't thought about what I was doing. I hadn't known any better, and I *should* have. I'm a Chant, trained and sworn. I sank my homeland beneath the waves and unnamed myself. I should have known better. I should have thought about it, and instead I . . .

Is it any excuse? I was drifting at the time; I'd lost myself. I had lost my connection to the world, to the people, to Chanting. Surely that has to count for something? Surely that has to explain, at least, why I could be so stupid and so blind, even when Mistress Chant was practically shouting in my face to warn me off it. She knew. I should have known already, or I should have listened. I shouldn't have made excuses for Sterre just because she was giving me a place to belong and—and making me feel like she'd scooped me up from the roadside where I'd been abandoned.

No excuses now. No room for them. I'm responsible for the people around me, and for the power I wield.[309]

Stories are powerful. Stories are arrows and swords. Written down, they become a copy of a mind. These words right now, on the pages under my hands—what am I doing with them? What power have I put into this? Is it safe? Is it right? How am I to know, when half of a Chant's purpose is to embrace the possibility of new knowledge lying just over the horizon? How could I ever know if this is right, when I might be proven and disproven a thousand times?[310]

And the words I put into the world, the stories I told in the Rojkstraat and the salons—it's too late for those. I was irresponsible.

I don't know what to do.

---

309 Yes. Yes! At last. Good!
310 Exactly. You can't know. Once you write it down and let it out of your hands, you might as well be dead. You have no control over where it goes, or who reads it, or when, or how.

I had all these thoughts when I was in Gradenheelt Square, wet and cold and trying to find the bridge, and I still haven't found any answers hours later.

There's one person I could talk to. There's Orfeo. Orfeo knows about merchant things, and I've told him all about Chant things. Orfeo's *good*. He's so full of goodness—he found out that he was doing harm without meaning to, so he stopped, and he's learning to do better. He's making an effort; he's trying to think more about other people; he's caring and respectful. He tries so hard to be better than he is. And he loves me. He wants to keep me. He's going to give me everything I want, and if all I want is my name, he'll keep writing it back into my skin until it's mine again. He'd give me his own name if he could.

(Oh . . . Except he could. He *could*: Ylfing Acampora. Fuck, my heart's racing.)

(Later. Think of it later. Think of it, bask in it, ache for it later. It's a thought that deserves more consideration than what I can give it when I'm this angry.)

———◆———

To tell Orfeo what's going on, I'd have to break my promise to Sterre.

. . .

Or would I?

FORTY-THREE

The Story I Told to Orfeo Just Now, When I Sat Him Down and Said I Had a Hypothetical Question

A very long time ago and half the world away, there was a baker. He made the best bread in all the city, and everyone bought lots of it and ate it, and it was delicious and nourishing and good. He had all kinds of bread, but the most favorite kind was a rosemary-olive loaf. One day he found that the olive barrel in his pantry had spoiled several days previously. He knew that everyone who had bought his bread in the last few days would get sick, and he decided to keep it secret.

Was that bad of him?

FORTY-FOUR

Orfeo's Answer

Well yes," said Orfeo. "Was that the whole hypothetical question?"

"Think about it, though. It wasn't his fault the olives went bad, right?"

"Probably not."

"What if he'd left the lid off, and mice or maggots got in? So there was an element of carelessness involved?"

"Then it's his fault, yes. A baker should take care with their ingredients. If a carpenter left his chisel out in the rain and it rusted, that would be his fault too."

"But he made and sold the bread before he noticed that the olives had gone bad. Is *that* his fault?"

Orfeo tilted his head slowly back and forth, uncertain. "Yes," he said at last, slowly. "Because he should have been paying attention. He should have been more careful."

I relaxed all over and released the breath I'd been holding. "All right. Yes. Good."

Orfeo left his head tilted to one side, smiling a little at me. "So what's the ending? What happens to the careless baker?"

I fidgeted. "I'm still trying to figure that out."

Orfeo gave me a strange look. "I thought you said Chants don't make up stories."

"We don't. We only carry them and pass them along. They're not ours to mess with."

"So what's this about?"

I took a breath. "There's something I'm trying to figure out, and I promised someone I wouldn't talk about it, but I needed to. I needed to say it aloud to understand it. And you . . . I trust your moral compass. You *think* about how to be good."

He propped his chin on one hand and grinned. "That's sweet. Thank you. Did I help?"

"I still don't know what to do, but . . ." I looked away.

Orfeo caught my hands in his and kissed my knuckles. "Do you want to keep talking about it?"

"Maybe later." I sighed. "I'm sorry. I'm not going to be very good company today."

"You don't have to be anything except you."

"Yes," I said. "That's rather the problem. I'm still figuring that out too. Still. I'm sorry, I know you thought I was all finished and fine."

"You're getting better, though."

"Am I?"

"You're in the middle of it all, so you can't tell, but you're getting close to the end. Then there will be something new on the other side." He rubbed his thumb across my wrist.

"How can *you* tell?"

"Because you don't have nightmares anymore," he said simply.

I stared at him. I'd never mentioned the dreams to him, not once. Not *once*.

He squeezed my hands. "You've slept in my bed every night for weeks," he said. "I notice these things. You used to wake up a couple times every night, flailing in the sheets like you were drowning."

"You never said anything," I said faintly.

He shrugged. "I was waiting for you to . . . reach for me, I suppose. Or to wake me and ask for comfort. I didn't want you to think you'd troubled me, because you hadn't. But you never asked; you never reached. You always just breathed for a few minutes and then curled up in a little ball all by yourself on the other side of the bed, so I thought you might not want to be touched, or that it might embarrass you. And then eventually, the nightmares seemed to stop, because you were sleeping through the night most of the time."

Not . . . stopped. But changed. I'm still dreaming of the marsh every night, of sitting silently in the boat with the figure and the cormorant. None of us makes a sound; there's not even a breeze to rustle the stars-in-the-marsh around us. But the sky above has pinpricks of stars now, and the cloudy spiral of the Eye of Shuggwa has grown much clearer.[311]

---

311 But how? Why? Why is this happening? Magic comes primarily from the earth and water, you know that—you've talked about the Hrefni runes that stop working when you go too far away from the land. And magic comes, rarely, from the heavens—which you might not know in your head, but you told the story of the Trout of Perfect Hindsight gaining his power from a chip of heaven-stone, and I daresay you have other stories with similar patterns. So what's happening here? It doesn't make any sense—what pieces of Shuggwa that came from Arthwend with the ancient Chants faded to a ghost of what he once was by the time they settled in Kaskinen, and never reached any farther. You could make a map of his reach, almost, if you had enough time and enough information. For every new tale of Shuggwa or Skukua, you could mark on a map a dot of ink or a pin for where you collected it, and they'd all be clustered in Kaskinen and the Issili Islands. And then, here, something new wildly far afield, an outlier. And it's too consistent to be merely a dream, and you haven't invented it from your own head, because there's all the symbols that you apparently don't know, or else you would have recognized them and identified him by now. So what is it? And how can it possibly be?

"And," Orfeo added, "I know it's not just that I got used to it, because I wake up if someone so much as whispers in the next room, always have. I wake up whenever you get out of bed in the middle of the night, and I wake up again a few minutes later when you start scribbling upstairs."

"I'm so sorry. I don't mean to disturb you."

"It wasn't a disturbance. I go back to sleep right away. The point is that you're getting a little better, whether you've noticed it or not."

"I still don't know."

He kissed my knuckles again, murmured "Ylfing" against my skin as he always did, and I closed my eyes and breathed and felt another tiny bit anchored into the world.

Acampora, my brain added. *Ylfing Acampora. You could have all the names you want, a name that's you and a name to tie you to something real. All you have to do is tell him you want it, and it's yours.*

The old Ylfing would have dropped everything and followed him across the—no.

No, wait.

That's not true, is it?

Because the old Ylfing didn't do that. The old Ylfing was apprenticed to Chant, and followed *Chant* across the world because . . . that's what he wanted. He wanted to be a Chant. He didn't really want all those boys he loved the same way he wanted that.

Oh.

The old Ylfing loved them, loved them wholly, with his entire heart, loved them like the world was ending and the sky was falling, loved them like they were each the great and all-consuming love of his life. But then when it was time to leave, he left them. He left them, and he was sad, but not as sad as they were, because the thing he really wanted was somewhere in Chant's head, or off on the horizon, something huge and beautiful and important, something infinitely rare and precious, something lost and forgotten. And then, whenever we stopped somewhere new, the old Ylfing went and loved the next boy just the same, just as wholly and sincerely. He loved, and loved, and loved. And then left, reaching out for something more important than that.

Oh.

————◆————

I've been sitting here staring at those words I just wrote for the last few minutes. I don't quite know how to go on from here. I've just discovered something about myself that I didn't know before—a whole new perspective on myself, a perspective of how I must have looked from the outside. The story I've been telling myself *about* myself isn't wrong, per se, but it is ... skewed, a little. Offset by twenty degrees or so.

I wonder if this is how Orfeo felt when he realized how many people he had inadvertently been hurting. I made those boys sad—I hurt them—because I loved *at them* with all my heart and then whisked it away without much of an explanation. I wonder how many of them were confused; I wonder how many of them thought I meant it.

Beka—no, I didn't love Beka.[312] He liked me, and I blocked him off because I was too deep in my grief to give him my heart, too afraid of being hurt myself. Again.

Ivo, then—no, Ivo was a little like Orfeo used to be. Ivo wanted affection and attention, but he didn't want to be *adored* with that intensity, and he began to push me away when it got too much for him.

All right, that's two that I don't have to feel bad about, at least. That's two I didn't lie to.

---

312 Who the hell is Beka? Have you ever mentioned—oh. The boy from those pages I threw in the fire, the one who took you to see the dragons hatching?

All Chants are liars, didn't I say?

Before Ivo was ... shit, what was his name? That boy in Enc—pretty brown eyes, had a little flock of goats, didn't mind that I couldn't wrap my tongue around the language without stammering ... Mev, I think? Probably Mev. He barely counts either, because we only kissed for an afternoon, and then Chant and I continued down the road the next day—surely I wouldn't have had time to give him any impressions beyond that massive love-mark I left on his neck.

Okay, no, I'm not going to go through the whole list of them—skip to one I know I hurt. Like Selim, then, the cabin boy on the *Koşucu*, when Chant and I were sailing from Map Sut to Kafia. I was a little older than fourteen; I'd only been traveling with Chant for not quite half a year. Nearly a month we had at sea, and both of us just boys who had never done anything with anyone beyond kissing until each other, and I told him he was the most beautiful person I'd ever known, and that was true. And he told me about his mother in Araşt, and how he'd take me to see her and she'd make me lentil soup—the best lentil soup in all the world, Selim said—and I said I'd go with him; I said I wanted to meet her. And then, a few days later, Chant told me about the alabaster temple at Mount Eikat, which we were heading to, and I was thrilled, and I told Selim I wasn't going to come meet his mother after all.[313]

How many times did I do that, or something like that? And never in my life did I ever think about it as a *pattern*.

I think I'll just have to sit with this for a while. I have to find a way to fit this big ugly thing into the rest of what I know about myself.

---

313 Wow, such a stunning betrayal of some kid you barely knew. What a horrible, unforgivable thing. You're definitely the worst person in the world. It's not like you're ever allowed to change your mind or anything! (Is the sarcasm coming through here or should I go on?)

If you'd asked me five minutes ago whether I love Orfeo, I would have said yes. If you'd asked me whether I was in love with him, I wouldn't have considered that a distinct question. I do love him; he's so dear to me, and he deserves to be adored and cherished and—

Have I ever been in love with *anyone*? Really in love? Chant used to make fun of me, saying I'd fall in love twice a week given the opportunity. But it was always more genuine and sincere than infatuation,[314] at least by what I understand infatuation to be. Perhaps I just fell in affection with everyone who caught my eye.

Have I ever cried over someone? Yes, many times. So many times. But that seems different, somehow. I suppose it's that none of the boys I loved ever left me before—not in the abrupt way I left them, again and again. Some of them drifted away from me, a little at a time. I've been hurt before. I've fought with boys I was affectionate towards. I've been betrayed. But did they *leave me*? Did they steal away in the dead of night? Never. Maybe leaving is just what Chants do.

Even when I was an apprentice, when I was young and full of feelings so intense that sometimes I thought they'd tear me apart . . . even then, I never met anyone who I was prepared to leave my apprenticeship for. I chose the road and the horizon; I chose cold nights without a windbreak and blazing hot days without a speck of shade. I chose loneliness and hunger, broken occasionally by an unexpected friend and a feast. I chose the world laid out before my feet. I chose everything that's in it.

Everything—that's the only thing that would have been enough, before. The only thing that could have filled up my heart.

---

314 On the previous page, you talk about a boy whom you spent a whole afternoon kissing and putting love-marks on, and you couldn't remember his name at first.

Chanting is the only thing I've ever been that devoted to.[315] It's the only thing I would sacrifice things for without expecting anything back, though I hope and hope and hope. I've been prepared to burn my entire self on that altar, and when I was told to do it, when Chant said *All right, let's get it over with*, I didn't hesitate. I didn't think. I threw myself towards it with my arms outstretched, I gave away my heart entire, and it wasn't until later that I had any regrets.

It's not the love you find in real life. It's love from stories, love like the tale of Hariq and Amina that ends with the two lovers throwing themselves from a cliff to their deaths. In real life, the best you get from love is two people who have been together for decades, who still care, who still want to be near each other, who still look to each other for comfort. And that's not nothing. But it's not the thing that burns at the heart of Chanting either, the thing that might fill up the empty space in my chest if only I could reach it.

Chanting says, "Come," and I go to it blindly; I follow wherever it leads, waiting-hoping-longing-*yearning* for some promise to be fulfilled and yet never knowing that it will be. I walk across the world; I run until my feet are bloody; I climb up mountains; I row down rivers; I cross borders.

And when I come to the end of the world, when I reach the horizon and lay hands on what I find there, what *Ylfing* will I find there? Who the fuck will I be?

<hr />

And on the other side of the argument, there's Ylfing Acampora.

It's a quiet thing, in comparison. Small, in comparison. Anything would be small next to the whole world. But also *certain*. Defined.

---

315 Glad to hear it.

Ylfing Acampora is a name that says, *Someone loves me. I belong somewhere.* Ylfing Acampora is a space with edges—not loneliness and hunger and something huge and unreachable. It's cold nights spent in a warm bed, and blazing hot days in the shade of a villa somewhere. It's someone listening beside me, always. And there would still be enough of the world to sate me, to soothe my feet when they itch to chase the horizon—the Acamporas are merchants. They travel. There would still be knowledge enough to keep me occupied for years—the language, to begin with, perhaps later one of the universities if I wanted. Anything I want, Orfeo said. He'd find a way to give it to me.

Ylfing Acampora has a home and someone who loves him— maybe many someones. A family. Ylfing Acampora could have nearly everything the-Chant-called-Ylfing would have, adapted and circumscribed and made civilized.

I know *exactly* who Ylfing Acampora is. The-Chant-called-Ylfing is . . . uncharted.

FORTY-FIVE

I wandered back down to Orfeo's room after that weird moment of self-examination, and I crawled into his arms in the dark and curled up against him.

He woke up a little and rubbed his face on my hair, and sighed. "Ylfing," he mumbled, because it's just habit by this point.

"Go to sleep," I whispered, and he nestled in close and drifted off again, and I lay there in the dark and . . . fumed.

Fumed at the world, fumed at Chant and Mistress Chant and Sterre, for being imperfect and selfish. Fumed at myself for being so stupid and naive, and for not knowing who the *fuck I am*. Fumed even at Orfeo, for giving me options, for making me choose, for requiring me to do something besides passively accepting whatever fortune the open road and the horizon handed me, for leading me to a crossroads, which was a ridiculous thing for me to be angry about—but there you have it; that was my honest feeling.

Somewhere in the dark, I think I found something.

Who you are isn't the thoughts in your head or the fears in your heart or the name someone else gives you or takes from you.

Who you are is what you *do*. It's the actions you take, or that you don't take. It's the way you help people, or don't. It's the good that you put into the world, or the bad.

Which means—again, again I come back to this conclusion—that you can *choose* who you are. There's always a choice. I don't have to be Chant, or the Chant-called-Ylfing, or Ylfing Acampora. I just have to be the person who made the choices that I want to make. I can choose Chanting, choose to forever chase the dark-burning thing that hangs just out of my grasp, the thing I will never quite reach. I can choose something else. I can choose Orfeo.

———————————

I dreamed of the marsh and the boat, the figure and the cormorant. Just the same as last time. Except I was angry still. Fuming and bitter, and wanting to seize hold of something and shake it until a decision fell out.

And I found that I was more in control of my dream-self than I had been before.[316] Usually in dreams you find yourself acting without making decisions or thinking about it, but this time I was able to think and reason and assess consequences, and remember the emotions that I'd gone to sleep with, even though it was all a little hazy.

I reached out and put my hands on the gunwale; I touched the surface of the water with my fingertips. I even stroked the cormorant, and it allowed me.

---

316 And you don't even think it's real. Well ... maybe it's not. Maybe. I once met someone, a monk, who tried to reach a moment of divine epiphany by meditating night and day. He drank only milk and ate only plums for seven days, and didn't sleep a wink. He said that by the end of it, he was seeing shadows and demons everywhere—not real ones, just hallucinations produced by a brain under great stress. Perhaps this *is* what is happening to you. (I feel such a damn traitor, admitting this. But selfishly, I'd rather that it was just a dream. I'd rather think that it was that. It makes more sense than the alternative—that's the reasonable explanation. But my faith clashes with my reason when it runs up against logical arguments like, "What motive does this little upstart have for lying so exhaustively and elaborately? What motive could he possibly have? What could he gain from this?" And the answer is ... nothing. There's no reason that you'd lie, nothing for you to gain. So it must be something else.)

"Ylfing," said the figure in the stern of the boat, the first word they had said in ages, and I turned to look at them.[317]

I took a breath. "Thank you," I said. "I should have said that before. Thank you for saving me when I was about to drown."

The figure inclined its head just once. The lamp behind it guttered briefly.

"You know my name," I said. "Do you have one too, or are you just a dream thing?" The cormorant cawed as if it were laughing, and I somehow, *somehow* knew the shadowed figure was a little affronted. "I'm sorry," I said. "I don't want to offend."

Another slow nod, begrudging.

They didn't tell me their name. I sighed. "Is it all right if I talk?"

A nod.

But then I didn't know what to talk about. I twisted my hands in my lap. "Do you know anything else about me, besides my name?"

Nod.

"I suppose you would, if you're a dream thing; you'd know everything I know."

Silence. Faintly annoyed?

"The flowers are going to start dying, and I don't know what to do, but I have to do something. And then when it's over, I have to figure out whether I'm Ylfing or Chant or something in-between. I could stay by myself or go with Orfeo back to Pezia."

The cormorant croaked.

The shadowed figure twitched their left hand,[318] covered in the

---

317 I hate this.

318 I have just groaned aloud. This is another part of the argument for Faith over Reason—you keep citing these details and symbols, and I am *dead certain* that if I asked you about Shuggwa's iconography you wouldn't be able to tell me anything significant. And yet here they are—the boat, the lantern, the cormorant, the cloak of rushes,

cloak as always, and the boat stopped dead again. They stood slowly—
and of course, because it was a dream, the boat didn't pitch from side
to side with the change in balance. It was as steady as solid ground.
The figure looked off into the distance for a long time, then extended
a hand, still draped in part of their cloak so I couldn't see their skin,
just as they'd done when they touched my face.

I took it without hesitation, and the figure pulled me to my feet
and pointed off to the horizon.

The stars-in-the-marsh were only waist-height here, and they
went on and on as far as the eye could see in every direction, swaying
and gleaming and glittering in the dark. The disease was spreading,
I could see. The flowers were all more golden than blue-white. And
in the eastern sky, a whisper of light. Dawn approaching. And on the
opposite side of the sky, the two moons setting, one below the other.
"Since you come from my head, I suppose you have all my memories,"
I said. "So I suppose you remember when I was in Xereccio and I saw
the hatching dragons with Beka."

Silence. A slow shake of their head.

"Oh. It was like this, a little. Dawn, and someone next to me as
we look at something both beautiful and horrible. But I'm less sad
than I was then." The figure nodded, sat down again. "You know what
a Chant is?"

A nod, and I couldn't have been imagining the wry air to it.[319]

"I think I might stop being a Chant."

The figure didn't move at all, didn't give any indication that they

---

the left hand. Always just exactly right. But perhaps your master told you the symbols
long ago and only your sleeping mind remembered them. Perhaps it is just a dream
after all. That's the thing that makes the most sense. It's the most mundane explanation.
319 Okay. Okay. Okay. Here's a third option: It's not a lie, per se. You're just fucking
with me because you know all this will tie me in knots and keep me up at night. Faith,
Reason, Prank: those are the three current possibilities.

had even heard, but suddenly I sensed that all their attention was on me. Slowly, they shook their head.

"Well, I don't see who *you* are to say whether I should keep going or not."

The cormorant laughed again.

The figure let the cloth covering their hands fall aside, and suddenly, again—

◆

I woke up, burning, my hands empty.

And it was morning, and Orfeo was dropping a scratchy, stubbly kiss against my neck that sang down all my nerves, except then he was climbing out of bed, and I sat up. "Orfeo," I said.

"Morning," he yawned. "Sorry to wake you."

"What are you doing?"

"Getting up."

"Oh. Don't do that."

He laughed. "I'm starving."

"Come back to bed."

"I have to get ready." He was cheerful, and he kept talking, something about Uncle Simo and plans, and I couldn't focus because my whole *being* was yearning for something, reaching out, and if Orfeo would only just come back to bed I could fix it, or sublimate it, make it about physical desire instead of this terrible undefined *wanting* that I didn't know how to answer.

"I dreamed," I said, interrupting him, and then bit my tongue. I had a sudden, pressing certainty that it was *not* a dream to share with Orfeo, for whatever reason.[320] It seemed . . . private. Chant-like,

---

320 Damn right it wasn't!

in a particular way that I didn't think he would understand, though I didn't know the significance of the stars, or the bird, or the boat, or the figure, or the lantern. So instead of telling Orfeo . . . "Sorry. You were talking. You're with your uncle today?"

"Yes, all day." He beamed sleepily over his shoulder at me as he brushed the sleep-wildness out of his hair. "He thinks you're a good influence on me, you know. They all do. They like you. But Uncle Simo particularly—he's been giving me more things to do lately. Important things. He said he was glad I'd gone to de Waeyer's party. He said he was *proud* of me for paying attention and noticing those things about her." He laughed. "Hell of a thing. I would have found a nice boy to introduce to them a long time ago if I'd known it'd pay off like this." He paused and suddenly turned back to me, leaning down for another kiss. "Of course, it wouldn't have paid off quite like this, because any other nice boy wouldn't have been you." He sounded like he was trying to reassure me, as if I were jealous. Perhaps he wanted me to be a little jealous, or at least a little possessive.

I watched him shave, willing him to turn towards me, to see me, to listen so that I could tell him—tell him what?

When he'd finished, he splashed his face with water, patted it dry, and rummaged through his sea chest for a fresh pair of pantaloons—dark blue ones today. He put on a clean shirt too, and a white doublet and his favorite simarre, the black one with the sable trim.

I eyed his clothes. "One of Uncle Simo's important things today, then?"

"Negotiations," he said, with great relish. "I'm allowed to come and watch. I promised I'd be quiet and good, and he believed me." He leaned in for another quick kiss, this one cool and smooth and a little clammy from the cold water, while he belted his simarre closed with a silver chain. I seized him by the back of the neck, tried to pull him down, but he ducked away, grinning. "All because of you. Not that I'll be doing anything but standing in the background and looking decorative."

"You're so good at that, though."

He laughed and sat on the edge of the bed to pull his shoes on. I stared hard at the side of his head. *Pay attention, Orfeo,* I thought at him as hard as I could, though I couldn't have told him where it was coming from. *Everything I want, you said: I'll have your eyes fixed on me, I'll have your heart in my hands, I'll have your breath tied to mine—you're no audience of thousands, but you'll do.* "And you?" he asked.

"I'm not going to work today," I said.

Orfeo glanced up at me. "Not feeling well?"

"There's just some more things I need to think about." I paused. *Pin him to the wall across the room with only words,* I thought. *Grip him and hold him, like you held them at the auction house.* Strange, the way thoughts intrude on your mind without your decision to think them.[321] "Are you in a terrible rush?"

"Not a terrible rush, not yet." He stood, looked into the mirror across the room, and finger-combed his beautiful curls until they fell just right. "Why?"

I watched him move around the room, finding the bits and bobs that he'd need for the day and tucking them into his pockets. That prickling feeling came across my skin, the same that I'd felt at the auction house.[322] I felt like a plucked lute string, like a cup brimming over, like the ground just before an earthquake, like a bird of prey right before it dives.

---

321 These ones seem unlike you. Were they yours?

322 That's a pattern. I told you just before you left, didn't I? I said my specialty was patterns. It wasn't just at the auction house, either—there were other times you've mentioned that prickling feeling. I think there was once in van Vlymen's garden when we were talking, and once in Sterre's garden when you and Orfeo were talking. . . . What's the common thread between those?

I wonder if other Chants have felt that. I wonder if they've felt a story bloom suddenly in their mouth without being summoned up. I wonder if they've suddenly remembered something they haven't thought of for years.

"Look at me," I said, barely recognizing my own voice. Orfeo turned, at last, blinking in surprise. I met his eyes, and I reached out with the hands of my soul and thought, *You want me.* "Listen."

FORTY-SIX

Aitiu and Nerelen

Nerelen, the god of wine and wildness and wilderness, came upon his heart's desire perched on a rock in a spring meadow: a shepherd youth of surpassing beauty, with auburn hair that shone in the sun, and long golden limbs, and sparkling eyes the color of golden acorns.[323]

From the moment Nerelen set eyes upon him, the sun lost its warmth, the flowers of the world lost their colors, food lost its savor, wine lost its sweetness, and Nerelen knew nothing more but want. *(Here, I got out of bed and went to Orfeo, touching the line of his jaw.)*

He appeared to the youth first in the form of a fox, creeping close as he played his tibicen, surrounded by his flock, his piping so keen and wistful that Nerelen's heart twisted in his chest even as his desire ran hot through his blood. *(I took Orfeo's hand, pulling him back towards the bed, tipping him onto the mattress—he smiled a little and went along with an indulgent air.[324])* Nerelen lay at the base of the rock,

---

323 Huh. I haven't heard this one before. At least, not this version. Good for you. I knew you'd have a new story for me sooner or later. (By the way, it's nearly four o'clock in the morning, and I'm too tired to work up the outrage to castigate you for writing this one down—I've already done that a few times already, so just do me a favor and take it as read, would you? You know the script.)
324 Ugh, enough of your personal life. I'm not interested!

full of agony, and his heart's desire looked down upon him and smiled and continued to play, unafraid.

He returned again the next day in the form of a wolf. The shepherd had woven flowers into his hair, and as the day was warm, he had cast off his tunic. He smiled at Nerelen as he walked up and lay in the grass by the rock, and then the youth took up his tibicen and played a plaintive folk song—there had been words to it, when Nerelen had heard it before, about a maiden longing for her lover. Nerelen yearned to reveal himself, to snatch up the youth and whisk him away to some secret place and make the youth as wild as he— and yet he held himself back. (*I remember that here I began to feel . . . unanchored. I was acting without conscious decision to act. Chills ran up my arms, and I felt a prickling on the back of my neck, like the feeling you get when you imagine someone's watching you. But there was only Orfeo. "Are you doing something to me?" I murmured, crawling over him. "Something with your magic?"*

"Gods, no! I wouldn't, I swear—" He looked horrified at the very thought and made to pull away. I caught him by the front of his clothes and pulled him back in, kissed him softly, toyed with the buttons of his doublet.

"Just asking. Be still."[325])

The next day, he went to the meadow again in the form of a lion, the ferocity of his form reflecting the ardency of his desire. The youth, surely the fairest in all the land, idly watched his flock as he sat naked in the grass by the base of the rock, his hair all disarrayed as if he'd just been tumbled. He smiled as Nerelen approached, and held out his hands (*and here I laced one of my hands with Orfeo's*), and Nerelen flung himself to the ground beside him. The youth sank his hands

---

325 Well, now I have a motherfucking dilemma. Skip the oversharing about your sex life, or stay for the new story?

into Nerelen's wild mane *(and here I combed my fingers into Orfeo's hair, scratching gently at his scalp until he shivered)*,[326] and exclaimed over its color, its scent like spring flowers, until Nerelen was trembling with the urge to cast his form aside. "How handsome you are," said the shepherd. "And how kind of you to keep me company. It's terribly lonely, all day with no one to talk to but the sheep. Will you come again tomorrow, I wonder? Though I don't know why you bother with a disguise," he added, startling Nerelen so sharply that he almost jumped right out of the lion-body. "There's ever so much more we could say to each other if you were yourself."

Nerelen did cast off the lion, then. The shepherd watched with a bright smile, twining his hands deeper as Nerelen's mane turned to hair. "Thou knew'st me?"

"Not the first day," the youth said, laughing. "But I knew the wolf of the second day was the same person as the fox of the first day, and there are not many who can take up and cast off forms so adeptly. Why did you?"

"I did not wish to frighten thee."

"I am not frightened." *(I kissed Orfeo.)*

"I did not wish to upset thee."

"I am not upset." *(I kissed him again.)*

"I did not wish to chase thee away."

"I am before you." The shepherd held him firm by the hair and leaned down to kiss him. *(I paused, just long enough, expectant, and Orfeo tugged me back down, laughing, and set his mouth against the skin just under my ear.)*

"I would have thy name," Nerelen said, as the wolves and lions of desire tore at his body and ran wild through his blood.

---

326 I think I'll just try not to read the parentheticals....

"Aitiu," said the youth. (*With Orfeo's teeth scraping my neck, my voice was as breathy as his must have been.*)

"Three days thou hast sat here and played, and three days I have listened and felt my heart moved."

"Only your heart?" he said, his voice full of amusement and warmth, and Nerelen surged up and twined his arms around Aitiu, kissed him and kissed him. (*Orfeo laughed again, winding his arms around me, pulling me closer. "Go on," he said. "I'm listening, go on. I've never listened so hard in my life."*

He bit me, more sharply, and a surge of chills ran across my skin. I drew a breath, and felt or heard the echo of another breath drawn, felt something whisper from Orfeo into me and then drawn from me to . . . elsewhere. Orfeo shivered a little, his voice catching, his grip on my shoulders going lax like the falling tide for a moment—just a moment, and then he groaned aloud and the strength of his arms around me redoubled, anchoring me close to him. The next words out of my mouth were not quite the ones I had composed when I first made up this story—I'd been sixteen then; I wouldn't have thought of anything like this. It was like the story twisted on my tongue.)[327]

"Fairest one, I would see thee draped in gold and jewels, wearing robes of bright-colored silk. I would hear thee play thy pipe until the moons fall from the sky and the stars go out, until the ocean rises and swallows up the land. What payment wouldst thou have for thy

---

[327] Wait. There's that pattern again. I don't get to skip over the parentheticals, do I? (And as long as I'm commenting on the parentheticals anyway—you *made this up?* Gods witness my suffering; it is too early in the morning for this and I'm not drunk enough to deal with it. Why are you making up a story about Nerelen, a god that *doesn't belong to you?* I'd show mercy on myself and go take a walk, but I don't want to still be reading this when dawn breaks. I shall content myself with rubbing my temples and sighing loudly until Arenza asks me what's wrong again. For the hundredth time.)

playing? Ask for anything, and it is thine." (*And then the feeling passed, and my tongue was my own again.*)

"I could not ask for anything of worth, my lord," Aitiu said.

"Then do not ask—command me, I am thine."

"Kiss me," said Aitiu. (*Cradling his face in both hands, I turned Orfeo's mouth up to mine. He sighed, yearning a little. "I'll be late," he whispered. "I really shouldn't—"*

"*Tell them it's my fault. You can say I wouldn't be denied.*"

"*Gods. Gods. Keep going.*" *He bit again at my neck, and I turned my head aside to give him space to work, wanting the bruise, wanting, wanting.*)

But Nerelen, overcome with love, knew too well how fragile mortals are, so when he obeyed it was with great care and delicacy and softness, though he strained and ached to devour him whole, to bring the wildness and wilderness upon him, to leave him as limp and light-headed as a drunkard.

"It wasn't just that I recognized you," Aitiu said. "I could feel your eyes on me as if you were already touching me. I was driven to distraction thinking of what I'd have to do to make you come to me. You should have waited until tomorrow—I had a lovely plan."

"Thou needst no plans, fairest one. Thou art temptation itself." ("*So are you," Orfeo growled, and another chill ran down my spine, another moment of drifting as if I were in a small boat at sea, the waves rushing beneath me. Another breath, and the echo of the breath, the rise and ebb of the tide running through me, and Orfeo went a little wild himself, as if Nerelen had brought the wilderness upon him. And I? I only turned my eyes to the corner of the room. Empty.*[328])

"And yet you show such restraint, such gentlemanly comportment, as if I were some delicate thing with hesitations about the

---

matter of being ravished," Aitiu said, lying back in the grass and pulling Nerelen over him. "I'd not imagined a god would be so shy."

Nerelen bit him sharply, pinning him still with mere power. "This? This, thou fox? If thou canst feel my eyes upon thee, then perhaps I ought only *look* at thee." (*I laced my fingers with Orfeo's again and pushed his hands above his head, holding them down in the rumpled bedclothes; he made a soft sound and squirmed beneath me, his eyes wide and dark. "Keep going," he breathed. "I'd listen to this all day."*)

"My lord," Aitiu gasped.

"What wouldst thou have done tomorrow when thou felt my eye fall upon thee?"

"I have been told," Aitiu said breathlessly, "that in the old days, those who knew your mysteries would drench themselves in wine and go walking in the forest. I would have done that, and called and called for you, and begged you to come to me, and when you came, I would have run and made you hunt me." (*"Fuck," breathed Orfeo. He shivered, and his hands clenched in mine.*)

"Thou knowest, then, the appetites of the gods."

It was a warning, but Aitiu did not hear it as such. "Not all the gods," he said, his eyes dark, his voice low. "But you, yes. For years, I have wondered, taking my flock to this meadow, if you might come to me. I have wished for nothing else."

"Thou dost not wish to be hunted like prey," said Nerelen, but he whispered it as a man whispers a secret he hopes to hear disavowed.

(*I lowered my lips to the edge of Orfeo's ear and whispered:*) "I do, if it is *yours.*"

(*Orfeo yanked against my grasp, twisting his wrists. "Ylfing, come on, yes, fuck." I laughed and held tight, my blood singing, my skin prickling like someone running their nails down my spine.*

There was a moment, looking down at him, watching and laughing breathlessly—for less than a heartbeat, for less than a blink, I thought he was someone else. Only briefly. It was like the flicker of a candle-flame, there and gone, and I felt like I'd just caught sight of something out of the corner of my eye, something I wouldn't have seen at all unless I had happened to look down right at that moment. And then it was nothing, it was just Orfeo, warm and present and very much himself, laughing and cursing me in turns.)[329]

---

329 And here it is again, the pattern. Except . . . every other time you had a prickly feeling, you were near one of the stars-in-the-marsh. Maybe I'm wrong, then, and this is just your brain playing tricks on you. In any case, this isn't much like you. All the other times you've taken Orfeo to bed, you got all coy and oblique about it, and thank the gods for that. Shit, wait, no—I was a few pages farther on and I just remembered something and came back: You still have that star-in-the-marsh in your room, don't you? And it was directly above you.

FORTY-SEVEN [330]

I leaned down and kissed him once more, then let his wrists go and climbed out of bed. "You're going to be late," I said, grinning. "And your clothes are all mussed up. You'd better run."

"Oh, don't you dare." He sat up, incredulous, still laughing. "Ylfing, come back here this instant." [331]

"Better not. I don't know how I could live with myself if I made you late," I said, blinking and putting on a most innocent face. I picked up my own clothes from the floor and began to dress.

"Ylfing!" He pushed himself up and swayed to his feet, light-headed as a drunkard, I noticed, pleased. He tried to grab for me, and I danced back out of his grasp.

"Later, later! Run, sweetheart! You'll be late!"

"More like unkindest one, not fairest one," he grumbled. We both heard the clock ring the hour, and he groaned, an entirely different note now. "Shit."

"Off you go!" I said cheerfully.

He groaned again and sat to pull on his stockings and shoes. "I don't even get to hear the end of the story?"

"They have amazing sex, and Aitiu begs for Nerelen to whisk him

---

330 No, dammit, no! Again? Again you grow bored in the middle of things?
331 Listen to Orfeo! Finish the story! Why do you always do this? At least I'm not the only one suffering.

away to the divine lands, and offers to look after the flocks of the gods, and to play his pipe for Nerelen whenever he likes. Offers to play Nerelen's pipe too," I added wickedly, and dodged the pillow Orfeo promptly flung at me. "Aitiu's suitors arrive to try to rescue him, but their plots are foiled and they're sent off empty-handed. Other than them, everyone lives happily unto the fading of the stars and rising of the oceans."[332]

Orfeo grumbled, and stood up to fix his hair in the mirror. "*Baciami*," he said when he finished, turning to me, and I obliged, giving him one more teasing kiss that made his breath stutter. "The story was good," he murmured. "Even if the teller is unnecessarily cruel." He drew back, looking at me with his head tilted a little. "You know, I've never seen you like this," he said. "I wouldn't have thought you'd—well. It's not what I would ever have expected from you. But I'm glad to be surprised, and—"

"You're going to be *late*," I said.

He caught me just once more, pressed me to the wall beside the door, kissed me so lightly I barely felt his lips. "But later, you said? When I don't have anywhere to be? Because I want."

"Later," I agreed, and then I pushed him out of the room.

And it wasn't until a few minutes afterwards, when I was combing my hair in the mirror, when his words started chafing at me: *Not what he would ever have expected of me.*[333]

That was not at all how I told the story when I made it up, years ago—it was much more chaste then, more about romance than sex.

---

332 This doesn't count!!

333 There, see. Orfeo noticed that something was odd too. Which, if I believe your account, proves that it wasn't just in your head. Not just a dream, so that knocks Reason out, and leaves only Faith or Prank. I am neither drunk enough nor sober enough to deal with this.

I don't know what came over me, telling the story that way.

And then writing it down! Gods! Should I get rid of this? All I would have to do is press it against my burning face right now and I bet it'd burst into flames.

——◆——

And then there's all the rest of it. The echoing of my breath, the whisper of something that passed from Orfeo and then not *to* me, but *through* me, like I was a conduit of . . . whatever that was. Orfeo said it wasn't him, that he wouldn't nudge me. I believe him.

——◆——

~~I'm not sure~~

——◆——

~~Perhaps I shouldn't~~

——◆——

~~Are you there?~~[334]

——◆——

Oh, to the desert with this, and with me. I'm being foolish. Never mind.[335]

---

334 Fucking hell, stop screwing with my head like this. You know what, fine! You've driven me to it! Either you're far more of a cunning little bastard than anyone gave you credit for and you're making your point seem sincere—performing hesitation for my benefit by crossing out your own false starts is both elegant and effective, well done— or . . . No, I'm not going to legitimize it by writing it down. Look what terrible habits you've led me to.

335 Oh gods, what hour is it now? Is it too early for a cup of tea? (Perhaps, under the circumstances, I should stop swearing by "gods.")

FORTY-EIGHT

As I was writing earlier, a couple hours after Orfeo left, a proper tempest blew up out of nowhere, and it rattled all the shutters on the windows, howled around the corners, slammed torrents of rain into the roof and the walls. It was loud enough and strong enough to be unsettling, and when the lightning started flashing, the thunder was *immediate*. No delay at all—those bolts were right on top of us.

I gathered up my papers from my room in the attic and stashed them in a box in Orfeo's room to be safe, just in case the shingles on the roof came loose and started leaking, and then I went downstairs. The inn's public room was all but deserted—almost all the guests had left for the day, and it was still too early for the patrons who came only to eat and drink. "Anyone about?" I called.

Mevrouw Basisi stuck her head out of the kitchen door in surprise. "Oh, it's you," she said. "Hungry?"

"I could eat."

"Come into the kitchen. Keep us company," she said, waving me in. By the time I crossed the room and came to the doorway of the kitchen, she was already busy at the cutting board. The inn's cook, Stasyn, stood at the hearth, already raking coals into a pile, ready for a pan atop them. "What are you in the mood for?"

"Seems like you're going to tell me," I said, eying her knife as it blurred its way through a pair of small onions until they were tiny, tiny cubes.

"Almost everything has onions in it," Stasyn said sagely. "That's where the tasty comes from."

"Tell us what you want to eat—anything," *Mevrouw* Basisi said.

I sat at the little table at the back of the kitchen by the door, well out of their way. "Not *anything*, surely," I said with a laugh.

They shot me an identical look. "Anything," Basisi said grimly, setting her knife to one side and leaning on the counter. "Do you think she's just a *cook?*"

"Of course not."

"You've been all over," Stasyn said, scraping the onions from the board into the pan. "You think you've tasted all the foods there are."

"Oh, definitely not all of them," I said, some of the old Hrefni perspective taking me over. "Only a lot." I've tried to break the habit of looking at the world like this. No one else quite understands what I mean. They think I'm being arrogant; in most places, it's politer to demur, at least nominally, rather than to admit to your real skills. But I was distracted still, thinking of that thing I'm not writing about.[336]

"You've noticed that we have the best inn in the city. I've met people from everywhere. They're all homesick. They're all here because they come from somewhere else, and they only stay until they get to go back. I have *everyone's* mother's recipes for *everyone's* favorite dish. So when I say *anything* . . ."

"We don't mess about, not in here," Basisi finished, grimly.

I bit back a smile and thought of how much I would have liked

---

336 Wait, what thing? The Shuggwa thing? I'm assuming the Shuggwa thing. Ugh—and now I have no way of knowing what you've left out, even though you obviously have left something out.

to introduce them to Lanh Chau. "I don't want to trouble you. I'd be fine with whatever's easy."

"Answer the question. Is it so hard to just pick something?"

Yes. I made myself smile and cast around for some memory of food that wasn't tainted by my master leaning over and muttering under his breath to me about the economic significance of some ingredient, or the historical reasons for the presence of one grain over another . . . "There was, um . . . I was in Avaris once, and I had this . . . it was like eggs baked in a little dish with cream and butter and herbs?"

"Shirred eggs," Stasyn nodded. "What else? Young *heerchen* like you, you can't eat just eggs. Come on." She snapped her fingers at me. "You're holding out on me. Everyone's mother's recipe, I said. You're from far off; you'll tell me something new."

"You can't make it, though; you don't have the things for it," I said impatiently.

"But I can get 'em," she replied, stubborn. "Or a damn close approximation, after some trial and error."

I cracked. "Fine. Smoked salmon," I said. "This bony silver fish called a *seolfring*, which you cook by laying it out flat, like a pinned butterfly, on a pine board in the bottom of a clay pot that you bury in the ashes of a banked fire the night before, so it's warm and tender in the morning."

"Too late to bake you a fish overnight, so we'll have to try that another time. What else? I can usually take a stab at drinks, too."

"An infusion of young pine needles in water. Creamed onions on bread. *Beorcswete*, which is really just hot milk and birch syrup—but it's for children—"

"I don't believe in some foods being only for children," Stasyn said thoughtfully. As I'd spoken, she had found a pair of small bowls and smeared butter on their insides, adding a splash of cream, a shaving of sharp white cheese, and a cracked egg into each one, topped with salt and pepper and herbs, just as I'd said. She set them on the hearth, and covered them with an iron pot that always lived by the fire, hot and ready. "Everybody eats. If you want it, I'm certainly not going to smirk about *childishness*, or whatever is the problem."

"I don't know that we have birch syrup," Basisi mused. "We have some smoked fish, though, and herrings. Won't be quite the same, but it'll do for short notice."

"I've got it. Sit down, put your feet up, Basi," Stasyn chided, flapping her hand towards the other chair at the table. She set another pan to heat on the fire, and fetched out the smoked fish from the larder. "Creamed onions—what is this flavored with?"

"Salt, and ... um, there was an herb. ... It only grew wild in the forest; it was called *eorðmistel*, I think? But sage would be close enough, if you have it."

"*If* I have sage," Stasyn scoffed.

"What do you do when someone asks for something you don't know how to make?"

She shot me another look. "I'm the best chef in the city. When that happens, I make them describe it for me—creamed onions on bread, I daresay I don't need much more information than that. I find out what the ingredients are, and I find out how it makes them feel when they eat it. I find out whether it's peasant food or noble food, what time of year people eat it, whether it's eaten for festivals and holy days." Stasyn threw the diced onions into the pan with a knob of butter and a generous pour of cream, and they sizzled loud, filling the kitchen a moment later with a smell that made my stomach pang with hunger—it's amazing how good plain onions frying in fat smells.

"What for? Why all the rest of it besides the ingredients?"

"Because in addition to being the best chef in the city," she said,

"I'm also a businesswoman. I know the prices of things; I know when they're in season. I know where food comes from, where spices come from. All of this is important. People who aren't chefs, they'll tell you all about a dish, but they don't really know what's in it. They don't know how it *works*. Suppose that nice young man of yours is pining away for some Pezian dish I've never heard of, and when he tells me about it, I try to make it. If I make it like a Heyrlandtsche dish, he's going to be disappointed. So when I cook a Pezian dish, I cook like a Pezian—olive oil, not butter. Hardly ever use lemon, compared to us. A mind-boggling variety of pastas. Stewed tomatoes in everything, because Pezians are rakes and lushes. Oregano, thyme, pepper . . ." She shrugged. "Everything is a little different. Even the way I chop the onions. It's a science."

"You didn't ask me any of that."

"Didn't need to. You were thinking of foods you liked when you were very small. You mentioned that birch syrup drink—you said it was only for children. And I didn't need to ask about the butter or olive oil, because, well . . ." She nodded to the pan. "Cream. So you had cows, so you had butter. And I didn't need to ask if it was a peasant dish or not because—" She nodded to the pan again. "Cream. Your family was comfortable, at the very least—you either had a cow of your own or you could afford to buy milk and butter and cream from someone else."

"You're a little like me, I think," I said, immensely pleased.[337] "You with food. Do you want to travel at all?"

She laughed and crossed her arms. "The world already comes to my doorstep without me having to take a step outside the city."

---

[337] She is, at that. I'd track her down and introduce Lanh Chau to her, but I'm waiting for him to come to food on his own. He's too contrary—if I shoved him at it and said, "Look, there's your heart's desire," he'd open his mouth and deny it categorically before his brain had time to catch up and think, and then he'd be stuck.

"I can't pry her out of the kitchen with a crowbar," Basisi muttered as Stasyn prodded the onions around the pan. "*Mevrouw* Chef does not understand the concept of a *day off*."

Stasyn rolled her eyes. "Oh, and *you* do?"

"Always things to do," Basisi said sagely. "Inns don't run themselves, and Nicasen can only manage so much by themselves at the house. Has trouble in crowds," she added to me. "The noise, the jostling—they find it very upsetting. They handle the accounts and so forth, all the things that require a great deal of focus and concentration and don't involve other people at all. Anyway, back to food. You were saying, Stasyn."

"It's important to get it right, isn't it? Not just for our reputation, although that is of *utmost* importance." Basisi grunted in what seemed to be agreement. Stasyn continued: "Doing something like this, you have to give a shit about people. As long as they can pay, you give a shit. Food is the best way to do that."

"Everybody eats," Basisi agreed. "Doesn't matter who they are or where they're from. They eat."

Stasyn lifted the iron pot from over the eggs and moved the two little bowls onto a plate with her bare fingers, unaffected by the heat. She turned towards our table. "Oh. Dear. Basi, the door—"

We both turned to look. There was a puddle of water coming through the crack at the bottom, and it was visibly growing. Stasyn dropped my plate on the table, and both she and Basisi leapt forward, seizing dishtowels and rags and cramming them into the crack. "This rain!" Basisi cried. "Damn this city."

I'd leaped up from the table to clatter through the cupboards, seizing what other rags and dishtowels I could find and tossing them over.

Stasyn said breathlessly, "It's wind. It's driving the rain through every little crack. I'd best go check the windows upstairs too—"

"But the wind is coming from the other direction," I said. "From the northeast." That was the opposite side of the building—the side Orfeo's room was on.

Stasyn and Basisi frowned, and then Stasyn shot to her feet and opened the top half of the kitchen door, just a crack. A gust of wind blew through the room as Stasyn peeked out. "Oh, shipwreck," she said, slamming it closed and latching it. She was wild-eyed when she turned back to us.

"What is it?" Basisi asked. Stasyn leaned down to help her up from the floor—Basisi's knees, I gather, aren't what they used to be.

"It's the water," she said. "It's . . . *high*."

Basisi froze. "How high?"

"High." Stasyn was pale and grim.

"I thought it never got high enough to flood the houses," I said. "Should we start moving things upstairs?"

"No," Basisi said. "*Things* don't matter at this point."

"I don't understand."

"One of the dikes went down," Stasyn said.

———◆◆———

We ran out of the inn, or rather *waded* out of the inn. We were wearing boots, but the water was already more than knee-high. Stasyn and Basisi didn't seem to care—what was so alarming about a potential infection and amputation when the water was going to kill us one way or another?

"How high does the sea get?" I shouted to Stasyn. We were weighed down with buckets and tools, and we had to fight against the wind and rain at every step. She couldn't hear me, or she didn't have time to answer. Down by the canal, there were rowboats tethered to cleats, covered in oilcloth tarps to keep out the rain—the cleats were under more than a foot of water, and the rowboats floated at the level of our hips. Basisi seized ahold of one boat, throwing off its tarp heedlessly, dumped her supplies into the bottom of it, and clambered in after them. Stasyn followed.

"Go back inside," Basisi shouted. I could barely hear her over the gale.

"I can help!"

She gestured firmly back to the inn, but I shook my head and climbed into the boat after them. Basisi sighed, and Stasyn, who had untethered the boat, set the oars in their locks and began to row.

We had to fight against the wind there too—it was coming off the sea, from the same direction we needed to go. I crammed myself into the prow, and for half an hour I had nothing to do but stay quiet and still and think about how if some of the stars-in-the-marsh had escaped infection before, they certainly wouldn't have done so now. The waters were too high.

"How do you know where the break is?" I shouted to Stasyn over the wind.

"I don't!" she yelled back. "Someone will find it and tell the rest."

I saw what she meant when we got closer to the edge of the city—there were more boats now, other people, all of us rowing out to the edges of the city, and I could imagine it through the rest of the city too: Hundreds of people flying for the closest dike, looking for the break. We hardly slowed our pace, though the canals were crammed. No one stopped; no one jammed up the rush of boats.

The dikes here are artificial hills, thirty feet wide or more, sturdy enough to resist the pressure of the sea. On the outer side, they're set with rocks and boulders to protect the packed clay from being worn away by the constant battering crash of the waves. And they're tall enough, twenty feet or so, that even a storm on the day of the king-tide wouldn't raise the seas high enough to spill over the lip—yet there's a three-foot stone wall running right along the top, just in case. Orfeo and I had walked along them before the storms came, throwing pebbles into the sea like young boys and ducking down together in the lee of the wall to stay dry when a wave crashed too close and cast its spray into the air.

And, set at intervals along the dikes and on either side of the locks that let ships in and out of the harbor, the windmills pump water from the harbor over the dike and dump it back in the sea. Or they're supposed to—in the stormy season, the gales blow too strongly. They'd break the vanes right off the mills like they were twigs, if the millers left the sails on.

—————◆◆◆—————

We turned a corner, and the harbor opened out before us. The waters were rougher here, choppy with the howling wind that slammed into us full-strength now that the shield of the tight-packed houses was behind us. Stasyn heaved at the oars as the boat floundered in the gusts, and I scrambled from my place in the prow to the thwart beside her and took an oar. Basisi squinted through the driving rain, shielding her eyes, then pointed suddenly, catching at Stasyn's wrist.

There it was—the break.

A gash in the side of the dike, as if someone had wrenched part of it free, and a powerful torrent of water was pouring into the harbor. One of the windmills lay, partially submerged, against the side of the dike, its very foundations torn out from the ground like an uprooted tree. The remaining crater had evidently been a sufficient enough weakness in the dike for the pounding waves to work their way past—and once a trickle made it through, the force of the water behind it would have eroded the crack, widening it more and more until ... this.

There were people swarming across the dike already, pummeled by the wind—people with tools, breaking up the stone wall on top of the dike into its component rocks; people frantically unloading boatfuls of spare wooden planks.

Stasyn brought us right up to the dike, one more boat in the row, and we struggled to alight, fighting against the heaving waters long enough to stumble from the tossing hull to land that squelched under our feet—I had a brief clutch of fear, a vivid memory of the nightmares, the mud sucking at my feet as I floundered through the marsh, and for a moment I couldn't breathe.

But Stasyn hauled me along with her, and we scrambled up the slope of the dike to the top, where the wind hit us in the face like a punch, throwing saltwater so hard it stung like needles against our skin. Basisi followed along behind us, a little more slowly.

The rest of it is ... vague. I've trained for most of my life to remember things as exactly as possible, and yet all I have from that moment on is glimpses:

We broke the wall for raw stone. Others, working in the lee of the dike, hammered the wood planks together into lengths long enough to span the gap, burying each end in the mud, with gaps between the planks so the water could continue rushing through without breaking the wood. We heaved the rocks from the wall into the gap; the planks held them in place, keeping them from being washed away into the harbor.

We labored for hours—my arms and legs screamed with effort, hauling rocks mindlessly, frantically. The gap was so large; I felt like we were filling in a vast ravine with mere pebbles. And the wind, battering and bashing at us like the punching fist of a god, over and over, unceasing, for what seemed like eons. I remember whispering the names of gods, requesting strength, or attention, or mercy. I even whispered Shuggwa's name, asked him to let his Eye fall on me.[338]

I remember feeling faint as I worked, as the hours wore on and on. I remember throwing another stone into the torrent and nearly falling in after it myself—but someone caught me by my sleeve, pulled me back from the brink. When I turned around, I didn't see who it might have been; I couldn't even thank them.

I remember more and more people arriving; I remember that some of them were turned away as there was no space for them to land their boats or move about on the dike. Some of them brought food and drink, casks of water and weak beer, cups that occasionally got shoved into my hands which I gulped down with rainwater.

So many people. So many, many people. And the ones that couldn't land on the dike, or couldn't get close enough, floated there in the harbor and watched, their boats flung about by the rough waves, the wind shoving at them until they must have been nearly as exhausted as we were, but they watched. They waited. When a space opened—someone exhausted leaving the work, or someone injured being taken away from it—just as quickly another boat would land, and another few pairs of hands would replace those that could go on no longer. The rain was so heavy we could barely see across the

---

338 Hm. I didn't think of it until you mentioned Shuggwa but . . . this is a little bit sinking-your-homeland-beneath-the-waves—the rocks, the water, the willingness to sacrifice. You know, most people only throw a pebble or a handful of earth into the water, but you threw wagonloads of rocks, eh? Dramatic little thing. Did you remember Arthwend, as the rites command, as you worked to save Heyrland from a similar fate? I don't expect that you did, or that you even took notice of the parallels. For a Chant, an awful lot of stuff goes over your head. But I suppose that's to be expected in one so young.

harbor, but there were more people watching on the docks, and flur-
ries of activity as they loaded boats with supplies or unloaded the
injured and whisked them safe inside.

The whole city, it seemed like, knew the dike was down, and all of
them were turning their entire attention our way, straining towards it
with their minds, if not their hands and backs.

I would have thought they would flee. In moments of disaster,
most people do. They run; they try to save at least themselves, if they
can't save their property. But the people of the city came out into the
water, into the rain and the wind, and they helped. We strained and
heaved and pulled while the waves crashed against us unceasingly,
only seeming to grow stronger by the hour.

But of course everyone was trying to save themselves. Of course
they were. If the dike had fallen, if the water had gone unchecked, we
all would have drowned. Everything would have been lost.

The dikes go all across this little country, a network of walls
holding back the tide against the will of the gods and the inexorable
pull of the moons. It is the material product of the struggle between
the citizens and the water, and in this struggle there is no room for
selfishness. Better for one person to fall than for the country to fall.
Better for exhaustion so deep in your bones you'd feel like sobbing,
if only you had the strength. Better to save yourself with a rock wall
broken to pieces and thrown into the torrent, standing alongside all
your kith and kin, working to save each other as much as yourself . . .

No lone person in Heyrland can keep the waters back. It takes a
city. And the city was *there* today. The danger was not yet past when we
left, trembling, weak, and too wrecked to even lift our oars. Someone
came for us, tumbled us into a rowboat, and took us back to land. No
questions asked; no conversation. They helped us step down into the
flooded street, and then they rowed back again, waiting for another

passenger to ferry across the harbor. When we left, supplies were still arriving: food, water, stone, and wood. There were people clustered around the other windmills then, I saw as we left—the vanes were lashed tight and still, the sails still off, but the pumps were going at full speed, powered by the hands and backs of the people who could do that one little thing.

There were people on the dikes carrying buckets of water from the harbor, up the slope of the dike, and tossing it back into the sea. Bailing out the city drop by drop, but that was one little thing too, and they did it.

They're out there now, saving themselves, saving the city. They all live, or they all drown, and they don't know if their efforts will be in vain. . . .

And they do the one little thing.

———◆———

I know what to do about the flowers.

FORTY-NINE

The water level stabilized by yesterday afternoon. It's been falling steadily since. Around three this morning, I think, the gale died down, but even when the sails were replaced on the windmills and the vanes began turning, even when the pumps sputtered to life and the people working them could fall back in exhaustion, the bucket teams stayed on the dike, draining the city by hand. Drop by drop. The one little thing.

This morning, the waters were still on the higher side, but most of the pavements had drained into the canals. There are new high-water marks on the buildings, thigh or hip-height in most places. Basisi's inn took a full foot of water, spoiling the food on the low shelves of her kitchen larder and almost everything that we'd left in the cellar but the contents of the watertight casks.

The Acamporas were taken by surprise in the torrent and waited out the storm at the house of their business contact; they returned this morning as I was leaving for Sterre's offices, bedraggled and damp and not in terribly good spirits.

As I walked today, I passed by house after house where I caught the faint rancid-meat scent that marked the presence of stars-in-the-marsh somewhere in the back gardens.

It's too late. The waters rose too high. A few days ago, before the dike fell, we might have had a chance of catching the plague before it spread, but now it is only a matter of time until all the flowers wither up, and then all the imaginary money that those people have accrued from passing around the futures contracts will disappear in a snap.

Sterre's office door was open when I arrived. I kicked off my water-boots and threw my oilcloak onto the floor without looking, and I charged through the front room, barely paused to knock at her threshold, and let myself in, shutting the door behind me.

She blinked at me. "Well, good morning," she said. "Bit of an upset last night, wasn't it? Teo said he saw you on the dike when he went out to help with the repairs."

"I can't do this," I said. "Rather, I won't do it."[339]

"I beg your pardon? Won't do what?"

I took a breath and steeled myself. "I won't lie for you. I won't tell any more stories for you. I won't let you use me like a tool.[340] Something bad is happening because of your choices and your greed, and I won't help you cover it up."

She stood slowly. "Think about what you're saying, Chant. You'll ruin yourself—no one in this city would hire you again. Your future, all your prospects . . . You'll be blacklisted forever."[341]

"I don't care," I said, because I didn't.[342] "I've never cared about

---

339 Yes! At last! All right, now the interesting parts, right? Now the parts where you tell Sterre to go to hell.

340 Yes! Yes! Yes, yes!

341 What a ridiculous notion. There are more places in the world than a Chant could ever hope to visit in their lifetime. You could make a project of getting yourself blacklisted from as many of them as possible, and still there would be places and people in the world left willing to listen to you.

342 Good.

that. I have to do the right thing. You made mistakes, terrible ones. The flowers are dying even now—after last night, it's a certainty. We can't cover it up, and we shouldn't have been trying to. We shouldn't have sold the flowers like that in the first place. The sickness has already swept through the city, and soon they'll all be dead, but it won't matter to you, because you're rich, right? It won't matter that people are going to be ruined, that they're going to *starve*."

"Do you think I'm happy about this? Do you think I wanted it to happen?"

"No, I don't. But you knew that it might, and then it did. I won't help you anymore. I'm already partly responsible for this."

"You promised," she hissed.

"I promised to help you fix it," I said. "And I will. We have to undo what we've done. We have to make amends. We have to rebuild with our own hands the thing we broke."

"Chant, have some sense!"

I drew myself up. "Don't call me Chant," I said. "My name is Ylfing.[343] And I'm going to tell the truth. It's the one little thing I can do to help."

She threw me out. She would have wrestled me into the canal, if I'd let her, but I squirmed out of her grip and ran—I'd left my boots and my oilcloak, and I lost my suede indoor slippers almost immediately, and then there was something lovely and freeing about feeling the light drizzle in my hair and the cold wet cobblestones through my socks—only rain, harmless, since the tides had begun to fall again as the moons waxed and moved out of alignment.

---

343 I'll let this one slide—if you felt like you had to be . . . *that* . . . in order to tell the truth, then fine. Fine.

I came to the Rose and Ivy, where Mistress Chant was staying, because there is no better place, I suppose, to make my confessions and to think about what I'll do.

She isn't here; the innkeeper said he expects her back later this evening,[344] so I've paid for a room and some paper and ink and settled in to wait for her.

Choices. Choices like telling Sterre my real name. Like Orfeo. Like writing down everything that happened to me because words on a page are real in a way that they're not when they're only in your head. In your head, they're shifting formless things, twisting and gyrating through the air with no heed to reason. But on paper, you can shape them. You can put some discipline on them. You can draw conclusions from them that you can't when they're mere nebulous thoughts somewhere in the dark. And sure, yes, maybe at some point they get taken from you and used against you.

Or maybe you give them away and hope that someone will understand you as well as you understand yourself. Because those weeks ago, after I'd spoken to Neeltje, when I said that something as small and inconsequential and powerless as being understood, however briefly, by someone who feels your pain as their own couldn't possibly help? I was wrong. It's not pathetic and it's not pointless. I thought it was nothing, but . . . One little thing like that can be *everything*.[345]

Here are the words I need to be real:

I'm Ylfing. I care about people, and I've been afraid because caring got me hurt, made me miss things that were right in front of me. Easier to just draw away, easier to run from it. But I care. I care

---

344 "There's some raggedy half-drowned young *mann* what says he's here to see you. He's got no shoes, but he had enough coin to buy a room. Weird priorities. Do you know him?"

345 Hm. I see. I don't agree, but . . . I do see.

and care and care, whether or not the person I care for deserves it. Everyone deserves understanding, at the very least.[346]

My greatest strength has always been in looking at someone and finding an inherent spark of goodness in them. This is not to redeem them. Some people are beyond redemption. But even they yearn to be understood, just as everyone does, just as I do. So I look into their hearts and find the jewel among the slop. Except the slop too has value and weight and importance. It completes a person.

People soften when they're around me. At least, they used to when I was young and small and cute. Perhaps they still do—I'll have to watch for it. I never did anything in particular to merit that softening, besides being soft myself, and kind, and loving. I just reached out to them with my heart and made a connection.

And maybe that's the key to all of it. Connections.

When I was an apprentice, my master-Chant liked to tell me about how valuable stories are. We need no material to trade, he said, besides words. He bragged about the times he'd wandered through an area gripped by severe famine. He would stop to ply his trade in the town centers, and at the end, he'd find that he had earned no money, but someone would have given him a crust of bread to eat. He said that's how you know the value of what you're doing. Because in a famine, the food should have been the most valuable thing, but they were still willing to pay him a crust to be taken away from their suffering. So the story was, therefore, more valuable than the food, right?

Right?

Right?

But that's not right. Not at all. Because people want to stay alive, more than anything, and if there had been any danger of someone

---

346 This, this I agree with.

truly starving, he wouldn't have gotten paid, not even in crusts of bread, no matter how good his story was. It wasn't about that. His methods were right, but his conclusions were wrong.

Telling the story connected him to them. It wove a bond between them. The food wasn't payment; it was a *gift*. It was just someone looking after their own, *because that's what you do*. You look after your people. You form bonds. And those connections—those are what matter most.

Those are the most valuable things in the world.[347]

Mistress Chant thinks that I'm a heretic for—gods, a lot of things. I don't even know the full list of things she hates me for or thinks that I'm doing wrong.[348] But I'll write this here and now, my confession: I *have* sinned, this last year and a half since I sank my homeland beneath the waves. My sin was in drifting unanchored through the world, in passing by people like a ghost, in failing to reach out to them, in letting my fear get the better of me, in thinking it wasn't *important*. My sin was the selfishness to think that *I* wasn't important, that I couldn't be important to the people I was passing. And that's not the sin of a Chant. That's a sin within the reach of any of us.

I can't save everyone completely. But maybe I can mostly save a couple people, or save most people a tiny bit. It's one little thing, and that's better than nothing. That's always better than nothing.

Sterre's going to have to see reason, before anything else. She's going to have to accept my help. When I reach out, tossing her a rope

---

347 Oh . . . Oh, you're right. My master-Chant used to tell me that little fable too. I don't know if it was ever true, but I can see how many Chants might have had similar experiences. But you're right—it was never really because the stories were that good. That's vanity. It was never about the stories. It was just . . . people. Of course.

348 "Hates" is an awfully strong word. I can be angry at you without hating you.

like she's drowning, she'll have to take hold of it. And then, together, we'll toss ropes to everyone, and maybe they'll do the same for other people, on and on until the city is a web, lashed down by a thousand ropes to weather the stormy season. That's the only way to survive misfortune and turmoil.

Heyrland knows about floods. They know about throwing ropes to the drowning. If I were anywhere else in the world, I don't think that this would work. But here . . . maybe. Maybe.

Here, there's a chance. Because they know what they need to do to keep the waters back.

⸻ ❖ ⸻

Mistress Chant returned. I don't have the strength to write about that now[349]—every time we speak I stagger away only wanting to sleep for a year, rolled up in a blanket in the attic of the inn where it's quiet.

---

349 Motherfucker! Fine!

FORTY-NINE ½

Some of Us Have Discipline, You Know

Except it has to be written, Brother-Chant, whether you feel like it or not—hell, even whether I do. The story has to be complete, and the talk we had that day was important, and it informed the things we talked about later. I still don't like this writing-things-down affair, but . . . the story has to be complete. It would be a greater sin to let it remain fractured.

So:

———◆———

"There's some raggedy half-drowned young *mann* what says he's here to see you," said *Mevriend* Otte, the innkeeper, upon my return. "He's got no shoes, but he had enough coin to buy a room. Weird priorities. Do you know him?"

It was the weird priorities that made me think it might be my brother-Chant. I sent Arenza and Lanh Chau to occupy themselves in the common room, and I followed Otte's directions up to Chant's room—the door stood open, and Chant himself sat at a small desk, scribbling what I thought at the time was a very long letter.

"And to what do I owe the pleasure today?" I said. He looked up—Otte's description hadn't been far off. His hair was half-dried, but his clothes were still sodden and dripping, and all he had on his feet was a pair of muddy socks. "Shouldn't you be at de Waeyer's offices?"

"We had a fight and she threw me out." He slid all his papers into a stack and put a blank sheet over the top to cover his writing—all I glimpsed was a few lines of Xerecci, written in a fair, clean hand.

"Glad to know you pick fights with more than just me," I said, making myself comfortable in the other chair.

"I was in the right. I told her ... Well, you probably don't want to hear about all that." He fiddled nervously with the papers. "Could I tell you a story?"

"Of course."

"A very long time ago and half the world away," he began, a little rushed. (See, Brother-Chant? I can take your butterflies and pin them to paper too. How's it feel?) "My master-Chant and I returned to my homeland in Hrefnesholt. He was old, you see, too old to be traveling that much anymore, and he longed to rest his feet. He knew I wasn't quite ready to go off by myself, but he couldn't lead me anymore, and I didn't want to settle. I wanted to go; I wanted to keep having adventures and meeting new people and discovering beautiful things. I wanted to see the Palazzo della Colombe in Pezia, and the dragons hatching in Xereccio, and the festival of lights in Tash. I was prepared to take the oaths. I had been prepared for years. I'd carried a rock around with me ever since I left home, but my Chant told me I needn't have.

"We went home, back to my own little village with the mountains hard at its back and the pebbly beach of the fjord at its toes, with the forests thick around, and the little plots of farmland. We went home, and I discovered it wasn't really home anymore. My parents were still alive, but we were nearly strangers to each other—we'd always been strangers on some level. That's part of why I left in the first place, because something in me had known I didn't belong there, that I didn't fit. I'd always been looking off over the horizon—before I met Chant, my biggest dream was of being taken to this competition between all the villages, called the Jarlsmoot. That was the greatest adventure I could conceive of.

"When we returned, I only found that I fit even less. The boy I'd been in love with was as grown as I, and he was taller and stronger and handsomer than when I'd left, and he'd taken up making-home with another boy we'd known as children. It was all just the same as it had always been, and I was nothing like the boy who had left. I'd seen more things and done more things than any of them could dream of. They welcomed me home with warmth, but when we sat down at the fireside and they asked me about my travels, they gawked at every word I said, and they swore it must be impossible, that the world could not be as big as I described.

"I had changed too much. I had already lost my homeland, pain-lessly and gradually, in bits and pieces, with every step away, and even with every step back to them.

"So early the next morning, when the sun had not yet burned away the mist veiling the surface of the water, I led my Chant a little ways out of the village, down along the narrow, rocky beach to a secret place I knew where a brook tumbled out of the pine forest into the fjord. It was quiet but for the birds, and we were well enough distant from the village that we might have been the only two people in all the world.

"'Last chance, my boy,' said Chant. 'Don't do it unless you mean it. There's time yet to think about it.'

"But I was ready, and though my heart ached for the homeland I'd lost, it was no worse than the homesickness I'd felt on the road a hundred times. I scraped up a handful of dirt and pebbles, and I said the oaths, and I wept for Hrefnesholt and for Arthwend, and then I waded out knee-deep into the cold water, and lowered my hands under the surface. I sank my homeland the way it had been lost, slowly and gently, first soaked to mud and then worn away in trickles between my fingers by the currents of the water, until all that was left was a little bit clinging to my skin and under my nails. And I washed that away too, and then I went back to the shore, and hugged my Chant, so small and old and frail, and wept while he clucked his tongue and scolded me in that way he had, and chafed my hands to warm them, and told me I was very stupid, which had always meant that he loved me and worried about me.

"We spent all day there, him giving me advice and chastising me about minding my manners out there in the world, and sometimes he said nothing, and we just sat together in silence, in the dancing, dappled sunlight that came through the pines. And when I'd stopped weeping, we told each other stories of all our best memories of those years we'd traveled together, and we laughed, and I cried again, and he told me I was an idiot.

"The next morning, I left. And Chant stood at the threshold of my mother's cottage and watched me go along the shore road, waving whenever I looked back over my shoulder, all the way until the forest blocked him from my sight.

"And that was how I became a Chant," he said.

I nodded.

"What do you think?" he asked.

"Does it matter what I think? It's your story, and it's a story for you. It doesn't matter what I think of it." He looked sort of upset, so I sighed. "It was a good story, Chant."

After a long pause, he said slowly, "You could call me by my real name."

"No. Absolutely not. You told a good story; don't ruin it with some . . . dreadful whimsy."

"It's not a whimsy. I've been thinking of it for a long time. Of using my name again, I mean. Don't you want to know what it is, at least? It's—"

"Hush!" I said sharply. "I won't use it. I don't even want to know it."

"It's my choice to use it. You could respect that. It doesn't have anything to do with you."

"You made an oath, and you would break it so easily? Pig trough or fjord, both ways you made the oath. I don't agree to be your accomplice in this. I don't agree to witness whatever damn fool thing you think you're doing, whatever adolescent tantrum you're having about it. Now, are you here only to tell me that story, or was there something else you wanted?"

"I want to know how to undo a story."

"Don't ask me questions you already know the answer to. You tell me how."

"Tell another, and hope that the first one is weaker, I guess," he said bitterly. "You were right, you know. About the flowers, about my part in it."

"Of course I was." And then, because I was feeling vindictive, I said, "You're a smart lad." I wouldn't speak his master's language. If I called him an idiot, he might think I approved of him.

"Would it really be so bad if I broke my oaths?" he said. "If I decided to . . . give it all up?"

"I don't know," I said flatly. "Would it? Could you live with yourself if you did?"

"You'd like it, me giving up Chanting. At least part of you would. But you'd be upset with it too. You want me to be better than that."

"Once again, it doesn't have anything to do with me. It's none of my concern. It's between you and your ability to sleep at night."

"Have you ever thought of it? Settling down? Finding one place to stay?"

"Of course I have. I plan ahead. How you imagine spending your twilight years, what with that ridiculous and unnecessary devotion to asceticism that you got from your master, I'm sure I don't know. Me, I'll have a house and food, because I've planned for it."

"Where will you go, when you're ready?" He glanced at me. "Inacha, I suppose. To be with the one you love."

"And that's none of your concern."

"I've been thinking lately that it might be nice," he said, fidgeting anxiously with the edges of the papers once more. "If I were married. If I belonged somewhere."

"You won't do it," I said. "You're talking about it, but you won't."

"How would you know?"

I snorted. "Have you found some all-consuming love, then? Something right out of legend? Some lover who, in giving you his heart, will eclipse everything else that came before? You wouldn't settle for anything less. A Chant never does."

"Is that His Majesty of Inacha for you, then?"

I spread my hands. "You see me sitting here before you in Heyrland, don't you? Chants don't settle down like that. We're too full of stories to find a human relationship stable or sustainable. No living man could ever live up to the myths you'd tell yourself about him. You'd make him into a concept, or an avatar, or you'd set him on a little pedestal and build a shrine around him. You'd expect him to move mountains for you or part the seas, or something else ridiculous like Tyrran's twelve tasks—you'd expect him to be a mythic hero. And he won't be; he'll just be a person, crushed to dust under the weight of your expectations." I leaned forward. "You might walk away from Chanting, but Chanting won't ever walk away from you."

"You don't know all that," he said softly. "Not for certain. You're guessing. What if my story had been that I went home with my Chant, and Finne wasn't making-home with anyone? What if he'd waited for me? What if I'd decided to stay?"

I shrugged. "You keep demanding answers from me, and I have none. All I know is patterns. I've made something of a study of them, you see, the way Lanh Chau does with music, the way he'll do one day with food, whenever that bolt of lightning strikes him."

He stood abruptly, shuffled his papers together into a stack, rolling them up and wrapping them in several blank sheets, presumably to keep them dry. He tucked them into his coat, and I folded my hands and watched.

"I'm leaving."

"You don't say."

"I'm trying, all right? I know you don't believe it, but I am."

Adolescent histrionics. I took no notice of them. "Well, have a good evening. Do come back again if you have any real questions. Maybe one of these days you might ask after me, instead of talking about yourself the whole time."

<hr />

There. That's better.

The other reason he'll never settle down and get married is because he runs away the second shit gets hard. No one ever taught him how to argue constructively. No, he'll stick with Chanting.

FIFTY

oday I went to the coffeehouse on the Rojkstraat, which was sleepy and smoky as usual. To my great luck, I happened to see Crispin sitting at a table in the back. I went up to him immediately and said, "Sir, we met the other day. You know me as Chant. I've been selling those flowers for Sterre de Waeyer."

"Oh, yes. Good morning," he said.

"I wanted to talk about the variant flower you spoke of before."

He smirked and poured me a cup of coffee from his carafe. "I'm afraid it's too late," he said. "I've already signed a contract with *Mevrouw* Valck. She's buying it, to be delivered as soon as the bulb can be moved."

"You have to cancel the contract," I said. "You won't be able to fulfill it. The flower isn't a variant; it's sick."

He set his cup down with a clatter. "Sick," he said.

"It's a disease that strikes the stars-in-the-marsh. First, the color shifts and the petals mutate. Then speckles of black grow over it: first the leaves, then the stalk, and the flower. Then it dies back." I bit my lip. "It spreads like a plague. Through the water. So your other flowers . . ."

He stared at me for a moment, then laughed. "Well, this is a clever strategy, but unfortunately it's one I've seen before. Listen—maybe try it on someone else. I don't blame you at all," he added quickly, raising a hand to quell my objection. "I'm not at all upset with you for trying. An enterprising youth like yourself has to take every advantage he can. I was just the same when I was your age. And really," he said encouragingly, "you almost had me. You were so close! Just keep practicing, and I bet you'll be able to convince someone else. Now, did you want feedback, or . . . ?"

"It's not a ruse, sir; I'm not trying to trick you. Your flowers are dying. If the others aren't showing the signs already, they will soon. You might as well pull them up by their roots and burn them."

His eyebrows shot up. "I beg your pardon, no."

"I'm not lying to you. Don't try to sell them on! You're already ruined." You have to speak to Heyrlandtsche in a particular way. "There is a great storm coming. Reef your sails or risk shipwreck."

"I appreciate the warning. If you'll excuse me."

So it didn't work. I went to a few of the houses of Sterre's other clients, people I was faintly acquainted with. I told them what I'd told Crispin.

Nobody listened to me. I've gone to everyone I can, pounded on their doors, begged to see their flowers. They—or more often their servants—refuse me entry and shut the door in my face.

But it's too late anyway: of the one or two people who remembered me from the salons and allowed me to see their gardens, each of them has at least one star-in-the-marsh that is exhibiting signs of the sickness. I've tried to tell them, but no one listens to me—they all laugh and wonder what incredible new plot Sterre has cooked up now.

The so-called variation is lovely, I'll grant them that—some of them are as yellow as lemons, some of them a glistening white-gold. The mutation of the petals is delicate and lacy, and of those which are far enough gone, the black spots spread across the centers of the petals like freckles across the bridge of someone's nose.

I don't have the right story. It's not strong enough to turn the tide against everything else I've been telling them for months, again and again and again. No, not a tide—I sang a *flood* into being, drop by drop, and now I am but one voice trying to repair the dike. It will take months again to make any progress against this thing I've built, and I don't have months.

FIFTY-ONE

Something happened and it wasn't a big deal.

There. That's the hardest part done—actually starting, putting words down instead of staring at a blank sheet of paper and feeling . . . I don't know. Feeling feelings.

If it wasn't a big deal, why do I want to spend the time and ink to scrutinize it? Orfeo said it was nothing, and he'd know better than I do. So why do I care? I should just forget about it, like he said. Nobody got hurt, not really. Just a little heart-bruised, but that's what happens when your hopes are disappointed. It happens every day, to everyone. It's not something to be having a crisis over.

I'm not having a crisis. Am I? Orfeo said I shouldn't. I'm fine, and he said it was nothing. He said it wasn't even worth writing about.

I think I'm going to write about it anyway. I'm only wasting my own time, after all.

───── ◆ ─────

It started in the dark with Orfeo, just as we were about to drift off to sleep. "So," he said. "I haven't wanted to bring it up, but . . ."

I held my breath.

"We're leaving. The worst of the storms have passed, and my uncle wants to be getting back. My cousins too. We're all getting homesick."

"Oh," I said.

"Have you given any thought . . ." His arms tightened around me briefly, then loosened abruptly, deliberately, like he was trying not to cling to me, like he was trying not to cage me, just in case I didn't want to be caged. "Come back with me. Come back to Pezia. I'll introduce you to my family. They'd like you—Uncle Simo already does."

"I don't know . . ." I said, thinking of the flowers, thinking of the flood and the dike.

Orfeo drew me closer, rubbing his nose against my neck and jaw. "You'd like Pezia," he said, low and beguiling. "And Lermo is a beautiful city, all wide streets and fountains, trees everywhere, ivy growing over all the buildings, orange groves—we have one at the country house. And at the city house, there's a covered walk around a courtyard, a cloister, all overgrown with wisteria. They bloom in the spring—I've never seen anything so pretty, except for you."

I laughed. "Are plants the main attraction, then?"

"You like plants, so yes."

"Do I?"

"Don't you? You're always on about those flowers. You have one in your room—you'd have to like plants to put up with the smell."

"I've never really thought about it."

"Well, there's other things. There's parties every night, if you know enough people or where to go, and dancing, and beautiful clothes—we could afford them. The family would give us a stipend, and I told you they'd give you a job, so there would be your salary too. We could buy all the clothes we wanted, and a new pair of dancing slippers every day, and—"

I laughed again. "I definitely don't like dancing enough to do it every day."

"Shit. Food, then. Everyone likes food." I let the silence draw out just long enough for him to scold, "*Ylfing*," before I burst into giggles.

"All right, sure, yes. Nearly everyone likes food, including even me. Sometimes."

Orfeo huffed and grumbled into my hair, "Being difficult."

"Sorry, sorry. I'm cooperating."

"Better food in Pezia, that's all I was going to say." He grumbled again and kissed my temple. "Other things too. All the things you like. If something's lacking, I'll . . . *unlack* it. Come back with us. You know you want to."

I turned and kissed him, leaned my forehead against his. "There's something here I need to fix, before I go anywhere. I can't leave quite yet."

He was quiet for a moment. "I could stay here with you until it's done."

That, of all things, made my heart skip a beat. But . . . "No," I said. "Your family—you're making so much progress on repairing things with them. Staying here is the *rake* thing to do; you have to show them you're reliable and sensible now, and make the reliable, sensible choice. Go back with them."

"Wouldn't it be nicer if I was here?"

"Yes, but . . . It's best if you go."

"I just don't want you to think that I've *left* you when I leave you. I want to keep you." He paused. "We could be married before I leave."

Tempting, actually—I didn't want to feel like he'd left me when he left either. I've had enough of being abandoned by a roadside for one life. But still . . . "That's even more of a rake thing to do, Orfeo. How would that conversation go with your family?"

"'I met someone in Heyrland, you'll think he's wonderful, just ask Uncle Simo.'"

"And then they ask when they'll get to meet me, and you have to say, 'Well, he's not here, and actually, you don't get a choice about having him around once he arrives. You have to take him, even if you end up hating him.' Reliable, sensible choices, Orfeo. Uncle Simo said I was a good influence on you, didn't he? Listen: they have a story about Orfeo in their heads that's been in the telling for twenty years. You can't change a story like that overnight."

He was silent for so long that I thought he'd fallen asleep, and I began to think about getting up to go to the attic to stare at the flower and wonder what the hell I was going to do. "If," he said suddenly.

"If?"

"If I'd said something else, would you have said something else?"

"What do you mean?"

"I didn't know what things you liked. I don't have any idea what things you like. If I'd known, just now, would you have agreed to leave with us?" He was more nervous than I'd ever heard him, even that time in Sterre's garden when he was beside himself with confusion, swamped and uncertain.

I kissed him again. "*I* barely know what I like; I wouldn't expect *you* to know."

"You like me, don't you?"

"Very much. You should have led with that! Pezia has Orfeo in it." I closed my eyes and nestled farther into his arms. "It doesn't really matter if you don't know what I like," I said. "You love me."[350] That was the moment it all started going wrong. Because as soon as I said that, he went tense and still.

"Orfeo? What did I say?"

"Nothing," he said, and I noticed, distantly, that he was using his

---

350 Unhealthy, Chant! Don't tell that kind of thing to a boy! He might get the impression that he doesn't need to give a shit or keep making an effort once he's got you as a sure thing.

rake voice, smooth and soothing and so much less genuine than he'd been a moment ago, even when he was trying to beguile me. He didn't sound like himself.

"Something," I insisted. "What's wrong?"

"Don't worry about it."

"Too late—I'm already worried. What is it?"

"Just something stupid." He cleared his throat, and shifted, and began kissing my neck in that way he knows I like, and slipped his hand under the covers, stroking my side, my hip. "Let me help you get to sleep, gorgeous."

I grabbed his wrist. "A Chant's job is to find things out—my master and I once walked fifty miles through a thunderstorm in the mountains just to find a woman rumored to have a talking cow. This, in comparison, is nothing, because you're already here in front of me. You're going to tell me this stupid thing. Don't lie and say it's nothing, because I can smell that it isn't."

"I don't want to upset you."

"I'm going to be upset anyway if I have to go to sleep thinking that I've offended you somehow. That ship has left the harbor. So what *is it?*"

"Did she have a talking cow? That woman?" he said, using his rake voice to sound interested.

"I'll tell you later. Why are you dodging the question? Do you think I—oh." I paused. "I only said I liked you very much, didn't I? Is that it?" He was silent, still tense. "You're upset because I haven't said I love you?" He got, if anything, tenser. "Oh, Orfeo. I'm sorry. Of course I do, sweetheart. Of course I do. How could I not?"

"That's—not," he began, strangled. "That's not. Fuck."

"What?"

"I . . . had not. Um. *Realized.* That's. Something that you might have ... wanted." He took a deep, slow breath. "You know what? I'm being stupid. It's nothing, really. I did say you could have anything you wanted. You want that, you can have—it." He choked a little there. "I'll take care of it; leave it to me."

"Now you sound like you're panicking." It was making me panic a little too, my heartbeat getting faster. "You didn't realize I'd want ... to love you? For you to love me?"

"Yes," he said awkwardly.

"But you want to marry me. Right? I didn't misunderstand that, did I? I come back to Pezia, I meet your family, they love me, you marry me, everyone's happy forever. That's the plan, right?"

"Yes, absolutely, yes."

"But you're not in love with me," I said blankly.

There was a long silence. "Not ... per se. Currently. I can work on it!"

I sat up, staring into the darkness across the room, empty and confused.

"Now you're upset," he said. "I knew you'd be upset. I told you it was stupid."

"No ... No, I think I'm the one being stupid." I should have laughed it off, maybe, lain back down and gone to sleep and decided that it wasn't important. There are plenty of places in the world where people marry for reasons besides love, where their families or a matchmaker choose someone for them. It works out there, sometimes better than it works with love matches. Families usually want the best for their children, after all. They want their children to be happy.

And there were all the people I knew in Nuryevet, who married for reasons besides love—for business purposes, or just to join households and have a life together with someone they could count on.

Love isn't required—I've seen people build strong and happy mar-
riages on friendship. I've seen them build their foundations merely on
the promise to guard each other's backs.

I shouldn't have said anything else. I should have agreed that it
was Orfeo's problem to worry about his own feelings. I shouldn't have
expected—assumed—

But Pezians have love songs, and dances like *amoroso* that are
about or for lovers. And *he wanted to marry me*. I just thought . . . "Do
you like *me*?" I asked.

"Well . . . yes? Yes," he said, more confidently. I put a hand to my
chest, feeling like I'd just been hit with the bewildering thump of a
crossbow quarrel. "I like talking to you, and I enjoy your stories. And I
very much like sex with you. And stories during sex: that was hot; you
could do that again," he offered. "And besides, Uncle Simo loves you."

"Yes, but I'm not marrying Uncle Simo," I said testily. "You always
say that, you know. You always say how much your family will love
me—"

He sat up. "But that's the point."

"—I just feel like an idiot for thinking that included you. Wait,
what's the point?"

"That they'd love you." I didn't answer, just turned towards him in
the dark, even though I couldn't see him. "You know, because you're
so talented, and you know so many things, and—I mean, that *auction*,
Ylfing. If I always say it, it's because it's true. You're too smart to be
wasting your time with people like de Waeyer. She doesn't appreciate
you. In Pezia, you'll be able to have your pick of whatever job you
want with the family."

He'd said that a thousand times before, but this time I heard something in it—a faint, distant sort of thing, like a drip of water into a tin
bowl in the next room. I breathed, took a moment to remember all

the Chantly wiles I'd learned over the years, picking them up like rusty, unfavorite tools. "That's true . . ." I said. "It would be nice to have that."

"Right?" he said.

"I suppose you and I could carry on just as we have been." I felt like I was feeling my way by touch, testing each floorboard delicately with my feet before shifting my weight onto it.

"Yes." He sounded relieved.

"I probably should have talked to you about expectations and things, like in that first conversation we had. I suppose I jumped to conclusions."

"It's all right. I forgive you." He laughed softly. "Shit, I feel like I just ran a mile."

I feel like I've been shot in the chest, I thought, *and I'm about to find out if I'm right to.* "So what would you do in the family?"

"Oh, I expect they'll get off my back if I'm married." He laughed again and fell back into the pillows. "Especially if I'm married to you. I'll be able to leverage that for *years.* 'What do you mean I'm not pulling my weight? I brought you Ylfing, didn't I?'"

I forced myself to laugh convincingly. "That would be a significant contribution, wouldn't it?"

"Gods, yes. You'll be brilliant."

"And what will you be?"

"Happy. I'll never have to worry about anything ever again."

There, there it was. "Really? Nothing?"

"They'd never disown me, because then they'd have to disown you too. They wouldn't cut off *your* allowance. I—we—could do anything we liked." He sounded dreamy.

"Yeah, anything at all," I said, matching his tone. "And that'd be worth a loveless marriage."

"That'd be worth any marriage," he chuckled.

It might work for the Nuryevens, but it wouldn't for me. Mistress Chant was right again—I didn't write about it, but she made a comment when I was at her inn the other day. She said I'd never settle for a love less than something of legend, that I'd build a shrine for my love and expect him to part the seas for me, until he was crushed to dust by the weight of my expectations. And she was right. She's always right.[351]

"You're no better than Sterre, you know." Silence. I sat there trembling. "Really, you're no better than my master was either."

"What?"

I flung back the covers, feeling around on the floor for my clothes and pulling them on.

The mattress shifted behind me as Orfeo sat up again. "Are you—? Where are you going?"

"Not to Pezia, apparently." Tears were stinging at the corners of my eyes.

The soft faint gold of Orfeo's witchlight bloomed from behind me, enough to see that I'd put on my pants inside out. "Wait," Orfeo said. "You've misunderstood. Ylfing, stop. Just for a second, stop!"

"What have I misunderstood? You want me to marry you so that you can drink and go dancing and gamble all you want?"

"I mean, yes, partly, but there's a lot more to it than—"

"So I swear myself to someone who doesn't love me and might never love me, and go to work for his family for *his* benefit? I'm supposed to carry you for the rest of our lives so that *you* don't have to do anything unpleasant?"

"For *our* benefit, surely. Don't pretend like you're not getting anything out of this."

---

351 I shall sing the praises of the gods for gifting me with this miracle. Also, Orfeo's trash. I've always thought so.

"Nothing I care about," I snapped, turning sharply to face him. "I would have done it because I cared about *you*, and I thought you cared about me. I would have done it if we were in love." And the witchlight now let me see the way he looked a little sick, the way his eyes darted towards the door. "Thinking of running off without your drawers?"

"Not at all," he lied. "Listen, I told you—I told you that I intended to give you everything you want. I meant it. I can be in love with you if that's what you want."

I pulled on my shirt, not bothering with the buttons. "Oh yes? How?"

"I'll—I'll have flowers sent to you at the office, and I'll buy you nice clothes—"

"With the money *I* earn?"

"And I'll take you to most parties, and—I don't know what else you want! I don't know what else to do! You can't be mad at me for that. You said yourself you didn't know what you wanted."

"Are you going to have sex with only me, no one else?"

He froze, but only briefly. "If that's what you want. I keep my promises." He was lying.

I climbed out of bed. "I'm not marrying you."

"Ylfing, wait, stop." He was panicking again, getting frantic, seeing his one last chance slipping through his fingers. I strode towards the door and he dove after me, catching me by the wrist. "Please, please don't go. It's late, we're both tired, and it's just a spat. Everyone has spats."

"I'm not marrying you."

"Five minutes ago you would have! You were almost there; you were about to decide to!"

"I don't like this anymore." I pulled my wrist away.

"I was honest with you; be honest with me about this one thing."

I looked at him—naked and wild-eyed and terrified, beside himself with it. "Yes," I said. "I would have followed you to Pezia. I would have followed you anywhere. It's kind of what I do with people I care about."

I stared hard at him for a long few heartbeats, then reached for the doorknob.

"Stay," Orfeo said, in a wretched voice. "Marry me."

I felt something, then, strange—it was like a pressure, but it wasn't physical. It was like . . . Like a suggestion of the feeling you get when someone wraps their arms around you, presses their palms between your shoulder blades, pulls you forward into a welcome kiss, and—

"Orfeo, are you nudging me?" I asked blankly.[352]

The sensation stopped immediately and

[353]

---

352 Oh, fucking *hell*. Are you serious? *Orfeo Acampora tried to nudge you?*
353 Huh. Okay. There's about fifteen different questions that immediately spring to mind, but I suppose the most obvious ones are "What the fuck?" and "Stopped immediately and *what*? What happened, what did he *do*? What did *you* do?"

Decided it wasn't nothing after all. Went to Simoneto's room. Asked him about it. He woke up everyone. It's being handled. [354]

---

354 Well, shit. "Being handled" is awfully vague, but considering they're the wealthiest and most powerful family in Lermo (and among the top five families in all Pezia), I can only imagine how little they'd want people to know that one of their scions used the Pezian curse against another person. I wonder if they disowned him outright, or if they've only dragged him home to keep him under private house arrest for a few decades.

Shame, really. I would have tracked him down and castrated him for you.

I'm having to remind myself that you were well enough to write all this down after the fact, and had the mental acuity and awareness to notice him doing it in the first place, and then the intuition to smell out that he was lying when he told you it wasn't worth being concerned about or writing down. Well done, you. Good Chantly survival instincts, there: When in doubt, run your mouth to someone. Always get a second opinion.

FIFTY-EIGHT [355]

Dreams.[356] Still every night, but now when I wake they feel ...
close. Like part of me is still in them, still dreaming, like the
dream is laid out behind me and even in the waking world I

---

355 Wait. The previous section was number fifty-one. Am I missing parts of this?
Did you misplace some pages? Except the rest of this was arranged so carefully....
Your numbering has been so tidy and careful up to this point, and the pages were
packaged so neatly. You wouldn't have lost them, not when the rest of it is here like
this. And *I've* been careful too, except for that section I tossed in the fire, early on. So
I haven't lost them.

Which can only mean that you removed them yourself. On purpose. You removed
six chapters, and blacked out the rest of the writing on the page you had to leave in.

What *in the name of all the gods* happened that night? How was it *handled*?
356 No! Don't go back to this; don't distract from the issue! Don't distract *yourself*,
~~Ylfing~~ Chant! (Ignore that.) You're just going to stonewall me on this? You're not
going to give away anything?

Damn your eyes, Chant, you're doing it again—the same thing you were doing
when I first found you. But this is your pattern, isn't it? You can't cope with betrayal,
and that's what the nudging was, wasn't it? If you won't tell me, then I'll have to
imagine it myself, or deduce it. So what have you given me to work with? Six missing
chapters, and a few paragraphs redacted, after an abrupt end. It should have been
a bittersweet recounting of separating with your lover—that's what you wanted it
to be, wasn't it? The whole preceding part, was that even true? Or did you edit it as
well, to make it tidier and more comfortable, less heartbreaking? Did you end there
because you couldn't wrench the story away from truth?

Or was it all true, and you stopped where you did because you decided that
was the only truth you wanted to keep? There are many truths—all Chants know
this. Are you choosing one in particular to be yours, the way I told you to choose a
different story about your master?

could just turn into it, wheel around like a cormorant on the wing, and dive back below the surface, straight into it.

The figure has moved, now. They sit closer to me, still silent. The boat moves through the marsh, and the flowers die around us. As they succumb, the putrid scent eases. As each flower dies, a new star appears in the heavens, more every night. The Eye of Shuggwa (called also the Woman's Clay Pot, or the Mirror of Heaven, or a hundred other names; but Chants call it this) is bright and clear now, and I can begin to pick out a few other constellations—the Plowshare, the Cat and Mouse, Ardi's Gold Ring, the Lamp, the Dragon.

I rarely look at the figure anymore, but they watch me, I think, though I can't see their face. Sometimes I think they're smiling.[357]

They look so dark and ominous. They should be frightening, or at the very least unsettling, but I don't feel that. I don't feel unsafe. They wouldn't have saved me from drowning if they wanted to hurt me.

In the dreams, I don't do anything but look and wait. Neither of us speaks, either—I watch the flowers die, or I look at the figure in the stern of the boat, or at the bird. I look up at the stars, or into the water where the stars are reflected.

It's strange. It's all knotted up in this thing I've been struggling

---

What do I know for certain? You excised six chapters and a few paragraphs. So you did write *something more*. You wrote something that you didn't want anyone to see, or perhaps that you didn't want *me* to see. Or . . . perhaps something that you wanted to erase from existence entirely. What was it you said in those first pages? Writing things down makes them real? Makes them a paper copy of a mind? I'm getting closer now, aren't I? There was something in those chapters that you wanted not just to hide but to *unmake*.

I'm sitting here quietly and wondering, suddenly, if I'll find Orfeo's name mentioned again even once through the rest of these pages.

357 And if it's not the Orfeo thing, it's *this*. I can't stand this. I can't understand. Why? Why would he appear to you? We're so far from anywhere he might still carry a whisper of power, so why . . . ? Is it your belief in connections? Is it something else? *Why?*

with, who I am and whether I should be a Chant and how to do Good. I think the dreams will stop when I've figured everything out. It's funny how your sleeping mind works sometimes. It's always gnawing on whatever's bothering you—it's funny how much it can sneak up on you and take over. It comes up with all kinds of wild fictions to help you make sense of the world.

———————•◆•———————

That's the sort of strange thing minds do when you're not paying close attention to them. The stress of everything—of avoiding ████ ,[358] of dealing with his family trying desperately to buy my silence,[359] of watching the flowers teeter on the edge of death while the city takes no notice of the end rushing up on them—it's overwhelming me, and I haven't been sleeping well. I lie awake in my attic, worrying all night, trying not to toss and turn for fear of disturbing Simoneto in the room below, now that he's taken it over.

---

358 Knew it.
359 Oh, shit. They found out, somehow, that he'd nudged you, then. Or you told them outright. Trying to buy your silence—so they're afraid you'll tell someone, and they're afraid of what would happen to them or their reputation if you did. From what I know of Pezians, they'll be dealing with Orfeo privately, keeping it a family matter.

FIFTY-NINE

It has been five days since I've been to Sterre's offices. I've been out in the city, telling the story of the disease, imagining myself singing a countercharm against a flood.

I was wrong before, when I said they didn't listen to me. They do listen; of course they do. But they don't believe, and they don't act. It is too terrible to believe in. But they listen. At first quietly confused, laughing it off. Later, with anger beginning like the bubbles at the bottom of a pot of water before it simmers.

But no action. Just silence, anger, resentment. Easier to dismiss me, even though they know me, even though they'd seen me at the Rojkstraat and at Stroekshall.

Funny how I've gotten exactly what I wanted, at exactly the time I don't want it anymore. I was longing for this, for them to ignore me, and now that I have it, I long for nothing more than that moment of influence that I had at the auction when I held the city rapt and beckoned them closer, inviting them to listen, to be swayed, to want what I offered, daring them to try to look away from me.

I went to Sterre again. I came into the offices and ignored the stares of the clerks as I walked through the long room, dodging and weaving in between the desks as I went, and I opened Sterre's office door.

"I've been talking to people," I said, before she could speak. "They won't give up the flowers, and the disease has spread. They know. I've seeded the story across the city, and it's beginning to spread too." It wasn't—not really. Those who thought themselves clever dismissed it as ridiculous rumors; everyone else was too fearful to speak of it—the same way they only speak the word "shipwreck" as a vile curse, for fear of bringing that misfortune upon them. The way the people of the ancient Chants in Arthwend spoke softly, walked softly, dressed blandly, and covered their heads so as not to draw Shuggwa's Eye. I don't know why that, of all things, was the metaphor I picked, but it's accurate.

Sterre sat back and rubbed her hands over her face. She looked as tired as I felt—bags under her eyes, and at least a day or two of salt-and-pepper stubble on her cheeks and chin. Her fine lace neck-cloth was wrinkled and stained with sweat where it touched her skin. "Shit," she said. I'd expected her to rage at me again, to throw me out, but . . . She was defeated. She was out of options and out of time. "It's done, then. It's over." She laughed, sharp. "I might as well run. Right?"

"No. You won't do that, and you shouldn't do that."

She got up, dragged her chair over to the window, and sat down again, looking out at the canal that backed the building. "You said . . . the other day. You said I shouldn't call you Chant anymore."

I settled myself in the other chair. "I did say that. My name is Ylfing."

"Ylfing. I'll call you that, then. I know something about changing names," she said wryly. "I changed mine once. There's still a few tiresome people who call me by the old one, foreign acquaintances I knew in my youth who haven't seen me in a while and who come from places where there are, allegedly, just *mannen* and *vrouwen*. Statistically speaking, that's wildly unlikely, but . . ." She shrugged. "No matter. Ought I offer congratulations on your change?"

"This isn't a change. It's an un-change. It's always been my name. Chant was—"

"Just a title," she murmured. "Yes, you mentioned." She paused. "Can I ask . . . why?"

"Why did I stop using my name?"

"No. Why are you going back to it?"

A big question. I could talk for days to tell her why. "It felt right," I said at last. "I don't feel like me when people call me Chant. I wanted to feel like myself again. I'm finding that it's easier for me to be sincere when I'm not lying about something that important. It's easier for me to do good." I gave her a look that I learned from my old master. "I have a story to tell you. Do you have time?"

"Are mobs going to arrive on my doorstep in the next hour?"

I leaned forward.

SIXTY

The Land That Sank beneath the Waves[360]
(As I Told It to Sterre)

A very long time ago and half the world away, there was a great and golden kingdom on a small continent in the middle of the southern reaches of the Unending Ocean. Their kingdom stretched from shore to shore, from the tallest mountains into the lowest swamp.

Or almost that far. There were tribes in the swamps that the kingdom had not absorbed, folk who had their own ways about them, their own stories, their own god: Shuggwa. A shadow god, a trickster god, a god whose Eye you should not draw, else misfortune and calamity befall you and those you loved. Unless, of course, you were a Chant. The Chants were Shuggwa's favored ones, and they called and called to him, drawing his Eye away so all the others could live in fearful, tiptoeing peace. The Chants lit great fires at night, danced and sang, and dressed in bright clothes and jewelry, tied bells around their ankles and wore clattering strings of beads in their hair. They did all this to protect the people of their villages, to shield them from

---

360 Fuck, no. What did I say before when you were trying to tell this story at van Vlymen's salon? This one's ours.

harm and misfortune, and they carried in their heads the wisdom and memories of generations, passed down in whispers from one Chant to the next.

Then one day, the great and golden kingdom angered the gods, and the water came. (*Here, Sterre stopped and looked at me, suddenly still, right on the cusp of haunted horror, and I felt a curl of pleasure, of certainty. The Heyrlandtsche know what it is to do battle against the sea.*)[361]

The waves rushed across the land, a cataclysmic wall of water that washed aside everything in its path. The kingdom drowned, every *mann* and *vrouw* and *niets*, every *vroleisch*, *tzelve*, and *loestijr*.[362] All the children and all the animals. The land sank and was lost.

But the Chant-people had their little flat-bottomed marsh boats, only big enough for three or four people each, and as the waters rose and swallowed up the land, they gathered up what few possessions and supplies they had and lashed all these boats together with ropes at the direction of their wise Chants. The Chants guided them, saved them. Every little village of the swamp found another village, and another, until all the Chant-people from all the villages were tied together into a great floating pontoon that shifted and flexed and rolled with the rise and fall of the waves. A single boat alone would have been capsized as the first wave hit, but when tied together with hundreds of others, when they became one big boat; they were too wide and too strong to be lost.

The Chants sang, begging for Shuggwa's capricious mercy, and they danced night and day. The Chant-people knew the stars, but not the sea, and they had no idea if there was land to be found,

---

361 Hm. Okay, I see why you chose this. But you could have given her "Paika and the Flood," or "Old Bagu's Dream" about the river god who rolls out of his banks, or literally any other tale about any other mythic deluge.

362 Good adaptation, fitting this detail to your audience. Makes it more real to her.

or how far it was, or in what direction. But they had their boats, and the web of ropes that lashed them together, and they had their Chants to guide them and carry them across the waves and sing to save them from the water.

They couldn't have done it alone. Even a Chant, solitary, couldn't have done it.

They danced for Shuggwa and sang to the heavens, and the ocean currents carried them north, in the direction of the Eye of Shuggwa (which you Heyrlandtsche call the Whirlpool) where it hung bright and low in the sky. And when they saw at last land on the horizon, the Chants fell down in exhaustion and had to be carried ashore, caked with salt but alive, and saved from the sea.

SIXTY-ONE

I leaned my arms on the desk. "Here in Heyrland, you live right at sea level—when the king-tides come, it's more like a few feet below, as much as a dozen in some places. Why is that?"

"Because it's ours. It's home."

"So you fight against the sea. Your whole country fights every day to keep back the water. Because if the dikes come down, *everyone* drowns." I leveled another look at her. "Sterre, when you brought the stars-in-the-marsh, when you employed me to make them more than they were, you built a dike that you knew might fail. You *knew* about the disease, and you knew that it strikes sooner or later. You built the dike and then you made me lie about it. You told me to tell everyone that it was good and strong and worthy of trust, and now the water is about to come rushing in, and people are going to be ruined. Some of them might die."

"You're embellishing the extent of my responsibility in this," she said quietly. "Everything has risk. We didn't tell them to trade the futures contracts. We didn't tell them to bid the prices through the roof."

"No. But you put me in beautiful clothes in front of them and told me to do my worst. You told me to pull them by their hearts, like—" I swallowed. "Do you know about the Pezian gift? Nudging?"

"Yes. A gift, you think it? Every Pezian I've known has called it 'the curse.'"[363]

That plucked a twisting note of sharp emotion on my inner strings. "Everyone can nudge like that," I said. "Or they could if they learned and practiced. It's no different than persuasion. It's no different than what I do, but I do it with words and stories instead of magic."

She quirked an eyebrow at me. "I don't think the Pezians would agree with you, nor do I. I'd call what *they* do coercion."

"You asked me to make the flowers irresistible," I said. "You asked me to nudge them into buying the flowers, and I did, with the tools that I had. I did it by hand; ▮▮▮ Acampora[364] could have done it by magic. It's no different."

"*Speech* is not considered criminal, the last I checked," she said flatly. "Using the Pezian curse on someone is. It's nearly a capital offense over there when it's used on a person. One step below battery or rape."

"What I did—what you asked me to do—isn't that much better. You lied, and you involved me in your lie. You knew the risk; you knew that the disease would come sooner or later. Can you accept the consequences of what we did? You know it was wrong. You asked me about angry mobs just now, and don't try to convince me that you were joking. You *know* you're ruined."

She flinched and dropped her eyes, twisting her hands in her lap.

"Your reputation matters to you," I continued. "And that's been destroyed, or it will be as soon as enough people hear the truth that I'm going to keep telling them. But . . . I think your community matters too, doesn't it? Everyone is part of the wall that keeps out the sea. If one

---

363 Told you so.
364 Well, that's one way to unmake him.

stone in the wall is weak, the whole thing comes down. You believe in the dikes, don't you? You believe like some people believe in gods."

"Yes," she said, very quiet.

"When the dike broke during the storm, where were you?"

"My warehouse by the docks."

"And what were you doing there?"

"I sent out a few boatloads of ship's rations—water, tack, dried meat, and fruit. A few barrels of nails, some tools, some oilcloaks—that was all we had that would have been useful. I lent *Mevrouw* van Petijer boats so her people could take loads of wood and stone out."

"Why did you do that?"

"It's just what you do. When the dike goes down, you run towards it, not away from it."

"Right. Even if you're scared?"

"Especially if you're scared."

"Because you have to be strong and brave to keep all that water back. You have to have a *conviction* that even enormous, impossible, futile tasks can succeed if every person shows up to help. If we all give what few useful things we have—a barrel of nails or water or hardtack, or a spare hammer. Right? And one day, the water's going to come in anyway, and Heyrland will be lost again. But for today . . . We can keep it back another day. If we do the strong and brave thing. If we fix the dike. I'm already doing all I can. I need you to help me."

She glanced up at me—her eyes had gotten red. "I never wanted this. I once dueled a man who called me a cheat, you know. Stabbed him in the arm."

I didn't think she'd want me to take any notice of her feelings or of the tears she barely kept in check. "I think that the sort of friends you have and the way they talk about you is . . . telling. You have a lot of acquaintances, but I've only met a few of your friends. They seem like good people, most of them," I said slowly. "And these good people seem to think that you're a good person too. You knew that the sickness would *probably* come eventually, but you didn't know when. If it had taken three or four years, perhaps the demand for the stars-in-the-marsh would have died out on its own, naturally and gradually, and it wouldn't be such a catastrophe. You aren't a cheat, per se, because you didn't design it this way on purpose. But you did conceal part of the truth. You're responsible for it."

"I was greedy," she said. "And incautious."

"Show me someone who isn't. If you do manage to find one, then they'll have different sins in place of those, I can guarantee that."

"When do we get to the part where you tell me how to lash all our boats together and navigate by the stars to guide us to land?"

I smiled. "There's only one thing to do. Your reputation is crumbling, but I can save it. I can save you. I can get you out of this, but you'll have to sacrifice something to do it. You'll have to give something up with the knowledge that you will get *nothing* in return. When I tell you to lash the boats together, I'll mean *all of them*, and . . . you seem to have ended up with the entire city's stock of rope."

"What am I giving up?"

"Everything," I said. "I can save you, but when I do, you'll be a pauper. You'll have nothing left. You'll have to start from scratch."

She stared at me in horror. "I'm only human," she protested. "How can you believe that I'm capable of that? Of giving everything up, of *knowingly* relegating myself to the poorhouses?"

Because, I thought but did not tell her, *if someone believes in you hard enough, sometimes it persuades you into doing the thing you thought impossible. Sometimes that's the only nudge you need.*[365] "You *are* capable. I know you are. I know you want to do the right thing, and that you have the means to do it. There's nothing stopping you except whatever is happening in your own head right now. So what's holding you back?"

"Oh, you know. Fear," she said, falsely airy, and pulled a lace handkerchief from her pocket. "My parents were poor. I grew up sleeping in drafty, dirty rooms and going hungry when the bread lines were a little short, and wearing ragged old charity clothes on my back. And you ask me to go back to that?" She shook her head slowly, incredulous. "I've been afraid this whole time, you see. Of that, of falling back into that. I've been running away from that fear like it was a pack of ravening wolves. I got lucky the first time. I can't count on luck a second time."

"You won't need to," I said gently. "Or not as much. Because you aren't the same person now that you were then."

She snorted. "Too right," she muttered, wiping her eyes with the handkerchief.

"It'll be easier than it was before," I said. "You have more know-how, and more connections. And surely a person of such unusual honor and selflessness deserves some assistance, does she not? People know you and they know the sort of person you are, and they'll know even better when the truth comes out, and you own up, and make amends. You won't live in the poorhouses—you have dozens of friends who will give you shelter, feed you and clothe you and provide you with a warm bed and a roof over your head, people with the money to spare to help you get back on your feet, to invest in

---

365 Don't align yourself with Orfeo, even like this. What we do is nothing like what the Pezian curse does. It grabs and yanks, and we outstretch our hand and wait for someone to take it.

whatever Sterre de Waeyer's next great project will be. Think of each person you've helped in the past—do you really think they'd let you drown? In every fairy tale, a good deed or a kind word is repaid three-fold. When the real dike broke recently, how many people lost their lives to fix it?"

"Seven. Four *mannen,* two *tzelven,* one *loestijr.*"

"Did you hear their names afterwards?"

She paused. "Yes."

"One of them was a pickpocket; did you know that? But now everyone says, 'Bardo Vanden, he was one of those people who died the other night, poor thing,' don't they? He was a hero. And you're going to be a hero, too."

"You can't know that!" she cried. "You don't know how it is here— people *care* about morality and goodness. And you expect them to just forgive me?"

"I *can* know that," I said calmly. "I made useless flowers into price-less treasures, didn't I? If you do things that a hero would do, then you're halfway there already. It can be easy and simple, if you decide that it is. Just give them their money back," I said. "All of it. We'll buy back every futures contract, and we'll refund everyone who purchased a bulb. We'll drain your coffers dry."

A long silence wound through the room. "That's crazy. You know that?"

"It's not crazy," I said. I stood up, clasped my hands behind my back. "Everything we do, we do because of stories of one kind or another. Sometimes they're small ones, like what color is fashionable this season, or how you can throw a penny off a bridge to make a wish, or whether penny-throwing from bridges is silly. Sometimes they're bigger ones, like manners and laws and the importance of keeping promises. We tell each other these stories, and then we all have a rough idea of how to behave to each other in order to get along. These are a crucial part of why it's possible for people to live all crammed in on top of each other like this without murdering each other," I said, gesturing around to indicate the city. "You think my idea is crazy only because it doesn't fit into the story you know: that a clever person can, with a bit of luck and a great deal of business sense, build herself up from nothing into the richest *vroleisch* in the city, and that she will then hold on to that place of comfort and security with both hands." I perched on the edge of her desk. "But you're going to flout the story, a thing that nobody ever, *ever* does unless they're pushed to it. And everyone else is going to think it's crazy too, at least for a little while. No one has ever done anything like what you're doing before. No one is going to know how to deal with it, or what to think of it, because you *do* have a reputation as a sensible, clever person with a canny business sense. You have excellent credit; you said so yourself. You might not have realized yet that your credit is not just financial, but—"

"Moral?"

"Social. People trust you. You break the story and they will be alarmed and confused. They'll try to think that you're crazy, but it won't fit with the stories they know about you, so they'll be forced to discard them. In time, all they'll be able to conclude is that you're . . . good. You're more good than they ever expected anyone to be."

"Does it even count as goodness if we're being so sneaky and deliberate about it?"

"Yes," I said firmly. "Yes. Because it's still the right thing to do, and we're still saving people and undoing the damage. We're fixing the dike."

I have to believe that's true. I understand why she was dubious; I do. But I have to believe that "good" is about the actions you end up taking and the help and healing you offer, and not about how much time it takes you to decide or what the thoughts in your head are beforehand. It's not wrong to have a plan—we just think truly good people are ones who do it impulsively and recklessly, and who never have to think about it. I used to be like that, and I want to be like that again, but . . . this is a really, really big mess. And when you're doing something big, you need a plan, and you need help. If I learned anything from my old master, it was that.

"You can fix the dike," I said. "Or you can let the city drown. You have boats; you have rope. You even have a Chant to guide you by the stars and sing the waters calm."

"And all I have to do is ruin myself." She rubbed her hands over her face. "I can't. Fuck. I can't do it."

I sat there in silence, looking at her for a long time, waiting for her to change her mind. And then I left.

So now I flex my hands and roll up my sleeves, and I get to find out what a solitary Chant *can* do alone. If any god is watching, I beg indulgence and mercy.

SIXTY-TWO

Except I'm not alone.

I went to Mistress Chant.

"I'm sorry," I said. "You were right." I stood in the common room of the Rose and Ivy, my hands empty. She had refused to go anywhere quieter.

"Of course I was." She was in the middle of a solo game of some sort involving dozens of hexagonal ceramic tiles, each with a different tiny picture painted on one side—a carp, a cherry blossom, a candle, a clock.

"I made a really big mistake. I didn't think that it was something that would have . . ." I shook my head. "I didn't think. And when you tried to smack some sense into me, I mostly didn't listen. That was a mistake too."

"Why are you here?" At last she looked up from her game.

"I need help. I asked you the other day about undoing a story. It's not working—no one listens, no one believes, no one wants to set aside their fear enough to accept what I have to say."

"Then your new story isn't strong enough."

"I know. I made the first one too big to control by myself. I just want to fix it, and help however I can. I want to make it right."

"And why should I bother helping? It wasn't my story. As you say, I tried to smack sense into you. What do I get out of this? Besides moral superiority and a warm feeling of having done the right thing, but I'm not short of either of those."

"What is it that you want? What's even within my power to give you? Money? I have some, I could—"

"I don't want a cent if you were paid it from de Waeyer's coffers." She paused over her game and folded her hands. "I want the story."

"That's it?"

"The whole story. The true story, as you saw it happen. I want to know everything you know about what's been happening, from the moment Sterre de Waeyer decided to import stars-in-the-marsh to now, this moment, this instant. I want you to tell me something real, and I don't want you to cringe away from the truth or make excuses."

"Why? Why that, of all things?"

She gave me a sharp look. "What did I say about asking me questions you already know the answer to?"

"So it's because you're a Chant and that's what you do? That's it?"

She sighed and sat back from her game. "Heyrland is in strong competition for the title of the second-biggest and most influential trade empire in the world, keeping good company with the rest of the pack as they all trail distantly behind Araşt, somewhere off on the horizon—nobody's arguing that *they're* in first place. Heyrland wishes it had one percent of the pocket change that Araşt left in last year's coat. Still, Heyrland's managed to beat off Avaris, Vinte, and Borgalos from establishing any kind of really reliable network here along these southern hemisphere coasts of the Sea of Storms, and they—*not* Araşt—have managed to wrestle an agreement for exclusive access to trade with the Ammat Archipelago, not counting smugglers and pirates.

"The short version, Brother-Chant, is that the ripples of what you've done here may well be felt as far north as Sdeshet and as far east as the Archipelago. I want to know the whole story, from your perspective as the man who was at the very center, at the eye of the storm, so that when I go elsewhere and a farmer or craftswoman or merchant complains about fewer Heyrlandtsche ships coming to port to buy their goods, I can tell them that I know the why of it, and I know the man who put his finger on the scales of fate. Rather like your master, isn't it?"

"At least I come by it honestly," I said. "And I'd like to undo it."

"It's not like everyone will be cursing you for a fool, though," she continued, as if she hadn't heard me. "Avaris, Vinte, Borgalos—they won't mind. They'd shake your hand. Tripping up the Heyrlandtsche a little bit, that's only to their benefit." She shrugged. "So that's my deal. I help calm the waters, and you give me the very, very long version of the story. Take it or leave it."

So I took it.[366]

---

366 And then you cheated me anyway! Left me this mountainous heap of rambling babble, when you knew I wanted the story from you in your voice, not by your hand.

SIXTY-THREE

istress Chant and I had agreed to meet at Sterre's offices this morning, but when we arrived, *Andeer* Janne, one of the clerks, told us she hadn't come in yet, that she likely wouldn't come in. We went first to her townhouse. She wasn't there either, but her butler, Lijsbet, whom I had met several times before, was eventually persuaded to tell us that *mevrol* had headed to her country house before supper the previous night.

We were obliged to hire a pair of horses for the hour's ride out, while I squirmed with embarrassment and tried not to look over at Mistress Chant too often to see whether she was annoyed with having to be involved in such a tedious production. We rode in silence. I noticed that she had a very good seat—she rode like a Qeter, in fact, and she has the look of that general region, though I might have guessed her for an Araşti or Kafian or Yama just as readily. I imagine it would be difficult not to become a good rider, if her homeland, growing up, had been Qeteren. The only people more devoted to their horses are the Umakh, far to the north.

We arrived somewhat before noon. I knocked at the front door, and we waited on the step for nearly ten minutes while Mistress Chant stood behind me and said nothing. "She has to be here," I said. "*Mevrouw* Lijsbet said she would be." I knocked again and got no answer, not even from a servant or the steward of the house. I tried the door—locked.

Mistress Chant snorted. "Are we going to break in?"

"I'm welcome here," I said. "We'll go around to the back. Perhaps she's in the garden and didn't hear us."

"If she's here, where are her servants?" But she followed me down the steps and the long, long path to the back of the house, where we did indeed find Sterre de Waeyer on the back porch, drunk and belligerent, even though the noon bell had not yet rung.

"No, not again," Sterre said miserably as soon as she saw me. "I told you, I can't."

"You can." I wrestled the bottle out of her hand and set it aside—it was empty, and there were two more, likewise empty, fallen to their sides next to her wicker chair. Mistress Chant made herself comfortable on one of the other chairs without waiting to be invited.

Sterre glared at her. "You've brought a guest," she said.

"You remember my colleague," I said. "I wanted to talk to you about things again, and . . . she's here to help. To be an outside perspective."

"You told her?"

"He did," Mistress Chant said. "But he's told a lot of people."

"He tell you what he wants me to do? He wants me to ruin myself. Give away my fortune, every penny of it, to—heal the wound, or balance the scales, or something. Some metaphor. Ropes, that was it. Ropes and boats and drowning. I can't do it. No one would expect me to do it. It's not my fault."

"Of course it's not," Mistress Chant said immediately. Not the position I'd expected her to take, honestly, but I occupied myself with collecting the bottles and bringing them to the door inside, very slowly to give them time to talk. "Your job is much like mine—you go to strange places, and find wonderful treasures, and bring them back for others to marvel at. You make people's lives better. And all this? Just an accident."

"Exactly!"

"You knew that the disease would probably strike eventually, but you couldn't have predicted that the city would flood like it did," Mistress Chant continued in a soothing voice. "But consider ships— every ship is going to sink sooner or later. That's no reason not to use them to get around, is it? And even if you buy a ship and it sinks on its maiden voyage, that's not really your doing, even though you know ships sink from time to time."

"Tell him that!" she said, pointing at me. "He just wants to make sad eyes at me and wobble his lip until I do something about it."

"He's like that. Ignore him. You know, there's a quote by a famous philosopher—something about how a person can take no responsibility over anyone but herself. Heile van der Laere, I believe?"

"She's a hack," Sterre said immediately. "I don't care what anyone says. Smug bitch. Holes all over her logic. Dreadful rhetoric, too."

"You disagree with her positions?" Mistress Chant said, and I realized she was faking.

Sterre bristled. "As anyone paying attention would! Any halfway good idea she ever had was stolen wholesale from better brains than hers—de Coronado, aj-Karani, Valerius. Fuck, even Fortanier, and nobody bothers taking Fortanier seriously anymore."

"So you think that a person does have a responsibility over others besides herself." Mistress Chant nodded. "I respect your position. You've convinced me."

"Have I?" Sterre said, squinting.

"Your arguments are simply unassailable."

"Oh. Good. Yes. Philosophy was quite fashionable, ten years ago or so."

"I see how much of it has stuck with you. Have you read *The Chrestomathy of Righteousness?*"

"No," Sterre replied slowly.

"An anthology of passages from several philosophers who studied together at the University at Thorikou. A lot of it is useless drivel about turning up one's nose at fashion and adopting strict asceticism, which I find tiresome but some people take to like gawky cygnets to water. But the core argument—and stay with me here—is that money doesn't really matter."

Sterre stiffened instantly. "I suppose you've never gone hungry, then, have you?"

"A few times. And you?"

"My parents were paupers. We would have starved without the bread lines and charitable strangers."

"Mm," said Mistress Chant, and sat back, folding her hands in her lap. She said nothing more, only gazed at Sterre for a long time while I lurked off to one side of the patio and tried to pretend like I was uninterested.

"All right!" Sterre burst out. "All right, fine. I was lucky that someone decided it was more important to keep me alive than to save a few duiten. But we're not talking about a few duiten. We're talking thousands and thousands and thousands of guilders."

"How much is one human life worth?"

Sterre's frustration collapsed instantly into misery. She looked around for the wine bottle and, finding none, slumped back in her seat. "It's an unanswerable question," she said.

"Mm," said Mistress Chant again, and got to her feet. "Well, remember that unanswerable question when you start hearing about children orphaned because their parents died of jail fever or consumption in the debtors' prison." Sterre flinched hard at that. "Good day, *mevrol*."

"Wait," Sterre said, miserably. "Fine. You win. You goddamn win; are you happy? Fucking Chants."

I slumped with relief. "You're doing the right thing, Sterre," I said, coming forward.

"What do I have to do?" she asked. "If any part of it requires me to sober up, then I'm out. I'll tell you that now."

"I need letters of introduction. I need bank drafts. I need . . ." I looked to Mistress Chant.

"A better story," she said. "But she can't help with that."

Sterre grunted. "I'll need to sober up to write the letters, I suppose," she said. "Fucking Chants. I'll send 'em along tonight. Dinnertime."

"Thank you," I said.

It wasn't until we were on the road again, back to the city, that I glanced over at Mistress Chant. "How'd you do that?"

"What, earlier? Persuading her?"

"Yes. You knew she hated van der Laere, somehow; you knew she'd react like that."

"She was drunk," Mistress Chant shrugged. "Made it easier. And at the salon, I was snooping through *Heer* van Vlymen's library. He had a copy of de Coronado with a handwritten inscription from Sterre, exhorting him to read something of note and value rather than van der Laere's drivel. Easy."

I was quiet for several more miles. "You hurt her, talking about the orphans."

"Yes," Mistress Chant sighed, as if the whole conversation was tiresome. "Her parents died in debtors' prison. Pneumonia. The wardens were still using duckings of cold water as corporal punishment in those days."

"How did you find that out? She doesn't talk that much about her parents, and I know you don't know her personally, not well enough to have her confide anything in you. Gossip from other people, I guess?"

A mild, one-shouldered shrug. "You find someone and tell them a secret, and then they want to tell you a secret in return. There are many people in the city who know things about *Mevrol* de Waeyer, and I'd hardly consider the things I know about her to *really* be secrets. It's basic Chant work, dear boy. But what next?"

"I'm going to go around to Sterre's rich friends and show them the letter. I'll offer to write them the bank draft there and then. I'll see if any of them take me up on it."

"Mm," said Mistress Chant, and we said nothing more.

SIXTY-FOUR

I paid my first visit to Ambassador Kha'ud of Tash with my letter from Sterre, and when I came in, I sat. "I'm so sorry," I said, never raising my eyes above the ambassador's hands. "This is going to be difficult to hear. Sterre de Waeyer imported defective product into the country. The bulbs of stars-in-the-marsh were infected with a disease and would have spread it to the healthy ones through water contact. Considering the recent floods, *Mevrol* de Waeyer and I are assuming that every flower in the city has been infected by now." I took a breath. "I'm so sorry, but your investment is about to vanish. It's dying out in your gardens, and when it's finished, you'll have nothing left of what you paid for. But . . ." This was why I had gone to the Tashaz ambassador first. The Tashaz won't interrupt unless it's a matter of life and death. I wanted to practice my presentation of this issue, and I wanted them to understand the whole concept instead of getting it in pieces. "If you have any contracts with *Mevrol* de Waeyer, consider them broken. Whatever money you put down as a deposit will be refunded in full, without question. And," I added, in a shaky voice. "If you have made agreements to sell original contracts of your own to anyone else based on next year's prospective offshoots, *Mevrol* de Waeyer will fulfill your buyer's financial obligation at one-third of the contracts' face value. You won't get back all the money you lost in this fiasco, but you'll get some of it. Enough that you won't be ruined.

And neither you nor your buyers will be able to sue for breach of contract." I folded my hands politely to show I was finished.

"Why does *Mevrol* de Waeyer care to refund so much money?"

"Because she feels that it was her responsibility. They were her choices. She's a woman of honor, Ambassador, and she would rather die than have her name tracked through the mud while she denies and denies and denies that it had anything to do with her. She's taking responsibility. *Full* responsibility," I added. "As much as she can. She has a reputation to protect. Coin comes and goes, but a reputation sticks with you forever."

"That's all well and good," said the ambassador. "But if I have purchased futures contracts from others? Private individuals?"

"We will also buy them at one-third of their value. Whatever you have that's related to the stars-in-the-marsh. You can also feel free to keep the flowers in your garden—the disease won't spread to other kinds of plants, and it's already too late to save the ones you have." I swallowed. "You might as well enjoy them while you have them."

"I'm going to have to think about this," they said. "Is there a time limit on this offer?"

"No," I said. "Not at all. Anytime you want to get out of the market, we'll let you out. We made a mistake, and it's our fault, and we want to do whatever we can to fix it. We want to erase it."

"Not whatever you can," they said sharply. "Or you'd pay the full value of the contracts."

"If it is a contract you bought directly from Sterre, we'll give you the full amount. But if you bought it from someone else at a markup, we can't honor that. We just can't. We're giving everyone their money back, but we only have so much to give—we can't make more money from nothing."

They tapped their fingernails slowly on the desk. If I had been so impolite as to glance up at their face, I suspect their eyes would have been narrowed. "This all seems so convenient. Where's the catch?"

That was as much as I'd expected. Of course they'd expect a catch—a catch was the only thing that would make this fit with the story in their head. "No catch," I said, which only made them more suspicious. "You get money back, and you get to keep the flowers."

"Why?"

"Because we're sorry, and it's our fault."

"But nothing has happened."

"It's going to. The flowers are going to die."

"Then I'll sell them before they do."

I put my head in my hands. "Just remember our offer, won't you? Please?"

"Fine," they said. "Was that all?"

"Yes. That was all."

Mistress Chant had contented herself to wait out on the street—she didn't care for the narrowness of the houses here, and she had mentioned she found it difficult to speak to the Tashaz, particularly dignitaries such as the ambassador, due to her annoyance with the eye contact thing.

"Well?" she said, raising an eyebrow and glancing me over. "I take it de Waeyer's pockets haven't yet been lightened."

"I couldn't get them to believe me," I said.

"Do *you* believe you? That generally helps."

"Of course I do."

She paused, and nodded. "All right. Why don't they believe you?"

"They thought there was a catch. Other people have too; the ambassador's not the first. I thought Sterre's letter would make a difference." I eyed her. "Do you know the answer, and you're just . . . I don't know, being didactic?"

"I don't know the answer, because I don't yet know the whole story." She sighed. "Let's find something to eat and a place to sit down. No use loitering like beggars."

She turned around without waiting for an answer and swept down the street. Here in the well-to-do quarter, the canals were wide and overhung with mature trees, which shaded the walks on either side and somehow muffled the noise of the city. Even in the depths of summer, it was cool and quiet.

Mistress Chant evidently knew exactly where she was going, for she led me to a small coffeehouse a few streets away and sat at one of the tiny empty tables outside. "What do you want to eat?"

"Oh, I'm not getting anything. I didn't bring any money."

"I brought plenty. What do you want? I'm buying."

"You don't have to. I'm not that hungry."

"You're—what, nineteen, twenty? Of course you're hungry. And I'd rather not spend all day with this problem, so you're going to eat and you're going to get your brain working, and you're going to fix your problem." The attendant arrived at our table. "Coffee for him, please, cream and sugar. I'll have—last time I was here you had a tea that tasted like a mouthful of campfire smoke."

"Nuryeven caravan?"

"That's the one. And we'll have bread and cheese and whatever cured meats you have, and something sweet for the boy, too—cake or pastries or what-have-you."

The attendant nodded, took Mistress Chant's payment, and left. "I really don't need that much food."

"I need you to have that much food. Coffee and sugar will make your brain work faster. I don't have all day." She folded her arms and looked at me. "I don't know the answer. I don't know the whole story yet. You, though. You are the only one who holds the whole story in your head. So you're going to down enough coffee and pastries to kill an ox, and we'll see if it jitters anything loose."

And indeed, she made me drink two cups of strong coffee and eat three sticky buns before she would return to the topic.

"They won't believe you. They think there's a catch. Why?"

"Because they know Sterre. They know she's cunning, and that she's got a mind for strategy." The coffee was actually making it harder for me to focus. "They think they've spotted something. Maybe some of them have gotten tricked before, or have heard of someone else getting tricked. They think Sterre is going to benefit somehow, and that if they can dodge her scheme, they can get some of the benefit for themselves. They still don't think the flowers are dying—I spoke to someone a few days ago who was overjoyed to explain to me that I was all wrong about the sickness. He said it was a natural life cycle of the flowers, nothing to worry my pretty little head about. Not exactly in those words," I added. "But that was the tone."

Mistress Chant sipped her campfire-flavored tea and tapped the side of the glass with one finger. "Have another sticky bun," she said, musing, and I sighed and obeyed—they were made of thousands of paper-thin layers of buttery dough, rolled into a spiral filled with warm spices and sugar and nuts, and baked with so much sugar and butter on the outside that the oven alchemized it into a thin shell of sticky-crunchy caramel.

"I can't convince them to think I'm telling the truth," I said. "They don't even think the sickness is real, let alone Sterre's offer."

"For that, at least, you only have to wait," she said, setting her cup down. "Your new story will only grow stronger with time."

"And by then it might be too late for Sterre to make a difference."

"Yes, that is the price. The ripples spread with every moment you wait."

"So why are we sitting here eating cakes?"

"It's an investment. We're taking one hour to save ourselves ten. Hypothetically, anyway. Assuming you get around to coming up with a solution," she added sharply.

"*You're* not helping much."

"I bought you lunch, and I'm asking you pointed questions. I'm helping all I can, kid." She tore off a piece of bread and smeared it with herbed butter, layering cheese and a shaving of red smoked pork on top. "It's simple, really. The problem is that they don't see what they stand to lose yet. Like you said, it's not real. Well, no more real than a ghost story." She chewed her bread and cheese and watched me. "You're too committed to this story," she said. "It's not working, and you're trying to think of how to *make* it work. Think of a new one. Something allegorical, something that will get under their skins. Maybe something involving the dikes and the sea; that seems to alarm them."

"No," I said slowly. "The story isn't the problem." Words from my mouth weren't real to them. They vanished away into the air like breath on a cold day. "I just need to make it real. Terrifyingly real."

"Wow, insightful," she drawled. "If only I'd thought of that. *How?*"

I stood up sharply. "Thank you for lunch. I think I know what to do, but I might need more help. I'll leave word for you at the Rose and Ivy."

She said something else, but I'd already whirled away and started running down the street.[367]

---

367 Yeah, I said, "So are you going to tell me what your brilliant plan is?" But you always do this. You always fucking do this.

SIXTY-FIVE

They didn't believe me when I spoke truth aloud, so I had to find another way.

Speech is as ephemeral as mist; words written down are more real, somehow. They're more permanent. Harder to deny. As I wrote before, they become a paper copy of a mind, capable of some of the abilities of its writer.

I had that thought sitting in my head like a heavy weight as I ran off from Mistress Chant, back to the Sun's Rest. The whole way, I thought in terror of how careful I'd have to be, how little room there was for error if I did this. And, floating above those thoughts like a vulture, the thought that what I was thinking of doing was something I'd seen done before. Something I'd taken part in before—in Nuryevet, we printed propaganda, and Ivo and I hauled them out into the streets by the armful and scattered them among the populace, sowing discontent and fear with them until the people chafed and itched and wept for mercy. We scraped them raw.

I'm just one man. One Chant, alone. Mistress Chant can stuff me full of sweetbuns and coffee until I jitter out of my skin, but she's right. She doesn't know the whole story, and she doesn't know where the snarls are. She can't really untangle it the way I can; all she could do, if she really had to, would be to add more tangles, ones that blocked off mine. But it wouldn't make anything better. It would just be a splint, enough to let things hobble along for a little longer.

No. This, this is mine. In this, I am alone. It's just me, my mind, my will.

So I thought ... I might as well make some help for myself. I might as well make paper copies of my mind.

So—back to the Sun's Rest. I rushed through the common room, heedless of the dour knot of Acamporas drinking in one corner, and pounded up the stairs to the attic. I scrawled out a draft, eight pages long, then swept it up, along with my pen and the pot of ink. I flew back down the stairs and out through the innyard to the street, towards a printer that Sterre knew of, a Vint named Monsieur Reinault.

His shop is about equidistant between the Sun's Rest and the de Waeyer offices, only a little ways off my usual route. It's in a surprisingly roomy building for the area, and from halfway down the street I could hear the thump and creak of moving wooden parts and smell the particular dark, smoky-earthy scent of lampblack overlaid with a single perfumy note of pine resin—the smell of ink.

Mssr. Reinault's industry is divided in two parts, I have since found—one workshop in a neighboring district, which produces daily newspapers for a small percentage of the city's population; and the other here, for pamphlets and books. Mssr. Reinault's specialty is illustrated tracts, longer than pamphlets but shorter than books, describing adventure stories by means of cunning sequential pictures with simply worded captions, the better to appeal to common folk who may not have a scholar's grasp of letters.

When I explained what I wanted to the assistant at the front of the shop, she had me repeat myself three times before she believed me, and then she wrote out the number on a piece of paper to confirm that I wasn't adding more zeros to the end than I intended, and then she ran off behind the curtain that separated the sales floor from the workshop. On my way from the inn, I'd thought of several more things to include in the pamphlet, and I took this moment to scrawl them out, my pages now a horrible mess of scrawls and splatters—my handwriting isn't so nice in Heyrlandtsche as it is in Xerecci. The assistant came back a few minutes later with Mssr. Reinault himself, a tall gentleman with broad, muscled shoulders, a shock of wildly tousled gray hair and beard, and deep lines etched into his face below steel-colored eyes. He looked like a thunder god, and the first words he said to me were, "*How* many are you wanting?"

"Five thousand," I said for the fourth time. I held out the pages I'd written. "As soon as possible, please. The bill to be sent to Sterre de Waeyer at her offices."

He took the pages from my hand with a little more force than most people generally use for freely proffered items and scanned over it. "Oh, you're *that one*," he said, and, turning away, dropped the pages to the floor.

I scrambled to pick them up, and by the time I'd gotten them in order he had vanished behind the curtain. I didn't spare a glance for the shop assistant and followed him. The space behind was cavernous; there must have been at least twenty presses going at once, each of them manned by two workers. "Monsieur," I said, switching to Vintish, "I beg your patience."

Reinault ignored me. He'd stopped by one of the presses. He smeared a pat of thick black paste onto a sheet of polished stone on the table next to the press, angrily dabbing and rolling the inking ball on it while it spread into a thin, smooth film. It made a sticky sound, and the smell of lampblack and pine resin grew stronger.

"Monsieur," I said. "If you'll read the pamphlet carefully, I—"

"My idiot son-in-law," Reinault rumbled, "spent a fortune on

those. I told him not to. I told him, and my girl Annette told him,
but the boy wouldn't hear sense. Took out a loan, even. Bought one
of those *futures contracts*, said he was going to sell it on in a month or
two." Reinault turned from the table and began banging the inking
ball across the type-form in the press with rhythmic, controlled
motions that did nothing to conceal his anger. "The flowers withered
up a week and a half ago." My breath caught—either the sickness
had progressed faster than expected, or Crispin's flower hadn't been
the first to show the signs (which was more likely). "Now he's ruined,
and my girl's going to have to divorce him or live in a poorhouse,
or debtors' prison, because I won't have the idiot living here under
my roof when they're evicted next month." He stopped and glared at
me with those steel eyes. "I won't have anything to do with you, monsieur," he said. "Not you, and not that Sterre de Waeyer, and not your
thrice-damned flowers. I won't have it. You're bilking honest idiots out
of—you see? That's what he was, my son-in-law. An idiot, but honest.
He didn't think that it'd be a scam. He didn't see how it *could* be one."

"We didn't mean it to be," I said. "I swear it. We're trying to make
it right. With this." I held out the papers again. "I want to print this.
Five thousand copies that I'm going to distribute in the city by my
own hand. I'll put one in your son-in-law's hands myself, and then I'll
get him his money back."

Mssr. Reinault eyed me.

"It really wasn't supposed to happen like this," I said. "Believe me.
We don't want your son-in-law to suffer for our mistake." He hadn't
taken the papers from me—my arm, still outstretched, was beginning
to ache. "Read it properly, and then if you still won't print it, I'll leave
and find someone else. But your son-in-law can claim his money back
regardless, whenever he likes."

"Words are cheap, monsieur," he grunted, tossing the inking balls onto the table. Another attendant, nearby, had already swept a new sheet of paper onto the tympan and folded the frisket down over it, and Reinault eased the whole frame down over the type, glaring at me all the while. "I know better than anyone."

"Then let me show you how much mine are worth," I said.

Reinault shoved the type-bed forward and yanked the pull with a mighty creak of straining wood, lowering the platen that squeezed the paper onto the type. "You *poets*," he snarled. "You're all the same. You all think you're the gods' gift to literature."

"I'm not a poet."

"Monsieur," he said, "whether you are a poet or no, *I* am a gentleman. But if you don't leave my shop at once, I will be forced to use some ungentlemanly language indeed."

"Send for your son-in-law! Tell him to bring his contracts. I'll take him to *Mevrol* de Waeyer's offices right now, and we'll come back here straightaway with a bank draft in his name. I made a *mistake*, monsieur, and I regret it. I am working to undo it."

Reinault pulled back the type-bed and lifted the tympan, peeling the paper away from the type in a smooth motion and revealing perfect blocks of flawless text. The apprentice removed the page from the frame and set it aside while Reinault, in silence, picked up the inking ball again. He said nothing to me.

"Monsieur," I said. "Please. Let me prove I'm serious. Look at me—I've got to be about the same age as your son-in-law, aren't I?" He spared me the briefest, briefest glance, measuring me up in an instant, and dropped his eyes back to the rhythmic press of the inking ball across the type. "I swear to you it wasn't malice—I was an honest idiot, and your son-in-law was an honest idiot, and now we two bumblers have both gotten ourselves into a mess. All I want is to do the right thing. Send for him. Please."

Reinault stopped and heaved a huge sigh. He glanced at his assistant and nodded, jerking his head towards the door. They nodded in return and jogged off. "Go outside."

"Monsieur—"

"Go wait outside! I've sent for the stupid boy, what more do you want?" he roared.

I held out the pages. "As soon as he arrives, we'll go and I'll be back within the hour. With his contracts refunded, and with payment for five thousand copies of this."

"If you think I'm going to print even one paragraph of that before—"

"I don't," I said. "And I wouldn't want you to. But start setting the type and I'll pay you five guilders of my own money."

He gave me another long, slow look. "You'll be wanting these in a rush, I suppose."

"Yes, as quick as possible."

"Five thousand?"

"Yes."

He flicked through the pages, counting them, scanning over my writing too fast to be reading it. Some of the really fine printers, the ones who know their business and could set a page of type with their eyes closed, can estimate the number of words on a page just by glancing at it. "Size?"

"Small. Pocket sized."

"Twelve pages of text. Title page?"

"Not necessary."

"*Title page?*" he asked again, in a dangerous voice.

"Yes please," I said.

"Twenty-one guilders. And I'll have all of it before I print a word of this."

Just shy of a duit and a half per copy, then, for what would come out to four sheets of paper, folded in half and held together with a single long stitch in the crease. He was overcharging me, but I didn't particularly care. "How quickly can you get it done?"

He sighed again, heavily, and pulled out a pencil and a roughly bound notebook from his back pocket, little more than a wad of pages tied around the fold with a string. He opened it to the middle and scratched figures on the page for a moment. "Call it a month."

"*Monsieur!* You have dozens of presses!"

"And dozens of orders to print," he replied darkly. "I can allocate two presses. Why? How badly do you want these?"

"I was hoping for three days."

"Then you can go on hoping, monsieur!" He shut the notebook with a snap.

Well, what's money for? What was I really going to use it for? "How quick could you do it with all your presses?"

He laughed. "Good day to you, monsieur. Come back when you've sorted out my idiot son-in-law."

"Could you do it in a week?"

"Good *day*."

"For fifteen guilders more?"

He paused. "Mind yourself, monsieur. I don't think your employer would take kindly to her money being spent like that."

"It's my money." It was in fact *all* my money, everything I'd earned that I hadn't spent on food. This was as good a purchase as anything else. "I'll pay it myself. This was my responsibility too, so . . . I'll pay it."

"Total of thirty-six guilders. For five thousand, in a week."

I nodded. "Let's just round it up to forty."

He laughed sharply and turned back to his press. "We can talk more when I see that proof you've talked so much about."

Reinault's son-in-law was indeed roughly of an age with me, a man named Emile, plain-faced but sweet-eyed, short and soft—in other words, nothing at all like ▮▮▮▮ but for his mop of black curls, which were close enough that it made my heart sour to look at him, so I tried not to. I whisked him off to Sterre's offices, explaining no fewer than three times along the way what we were doing and why we were doing it. He was bemused the whole way, bemused to hand over the contracts, and bemused when Sterre's clerk, Tyche, wrote out a bank draft for the full amount. He'd bought them from us, after all, so he received all his money back, rather than merely part of it.

"Burn those," I said, nodding to the contracts laid neatly on the desk under Tyche's hands. "Them and any others that come in through that door."

I took Emile back to the print shop, and he showed Reinault the bank draft, and then I showed Reinault the other bank draft, the one for twenty-five guilders from Sterre's accounts, and said, "I'll have to get the rest from my rooms. But you'll get started now?"

He sighed. "Five thousand in a week," he said slowly. "Will you be picking them up, or having them delivered?"

"The former," I said. "I'll come by once a day and take however many you've finished."

SIXTY-SIX

The first copy, the proof copy, went to Mistress Chant, to show her what I'd done. She took it between two fingers, frowning and turning it over like she couldn't quite believe her eyes. "You wrote it down?"

"Yes. Do you see? Do you see why? Do you see how it will work?"

"I see it," she said impassively.

"What do you think?"

"Too late for me to have an opinion, isn't it? You went haring off too quick for me to say anything. And you've clearly already chosen a path and run headlong down it," she said, tossing the pamphlet onto the table.

"Tell me anyway. For . . . didactic reasons."

She crossed her arms. "It's inelegant. You're solving a problem meant for a jeweler's screwdriver with a sledgehammer."

I shrugged. "Sometimes brute force is all you have time for."

"Quite." She paused. "You want me to tell you if I think it will work."

"Yes."

"I can't. I don't know if it will. I've never seen something like this before."

I picked the pamphlet up. "I have. That's how I know. That's what made me think of it. Would Lanh Chau and Arenza be interested in helping distribute these?"

She glanced at the pamphlet again. "Not Lanh Chau," she said.

"He's too young. I don't want you confusing him with your … ways. But I will ask Arenza if she's interested."

I nodded. "Have her come to the Sun's Rest or Monsieur Reinault the printer if she is."

———✦———

The first full batch of pamphlets went to all the buyers that Sterre had on record at her shop. I commandeered Teo and a couple of the clerks, in addition to Arenza, to help me with deliveries, and I myself went around the city to the fancy houses, one by one, and groveled and apologized.

The thing about printed words, a paper mind, is that they can slip in where a whole man is turned away at the door. If the servants denied us, all we had to do was put a couple copies of the pamphlet into their hands and ask them to pass along the message to their employers. All that was left, then, was to trust in gossip's ability to flourish.

And it has started to work. People have been suspicious of us at first—why wouldn't they be suspicious of someone on their doorstep handing them some unsolicited literature?—but the flowers are dying. Some of them now are fully black, and a few, like the printer's son-in-law Emile's, have already completely withered.

When I do manage to explain, when I make them read the pamphlet and really comprehend for once, when they see the realities laid out before them in clear language in crisp black ink on paper … It's different, wildly different, than one young man clutching at their sleeves on the street and desperately begging for someone to listen to him.

I get to watch, in silence, as it dawns on them that the disease isn't some clever scheme that Sterre and I cooked up. People rant at me, rail at me, cry at me. "We're ruined," they cry—if it had only just been wealthy folk, they could have afforded to take the blow. They would have cried and whined about it, but no one in their household would have starved.

The problem is, there are people who had bought one or two bulbs early on, like Emile, when prices were relatively cheap, and who, unlike Emile, had made a fortune (and then *spent* the fortune) selling the futures contract for the flower that now rotted in their garden. As I told Ambassador Kha'ud, we honor every contract that had been made with us directly. We gave back every penny they'd paid. But the vast majority of contracts were ones that hadn't been made with us— perhaps as many as two-thirds.

Yet we honor as many of them as we can.

Days have passed, and the pamphlets trade hands as fast as the futures contracts had, and people come to our offices by the score with their palms outstretched. Not once have we turned anyone away. And we must be making a difference—we *must*.

Sterre has dismissed her employees (granting them each a comfortable lump sum and glowing references, sending most of them to her rivals with personal recommendations), sold her properties, and gotten rid of everything she could possibly get rid of, all to fill the palms of the people whose pockets we've picked.

She does it whenever I ask. She pays whoever I tell her to pay.

The sickness sweeps across the flowers in the city. Every day more and more of them fall to the black-speckling illness.

People don't care anymore that it is beautiful. They try to isolate their gardens, to no avail. Inevitably, a flower takes on a tint of yellow, and then folk come to us to demand their money back—that knowledge spreads at the same rate as the disease.

SIXTY-SEVEN

I've stopped dreaming.[368] I don't remember which was the first night I slept straight through, but as we heal the city, my guilt, I suppose, lessens its grip on my sleeping mind.

I don't know what to think of it, if anything. Surely it was nothing, but—well. The coincidence, that the dreams would start when they did, and then stop when they did. It's a little convenient, isn't it?[369]

Yesterday I walked Arenza back to the Rose and Ivy, after handing out the last of the five thousand pamphlets. I'd tried to start several conversations with her, but she didn't seem terribly interested in talking. She's always on the edges of things, always watching, always listening. Always paying attention. I think she'll be a good Chant one day, a better one than me, probably. A different one than me and my Chant, certainly.

"Thanks for your help, these last few days," I said.

"Of course. Thank you for the lessons."

"Lessons? I don't remember saying anything that you wouldn't have already learned from your mistress."

---

368 Suspicious coincidence, which means it's not a coincidence.
369 Exactly!

"Sometimes a lesson affirms something you already know."

"Like what?"

"Like caution. Like resisting impulsiveness. Like thinking before you speak, and looking before you jump. I'd rather do things slowly and properly." She seems so cold sometimes when she says things like that. I think she must be very methodical and cerebral about these things, which is strange to me. So much of Chanting for me is *feelings*.

When we arrived, Mistress Chant was sitting on the tongue of her wagon in the innyard, tuning a lute, inasmuch as a lute can be tuned. "Evening, Chant," she said. "Care to sit for a while?"

I sat, and Arenza drifted away, wordless, as was her wont. Mistress Chant eyed her as she went. "She talk to you at all?" she asked, when Arenza was out of earshot.

"Not much."

"Hm." She went back to tuning. "Perhaps it's just teenage melancholy and I have no reason to worry."

"She's unusually . . . serious," I said, careful and tactful. "She's, what, sixteen? Gods know I was nothing like that at her age."

"What were you like?"

"Excitable. I loved everybody I clapped eyes on. It was stupid of me. My master always used to say so."

Mistress Chant plucked a few notes on the lute and frowned, making some adjustments. "People will tell a lot of secrets to someone who loves them," she said. Another few notes, and a sigh. "Arenza will make do with whatever path she chooses. If she chooses."

"You think she might not stick with Chanting?"

"Hard to say. Maybe, maybe not. She's got that bloodless way about her." Mistress Chant shook her head. "I'd worry, sending her out all on her own. Perhaps I'll see how she feels about being set up at one of the universities. Thorikou, maybe, or Akang or Khabi or Ahz-Jarea. It might suit her better. She likes facts."

"Is there such a thing? Really?"

Mistress Chant gave me a half-smile, which nearly sent me stumbling with shock. "At Khabi and Ahz-Jarea, I have heard there are people counting the stars."

"Stars die from time to time. The number is not constant." I paused. "She'd need passion to count the stars," I said. "It would involve a lot of sleepless nights. You don't do that for something unless you really care about it."

She sighed and plucked out a few phrases of a melody. "So how about that story?"

"Which one?"

"Yours. The one you promised me."

"It's not over yet. I want to see it play out before I start telling you."

"As long as you remember your promise," she said mildly.

"I won't forget. You'll get the whole thing."

"Whole *and true.*"

"Yes," I said impatiently. "I keep promises. Whole, and true, and real." And . . . that was the moment that I had the idea to give her this, this stack of pages with my heart spilled on them.

To give *you* this, Sister-Chant. [370]

Hello. [371]

Sorry. [372]

I expect you're angry. [373]

I just wanted to explain, and you *did* want the true story, and there's

---

370 Gods damn you, Chant! This was premeditated!
371 No!
372 You'd better be, because I'm going to wring your neck if our paths cross again.
373 Oh, you know, only a little.

not much that I can do to tell you more truth than things I said alone in the dark when I thought no one would ever hear them but me.[374]

I'll tell you the rest now, tell you the things I forgot to say aloud, or that I kept secret.[375]

See, we were sitting there having the first friendly conversation we'd ever had, and something in my head crashed into something else and all of a sudden I asked, "Are you fond of bright colors?" I thought you must be, by the clothes you wear and the colors of your cart.[376]

You sort of shrugged and replied, "Personally? I have no feelings either way. But I, at least, feel some obligation to my duties as a Chant." You eyed my threadbare coat. "You ought to wear the clothes *Mevrol* de Waeyer gave you. Those were nice. Chantly."

Of course I already knew you disapproved—I don't care as much now as I used to. Sorry, but I don't. Clothes don't have anything to do with it, not really. They're just one tool out of many. Perhaps I worded the question wrong when I asked, "What do your clothes have to do with your duties?" I meant to ask about *your* clothes specifically. What do they mean to you, Sister-Chant?

"The ancient Chants," you said. "Did your master neglect this as well? The ancient ones used to wear bright colors and light fires to attract Shuggwa's attention, to draw it on themselves, since they were the favored ones, rather than letting his Eye fall onto their village-folk and bring calamity. They used to sing, and dance naked, and swear, and talk loudly."

---

374 Fine. All right. (Coward, Chant. Where is the self-possession you had when you stood up in front of that audience of thousands at Stroekshall?) I'm almost finished here, and I've made the best of what you've given me. Might as well stick it out for the last bit. It's nearly dawn, and I've been at this all night.

375 About fucking time.

376 This is a little creepy, having you addressing me. Like I was looking at a painting or a statue and suddenly it turned to face me. I preferred it the other way.

"I know. You're trying to live as the ancient Chants did?"

"That's how my line has taught our apprentices for four thousand years. Discipline. We were always priests."

"But Shuggwa faded when the Chants and their people came to the Issili Islands and Kaskinen."

"So?"

This probably seems silly—I know you were here for this whole conversation, and I know you must remember it as clearly as I do, but bear with me. I want it to be fresh in your mind.[377]

"So those lands have nearly nothing of his power, just ghosts and memories—"

"And how does it matter how much power the god has left? The Chants were priests. There are other places in this world that have gods that faded too, or were forgotten, or were never real in the way Shuggwa was real. But people still pray, don't they? Whether or not your god can physically take you by the throat and drown you isn't relevant. That's not the important part. So why should it matter that Shuggwa faded when Arthwend sank and we floated away from the seat of his power? Why should we abandon him?"

I shrugged and picked at the hem of my sleeve. "My master never seemed to care. He didn't think it was important, so I never learned to think it was important either."

"You could learn if you wanted to," you said.

"How? The only people who know about that are the Chants, and if the rest of them are like you, then I guess I'll never find out anything for real."

---

377 Okay, yes, this is unsettling as hell. I was just about to scribble something about that. But fine! You have my attention.

You snarled. "Fine. You want information. You don't have to torture it out of me."

"I'm not torturing anything out of you. I was just making conversation."

"You worship Shuggwa by drawing his Eye, by performing or seducing his attention. He's not a difficult god to please, but he is capricious and elusive and, most important, *easily bored*."

I shook my head. "Really, you don't have to."

"The ancient Chants used to experience visitations from time to time. They'd sight him in the marshes, or he might appear on the other side of their fire, always just out of reach, but undeniable and impossible to dismiss. He traps people lost in the swamp."

My breath caught in my throat at that. It catches again, writing it down now. You know everything I know by this point. You probably spotted it before I did. You're more experienced than I am, and you're looking at it laid out all at once. You'll have to forgive me for not seeing it before. I was . . . distracted, and I didn't have all the information:[378]

"If a village experienced a lot of misfortune, then it suggested their Chant wasn't very good—they hadn't done their job properly, and someone else had caught Shuggwa's attention. He's a god of shadow. He plucked out his own eye and placed it in the heavens so he could watch eternally. He wore a long fisherman's cloak made of rushes, with a wide woven hat to shadow his face, and he sits in a boat that moves without rowing or poling. And he is attended by his servant, the bird Ksadir."

My breath had not just caught but ceased entirely. You didn't seem to notice. "What kind of a bird?"

---

378 Fair points. Too lost among the trees to see the forest. Next time, try to be sharper and quicker. You won't have me to spell things out for you.

"A gold-feathered cormorant."

"I see," I said.

My Chant must have told me all that. He must have, and I just forgot. Perhaps it was when I first started off on my travels with him; perhaps it was once when I was sick and feverish, or perhaps he told me when I was tired and on the edge of sleep. There's no other option. There are still tales of Skukua in Kaskinen, the impish trickster that Shuggwa became when he faded. I can believe that people have met him from time to time. Perhaps the ancient Chants' people, like Ylf and Tofa, had mud on their boots when they came out of Arthwend— earth and water, just enough to bring a whisper of him with them into new lands. But those places, those lingering whispers, are half the world away. If I were in Kaskinen, I might believe that I'd . . .

But I would never be in Kaskinen.

It doesn't matter now anyway, because the dreams have stopped.

But was it real? Possibly? It can't be, can it? Can it? How could it? Magic is tied to earth and water, and how much earth and water would you have to bring to Heyrland from Kaskinen to get enough to—

Oh. Earth and water. Who would bring earth and water from Kaskinen? Who would box it up and ship it across the sea to a brand-new land? And how would they do that, and why? Except . . . When you bring shipments of flowers, with the earth and water clumped to their roots. When you plant them and let them thrive.[379]

Shit. And now it's too late. The dreams—or whatever they were—have stopped.

I left abruptly after that, and you probably thought it rude of me,[380] but I was . . . preoccupied. I walked home to the Sun's Rest,

---

379 And you—you had a flower in your attic room, right above Orfeo's.
380 Eh. Faintly irritating. I've gotten used to you haring off in the middle of things.

looking to the north every chance I got, looking at the Eye of Shuggwa hanging low in the sky, mostly blocked by the houses, biting my lip and wondering and wondering.

If I'd been paying attention. If I'd told you about the dreams, or if I'd taken them more seriously. If I'd given any thought at all to that feeling of missing something just in the corner of my eye.

I spoke to him in the dreams. I could have spoken to him better if I'd known.

"Shuggwa," I whispered, looking at his Eye. "Shuggwa," I called again.

I felt nothing, not even a chill. He was out of reach, and my heart ached with regret. It should have been one of those once-in-a-lifetime things, like the dragon-hatching in Xereccio, a wonder and a treasure that a Chant holds most precious in their heart.

That was something real.

And I was stupid, and I missed my chance.

He pulled me out of the swamp. He saved me from drowning. He sat with me in silence. He was there at the auction when I was behaving as an ancient Chant would have, in bright clothes and with the attention of thousands on me and—and, fuck, he was there that morning with my lover, when I was acting unlike myself. Consider—that sensation of the rising-and-ebbing tide I'd felt, the way the story twisted on my tongue, regardless of my intended words, the way I looked to the corner of the room and found myself surprised that it was empty.

Stupid, stupid Ylfing! I expect you're saying the same, Mistress Chant, that you've been saying so all along. I expect you have all kinds of advice. I don't want it. I don't need it.

I still need to see the end of the story, and then . . . something. Then something.

SIXTY-EIGHT

Sterre has been reduced to bankruptcy, but our work has kept the city breathing. People are upset, but the money is flowing, and no one is starving. The flood of people demanding repayment slowed to a trickle, then a drip. Yesterday we didn't have any at all.

And now, I let out a breath that I've been holding for three weeks, since I gave the first pamphlet to the first former customer.

Sterre has no more offices. She has no more table at the Rojkstraat. She has no more frothing lace at her collar and cuffs, no more fine fabrics stylishly draped. Everything has gone to repay the city.

When I found her today, she was sitting in her empty warehouse with a bottle of extremely cheap brandy. Her clothes were old and shabby, secondhand at best (perhaps third-hand); her hair was mussed, and she once again had several days' worth of stubble on her cheeks. She'd sold all her jewels but one, the amber ring she always wore. Between every draft from the bottle, she'd look down at it and twist it around her finger.

"I don't have any more money," she said as soon as she saw me. "I don't have anything but the clothes on my back and—" She raised her hand with the ring. "This. Can't get rid of this, so don't ask me to. I won't do it."

"I won't ask you to."

"It's my dead wife's wedding ring."

"I definitely won't ask you to, then."

"She died in a shipwreck."

"I'm very sorry. You should keep it."

She drank. She said nothing for a long time.

"Did it matter?" she grunted. "Did it really make any difference what we did?"

"Yes," I said firmly. "It did. I'm glad that you cooperated with me—I know it was a very hard choice to make, but you redeemed yourself these past weeks. You did everything you could, which is not something that most people can say truly."

"I don't know why I fucking did that," she said. She drank deep from her flask. "I don't know how I let you and that *vrouw* convince me. Why not just take the money and leave the city? I could have bought a house on the river in Tash. I could have just walked away. And yet—" She glared at me, pointed at me with one finger from the hand holding the flask. "And yet somehow I listen to *you* instead. How old are you, twenty?"

"Thereabouts, yes," I said.

"Gods. You're so young," she spat. "And so full of fucking *idealism*. Tell me true: how'd you convince me?"

I shrugged. "I didn't, really. I think you mostly convinced yourself. There were things that mattered, and those were the things in danger. At the end of the day, you're a good and honorable person, and you made a mistake."

"I should have just walked away with the cash."

"Maybe. But you didn't. You stayed, because you have connections here."

She snorted. "Connections! You can buy connections if you're rich enough. You don't need them."

"Not business connections. You stayed because you *cared*. Because Heyrland is your home, and the people here are your friends and neighbors. You never wanted to cheat them. You wouldn't do that. You have a community here, and you knew that walking away would mean *hurting* people in that community. And you wouldn't do that. I know you wouldn't."

She seethed. "Do you do this a lot? Go around pressuring people into being good by sheer force of those huge puppy eyes? You just bombard them with how hard you *believe* in them and they fold to your will?"

"I guess so," I said. "If it works, then it works."

She shook her head and finished off whatever was in the flask. "I'm ruined now," she said with an obviously false jolly note. "But at least I have the comfort of my morality. I'm sure that'll keep me fed and clothed."

"What you have now is something more precious than gold."

"I have a city that hates me. I have *nothing*. Not even this warehouse—I sold that too this afternoon, to pay the last few debts. I'm only here to say goodbye. And to drink."

"The city resents you for now," I agreed. "But do you know how many people were confused when I paid them their money back? They all said, 'What's the catch? What's the catch? Why is Sterre de Waeyer folding so easily? Why is she doing this?' And every time I said, 'Because she's a good person, and you matter to her more than money does.' And every single one of them went away surprised, or confused, or deeply thoughtful. And none of them were *angry* anymore—or if they were angry, it was just an outward expression of that confusion. They had their money, or most of their money. The thing you did was huge, and unexpected, and illogical by most standards."

"No fucking shit."

"But it's not illogical at all if you accept the premise I gave them: that there are things in the world more important than money. You whine and complain and accuse me of leading you into ruin by force of will, but if you really believed something else, you would have brushed me off." I looked at her. I *looked* at her. I used to have that knack for seeing the truth of someone, for finding a tiny grain of goodness in the heart of even the vilest person. There was so much more than a grain in Sterre—there was genuine care and love for the people around her, and a willingness to help make their lives better with small things, things that were no trouble or burden for her at all, but which made a world of difference to the person receiving them. "You went along with it because you knew I was right. Because you agreed with me. There are things you care about more than money."

She stood slowly. "I haven't the foggiest idea whether you're right or not," she said.

"I am," I said. "It's hard for you to see right now, but it's true. And now you have an opportunity. You can find out what that most important thing is, and maybe you follow *that* this time as you rebuild your life."

"I'm old, Ylfing. I'm tired. I don't want new. I want familiar."

"Then do that. There's no shortage of people in the city who trust you now. Everyone knows you would do everything in your power to make amends, and that's . . . that's something special." I patted her arm. "I have a gift for you. In the spirit of . . . freely giving gifts to take care of the people around you."

"Kind of you," she muttered.

"Earlier in the year, right at the beginning of when I started working for you, I bought a star-in-the-marsh bulb. I planted it in a pot and kept it in the attic of the Sun's Rest, the inn where I've been staying. And I, uh . . . I was lazy, so I always got water from the rain barrel, rather than going down to the canal or to the district cistern." She was giving me a strange look. "It's alive. It was isolated. It's healthy, and it hasn't shown a hint of the sickness. I want you to have it."

"I doubt that anyone's in the mood to buy stars-in-the-marsh now," she said slowly. "Everyone's had their fingers pretty severely singed."

"True. It won't sell for much, but . . . you can probably get a little. There's *someone* in this city who wants to buy a healthy star-in-the-marsh, and then you'd have some coin. And you're Sterre de Waeyer—you could turn a few coins into hundreds, I'd bet."

"Too old to start from the beginning," she grumbled.

"But you're not starting from the beginning. In the beginning, you didn't have all the things you have now—friends, connections . . . A reputation, even though it's bruised. But now everyone in the city knows your name, and, more important, they know the sort of person you are. I swear it'll be easier this time."

"How the fuck would you know?"

I shrugged. "In terms of the mechanics of merchantry? I don't. But I know stories, and the story you carry with you is ironbound. People have built countries on less than that. People have torn countries down to their foundations with less than that." I gave her a bracing smile. "Sterre de Waeyer never dwells in a bad situation for long, right? You'll turn this around."

SIXTY-NINE

Well. I suppose I could call the story ended there. It's all over now. That's everything. I gave the star-in-the-marsh to Sterre, and she's taken it off to see how much she can leverage it to change her situation. And now I'm back where I started, approximately. I'm alone, and the world is open before me, and I . . . I get to choose now. Just like Sterre, I get to figure out what's most important to me. And then I get to start something new.

Here's what I know:

I know that when I was thirteen or fourteen and my master-Chant walked into my village, there was something about what he was that was *right*. There was something about what he offered that I wanted, that caught my heart on fishhooks.

I know that even in the deepest part of my grief, I still thought I could fix myself by writing it all down, by telling a story until I understood myself.

I know that I can't give myself up. I may have unnamed myself once, but being Ylfing is *important*. Chants are liars, but Ylfing tries to be good. I want to keep trying.

I know that my master-Chant was human, and fallible, and made mistakes, and screwed me up. I know that the Chant *he* was apprenticed to was all those things as well. For all that the Chants believe in remembering everything and passing the important things down . . . Humans forget things.

Sister-Chant, I know you're angry. You're angry that we ended up so different—perhaps you were thinking about your own teacher and wondering what things they forgot or fouled up—but when you have lines of teachers and apprentices, for four thousand years, and you don't write anything down, then of *course* things are going to get muddled. It's a miracle that we're even both still called Chants and that the basics of it have endured even if our practices have diverged.

I still don't think the practices matter very much—I think there's a core of something that's important. And . . . I think I'd like to find out what it is. Maybe then I'll be Chant instead of Ylfing. Or maybe I can just be both.

Hello, I'm Ylfing, but you can call me—no, that's not it.

Hello, I'm Chant. Call me—no, not quite.

My name is Ylfing. I'm a Chant. Possibly?

I'm a Chant. You can call me Ylfing. Also possible.[381]

I suppose I'll just have to open my mouth and see what comes out.

——◆◆◆——

I took a break and went for a walk. I thought about the other things I know.

I know I'm afraid of taking an apprentice. Part of me wants to wait until I've figured everything out, so there's no chance of hurting them like I've been hurt. Part of me, the braver part, thinks that maybe teaching someone else would be a good way to find my path to the center of things. And I have to admit . . . The road is lonely. It would be nice to have a friend with me.

---

381 Hmph. I suppose you earned the right to call yourself whatever you like. And Shuggwa clearly doesn't care—in a way, I suppose it makes sense. The ancient Chants attracted his attention with taboo behavior that flouted their social rules. Being a Chant and taking your name back is . . . taboo. And therefore . . . Well. It's not for me. But evidently it's working for you, so have at it.

I won't go looking for one. I'm really not ready for that yet, and there's no rush. But if circumstances lead me to someone, then I'll ... No, I'll think about it when the time comes. Hah, do you see this, Sister-Chant? I'm getting so practiced at making choices that now I'm trying to choose a path before I've even reached that crossroads.

Whatever happens, if I do meet someone, I'll tell them the truth. And maybe I'll teach them differently than I was taught. We'll see. We'll just see.

SEVENTY

I've been thinking about it a little more. All Chants are liars; I stand by that. But . . . not all lies are bad things. Not all lies are destructive. And, you know, it depends on how you define a lie.[382]

By one definition, most stories are lies. There was never a real time that Ylf and Tofa lived, for example. That means they're not true, and anything that isn't true is a lie, right?

But maybe I'm changing. Maybe I'm growing, like I told my lover I wanted to. Because now I think you have to consider the definition of *truth* too. I used to think of truth and lies being two ends of a spectrum, and stories being somewhere in the middle of that spectrum, depending—some are more true than others, after all. Some are more factually correct. There *are* stories about people who had real lives, who were born of a mother in a year that we can number, instead of simply *a very long time ago and half the world away.*

There's truth. There's lies. But above those, transcending those, are stories. They exist in a space entirely outside the spectrum, outside those frail, faded mortal concepts.

Sister-Chant, that night you told me to armor my heart with the

---

382 Okay, make your argument. I'm listening.

story I deserved—with the lie that I needed.[383] That night when I told you what my former master would have said: "It doesn't matter if it happened that way in real life, as long as the story is good, as long as it's truer than truth."

Do you remember? Because I have one more story.

---

383 Aha. I suppose I am forced to concede the point.

SEVENTY-ONE

A Good Story[384]

My lover left on a bright, sunny morning. There was a whole dizzying whirl of activity and noise and confusion, all completely alien to me, as his family packed up and vacated the inn. I have so few things, and departures have always been a more subdued affair, even when I was apprenticed. At the very most, whoever we were with, our new friends or old ones, used to see us to the door and kiss our cheeks and wave as we ambled down the street with only a single small bag slung over my back. (*This, at least, is true. Every lie burns brighter with a core of truth.*)

My lover's family ran all over the inn from early in the morning until the porters arrived to haul all their things—so many things!—to the docks. I didn't let go of my lover's hand except when absolutely necessary. "I'll come down with you," I said, and he gave me a smile both grateful and sad.

The whole caravan made it down to the harbor in fairly short order, and then there was the whole headache of getting so many people and things on the boat. My lover[385] stood with me off to the side

---

384 Yes, I expect it will be.
385 A more elegant solution than blacking out the name, by the way. I thought before that it was merely an epithet, but no—you've *unnamed* him. Because of course you, of all people, would consider that the most terrible curse you could inflict upon him.

as long as he could. We clutched each other's hands and hugged, and at last, in a broken voice, he said, "I feel like we're saying goodbye forever, and I can't stand it."

"Not forever," I said. "May I call on you, if I find myself in Pezia?"

He kissed me sweetly, cradling my face in his hands. "Yes. Please do. My door is always open to you, and I'll tell my family too—even if I'm not there when you arrive, I'll make sure you'll have a roof over your head and a bed for the claiming."[386]

"I'll never forget you," I said.

"You could write to me," he said, a little desperate. "If you felt like writing. I'd be so happy to receive a letter from you. But you shouldn't feel like you have to."

I recited the address of his family's house—in the Jasmine District in Lermo, a large port city of Pezia. He hugged me. He was trying not to cry again, and when he pulled back I gave him a bracing smile. "It's all right. I won't forget the address. Chants remember."

"Will you go on Chanting, then?"

"Now, now," I said, trying to tease and failing utterly. "You're trying to get me to spoil the rest of the story for you. Don't you want to wait for your letter to find out what I ended up doing?"

Simoneto called his name then, waving from the boat. We both flinched and looked at each other helplessly.

"I have to go," he said, shattered. "You're—I really loved you," he said. "And I love you still. And part of me always will."

"You saved me," I said. "You brought me out of the dark. I'm going to remember that too, for always. I'm going to hold it in my heart, and

---

386 I smiled at this, just now—very Chantly of you, this line. The promise could have been anything, but it's just about a place to stay when you're in town, in perpetuity? *Very* Chantly of you, Brother.

I'm going to *keep* it. That memory—that story—is mine, and I won't let it go, not for anyone."[387]

He took my face in his hands and kissed me, and then looked at me. "Ylfing," he said quietly. "Ylfing, Ylfing, Ylfing, Ylfing." Just like he'd done in the beginning when I'd first told him my name. He whispered it over and over until I was laughing, and he was crying, and then—then he let go of me. And he backed away a couple steps. "Be safe. Please, please be safe," he said, moving towards the boat.

"You too," I whispered.

"Write to me. When you can." And—then it hit me that he was going, and I was staying, and . . . maybe I'd never see him again, maybe I'd never hold his hand or kiss him, maybe this was the end of everything. And something cracked in my chest. I turned away so he wouldn't see the tears coming up in my eyes and spilling over. I didn't want to make it any harder for him than it already was.

I only looked back when the little rowboat was safely a dozen feet from the dock, and I watched my lover watch me all the way across the harbor until they reached the ship, and then I watched him stand on the deck while the sailors weighed anchor and loosed the sails, and I watched until the ship passed through the locks and out of sight behind the wall of the dike.

I made it home to the inn mostly by muscle memory, since I was sobbing nearly too hard to see. It's been years since I cried at all.[388]

---

387 And that's the thesis, isn't it? Pointed and deliberate—angry too, just a little bit, if I squint and tilt my head. Yes, it is yours. You got something good while you were together. You grew, and him turning out to be an asshole doesn't invalidate that. I'm glad you found a way to keep the good thing, that you decided not to let that boy take it from you.

Same goes for your master-Chant, but I expect you've already realized that. "Don't let boys spoil things for you" is a great code to live by, not that my approval matters in the slightest.

388 Wow, talk about all Chants being liars. That's a big juicy ten-foot-tall lie lit by fireworks and sparklers.

I couldn't sleep in my lover's room anymore. My feet, treacherous things, took me up there first, but it had already been cleaned and tidied, and there was no trace of my lover left there.

My only consolation is that the whole time on the docks and on my way back to the inn and on my pallet of blankets in the attic this afternoon . . . I never felt like I'd made a horrible mistake. I never thought of changing my mind.

——◆——

I don't have any tales of partings like this to use as examples or models—in all the stories, when a love ends it's because one or both of them died, or they had a falling-out, or something equally catastrophic. There aren't any stories about love ending because it was the natural time for it to end. There's none about people in love separating as still-beloved friends.[389] And in all the stories, the loves ended because they were bad or wrong or flawed, or the fact that they ended *was* the flaw, or the end ruined everything that came before.

My lover came into my life and he was full of joy and light. He

---

389 Ah, child. You are still so young. If we had been able to meet as friends, I might have told you some stories about these kinds of endings. You'll never read what I've written here, but I'll write it anyway: There's no way to feel but how you feel. When you one day have a love like this, a real love and not just armor on your heart, when you one day part with someone like this, remember that you haven't lost them— they've only gone away a little distance. Your paths will cross again if they are meant to. Fear not, Brother-Chant. And yes, in the meantime, write to them, one day when you have someone worth writing to. There's not much you can do to get letters back, except hope for a miracle, and tell everyone where you're going next, and then stay in one place long enough for the mail to catch up. Or, if you find yourself returning to one place again and again like it's the center of the spider's web that your path takes, just ask them to hold your letters for you. You go back once every year or two and there's a wonderful box of them waiting for you, from all the people you love best in the world, and they're all commenting on mundane little things that you'd told them about and set aside, and you can remember and be warmed.

took me dancing. He kissed me; he whispered my name into my skin until I felt like myself again. He anchored me into the world. He brought me back. He was good and kind, and patient and under-standing, and he never asked me for anything but what I was willing to give him. Just because it didn't last our entire lives doesn't mean it wasn't important or precious.[390]

That's the story I've decided on. That's me armoring my heart.

---

390 This was a good story. May it keep you warm for years to come. He did bring you out of the dark and back into the world, and that's . . . well. That was his *one little thing*, wasn't it? Even if he spoiled everything else. Even if nothing else was worth remembering—and here I mean "remembering" in the way that Chants mean it, car-rying it in your heart from place to place and giving it away again and again so it stays strong, so it survives.

SEVENTY-TWO

Well. There's nothing left in this city, I guess. Sterre sold the flower I gave her for a paltry twelve guilders, and she dumped all of it into buying a few shares of an overland trade caravan to Ancoux, the capital of Vinte—her friend van Vlymen, the tailor, whispered to her that he's planning on bringing silk jacquard back into fashion next year.

It's all just as I told her. Maybe not everyone will forgive her, but she strengthened bonds with her closest allies, and they'll see that she gets back on her feet.

So I'm done with Sterre, and my lover is gone, and . . . why was I here? Why did I stop, here of all places?

It's a beautiful city. I can see that now, easily. There are cascades of flowers and trailing vines hanging from every window box and balcony, and here and there, in unexpected corners of the canals, you'll find little lush floating gardens of lilies and rushes and all manner of water plants. There are trees, carefully tended, that shade some of the streets and overhang the canals, and in some places people have hung ribbons and lanterns from their branches. The canals are like veins— they're as alive as the streets in any other city, with people paddling about or poling boats of all sizes.

I'm about to leave it. I keep putting it off—tomorrow, then the next day, or next week. There's nowhere in particular that I desperately need to go, and I'm . . . You know what? I'm enjoying seeing the city for myself. My lover and I used to go on walks, but everything was hazy and rosy-colored around the edges when I was with him. It's different when it's just me.

Yesterday, I sat on the Swordfish Bridge with a bag full of sweet-cheese pastries from the Vintish bakery down the street from the Sun's Rest, and I just watched the traffic on the canal and the people walking by, and practiced *seeing* again. When I was an apprentice, Chant used to send me out to wander a new city alone, noticing things and getting to know the streets, feeling out its pulse. In the evening, I'd come back to wherever he was, loaded down with little scraps of gossip, and sometimes he could quilt them together into a whole pattern—"Mm," he'd grunt. "So they don't like the prime minister at the moment," even though I hadn't mentioned anything about prime ministers or government at all. It was amazing at the time.

I'll stay a few days more. Just a few. It's time to move on. I've done what I can here, and I think I learned almost everything I needed to. I'll just stay a few more days, and then I'll go visit you, Sister-Chant, to say farewell, and to give you this story.

It was as true as I could manage—truer than I'd like, actually. I know there are things in here that I don't much want you to see, but it would take too long to go through all these papers to find them, dispose of them, and then disguise the omission. The only things I'm leaving out are the things I promised other people that I wouldn't speak of—and not for money, either, so you can relax. I daresay you'd see through any attempts I made to disguise things anyway, and that wasn't the promise.

One story, whole and true and real.

And that's where you end it.

That was not as entirely useless as I was expecting, Brother-Chant. It's a ridiculous mountain of paper, and I'm not sure what to do with it, but without a proper ending it's . . . pointless. If you set out to tell a story, you owe your audience some kind of resolution. Or else they think that you've just wasted their time with anticlimactic babble.

Strangely . . . I don't feel like I wasted my time. If your purpose was to explain yourself, then I suppose you succeeded. My anger is quenched, and I . . . understand, at least partially.

I suppose that I see a possibility here. What am I to do with this mountain of paper? You must have known, when you handed it to me, that I'd be unable to just destroy it, whatever my threats were. It is a story, even if the ending is nonexistent, and I'm bound and sworn to keep stories and pass them along. I don't know who would be interested in this—maybe the people of Heyrland themselves? Perhaps they'd like a chronicle of what happened these past few months. Perhaps they'd like the perspective of someone intimately involved with that fiasco. Maybe I'll track down Sterre and dump it on her. Perhaps she'd like to branch out into a printing business.

So for their benefit, I'll do your work for you, Chant-called-Ylfing. I'll finish it properly.

SEVENTY-THREE

A Proper Ending

The evening was young, the light not yet entirely faded from the western sky. I was plying my trade in the inn where I was staying with my apprentices. Lanh Chau had convinced a pair of musicians in the corner to sing for him, and he was sitting perfectly still on a stool in front of them, watching and listening with the entirety of his attention bent on them. Arenza was doing as an apprentice does, circling the room and talking to people, making friends and scraping up trinkets of information. And I, I was lounging comfortably by the hearth and trading gossip and news with a pair of sailors, one from Cormerra and one from N'gaka.

It was then that my brother-Chant appeared in the room, carrying a hefty parcel tied up with string.

I knew as soon as I laid eyes on him that something had changed. There was a look to him then, the look of a man who has made a decision and intends to embark upon it. I knew, too, that he must have come looking for me—he knew that inn was where I was staying, and he had come to see me before. He had no business there except with me.

I braced myself for another fight. Every time we spoke, we fell into one sooner or later. I couldn't help but snipe and pick at him. I nodded at him and gestured towards an empty chair. He perched on it and set the parcel on his knees, folded his hands neatly on top of it, and waited.

I'd been in the middle of something with those two sailors, entertaining them with amusing stories and weaving throughout anecdotes of my travels, the news of far-off lands, and the sort of advice that all travelers share freely with each other—have you heard the Warden of the Marches is doing something about those highwaymen on the mountain road? That sort of thing.

My brother-Chant waited politely until I was finished. I gave him opportunities to step in, to take part, to contribute to the banter that I had going with my little audience. We could have had a bit of a double act, if he'd taken the cues, but he just sat and waited.

When I excused myself to refill my beer, he got up and followed me. "Hello," he said. "I thought you'd be happy to know—the whole thing is over. I fixed it."

"So I heard," I said. "Do you expect me to give you a little sugar-cake and a pat on the head?"

"No."

"Good. You did the bare minimum required by moral duty. You undid as much of the mess as you could."

"Yes," he said. "I tried. I suppose that's all I can do." I snorted, and he gave me some kind of reproachful look. "I'll do better next time, you know. I'm only human. I made a mistake."

"Our ways will part sooner or later, and that will be the end of our acquaintanceship. But before that, you have a debt to repay. You said you wouldn't forget."

"Actually, that's part of why I came to see you," he said.

I knew then: he was planning to take leave. It relieved me at the same time as it pained me. I've never met a Chant other than the one who taught me, and I'd known her all my life.

She'd gotten footsore, as Chants sometimes do, and she'd come to rest in my village in the mountains of Qeteren, meaning only to stay for a year or so. But people have a way of putting down roots when they stay too long in one place, and my Chant's roots took hold firmly. I met her first when I was four or five years old, and if you believe her stories, I hounded her daily, appearing at the window of her little cottage where she brewed medicine for the villagers. Everyone knew what she was—she'd explained it when she first arrived.

She always had the best stories out of anyone. She had seen more of the world than anybody in the village could believe, and there were plenty who didn't believe her. But I did. She was kind to me. She never tried to chase me away, except when the shadows grew long in the evening and it was time for me to run down the big hill to my mother again. She taught me all there was of the ways of the Chants by the time I was twelve years old. I knew I wanted to be just like her. I wanted to see the world as she had. We had a few spats about it, then, because she wouldn't apprentice me unless she was going to do it properly, and doing it properly meant tearing up her roots, putting her traveling shoes back on, and going once more into the wide world. She was still footsore in her heart, even after more than a decade. I was sixteen when she finally agreed, making me promise that I would learn as ardently and quickly as I could so that she could return to her cottage in the mountains. We went home again when I was twenty-two, and her cottage was still there, tenderly cared for by my parents. I sank my homeland beneath the waves of the little brook that trickled past not a stone's throw from her front steps, and I stayed for a year, and then off I went, to be a Chant properly, as she'd taught me. Before I left, she told me that I'd probably never meet another of our kind, but if I did, I must greet them as a long-lost sibling and open my arms in embrace to them, and offer them blessings and hospitality.

And here I was, facing the only other Chant I'd ever met, standing by a pillar on one side of the room and looking like two very awkward people attempting to pass by each other in a narrow corridor. I thought then that he would have been such a disappointment to my teacher. I was glad to know we were going to part. And I wished with all my heart that he'd been different. I wished I could have embraced him as a true brother.

"I'm leaving," he said, which was both belated and redundant, as far as I was concerned. But there were things to say. It was my duty to offer him blessings. "So yes, as you said, the debt. I know we've had our differences," he said awkwardly. "Even without the debt, I . . . I wouldn't have wanted to leave without explaining myself. A Chant seeks understanding, and I thought I'd leave you with the opportunity to understand me. If you wanted. You don't have to take it. But here's the story I have to tell you." He held out his parcel. "This is for you. For the debt. I've been writing a lot of my thoughts down since . . . well, since I got the job with Sterre."

"Your thoughts?" I said. My skin prickled with suspicion.

"Yes. At first I was just talking to myself, or to someone I didn't know. I was seeking my own understanding. I thought if I wrote it all down, it might get out of my head and be easier to deal with when it was in front of my eyes. So this is the whole story. It's about what happened to me, and what happened with the flowers. Whole and real and true."

"No," I said, stunned. "No, this wasn't the deal."

"The deal had nothing to do with how I'd give it to you. All you said was that you wanted the entire thing. I can guarantee you anything I told you in words would be less entire than this."

"So you wrote down the story?" I hissed.

I expected him to flinch. He'd flinched at my rebukes a dozen times. But this time . . . This time he met my eyes seriously. "Yes," he said. "I did. It was what I needed to do. I see nothing wrong with it, but if you feel strongly about it, then I'll hear your arguments." He smiled a little then. "But before you say anything, you should know that this particular heresy is one I made up myself. I didn't get it from my Chant. He would have been appalled at me for it. So if you'd like to scold me, you may, but it ought to be specific to me as an individual. My line has no part in this."

"Well, it's too late to undo it," I snapped at him.

"Yep," he said, entirely too cheerful. "And now I'm leaving, and what I wrote down is yours to do with as you like. You can keep it, or burn it, or read it, or dump it in the canal. It's out of my hands. It doesn't belong to me anymore. You can read Xerecci, can't you?"

"Can I read Xerecci," I scoffed. "What do you take me for?" I confess, I was curious. Dead curious. A Chant has to be curious—without that, they're barely a Chant at all. I did want to understand him, and I wanted him to prove me wrong. Prove that he had methods that were worthy of respect, if not imitation. "Where will you go next?" I said. I wanted to make sure we wouldn't meet each other on the road.

He brightened at my question. "I'm going to Xereccio. I'm going to see the dragons hatch again—there's something about that in there," he said, nodding to the bundle on the table. "And after that . . ." He looked away. "I think I might go to the Issili Islands. To the Jewel Coast."

"What in the world? What for?" At the time, of course, it meant nothing to me. I didn't know about his dreams, about the whisper of power that the stars-in-the-marsh had brought with them.

All he said was "Personal reasons."

"There's nearly nothing there. They're barely more than sand and palm trees."

"Have you been there?" he asked. I had to admit that I hadn't.

"Then how do you know there's nothing?" And he asked it so reasonably that I couldn't be offended. "I want to go. Even if there's nothing there, it doesn't mean I won't find something else."

"Find something? Are you looking for something?"

"Maybe. I just want to stand there and look at the ocean."

"You can go out to the dikes and look at the ocean all you want from here."

"It's not the same ocean," he countered. "I want to look at that ocean."

"Oceans look much the same wherever you go."

"They don't," he said, still so reasonable and calm. "The Sea of Serpents is aptly named, and likewise the Sea of Storms and the Amethyst Sea. The Unending Ocean is an exaggeration, admittedly, but if the stories are right then not by much. My master had maritime stories from his master. She loved the sea. It seemed to be her area of expertise."

"Then what's so special about that particular bit of ocean that makes you so keen to look at it?"

"The ancient Chants," he said, and . . . I was floored. "Right? Arthwend was somewhere to the south of the Jewel Coast before it sank. And then the Chants and their people came north on boats and hit land on those islands. So I'm going to go there, and I'm going to stand on the ground they stood on." He smiled again. "And if I don't feel anything, then I'm going to stop being a Chant for good and find something else. But . . . I think I'll feel something." Shuggwa, he meant. I know that now. At the time I only thought him . . . puzzling, excessively mysterious, and somewhat soppy—I mean, "I'm going half the world away to look at a specific ocean because I think it will make me feel something"? What insipid tripe. But now, having read all this . . .

He's going looking for Shuggwa, and he's pretty sure that he'll find him.

But, again, at the time, I thought only that it was silliness, much in line with his usual flavor of silliness. I gathered up everything I had learned from my teacher, all the patience that she had so vainly tried to teach me, all the grace. It was a moment for courtesy and respect. It was a moment for sincerity: "May the road be kind," I said, echoing the words my master-Chant had given me upon our parting. "And when it is not, may you find warm shelter. And when you do not, may the rain and snow and wind harry you to wherever you are meant to go." And I managed to be sincere when I said, "May you be worthy of drawing Shuggwa's Eye."

He looked a little startled. I didn't think at the time that he would find any value in my blessing, but since it was for me more than it was for him, it didn't matter—except now I know otherwise. I know he heard something in that blessing that I couldn't have begun to guess. I suspect it meant more to him than I ever intended: May you be worthy of drawing Shuggwa's Eye.

May you be worthy.

And he said, "Thank you. Same to you." I thought about offering to buy him a drink. I thought about asking him for one more conversation. I thought about offering to trade stories with him as we should have been doing this entire time, doubling our own knowledge by giving it away freely to each other. But I didn't, and I don't think he would have accepted. He looked at me, and for a moment I thought he was looking into my very soul, and he said, "You love your work, and you love your apprentices. You have a lot of discipline, and your devotion never wavers. I love you for these things."

And then he gave me this . . . smile. He'd smiled before, but this one was like sunshine bursting through clouds after a long winter. It blinded me—it must have blinded his lover, too, must have made him stumble a step or two.

And then that ridiculous, beautiful creature just . . . left. He walked out of the inn with no fanfare, just as he'd walked in. He walked out of my life. And part of me wanted to call him back and do things the proper, rightful way.

And I didn't. So I unpacked his parcel, and I sat for a while glaring at it, and then I asked for a pen and ink, and I sat in the middle of the inn and read until dawn, scrawling all over his pages as thoughts and outrage occurred to me.

———◆◆◆———

That's the end. I shall give this mountain of pages to Sterre de Waeyer after all, I think, and she can do with it as she will. In another few weeks, I'll head out of this city as well, and you can be assured that I won't be going anywhere near Xereccio or the Issili Islands for at least the next three years. Perhaps I'll go north, up the coast to Echaree or Cormerra. I'd heard rumors of trouble in Nuryevet a couple of years ago, even before Chant-called-Ylfing owned up to it. If it has settled by now, there may be fresh stories there. Perhaps someone there remembers Ylfing and his master.

Acknowledgments

Second books are much harder than first books, as it turns out—this was one of the most difficult things I've ever written, both emotionally and in terms of technical skill, but I survived it, and I'm so honored to be able to put it into your hands. Thank you for being here.

The godmothers of this book are Freya Marske and Jennifer Mace. They read the very, very rough first draft of this book when our friendship was still quite new and untested, they thrashed it into shape, and they tactfully and kindly didn't tell me it had been genuinely god-awful until much later, after I'd already fixed it. This book would not be what it is without them. Thank you, friends. (An individual thank-you to Macey for teaching me her method of planning a revision (murderboards!), which *saved my ass so hard*. Another individual thank-you to Freya for holding my hand and coaching me through how to write a sex scene.)

Navah Wolfe, my editor and the actual light of my life, must be damned with faint praise when I say: "Wow, she's really good at her job." Her faith in this book and her patience were unwavering, even when she was doing dramatic public readings of a hilarious writer tantrum I sent her during the first round of revisions. She is a gift, and I feel so lucky just to know her.

Meg Frank let me crash in their apartment, fed me curry and

cookie dough, and listened to me cry a lot when this book was hard. I planned the war campaign for the revision of the (god-awful) first draft on the back of a door in their apartment with (I believe) every Post-it Note that they owned. They are so good at creating "home" wherever they are for the people around them, and I'm a better person for knowing them.

Deanna Hoak copyedited this book with exquisite grace. She brought a real artistry and elegance to a process that so many people consider to be staid and unlovely, and I profess myself awed. The artist of the spectacularly beautiful cover was Ryan Begley, the gorgeous map was drawn by Drew Willis, and the designer was Nicholas Sciacca—I am convinced that no one who does such splendid work could be anything but splendid people as well. Brilliant work, all of you.

My little coterie of writers, the Author Sack, is a source of so much love and support—I'm so glad I have you guys, but I'm even more glad that you also have each other. Writing is a very lonely job sometimes, but it's a lot less lonely with you nerds in my life. Thank you.